ACCLAIM FOR TIM GAUTREAUX'S

THE
CLEARING

"A compelling look at one man and his family, barely alive but deeply human. In him, it is not hard to recognize ourselves."
—*San Francisco Chronicle*

"A postmodern masterpiece. . . . Gautreaux has created, out of antique characters and a 1923 Louisiana backwater, a parable about coping with modernity. About us. And he reminds us that great writing is a timeless art."   —*The Miami Herald*

"*The Clearing* is his very best yet, and to say that of Tim Gautreaux's writing is to say something is very fine indeed. . . . Wit, wisdom, and heart are all combined in perfect proportion in this astonishing and unforgettable novel."
—*The Times-Picayune*

"Tim Gautreaux's *The Clearing* presents the reader with an interesting dilemma: do you give in to the stifling suspense and read quickly, to find out what happens to the novel's vivid characters, or do you go slow, savoring each delicious sentence, and thereby risking, by the climax, a nervous breakdown?"   —Richard Russo, author of *Empire Falls*

"Inventive, carefully conveyed and energetic. . . . Tim Gautreaux has written a somber, serious, historical novel that assures us all that he is a rising force in fiction."
—*Chicago Tribune*

"The finest American novel in a long, long time."

—Annie Proulx, author of *The Shipping News*

"At once tender and unrelentingly exciting. There are enough ghastly creatures slithering through this swamp to hold anyone's interest, and enough moral insight to enlighten anyone's conscience." —*The Christian Science Monitor*

"Set in backwoods Louisiana after the First World War, this taut and unsettling novel . . . uses prose as rich and teeming as the swamps he brings to life." —*The Baltimore Sun*

"As a reader passes through the contagion of violence within this story, what is remembered are the tendrils of compassion and tenderness, small but enduring. Tim Gautreaux is a wonderful writer, and *The Clearing* is a unique and fascinating story." —Rick Bass, author of *The Hermit's Story*

"You can cut the atmosphere with a knife. . . . Exotic and electric." —*The Denver Post*

"Classic Southern storytelling, hallucinogenic intensity of description, and obsessive and authoritative attention to historical detail." —*Elle*

"Extraordinarily compelling and unsettling." —*Chicago Sun-Times*

"A dense, masterfully written story of filial ties and a struggle for decency and redemption in a heart of darkness. . . . The tale is imbued with such delicacy and even beauty that it not only affects but astonishes." —*Entertainment Weekly*

TIM GAUTREAUX

THE
CLEARING

Born and raised in Louisiana, Tim Gautreaux is
Writer-in-Residence at Southeastern Louisiana
University. His work has appeared in *Harper's*,
The Atlantic Monthly, *GQ*, and *Zoetrope*, as well as
The O. Henry Prize Stories and *The Best American
Short Stories* annuals. His first novel, *The Next Step
in the Dance*, won the 1999 Southeastern Book-
sellers Award, and he has also published two col-
lections of short fiction.

ALSO BY TIM GAUTREAUX

Same Place, Same Things

The Next Step in the Dance

Welding with Children

THE
CLEARING

THE
CLEARING

TIM GAUTREAUX

VINTAGE CONTEMPORARIES

VINTAGE BOOKS

A DIVISION OF RANDOM HOUSE, INC.

NEW YORK

FIRST VINTAGE CONTEMPORARIES EDITION, MAY 2004

The Library of Congress has cataloged the Knopf edition as follows:
Gautreaux, Tim.
The clearing / Tim Gautreaux—1st. ed.
p. cm.
1. World War, 1914–1918—Veterans—Fiction.
2. Wilderness areas—Fiction. 3. Lumber Trade—Fiction.
4. Brothers—Fiction. 5. Louisiana—Fiction. 6. Psychological fiction.
7. Historical fiction. 8. Domestic fiction.
PS3557.A954 C56 2003
2003065956

Vintage ISBN: 978-1-4000-3053-8

Book design by Soonyoung Kwon

www.vintagebooks.com

Printed in the United Sates of America
14

To Winborne

I'd like to thank my editor, Gary Fisketjon, who does his job the right way, with precision, hard work, and heart. Nobody does it better. Thanks to my agent, Peter Matson of Sterling Lord Literistic, for his excellent advice and guidance. Much gratitude goes to my mother, brother, and sister, Florence, David, and Lyn, for facts given and love shared, and especially my father, Minos, who took me into the swamps to show me the remnants of things. For Clarence Adoue, who suffered in France and lived to tell the tale. My thanks to several old men, now dead, who didn't know I was listening.

THE
CLEARING

CHAPTER ONE

1923

At a flag stop in Louisiana, a big, yellow-haired man named Jules stepped off a day coach at a settlement of twelve houses and a shoebox station. He was the only passenger to get off, and as soon as his right foot touched the cinder apron of the depot, the conductor pulled the step stool from under his left heel, the air brakes gasped, and the train moved in a clanking jerk of couplers.

Remembering his instructions, he walked south down a weedy spur track and found a geared steam locomotive coupled to a crew car and five empty flats. The engineer leaned out from his cab window. "You the evaluatin' man?"

Jules put down his bag, glanced up at the engineer and then around him at the big timber rising from oil-dark water. "Well, ain't you informed. I guess you got a newspaper back in these weeds or maybe a sawmill radio station?"

The engineer looked as though all unnecessary meat had been cooked off of him by the heat of his engine. "The news goes from porch to porch, anyhow." He spat on the end of a crosstie. "I know somebody better buy this place who knows what he's doin'." He nodded to the rear of his train. "Load yourself on the crew car."

The locomotive steamed backwards into a never-cut woods, the homemade coach rocking drunkenly over rails that in places sprang down under mud. After a few miles, the train backed out of the cypresses into the smoky light of a mill yard, and Jules stepped off the car as it drifted on like a wooden cloud making its own sleepy thunder. Surveying the factory, he saw it was larger than the Texas operation he'd just helped to close down, which was already rusting toward oblivion, marooned in the middle of eight thousand acres of drooling pine stumps. The new mill before him was a series of many iron-roofed, gray-plank structures connected with the logic of vegetation: a towering saw shed sprouted a planing section, and suckering off of it was the boiler house and many low-peaked shelters for the finished lumber. He stood in an evil-smelling mocha puddle, looking in vain for dry ground, then bent to tuck his pants inside his boots. As he straightened up, a man in a white shirt and vest came out of the back door of a weatherboard house and began walking toward him. When he was two hundred feet away, Jules could tell by his star that it was only the constable come to see what outlander had happened onto the property. Beyond him, the sawmill gnawed its trees, and jets of steam plumed high over the cinder-pocked rooftops, skidding off to the west, their sooty shadows dragging across the clearing. A safety valve opened with a roar above the boiler house, a man hollered down at the log pond, and a team of eight fly-haunted mules, their coats running with foam, dragged a mud sled overloaded with slabs bound for the fuel pile. Jules looked at his watch. It was a half hour until lunch time, and everybody on shift was working up to the whistle.

The constable, a solemn-looking man, big in the shoulders, walked up slowly. "Do you have business here?" He pushed back a one-dent Carlsbad hat and stared, deadpan, like an idiot or a man so distracted he'd forgotten to control the look in his eyes.

"I got an appointment with the manager to go over some figures." Jules reached out and took the constable's hand but dropped it as soon as he could without giving offense, thinking that if a corpse could shake hands, it would feel like this.

"Some figures," the man said, as if the phrase held a private meaning. From behind him came a strangled shout and the report of a small pistol, sharp as a clap, but he didn't turn around.

Jules stepped up onto a crosstie. "I helped ramrod the Brady mill in east Texas until we cut out last month. The owner, well, he lives up North and sent word for me to come over into Louisiana to look for a new tract. Maybe two, if they're small." In the distance three men fell fighting out the doorway of what Jules guessed was the company saloon. "This is my eighth mill in as many days."

"I was from up North," the constable said, turning to give a brief look at the commotion and then swinging back.

Jules noted how he stood, hands in pockets and thumbs flicking like a horse's ears. "The hell you say. What you doing down among the alligators?"

On the porch of the saloon, two men were tying the other's hands behind his back, one making the knot, the other kneeling on his shoulders.

"The mill manager's office is through that red door over there in the main building," the constable said.

"Say, why don't—"

"Excuse me." He began walking toward the fight, taking his time going around a broad mud hole, and Jules followed for over a hundred yards, stopping in a plinth of shade cast by the commissary. At the saloon, two men, wearing dark wool caps and suits that fit like a hound's skin, hauled the squalling man off the high porch and over toward the millpond, and the constable caught up with them as they mounted the levee. Jules barely heard him say, "Stop."

One of the men, barrel-shaped, his bare chest visible under his suit coat, motioned toward the water. "We gonna give the sonamabitch a swimming lesson," he called. "He owe the house fifty dollar he don't got."

The bound man, a big sawyer in overalls, bent his knees and sat on the ground. "Mr. Byron, these Eyetalians is tryin' to drown my ass."

"Aw, naw," the fat man said. "We just gonna watch him blow bubbles, then we gonna fish him out. That right, Angelo?"

His partner was slim, with a face full of splayed teeth; his response was to tighten his grip on the sawyer's denim collar.

"Cut him loose."

"I don't think so," the fat one told him, and in a single motion the constable reached under his vest, pulled out a big Colt pistol, and swung it like a hatchet down onto the man's head, putting his shoulder and back into it. Jules stepped closer to the commissary wall, even at this distance seeing the brassy jet pulsing through the dark pants as the man fell sideways and rolled like an oil drum down the levee. The skinny fellow stepped away from the sawyer, showing his empty palms.

Above Jules, on the commissary porch, a clerk began sweeping boot clods to the ground. He glanced over toward the pond. "Well," he said, as though he'd spotted a small, unexpected rain cloud.

"A little trouble."

The broom did not break its rhythm. "He ought to know better than to hammer them dagos," he said, turning and working the front edge of the gallery.

Jules put a hand to his chin and watched the sawyer stand up and offer his bindings to the constable's knife. He was thinking of letters he'd exchanged over the years with a man he'd never seen, the absentee owner of his now defunct Texas mill. "What's that lawman's last name?"

"Who wants to know?"

"The man who decides whether this mill gets bought."

The broom ceased its whispery talk. "You the evaluation man they said was coming? Well, you can look around and see the timber, but these fellows running things can't sell it. They poke around sending telegraphs all over but they couldn't sell harp strings in heaven."

Jules looked directly at the clerk, a pale man with skeletal arms. "Tell me his last name."

The clerk plucked a wad of chewing gum from his broom bristles. "Aldridge."

Jules glanced back at the millpond, where the smaller man, Angelo, was crouched next to his partner, slapping his bloody jowls. "You think your manager's in his office about now?"

"That's the only place he can be. Fell off his horse and broke his foot last week." The clerk made a final pass with his broom and stepped inside the commissary's syrupy darkness while Jules walked off toward the grinding thunder that was the mill.

At dusk, after examining the sales accounts, maps, invoices, payroll, pending orders, and the living mill itself, Jules put on his hat and walked toward the constable's house, glad he'd worn his old scuffed riding boots. A late-afternoon thunder-shower had turned the mill yard into a muddy reflecting pond where the images of herons and crows skated at cross-purposes. The mill was losing money, but only because it was operated by an Alabama drunkard; it was a financial plum, heavy and ready to be picked.

The site itself, called Nimbus, though that word was not apparent anywhere, was composed of brush-lined lanes twist-ing among stumps as wide as water tanks. The various fore-men and the constable lived in a row of large unpainted houses not far from the railroad. Jules raised his head toward an inconsequential guitar music tinkling down a lane and sound-ing like raindrops striking a trash pile of tin cans. He recog-nized the watered-down noise of a Victrola coming through the screen door of the constable's house, the man himself sit-ting on the porch in a hide-bottom chair, a flushed and wan-ing sun behind him, his eyes squeezed shut under his stained hat. Jules walked up and listened to a whiny lyric about a sweet old cabin in the pines where a mammy waits with open arms. The constable's eyeballs moved under his lids like nether creatures, not in time with the music; Jules was at pains to reconcile the saccharine song with the afternoon's violence. He coughed.

"I know you're there," the man said, not opening his eyes.

Jules took off his Stetson. "That's some music."

"I'm trying to go back to how it was," the constable said quietly.

"Pardon?"

"This song. It used to be one way. Now it's another." Inside the house the music died and the record clicked off.

Jules settled his sweaty hat higher on his brow and looked up over the sun-gilded porch boards. He'd seen a picture once of a younger man, but this was the one they'd been hunting for years. "Things change when that old clock goes 'round," he said.

When Byron Aldridge opened his eyes, they were like those of a great horse strangling in a dollar's worth of fence wire. "Can I last 'til things change back?"

CHAPTER TWO

When the telegram arrived at the Pittsburgh office, Randolph Aldridge read it and looked out the window as if he could see the thousand miles of bird-limed copper wire that carried this information from New Orleans. Telegraphy interested him because of the way it compacted the world, destroying its mysteries, good as well as bad.

Jules Blake, an employee, had located his brother. Randolph told his father, Noah, and when they examined subsequent messages arriving later that day, they decided to buy the Nimbus tract, brother and all. The following week, at the father's large house just beyond the sootfall of the city's smokestacks, they went into a drawing room and spread open a map.

"You can stay for three or four months," his father told him. "Just to straighten things out and convince your brother to come back."

"It'll be hard on Lillian," he said.

"Bringing Byron home will outweigh that." Noah bent closer to the map. "A good wife will understand."

"What about City Mill?" Randolph thought of the gleaming plant his father had placed in his charge, a small but modern hardwood mill with paved lanes, in fact a company village stippled with white cottages, electric engines, boilers fueled with clean-burning anthracite, where the title of mill manager held a weight similar to that of mayor or judge.

"You've done such a good job there, the place can run itself for a while." His father looked up as if to check him for doubt. "Suffering down South will make you appreciate what we have here."

Randolph had heard a great deal about suffering but had experienced none of it and discounted even his father's tales of his own hard youth; it was his grandfather who had built the company, starting with a third-hand steam engine after the Civil War and cutting crossties for government contracts. Randolph bent down to the broad mahogany table and set his brandy glass on a corner of the map. Below this Louisiana mill was a spongy green area, a cypress swamp that had been explored mostly by snakes, and below that a thin picket of marsh above the pale blue waters of the Gulf. Twenty-five miles to the west of Nimbus, the map showed a town they'd inquired about, a hard-drinking place called Tiger Island, a port on the Chieftan River and a small railroad hub. Some twenty miles to the east of the mill tract was Shirmer and the sugar cane plantations of the Terrebonne region. Directly north by five miles was a particle on the Southern Pacific main line named Poachum, and north of that was seventy miles of uninhabited land visited only by survey crews planning its destruction, for it was pregnant with oil, timber, natural gas, sulfur, and fur-bearing animals.

He had read Jules's much-misspelled but lengthy report and knew that this country was packed with soaring tidewater cypress, bug-proof, rot-proof shafts of butter-smooth grain, trees nine feet thick at the base, waiting to be made into boards that would outlast by three hundred years the bankers and lawyers sitting on their lake-cottage porches and smelling the sweet, peppery wood taken off the earth to furnish their leisure. Randolph put a forefinger down below Poachum but could not picture this teeming sponge of land, nor could he imagine his brother in such a place, serving law and making enemies at the edge of the world. He picked up his glass and took a drink. "This is two birds with one stone. A good mill and Byron both."

His father straightened up and pinched off his glasses. "I've given instructions that the purchase not be noised about that camp until you arrive."

"Think he'll bolt?"

"He will if he hears about it before you step up on his porch." His father touched him briefly on the shoulder the way a waiter might. "You're the one who can bring him back to us. You've got to remember that."

"My wife—"

"You're the one," the old man repeated, turning and leaving the room.

Randolph walked over to the piano and pressed down a C chord. His older brother was well educated, big, and handsome, and in spite of a disposition oscillating between manic elation and mannequin somberness, he'd been destined to take over management of the family's mills and timber. Then he'd gone off to the war, coming back neither elated nor somber but with the haunted expression of a poisoned dog, unable to touch anyone or speak for more than a few seconds without turning slowly to look over his shoulder. Randolph saw on the mantel the sepia photograph of a young man with dark hair laid over to the side, a sharp-eyed fellow who looked as though he had a politician's gift for talking to strangers and putting them at ease. After France, Byron spoke to people with his eyes wide, sometimes vibrating with panic, as if he expected them suddenly to burst into flames. Late in 1918 he had joined the police force in Pittsburgh, his father angry and ashamed that his eldest son would rather wrestle with the city's thugs and factory trash than come to work in the business he'd been born to.

After six weeks Byron disappeared, and Randolph was given the task of finding him, but none of the investigators he hired turned up a trace.

When letters began arriving in 1919 from Gary, Indiana, his father sent a detective to find him, but without success. Two months later, a postcard appeared from Cape Girardeau, Missouri, then a one-sentence note from Heber Springs, Arkansas.

After that came a long silence when the family could speak of him only in the polite evening language of holidays and Sunday dinners. In 1921 a paragraph from a little town in Kansas told of police work and jail tending, followed by a penciled note from farther west in Kansas, and a month later one from a New Mexico town that didn't appear on any map. Then, for a year now, they'd received not a word, as though Byron had at last found a place in which he was the only citizen, and somehow had gone beyond even that in his solitude.

In his brother's absence, Randolph began to understand that most of what he knew about music, women, or the business, he'd learned from Byron. He and the old man brought out detailed timberman's maps, running their fingers down canyons, across state lines, out of forests and into the white space of deserts, guessing at where he was. Now they knew, and their spirits lifted.

Leaving Pittsburgh, Randolph kept his face at the window of his sleeping car as it rolled down through the ordered farms whose crops covered the low hills like squares in a quilt, through modern towns and their scrubbed and turreted brick stations, their electric streetcar lines, their corn-rows of automobiles parked in front of stores burgeoning with anything an American could want. His efficient eye noted the just-built macadam roads, and he imagined a view of the region from an aeroplane, the new avenues spidering out to highways and turnpikes, webs of pavement binding tight the prospering soil.

He changed trains in Richmond, boarding an older coach furnished with plush seats and varnished wood worn to a satin finish, and then watched the night country fly by as the station buildings became smaller and more decrepit, the roads behind them now made of graded gravel. The next day further south he changed trains again and saw gaunt men standing in the fields as if sunstruck, their clothes a sagging second skin of denim and copper rivets, their tobacco crops bug-bitten and jaundiced in the heat. Here were no stone houses at all, no paved thoroughfares, and only a few factory smokestacks divided the horizon. Randolph wondered if the sun-blistered barns of Georgia could offer some clue to his brother's wanderings. Why *this* direction, he kept asking himself. Away from money, and from people like him? He stared out at this strange country, the South, at the dark heat, and the used-up, coppery soil scratched over by mules.

At dinner a steward seated him with a woman wearing a stylish drop-waist dress, whose young daughter fidgeted at her side. Randolph envied the energy and quickness of children, and for six years had tried with his wife to produce a baby. He ordered, then fixed the child with a flat look. "Tell me a joke," he said.

The girl looked at her mother, who shrugged politely. "Don't know one, mister."

He was stuck by her accent, backwoods, whiny. "Sure you do. Smart girls like you can remember all sorts of jokes. Think of one your grandpa told."

The girl rolled her eyes under her bangs and said nothing. The waiter brought salads balanced up his arms and refilled the water glasses with long streams that took on the sideways jostle of the coach. The mother said little, only that they were going to a funeral, and Randolph worried that neither of them was very bright.

After the lettuce and the pork chops, the apple pie and coffee, the mill manager looked at his check and stretched a foot out into the carpeted aisle.

"A lady asked a farmer," the girl blurted out.

"What?" He was in the act of hoisting himself out of the chair. The mother turned her face to the dark window, and her reflection was not amused.

"She asked him how deep was his pond." The girl's pink hand flipped through her blond hair like a butterfly, then dropped into her lap.

"And what did he tell her?"

She straightened in her chair and drew a line with one finger along her collarbone. "He said, 'It comes up to here on my ducks.'"

At first, he was too startled to laugh, and then did, excessively, complimenting the woman on her daughter's sense of timing before wishing them a good evening and heading back to his compartment. He knew he'd behaved oddly, acting too surprised, but the joke was one his brother had told twenty years before, when they were lying in the big carpenter-built tree house behind their country place south of Pittsburgh. Byron had been a natural joke teller, easing a listener into what seemed just a bland story and then springing the punch line like a slap on the back. The mill manager stared down out of his window at the edge of roadbed racing past in a rectangle of light, remembering other answers the farmer had given about the depth of his pond. "Why, it goes all the way to the bottom," and "Deep enough to walk away because it's got at least two feet in it." He saw each line formed in his brother's mouth and closed his eyes as the words came back to him.

At first light in Alabama, he saw that the stations were mostly board and batten, indifferently whitewashed, and the rouge-colored mud fields fit only for making brick. He changed trains again—the coaches older, the locomotive smaller—and watched the field workers as they bent between the cotton rows or sulked away from the sun, lounging on loads of melons in dung-spattered spring wagons. In Meridian, Mississippi, stepping out into the humidity, he recalled that his grandfather had been a captain there with Sherman. Meridian was where war had been invented, the old man had told him, where the general had first ordered his troops to dismantle every machine they could find and beat the gear teeth with mauls, pound open the boilers, fracture the castings of steam engines, bend rails around trees, and roll all flywheels into rim-cracking fires until the town held not a single working mechanism. Randolph noticed only two sets of factory chimneys before he was called back aboard, and as the train snaked south into even denser heat he wondered what industries would have been steaming along in town had there been no war, what prosperity would have graced its people, what forest of black iron stacks would have risen into the sky like the masts of ships in a harbor.

That afternoon the train left the last belt of pine and slid down into a marshy lowland, rocking over a series of longer and longer wooden trestles until it broke out over the inland sea of Lake Pontchartrain. On his way to the dining car, Randolph passed through several day coaches where passengers wore bandannas around their sweating necks to keep the soot off their collars. The windows were wide open in the heat, the locomotive's stack trailing a roil of cinders that flurried down the lurching coaches, blowing in the eyes of anyone foolish enough to hang his head out in the waterlogged breeze.

His sleeper rolled into New Orleans, and he got off in a warm rain. In the station he was told by a ticket agent wearing an enormous mustache that the railroad trestle at Lafourche Crossing had collapsed into the bayou and he would have to take a steamboat all the way to Tiger Island, then double back east on the train to Poachum, the town at the end of his ticket.

The little man made a show of pulling out forms and pounding them with rubber stamps. "You can wait four days for the line to open up, or I can call and book you on the *E. B. Newman* for Tiger Island."

Randolph put a thumb in a vest pocket. "I want to go to Poachum, and not by boat. Isn't there a bus?"

The agent glanced up. "You not from around here."

"Pennsylvania."

The man jerked another form from a slot. "Mister Pennsylvania, we don't have too many paved roads. It's rained every day for three weeks and Highway 90 is no better than a slop jar. A bus can't hardly make it over that swampy stretch in good weather."

Randolph looked at his porter, who was balancing his luggage on a dolly, ignoring the conversation, and then turned back to the agent. "I thought passenger steamboats were a thing of the past."

The man studied Randolph's clothes, as if trying to figure out what the place he called home might be like. "Mister, we still got towns down here with no roads going to 'em." He pulled a scissors phone away from the wall, and booked passage on the *E. B. Newman*, stamped another sheaf of papers, and handed Randolph an elaborate green ticket running with the filigree of currency. "When you get off at Tiger Island, you can make a connection with a mixed train for the last twenty-two miles to Poachum."

The mill manager looked over his tickets, unable to read the tiny print. "Is there a station building there?"

"You could call it that."

"And there's a lumber-company train from there to Nimbus?"

The agent glanced down at Randolph's gleaming leather luggage, then laughed meanly. "Nimbus," he said. "I hope you got boots."

The *E. B. Newman* was a ghost of a boat, a listing stern-wheeler buckled in the hull, its paint sliding off like burned skin. Two rusting smokestacks stood in front of a pilothouse edged above the eaves with sooty gingerbread. In Randolph's dark and boxy stateroom he removed his shirt and scrubbed the train's grit off his face, soaping his underarms using a pitcher of river water and a varnish-colored bar of soap. He brushed back his hair and dried off with a limp towel stained by the imprint of a rusted nail driven into the wall above the washbowl. The air in the room was thick with mildew, so he went out and stood on the boiler deck, resting his elbows on the rail and looking down to the stage plank where roustabouts were carrying on their backs wooden boxes marked BLACK IRON ELBOWS, and sacks of cottonseed the size of stuffed chairs.

"Go on you crippled sows," the big chief mate hollered when the line of sweating men backed up on the plank. "You load like mammys slipping in pig shit." The mill manager was impressed by the man's businesslike anger, since efficiency of any type—long his father's obsession—turned his head like the clink of a silver coin on pavement. Efficiency was the one thing his father had ingrained in him. He studied the men straining up the stage plank through a sweating cloud of profane guidance and graded them like lumber, knowing these to be hardwood, twisted in the grain.

After the freight was brought on board, it was time for a herd of mules and donkeys to come over the stage and step into a roughboard pen ahead of the boilers. The first mule balked at the ramp, and Randolph was amazed when four blocky young rousters put their shoulders next to the animal's legs and lifted him up, eight hundred pounds of live weight. The lead man arched an arm over his head and twisted the mule's ear like a dishrag while it pissed a splattering stream up the ramp. The rousters loaded six more plow mules and then five of the donkeys without trouble until the sixth backed down, braying, his eyes rolling up in a wooly gray skull. Two men hoisted him along and threw him like a loaf into the straw and droppings of the pen.

The last mule was a big hinny, long in the pastern, a bridled riding mule that stopped dead halfway up the ramp. No amount of bootblows or lashes with a deck rope could convince it to board. The chief mate, bearded, sunburned as a brick, pulled a hickory shaft out of a capstan and struck the mule a blow between the eyes that brought it down in a rumble of skidding knee bone. Randolph heard a sash slide open above him and looked up to the pilothouse, where the captain leaned out in a blue deepwater uniform. "Mr. Breaux, has that animal hurt himself?"

The chief mate pushed up one of the mule's lids with the hickory. "No sir," he called. "The big screw's just been educated is all." The animal drunkenly tried to stand, but two legs went over the edge and it fell thrashing into the river, detonating against the water's surface. "Lollis," the mate hollered, and a black rouster crabwalked down the canted wharf and jumped onto the mule's back, fishing up the reins and slapping its rump until his mount's forelegs caught lumber and pulled them both from the current. The rouster gave a whoop and rode the bleeding mule around a pile of coffee sacks in a barrel-race sweep and thundered up the stage plank into the deck pen, where the animal skidded on his iron shoes across a glaze of shit and slammed broadside against a bulkhead.

Randolph turned to the main cabin, where he was seated at once by the Negro waiter, and ordered a meal. He was sipping lemonade when the drone of the whistle sent his table's china into a sympathetic buzz, and he saw the dock drift away as the boat backed out, the paddle wheel biting water in a susurrant rush.

The waiter set down a plate of chops and potatoes with a little mocking bow of the head. "You need something else, sah?"

The mill manager looked up. From a distance, the man's navy, brass-buttoned uniform had appeared immaculate, but on close inspection it was like everything on the steamboat, carefully patched and dull with wear. "You'll be waiting on me for a day and a half. My name is Randolph Aldridge. What's yours?"

The Negro's face, nettled with a short stubble, did not change. He bowed closer. "They calls me Speck, sah."

"What's your real name?" Randolph spread a cloth napkin in his lap.

"I reckon that's it," he said, his eyes taking on the throb of the yellow electric light that pulsed under a dusty ceiling fan.

"Do you live around Tiger Island?"

"Not that place. No indeed." He shook his head glumly. "The engineer stay there, though. That be all, sah?"

The mill manager took a sip of his drink. "How much do you make, Speck?"

The man's dark eyes flicked toward the far end of the cabin, where a large gilded mirror doubled the room, to make sure the head steward wasn't watching. "About a dollar a day, plus a crib and my eats, sah. And some people's nice enough to leave a nickel under they plate if I gives good service." He tucked the tray under an arm and backed off, ending the conversation. After Randolph finished eating, he drew out a handful of pocket change and slipped a coin under the edge of the plate. Four quarters remained in his palm, and he closed his hand into a fist and thought about the man he held there, for a day.

The next morning the *E. B. Newman* discharged its animals at a dirt landing called Vane, where a band of half-naked drovers caned them up the levee in a struggle of flying mud. The boat waddled back out into a high river and the pilot began searching for easy water along the insides of the bends, as though the engines hadn't the strength to fight the current coursing midstream in mud caps. About sundown the boat drifted into the stained concrete vault of the Plaquemine lock. Randolph watched the chamber pump out and the boat go down like a coffin after prayers. He entered the cabin for supper and found only three other tables occupied and those by men without ties, their oily pants hitched up by suspenders. The lights burned infirmly, pulsing with every turn of the generator. After his meal, Randolph stared at the bulbs' convulsions above the filigreed turmoil of the salon, then walked down between the tarnished brass rails of the grand staircase to the main deck, moving aft toward the engine room. Inside, an oiler was filling the brass drip cups on the port engine, oblivious to the tons of machinery flying back and forth an inch beneath his arms. On a chair next to a wall of gleaming bronze steam gauges sat the chief engineer, a short man with a big mustache and hair the color of steel wool. He wore navy-blue pants, a black vest, and a string tie drooping over a white shirt, the cuffs held off his hands by garters.

"Mind if I come in?" Randolph asked.

The little man looked up from his chair, then down at Randolph's expensive shoes. "*Mais*, you can come in if you want, yeah," he said.

The mill manager stepped into the smell of hot enamel

and the oaty essence of saturated steam, looking over at the generator and its attendant electrical panel, a black porcelain expanse containing meters and knife-blade switches and one rheostat the size of a small drum. He reached out and rotated its handle an inch, and the lights came up, their pulsing diminished. "Some of the contacts are dirty."

The engineer looked away.

"Where's your home?"

The man looked back and saw the suit, the gold watch chain, the clean collar. "My house is in Tiger Island."

"You must know the other licensed engineers in town."

He nodded. "I know some. At the mills."

"What about at Nimbus?" Randolph blinked at the tap of a gong bolted to a beam above his head. The engineer stood up, gave a gleaming steel wheel a half turn, and the port and starboard piston rods slowed.

"That's way out in the swamp. I don't hear much about him, me."

"He's a German, I believe."

"That's what I hear," the engineer said, giving the throttle wheel another nudge. "A damned hun."

"You hear any news about that mill?"

"What kind of news you want, you?" He leaned on the hot wheel and narrowed his eyes.

"My brother is the lawman for the mill town. I haven't seen him in four years."

A small bell hanging overhead on a spring coil rattled, and the engineer slung the valve wide, the engines paying the wooden pittman shafts out to the paddle wheel faster, the polished valve gear clacking up and down. "Wish I hadn't seen my brother in four years," he said. "I'd still have me a bank account." He walked over and said something in French to the oiler, who nodded and walked out into the night.

Randolph stood next to the starboard engine, watching the seven-foot piston shaft play in and out of the cylinder. "Are the valves always this noisy?"

"Aw, that's California cutoff for you." He wiped his hands

and shook the rag at the engine. "The damned machine's older than me. Another ten or fifteen year you won't find a engine like this working noplace. Things are changing over, yeah." He stuffed a corner of the rag in his back pocket.

"What do you mean?"

"I been reading some." The engineer held out his pointing finger. "A diesel engine turns thirty percent of its fuel to mechanical energy. With steam you lucky to get five percent." He swatted the engine's asbestos lagging, which was as white as a plaster cast. "You watch. Ten years. It's scary, the way things go."

Randolph talked about steam engines, for that, too, was part of his education. After a while, the little engineer put on a glove and reached in between two rising and falling poppet-valve levers to retrieve a Mason jar of hot coffee. "You want some? The galley sent it down a couple hours ago." He retrieved two ironware mugs from hooks under the main steam gauge and poured.

The mill manager took a swallow of the strong dark roast, noting how it endured on his tongue. "Many boats like this still running?"

The engineer sat down in his chair and put a foot against a long lever. Behind him, the piston rods hissed and spat like cats fighting. "*Non*. Maybe two boats on the Natchez trade, one on Lake Pontchartrain and that direction. One on the Atchafalaya and Bayou Teche. Captain Cooley, he still runs up the Ouchita River where them poor people got no roads." He took a drink. "But nobody's making money. If our pilot put a log through the hull of this thing, we'd row home in the skiff and forget about it."

"Where would you work then?"

"Ferries. The icehouse. Maybe a sawmill. They got some pissant rafting steamers I could work on." He looked up at Randolph. "What you do? Lumber buyer? You dress too good for a salesman."

"I'm the new manager for Nimbus. My name's Randolph Aldridge."

The engineer seemed unimpressed, but he put out his hand anyway. "Minos Thibodeaux," he said.

"Your family always live in Tiger Island?"

"Since caveman days." He poured another slug of coffee into his mug, then the mill manager's. "Where you from?"

"Pennsylvania."

"That's where that snow flies."

"I haven't heard much from my brother," he said, pretending to read a gauge.

Minos looked away, sniffed his mustache. "You lose track of him, yeah?"

"He disappeared out west for a while."

"You come to check up on him or something?"

"I'm going to run the mill and make sure he's doing a good job."

The engineer gave him a hard look. "You'd fire your own brother?"

"No. I mean, I'm worried about him."

Minos seemed to think about this. "Maybe you need to."

Randolph put his cup down next to an oilcan. "Why's that?"

"Some 'talian gentlemen down at Tiger Island would like to send him back to Pennsylvania."

The mill manager laughed. "He can get people perturbed, all right."

"Cut up in a jug."

Randolph turned his head away. "He's a lawman," he mumbled. "He's bound to make a few enemies, I'd guess."

"These enemies was made before he met 'em."

Just then a big silver backing gong banged and Minos leaped to his throttle wheel and lever, reversing the machinery. The boat shuddered, backing out of whatever problem the pilot had steered it into.

Randolph went up to the dark cabin deck and felt his way along the outside rail. The boat struggled along a bayou as narrow as a ditch, the icicle beam of the carbon-arc headlight igniting the tops of stumps rising from the obsidian water.

Something like a longhaired wolf drifted toward him over the rail, and he flattened against the bulkhead as the moss-eaten limb gouged the window next to him and then retreated like a monster's claw. His heart bumped up in rhythm as the branch dragged a life ring off a stanchion. The boat heeled, the pilot skinning the bank with the stern and heading for midstream, following the deep water of his memory.

Later, from his hard, sour bunk, Randolph heard the sonorous whistle call its name to a landing, and for an hour he listened to the tolling of wooden barrels and the molten cursing of the mate. Then came the profound tone of that same oversized whistle and the sense that the boat was rocking away from more than just a mud bank, the paddle wheel slapping down the tarry water on a voyage beyond the things he knew. He thought again of his brother, a good swimmer who never feared the water, not even at night, and he fell asleep remembering the time he learned to float on his back, Byron's fingertips training the bones in his spine to drift level and rise toward the air.

The next day came on hot and foggy, and the steamer picked around fallen trees lined with red-eared turtles and fought pulpy rafts of water lilies, once yawing into a mile-deep carpet of the plants, and stalling. The mill manager was again in the engine room, speaking with the engineer when the pilot rang a bell for more power. Minos forced the long lever into its last notch and yelled for the firemen to shake the boiler grates. "*Fil d'putain*, we won't tie up until t'ree o'clock."

And he was right. The steamer rounded out of a bayou into a wide bay filled with salt-smelling water. On the eastern bank was a low town of wooden store buildings and warehouses, two large sawmills anchoring the upstream and downstream points. The *Newman* nosed into the public dock at two minutes past three and tied up among rafting steamers and hissing propeller tugs. The air smelled of coal smoke and stinking oyster shells, and beyond the muddy dock ran a street lined with several spattered Ford trucks and two caked wagons pulled by swaybacked mules. Randolph came down the stage plank between roustabouts and shouldered through a group of merchants and clerks come out to meet the boat. He navigated across the slurry of mud and clamshells that was the main street and got up on a boardwalk, knocking his shoes clean on the edge of the planks, then walking south toward the railroad station where the agent told him the train to Poachum would leave at six o'clock in the morning.

He looked out at the track. "I thought it left at six in the evening."

The agent spat a slow rill of tobacco juice into something behind the counter. "Sometimes it does. Tomorrow it leaves at six in the morning."

He wanted to ask what kind of railroad allowed a twelve-hour variance, but he could sense already that he had to be careful in this town.

The agent smiled a brown smile. "You from up North, ain't you?"

"Yes." Randolph told him who he was.

"Laney," the agent said, not offering to shake hands.

"Is there a place where I can hire an automobile?"

The agent's smile expressed an amber drop from the corner of his mouth. "Yeah. But what would you do with it?"

"Pardon?"

"The highway's got water over it. You might get to Poachum. You might not."

Randolph pulled out his watch and wound it, matching it against the station clock. "Well, where's the livery stable?"

The stationmaster spat again. "Mister, you'll tear the wheels off a buggy in them ruts out that way. And if you want to ride twenty-two miles horseback through the rain and flies, that's okay by me, but you better get a fat horse that'll float. If you don't break off his legs you'll have to row him through some low spots, and when you get where you're going they'll be more mud on you than him."

He looked through the bay window at a dark sky. "Is there a phone I can use?"

"Where you want to call?"

"Nimbus."

The agent chuckled while lowering his pencil to a form. "Phone line stops at Poachum. The agent does have a local wire going down to Nimbus." He looked up. "I've heard even a big owl can take 'er down."

"I want to call the lawman down there."

"What for?"

"I know him."

The agent bobbed his head. "And you still want to talk to him?"

Randolph pinched the fat under his chin and took in a long breath. "When does the mill train get to Poachum so I can ride it to Nimbus?"

"It don't run regular."

The mill manager cocked his head and arched an eyebrow.

"Okay, I'll raise my man down there, if you can call him that." The agent went to a wall phone, one of three in a line, and turned its crank a set number of turns, waited, cranked again, waited, then cranked once more, sending a short burst of electricity into the eastbound wire. When no one picked up on the other end, he walked to his telegraph key and sent a call. Both men watched the sounder in its resonator box, and in a minute it began to knock letters into the air.

The mill manager shifted his weight when the message stopped. "Yes?"

"Nimbus train gets into Poachum tomorrow around eight. You'll make the turnaround for the mill, mister."

Randolph headed for the door, then stopped and looked back. "What do you know about that lawman down at Nimbus?"

The agent unwrapped a plug of dark tobacco and opened his clasp knife, which he'd sharpened down to a talon. "I hear he don't like garlic."

CHAPTER THREE

A short man, his hair like cotton in an aspirin bottle, walked through the station door carrying a double-barreled shotgun, a marshal's badge dangling from his sagging coat. Behind him was a big, balding priest, smoking a briar pipe with a bent stem. "Sid," the marshal said, "what'd that man want?"

"Ticket to Poachum. He was asking about your friend at Nimbus."

The lawman looked after the mill manager, who was walking north along River Street. "His clothes fit too right."

"Sounds like he's from up North," the agent explained.

"What's he want with Byron?"

Sid Laney shrugged. "At least he don't look Italian."

The priest slapped his forehead like an idiot, chuckled, then followed the old marshal out into the sun. They walked down River Street among the musky trappers and wormy dogs to the office, a high-ceilinged box with a rusty jail cell at its rear. "Ah," the priest said, stepping into the shade.

On the main desk sat a pail full of murky ice holding two crockery bottles, their stoppers wired down tight. The men sat in a pair of squawking steamer chairs and slopped beer into a pair of mugs. The priest took a long draw, and the marshal came up for air with his white mustache sopping. They both blinked and for a long time said nothing. Across the street, a tugboat whistle gave a long hoot and a pilot cursed a deckhand in a rising harangue. The priest cleared his throat and Merville looked at him.

"I'm giving a good homily this Sunday. It's about Jesus throwing the money changers out of the temple."

"Methodists can't go to no Catholic church."

The priest took another drink. "You're not a Methodist."

"I was baptized one, me."

The priest leaned a black elbow on the desk. "You never darkened the door of any Methodist church. Your father was Catholic."

"Religion comes from the mamma." The marshal waved his hand as though brushing away a fly. "You can give me the short side of your sermon right now."

The priest folded his hands. "It's something you can relate to. It's about how even though anger is natural, and sometimes to a purpose, it always has to be controlled."

The old man sucked his mustache. "Why you telling me that? You still mad I knocked down that trapper?"

The priest shook his head. "The Walton man took thirty-six stitches and was unconscious for two days. You can't tell me you weren't excessively angry."

"Mais, non," Merville said. "He was full of radiator-made and trying to kill little Nellie the whore with a beer bottle over at Buzetti's. I wasn't mad. I just did what I had to do, me."

The priest looked at him with expressionless eyes, a trick he used to make his parishioners form their own notions about how things really are. "Somehow I can't believe that."

Merville took another drink. The beer had warmed and the mug formed no ring on the desk. "Father, if a nun had to face two drunk deckhands swinging razors on each other in a alley, she'd at least lasso one of 'em with her rosary."

The priest stood and drew off his mug, then wiped a finger over his long upper lip. "I'll come by tomorrow, maybe."

"If she had a shotgun," the marshal grumbled, "she might of used it. You can't let people kill each other."

"Goodbye," the priest said.

"If you see that Yankee, let me know what he does. I don't

want him messing with Byron. Poor bastard's got enough on his back as it is."

The priest's face brightened, his hand on the doorknob. "You could pray for your friend."

Merville looked down at his empty mug. "I think God done fooled with that one enough."

Since the *E. B. Newman* wasn't leaving until late the next morning, the captain allowed Randolph to keep his stateroom for two dollars, and he killed time at the boiler deck rail watching roustabouts roll two hundred barrels of molasses up the stage plank before nightfall. Later, he witnessed a thunderstorm walk in from the west and at sundown saw a ripping bolt take out the few electric lights along the street. When the rain stopped, he walked out on the cabin deck and listened to fast dance music—weeping clarinets and a stuttering trumpet coming from down an alley—and remembered it was Saturday night. A street lamp came on slowly, like a candle warming up, and he could see men, their boots lacquered with mud, slopping in and out of a doorway like bees in a hole. Somewhere a transformer detonated, and the lights failed again. On the wharf below, a sooty lantern rose above a crap game, then a short burst of doggy laughter split the air and a roustabout fell down with a bottle in his hand, the ocher glass shattering in the kerosene light. Three mosquitoes stung the back of the mill manager's neck and he hurried inside.

Hours later, awakened by a crescendo of angry hollering, he pulled on his trousers and walked barefoot through the carpeted salon back to the rail. Minos, the engineer, was standing forward, his shirt off. "It's the rousters," he said, when Randolph walked up. "They getting in it now with them bastards off the *Edenborn*."

A crash of drunken shouts sailed up from the wharf, then a single yell and a skitter of boots. On the top deck, someone ran to the wheelhouse and a spotlight fired up, shining on the dock where a dozen black men grappled and rolled, their rotten shirts ripping, loose overalls straps whipping the air. Suddenly, two of them pulled straight razors and began a ritual circling, then another unfolded a long blade and swung into a screaming curse. The captain walked out on the roof of the Texas and hollered down to the big rousters, who were deaf with drink. The hulking mate, yawning and pulling on his galluses, walked up next to the captain, who told him, "Go down there and put an end to it."

The mate spat over the rail. "Can't nothing stop them now."

The captain twisted around and called up to the pilot in the wheelhouse. "Blow shorts and see if that brings the policeman. We can't load freight with dead niggers."

The whistle coughed up a gallon of water and issued a series of yelping blasts. Another razor came out of a shirt, and the mill manager's mouth fell open as the blade drew a long red line across the face of the rouster who'd ridden the mule out of the river. Three men ran over from the downstream steamer and began swinging boots and fists. A man shrieked and fell on his back, bloody fingers pinching his stomach together as the riot closed over him like a muddy surf.

Minos bumped the mill manager's elbow. "Here come Judgment Day," he said, pointing.

Randolph looked and could make out a little man with uncombed white hair advancing quickly from a side street. A badge winked on his coat and a double-barreled shotgun dangled at his side, but when he stepped up onto the dock and yelled at the men, his words might as well have been puffs of steam. So he pulled the forearm off the shotgun, dropped the barrel from the stock, grabbed the twin tubes on the smaller end, and swung hard against the skull of the nearest man, sending him to the dock like a stunned cow. A few dark faces went up at that, and he swung again, his white hair shocking up on impact, and then again, sending a third man screaming into the river, and the others began to scatter and run. Five men lay sprawled on the dock, and the one who'd been cut across the stomach was not moving. The marshal straightened up over him, put his shotgun back together, and dropped two shells into its barrels.

"*Alors, quoi c'est son nom?*" he asked.

The engineer yelled down in French that he was not on the *Newman*'s crew.

A rouster sat up, holding his bleeding head as if afraid it might roll off his shoulders. "Don't shoot me, Mister Merville."

The marshal slid the gun into the crook of his arm. "A high-brass shell costs seven cents, and the bastard of a mayor we got would charge it against my pay." He pointed to the dead man. "You know him?"

"He on the *Drew* with us."

"He got a family?" Merville checked the corpse's pockets, found a silver dollar, and put it in his vest.

"He from way up the country." The rouster took a hand away from his face and looked at the blood. "He ain't got no people."

The marshal slid his shotgun under the shining waist, lifted, and rolled the corpse over, repeating the motion until it tumbled into the river. He looked toward the wheelhouse and shaded his eyes. "You can kill that light, yeah," he said.

The engineer spat over the side and turned to Randolph. "So much for that."

The mill manager finally closed his mouth. "Is that how you have to operate around here?"

"It is now." Minos looked down. "In ten years or fifteen years, maybe it'll be different."

"Who's the policeman?"

Minos turned his head to where the old man herded three limping men back to their boat, the bloody shotgun sideways against their backs. "Him? That's my daddy."

Randolph climbed onto his thin mattress and lay awake and sweating until he heard a tap on the door at five. Speck, doubling as porter, cleared his throat and the mill manager told him fifteen minutes. He got up and washed at the basin, shaved, and put on a fresh dark wool suit. In the narrow main salon he sat at a naked table in the dark, smelling the enamel and tobacco latent in the air, imagining the carnivorous swamp he was traveling toward and wondering how all the fine books his brother had read could have prepared him to police its mill saloon. He remembered the thump of the shotgun barrels on the skulls of the roustabouts, then looked up to where first light spangled in the textured glass of the clerestories, sooty greens and golds flaring dimly like fire seen through mica. He moved through the tinted light down onto the foredeck and stood among the freight boxes and sacks to wait for his luggage. Hearing a noise he turned to see the rouster who'd been cut in the face. He was sitting back against a pile of rice sacks, moaning like a record played much too slowly, and the mill manager lifted a deck lamp off its hook and walked back among the crates, thinking that it would be a shame for such a worker to be ruined.

He raised the light. "Is someone going to get a doctor for you?"

A pair of eyes opened, boiled eggs floating in a tabasco of pain. "Ain't one'll come."

Speck, the waiter, suddenly loomed at Randolph's back. "You want me to carry these bags up to the depot on the dolly, sah?"

The mill manager stooped down. "Do you have any alcohol and bandages on board?"

Speck sniffed. "Seem like some niggers done had enough alcohol."

"He needs some for the outside. And bring me a roll of gauze and a strip of salt meat from the galley." He looked up and couldn't make out the man's face, but he could smell his sour black uniform. "There'll be more than a nickel under a plate."

"Sah," Speck said, turning for the staircase.

The rouster raised his head and the gash in his face opened like a long, red mouth, spreading from above the temple, across the cheek, down to the chin. When the waiter returned with a bottle of straight neutral spirits, the mill manager poured it onto the cut, some trickling into the man's left eye, and he hollered out to God Almighty, thrashed his arms, and fell back against the sacks, trembling like a mule shaking off flies. Randolph wiped the wound clean, then he disinfected his penknife and cut a strip of salt meat out of what Speck had brought, laid this on the gash, and tied it in place with five separate bands of gauze looped around the man's head. Each time he drew a knot closed, the rouster cried out.

The mill manager put two fingers on the bloody neck to check the pulse. "Tomorrow, pull all this off at daybreak and throw it in the river. Burn the cut out again with this alcohol and tie on another strip of salt meat, just like I tied this one. Don't strain your face for three days or it'll split like a tomato, you hear?"

"I hear," the man whispered.

Randolph pushed the cinched chin sideways and examined his work. "If I had a suture kit I'd try to sew you up." He wiped a clot from the man's neck with a wad of gauze and threw it overboard. "Keep your face washed every day for ten days or they'll wind up rolling you into the river like they did that other fellow. The waiter here will give you the meat and gauze when you need it." At this, the rouster settled onto his side and closed his eyes.

Speck hoisted a trunk onto his shoulder. "Got no mo' manners than a hog."

The mill manager looked up at him, slipping the cork back in the bottle. "I don't think he's feeling very civil at the moment."

"No, sah."

"You take care of him and next time I see you, I'll remember."

"I bet you will, sah." Speck ducked his head at the rouster, then turned away, swinging the heavy trunk wide.

At six Randolph climbed onto a sun-peeled wooden coach tacked to the end of an eastbound line of freight cars. Across the aisle sat two men wearing long boots and holding taped-together shotguns between their knees, and behind them an Indian man and three hatless women in faded housedresses made of flour sacks swayed with the motion of the coach. The men stank, but so did he, a fact of life, he realized, in a place where a man could break a sweat by walking to the privy. He put a hand out of the window and hefted the air. The train rattled past the edge of town, its five-chime whistle scolding road crossings until there were no more and the little locomotive entered a sun-killing forest of virgin cypress, the rails running into a slot capped by a gray ribbon of sky. Drifting back from the engine a sooty mist coated the cars, and the mill manager considered Minos's predictions regarding the decline of steam machinery. He wondered what smokeless boxlike machine, easy on the ears and clothes, might pull the trains in fifteen or twenty years.

At a quarter to seven, the brakes came on with a jerk, and the train stopped at the dozen houses that made up Poachum. The baggage handler cast Randolph's fine trunks onto the platform of the little plank station as if they were boxes of trash. The train whistled off, and after the last coach passed, he looked across the tracks at the swamped, axle-bending road that led back to Tiger Island. Eight trapper's shacks built up on cypress stumps and four shotgun houses of raw wood were arranged with the logic of an armload of tossed kindling. A siding west of the station was loaded with flatcars of pale aromatic cypress planks waiting to be shipped, and a spur track plunged south from the main line, into the swamp toward Nimbus.

The mill manager entered the station where a dark-haired boy was sitting under a clock, wearing a green visor. The agent told him the mill had just phoned, and that the lumber train would arrive soon. Randolph watched him struggle to fill out waybills for a minute, then asked if he knew the lawman down there.

"I don't see him much," the boy said without looking up, his thin arms moving over his forms.

"He doesn't send messages out?"

"He keeps his business back in the woods." The agent began to sort invoices, frowning at each in turn.

Randolph walked out and looked down the kinked railroad to Nimbus that led into a tunnel of bearded cypress trees, the shallow water on either side carpeted with apple-green duckweed. In the distance he heard the exhaust of a locomotive, and in twenty minutes the train came wobbling into sight, dragging cars of kiln-dried one-by-twelves, six-by-six timbers, beams fourteen inches square, and racks of weatherboard, all red Louisiana cypress, fine grained and fragrant in the heat. After the engine drew the loads out onto the main line, then shoved them back into an empty siding, the mill manager pulled on the grab irons and mounted the locomotive.

The engineer studied his suit and shoes. "What?"

"I'm Randolph Aldridge."

"The devil you say."

"No, the mill manager. You and your fireman get down and put those trunks on the tender." He watched as they stepped down and considered his luggage a while before pulling off their oily gloves.

Randolph ran the locomotive himself through the hundred-foot trees back to Nimbus. The wood slabs the fireman tossed into the firebox were free fuel, and the smoke smelled like efficiency. The reports he'd received about the site had not drawn him a picture, but he hoped for an adequately maintained property that he could fine-tune. However, when the train clattered into a clearing of a hundred stumpy acres, the settlement lay before him like an unpainted model of a town made by a boy with a dull pocketknife. Littered with dead treetops, wandered by three muddy streets, the place seemed not old but waterlogged, weather tortured, weed wracked. He stopped the engine and blew the squalling whistle once, gazing out from the engineer's seat, his feelings sinking like the crossties under the locomotive's axles.

A two-story barracks for the single workers rose against the western tree line, and in front of it, on both sides of a rain-swamped lane, ran two rows of shotgun houses, paintless, screenless, not a shutter on a single one of them. South of this row by a hundred yards he spotted the manager's house, a square, porched, steep-roofed structure of raw, pink-tinged weatherboard, to the rear of it a cabin and tiny stable, then a short crude fence of cypress bats, and beyond that a wide canal, its surface broken with trunks drifting like reptiles in ambush. Between the house and the mill was the looming commissary with its muddy porches, and a good distance behind it was the low saloon, carelessly built and rangy, sagging back from a wide gallery bearing a dozen scattered hide-bottomed chairs. To the rear of the saloon three cabins and a line of privies perched at odd angles on the berm of the canal. On the other side of the soaring mill was a longer double row of forty shacks without porches or steps—the black section, he supposed—and two more of the featureless, rain-streaked barracks. Not far from Randolph's position in the locomotive's cab, he could see a line of low houses with screened windows and balustered porches facing south. In one of the backyards he noted a broken steam-engine flywheel, a set of rusty hand-cuffs dangling from a spoke.

In the middle of the clearing roared the mill itself. Out of every metal roof rose jetting exhaust vents or hundred-foot black iron smokestacks streaming flags of woodsmoke. Randolph figured that some five hundred people worked in the mill and in the woods beyond. He stepped down from the engine, felt the unsettled land devour his shoes, and suddenly understood something about this place: two years before, the loudest sound had been the hollow calls of slow-stepping herons.

Walking around watery gouges rippling with minnows, he made his way to the office upstairs in the mill. In an unpainted room made of glowing beaded board he met his assistant manager, Jules Blake, a rough, hungover-looking fellow, who said he was from Trinity County, Texas. Randolph asked him questions for two hours, watching him nervously build the wad of tobacco in his left cheek as he gave answers.

He tried to put the man at ease. "Just because ownership switches doesn't mean we have to do things any differently. But I do think we need to clean up some."

Jules looked out a sawdusty window. "I thought that myself when I come on a few weeks ago. But it rains ever afternoon and the weeds grow up faster than you can spare a man to cut 'em. The stumps won't burn, and we killed an ox trying to pull up a little one in the middle of a road."

"The last manager, how did he make out here?"

Jules put his boots up on a desk, crackling its loose veneer. "From what I hear he weighed down the incoming order forms with full jiggers. Did what selling he could over the phone there, going through that child at Poachum like we got to do. He counted the lumber when he could see it." Jules shifted his wad. "Worst thing he done is hire up a bunch of jarhead white trash and single Negroes as big as bulls from those east Texas mills." He spat expertly into an enameled cuspidor by his desk. "They just like oxes. I moved here to get away from such as that."

Randolph looked out to where a stray mule stood next to a house, its head in a window chewing on the curtain. "We can't run the place with schoolteachers. I'll just do the same paperwork as the last manager. You keep after the men as you've been doing, and I'll watch the mechanics of the place. What kind of engineers do we have?"

"Just good enough to keep from gettin' blowed up. You got to check on 'em come Monday, see they ain't workin' with the alcohol flu." Jules gestured over toward the boiler house. "The German's the chief engineer, and he's fair, but when he gets blue he sure likes that sauce."

"How's the fights?" Randolph asked, looking out the window at a rising rain cloud.

Jules stared down at the dried mud under his desk. "We got a graveyard with thirty bodies in it."

"Good Lord. Who put the most of them there?"

The other man pinched his nose, put his boots down, and sniffed. "Is it true your old man bought this mill because he found out your brother was working here?"

Randolph sat down at a rolltop desk and tried a drawer, but it was swollen shut. "That's right. Have you seen him today?"

"He's making rounds."

"Someone in town told me he's had a brush with some Italians? We heard about it up North, too."

Jules leaned over the spittoon for a moment, but held in. "Don't fool with me."

Randolph looked away. "All right, then."

"I hope the hell you've come down here to help him."

The mill manager gave him a look. "Isn't that what family does?"

Jules thought a moment. "Good family."

"Tell me about the Italians."

Jules shrugged. "A bad batch of Sicilians. The saloon's in their pocket, on a piece of property the last owners let 'em have. They own the thing, so you can't just run 'em off. Some time ago they wanted to put in two more card games, more slots, a couple new whores, and he's been bucking 'em."

"That's understandable."

Two floors below the office the band saw began to shriek as though binding in a log, and Jules stood up, stretching his arms. "The damned place just causes us trouble. The married men lose their pay and go home and beat on their women. Some of the kids around here look like sticks they eat so poor. The young bucks, they lose their scrip and start poundin' hell out of each other." Jules opened the door, listening to the engineer yell something in German down in the plant. "But you might tell your brother to ease off a bit. Those boys are from Chicago."

Randolph laughed. "This is a little saloon back in the swamps."

Jules turned and looked at him. "Mr. Randolph, one thing

I know. To a Sicilian, nothing's a local problem." He spat into the hallway. "They're just about like the federal government."

The mill manager watched him leave, guessing he was wrong. Looking out at the tree line where the land rolled down into black swamp water, he wondered how many people even knew Nimbus existed, this dot at the heart of a great forest-green blur on his father's map. He got up and found an old pair of high leather boots in a locker and walked down a rutted lane to his house, trying to ignore a man sitting wall-eyed on a stump next to the road and a noisy group playing cards in the shade of a shack, their commissary tokens glittering on scrap planks thrown across sawhorses.

There was not a speck of paint on or in his house. Walking through the rooms touching the naked wood, he felt like a beetle inside a tree. In the backyard an old mulatto man drowsed on the porch of a cabin while next to him a young light-skinned woman washed clothes in a galvanized tub.

"Are you the housekeeper?" he called, looking around the bald yard.

"Yes," she said. "This is my daddy." She nodded to the man with a respectful motion.

"I'm the new mill manager. Can you find me something to eat?"

She dried her hands in her apron and walked past him into the big house, glancing across her shoulder at his face.

Randolph found a nearly blind horse in the small stable behind the yard, its eyes the color of a sun-clouded beer bottle; he saddled him, and set out to ride the whole mud-swamped site, aiming to find his brother, and also wanting the men to see him moving among them, laying claim. The horse was slow but the mill manager sensed it had memorized the place, so he dropped the reins and allowed it to take him on a logical circuit. In a half hour he had not seen his brother, so he retook the reins and turned back to the houses near the railroad, riding to the one Jules had pointed out earlier and tying the horse to a porch post. He was surprised to hear a phonograph keening inside, John McCormack, the Irish tenor, singing "I'll Take You Home Again, Kathleen" in an impossibly high voice. When he knocked, a sandy-haired woman in her early twenties came out as soon as his fist touched wood.

She wore a patterned housedress and her hair was pinned up in back. Looking at his clothes, at the way he carried himself, she began wringing her hands. "He's resting up," she said. "He just came in."

Randolph smiled, thinking the woman a rascally surprise Byron had kept from them all. "I'm his brother, the new manager. And you?"

Her mouth dropped open and she glanced behind her, then gave him a shy look. "Well, I reckon you'll find out soon enough," she said. "I went and married him." She had the direct gaze and chapped hands of a farmwoman. "My name's Ella."

"I'm happy to meet you," he said, at a loss. "This is, well, it's nice to . . ."

"He's right inside."

She stepped back and then disappeared into the rear of the house, so he entered the front room where his brother was seated in a Morris chair, his eyes closed, a large Victrola quaking before him. His brother's upheld fingers trembled in the air along with the exaggerated wavering in McCormack's throat. He was, at thirty-six, already graying, the scoring along his eyes and mouth showing all the bad weather of France and Kansas. His hair was close-cropped, as though the woman had cut it with a big pair of shears. Randolph felt a lightness in his chest, just as he had as a young child when his brother came home from horseback riding or hunting.

When the record finished, the automatic cutoff clicked and the turntable stopped with a whistle. "Byron?"

He did not turn, but finally said, "I wondered how long it would take for him to send someone."

"It's Randolph, By."

And then the lawman, showing his big teeth, stood and grabbed his brother's hand, squeezing it too hard, not shaking but vibrating it like a man being electrocuted. Randolph stepped forward and gave him a hug, taking in the scent of him.

"My own little board-measuring brother," Byron said, backing away. "The best of a good lot has come to lay eyes on me at last. Well, gaze upon this ruin."

"You look good," Randolph said, taking back his stinging hand and putting it carefully into his pocket. "You've gained weight. Married life must agree with you." He still felt small around his brother, always too naïve and simple. "How's the life of a policeman?"

Byron sat down and pointed to a chair. "I'll bet you want to know a lot of things, don't you? Why won't I go home and work for father and get rich, right?" He leaned toward his brother, his eyes pulsing like a flame in an opened firebox. "Let's get this straight right now. I didn't want to join the army. Even though I was already working over there, I'd seen enough of it. When Wilson declared war, Father wrote and told me it was my duty because I was the fittest of his sons." He made a mocking, backhanded sweep. "Little Randolph was a bit portly and had flat feet, so I would have to be the family's glory. I turned off my brain and believed him. He made me a patriot." Byron glanced toward an interior doorway where the tip of Ella's nose was visible. "I shouldn't blame him, not really. His head was full of patriotic songs. After a while, so was mine." His shoulders rose and fell in his denim shirt. "I guess it still is. Once you start singing the damned things, it's hard to stop, you know."

Randolph straightened in his chair. "You made it through. You came back." He tried to keep accusation out of his voice.

"He still had the songs in his head when I came back, but you don't want to know what was in my head, Rando. You couldn't imagine."

"By—"

"When I got wind of the fact he'd bought this mill, I started to light out again. I thought he was planning to get me back in a suit and under his thumb." He laughed then, a booming laugh. "Can you see him coming down in these swamps, as much as he hates dampness? No danger of that. I figured he'd send you."

"You knew about the purchase?"

"Rando. I'm a policeman."

The mill manager looked again to the hallway door, which now was empty. "Your wife. She's pretty."

"I'll never inflict the family in Pittsburgh on her, that's for sure." He jumped up and wound the Victrola twenty times. "You asked about the police life." His voice wobbled with the turns of the handle. "Well, they ran me out of a town where I wouldn't kill a man, and they ran me out of another where I did. I ended up riding fence out West and chasing off rustlers until the marshals and their damned cars arrested them all and put me out of business." He sat back and seemed to try to think of something else to say, putting a hand to his forehead, then taking it down quickly. "The rest you don't want to know about. I just bang around from badge to badge trying to make fellows do right, that's all." His voice was too loud, and Randolph remembered that his hearing had been damaged.

They talked for an hour, Byron at times evasive and even incoherent, especially about the war, as though he didn't have a firm grasp of his own history. "I was there too long," he said, running a thumbnail over his eyebrows. "Remember, Father got me a job with the powder company, which sent me to Verdun as an observer." He lifted a hand and let it drop. "I saw the French go in and in, when they shouldn't have. You remember the lemmings the old man told us about? How that's what would happen to you if you didn't think?"

Randolph took a cigar from his coat and offered it, and Byron waved it away. "By, Father's worried about you. It's been years."

"Yes," he said, but he was shaking his head, *no.* "He needs me to run one of his damned mills."

"You could do it."

Byron gave his brother a rocky look, then glanced away. "I want you to hear the new records I just got in. John McCormack, damn his eyes, singing like an angel. Caruso, the dago bastard, tearing up *la donna mobile*. Riley Puckett doing "Silver-haired Daddy of Mine." He picked from a container of needles a bright point and inserted it into the arm. "Listen to this thing. It's a model fourteen I brought in from Tiger Island." Randolph thought it was indeed a good machine, and there was no hiss on the new record. Soon a brass group began playing, heavy on cornets, saxophones under that, and John McCormack began a patient, understated beginning: "There's a little bit of heaven floated down to earth one day. . . ." Byron threw out an arm and in the Morris chair began to pantomime the song with great feeling, weaving from the waist up, his head rolling. Ella appeared in the doorway and leaned against the frame, looking at her brother-in-law. After a while she placed a finger below a dry blue eye. At first Randolph didn't understand, but then he turned and saw that Byron was crying, his lips formed carefully around each note of the song issuing thin and one-dimensional from the mahogany cabinet. Randolph sat as still as wood, his lips parted, his disbelieving breath coming lightly between his lips. Out in the mill yard, rain began to fall, and the house shook as the blind horse bumped its head against the porch post.

CHAPTER FOUR

March 9, 1923
Nimbus Mill
Poachum Station, Louisiana

Father,

I wanted to call you to let you know I finally arrived, but we as yet have no direct telephone line out of the mill, and I'm not sure what the network is like beyond Poachum. The phone we do have is a local battery unit connecting me to a grown child of a railroad agent who has to take everything down by hand and relay it over his own direct line or send it out by telegraph. Some of the managing workers have to dictate personal letters to this boy when urgency is an issue, which he repeats aloud to the entertainment of whatever trapper or farmwife is in the waiting room.

I have met with Byron, and physically he seems strong, is well tanned and clean-shaved. I don't know what to tell you of his mental state yet. The tremors seem to have grown less severe. He wants nothing to do with any position other than the one he has. As far as I can tell at this early point, he has the camp well under control, no mean task as the felling and bucking teams are not all white, and are as coarsened by their labor as any I have ever seen. Most have been hired away from east Texas mills and are loners with no family in evidence. They are generally uneducated, and *while they can't count their money, they know how to spend it on bootleg.*

I tried to feel Byron out about France, but he gave only general statements which nevertheless let me know he is still disturbed about what went on there. I have no idea about what, but I'm sure he will begin to forget, and I will do my best to bring him back to us. He is very different from when we last saw him. I offered him a cigar and he declined. When I asked if he still played cards, he laughed and said that nobody had anything he wanted to win. But he is here, and working daily for us. It felt good to lay my hands on him. As I learn more, I will let you know.

The mill is, as the reports told us, a good purchase. If prices hold on siding and joists, we will do very well here because the stand will take about three years to cut out. I can't say enough about the workers, who are rougher in this whole region than any I have seen in West Virginia or Michigan, having a character that originates in something I don't completely understand, some sense of deprivation or old wrong being done that has gone into their bones. The men suffer more than our northern lumbermen because of the heat, which even now is bad, and from the dampness, which sometimes makes it hard for me to draw a breath. They experience the usual problems with sunstroke and insects, but with the addition of alligators capable of taking off arms and feet. Many of the tree fallers here have teeth marks running up their legs like zippers. I've already seen more snakes than I thought were in the world.

As the transfer states, the millpond is supplied by a narrow-gauge railroad running out on a canal levee into the swamp. Steam pull boats are in the canal winching the trees out of the woods with cable, and a little paddle steamer rounds up logs in other waterways, rafting them down the canal to the mill. The pull-boat cables are continuous, hooked like pulleyed clotheslines way back off the watercourse. Sometimes the water is high enough that two men have to cut trees while standing in little boats floating on opposite sides of the trunk. They then top them, buck them into twenty-footers and pole the logs out to the cable while standing on them. In low water, cabling them out is harder work and requires more ingenuity, even more than the dryland work with which you are familiar.

There are few women in this camp and almost no children, which contributes to a rather hard-nosed, uncivilized attitude all around, I'd say, there being little sense of family order or regularity, no church or school, and only a vast saloon owned privately on a postage stamp of land at the back of the mill, also noted in the bill of sale and survey. I have not been in it, but it sells hard liquor openly in spite of the law, which is only Byron, who operates under the authority of our salary and a minor deputy ranking with the parish sheriff. He hates the building but sees the practicality of it, for if the men could not blow off steam drinking here at night, they would somehow get into Tiger Island from where it is obvious that several of them per week would never return. So the building in some backward way keeps our board-feet quota met, though it causes Byron many problems.

It is eight o'clock at night, the third night after I've arrived. It is raining so hard that the little domed ridge on which the mill and village have been laid out is completely underwater, and now I know why every building is up high on stumps or piers and why all the privies have ropes tethering them to saplings. I will stop writing now and prepare tomorrow's sales offers, which I must give standing in the windy office in Poachum over the baby agent's phone.

Please give Lillian this letter and my love. I have not asked Bryon to write, and he has not offered, but he does send his regards. I know you want to hear more about him, but I have found out little and don't dare drive him off with my questions. I have written to Lillian already, and I wish you would send her whatever portion of my salary she says she requires. As for me, petty cash here will do. If I wanted to spend money, I'd have to hire someone to figure out how to do it.

Your son,
Randolph

After he finished the letter, the nine o'clock whistle roared one short blast and the mill's light plant was shut down, the bulb in Randolph's desk lamp dimming as the dynamo slowed. The housekeeper, May, brought a kerosene lamp, placed it at his elbow and set the wick, then walked back into the kitchen. He had considered writing his father about Byron's wife, but his brother had told him not to or he would move on. For now, he would take his brother's side, simply because Byron needed his help the most.

The first week, he settled into the rhythms of the mill, studying the plant's details from the leviathan steam engine that powered everything to the least entry in the commissary ledger. He began to memorize the faces and names of sawyers, millwrights, foremen. The horse knew the compound better than he did, and its paces seemed to quicken now that it was taken for long periods out of its dark stall.

One day, at the edge of the rack yard, it refused to walk between tall stacks of drying weatherboard. Randolph gave it a light spur, but the horse turned its head aside and ignored him. Finally a dusty stacker walked out of the maze of boards and noticed horse and rider standing like an equestrian statue.

"Boss man," the stacker called, "that old hoss won't walk next to a rack."

The sun felt like a hot iron on Randolph's shoulders. "Well, why the hell won't he?"

"The piles is sittin' on crosspieces under the mud. If he step on one, the whole pile fall over on top of you." He was holding a work glove by the thumb, and he saluted the animal with it as he walked by. "*He* know that."

The workers had come to Nimbus because they were paid two dollars and twenty-five cents a day, a quarter more than at other mills. Though he wasn't happy about it, Randolph had to expend this salary to keep a workforce out in the swamp. The state government let him pay in brass tokens redeemable for goods at the commissary, and of course in the saloon. The day before, as he'd made an accounting of the financial records, the bookkeeper reminded him that their commissary's inflated pricing made up for the extra daily quarter. No one could save a nickel, but then, the mill manager had never known a common worker with a bank account.

When the knock-off whistle roared from the saw shed roof, he looked out the office window and saw his brother step up on the commissary porch, wearing a small, sweat-stained cowboy hat left over from his days in western Kansas. No one greeted him, but the mill manager saw that everyone knew he was there. A few white workers sat on chairs or on the edge of the porch while several Negroes hunched on blocks in a side area paved with clamshells. Randolph's attention drifted over to where the green-stained bulk of the saloon waited for sundown, its wooden swing-up windows propped open with broken stobs of lath. On its canted porch a man got up from a chair and walked inside, scratching his behind as he disappeared into the smelly dark.

Leaving his office, Randolph walked down and stood in front of the saloon noting two entrances right next to each other, one for each of the races; peering inside he saw a wall bisecting the building into sprawling rooms, each holding a bar and a thicket of scrapwood tables. In the center of this wall was a narrow opening covered with a curtain for the bartenders to pass in and out of the different worlds.

His brother came up behind him. "What do you think?"

He didn't turn around. "It's a waste of cheap lumber." He looked at a blood-spotted rag hanging off the back of a porch chair. "When do they start up in there?"

"Tonight's just practice. Saturday night comes the main event." He slapped Randolph so hard on the neck that his hat nearly flew off.

"What was that for?"

Byron opened his hand and showed an inch-long horsefly. "You wouldn't think it, but Sunday night is the worst. Not so crowded, but that's when the dumb bastards who didn't learn anything the night before come back." He dropped the horsefly and turned his boot on it. "Sunday nights are shooting and sticking time."

His brother turned away from the building to stare over at the railroad equipment. "The foremen, the engineers and such, are they in there on Sundays?"

Byron spat. "That old kraut in the boiler room is, sometimes. You'd think that someone who survived German army service would take it easy on himself."

"We need that engineer in one piece. Can you keep him out?" He looked up at his brother. "The Italian that runs the place, what's his name?"

"Galleri. Somebody Galleri. He might own the building and operate it, but a man named Buzetti controls everything. Galleri is all right. He's not like Buzetti and his Sicilians."

"Can we convince him to keep the German out?"

Byron shook his head. From inside the saloon came a rasping cough and then a whore's rising laugh. "I want to close the place down on Sunday. The last mill manager wouldn't let me. Galleri himself doesn't want to open on Sundays."

Randolph stepped closer and looked into the dim interior, now smelling something sour—beer spilled, passed, or spewed. "Well, why the hell does he?"

His brother looked at him and laughed. "Little brother, you're starting to talk like the locals already."

"I don't speak like I'm in the parlor all the time."

"We'll see how bad you get." Byron pulled up his gun belt. "As far as Galleri's concerned, the nice fellows that bring in the liquor make him stay open. If he didn't, they'd come up the canal in their motorboat and pay him a visit, as the oily bastards say."

Randolph looked at his brother and frowned. "We do business with Sicilians in Pittsburgh, the Grizzaffis. They're fine people."

Byron shrugged. "Most of them are. But 'fine' is not a word I would use to describe Buzetti."

Randolph looked down at what appeared to be a small lobster backing out of a cloudy puddle, as though the saloon's reflection was enough to poison the water. "I don't like men getting drunk on Sunday nights. They answer Monday's whistle and then we have accidents. You remember the sawyer at Brinson who passed out in the saw shed?"

Byron laughed out loud. "Fell down on the carriage while it was moving toward the band saw, and got made into a six-by-six."

Randolph looked at his brother hard and took a step away. "The accident shut us down for most of a day. Tell this Galleri he's closed Sundays. If he refuses, we'll issue notices to the men to stay away." He looked into the void beyond the door on the left. "How'd Buzetti get a lot in the middle of the tract?"

"Last owners gave it to him." Byron threw his head back and watched a hawk kiting over the mill yard. "They were under some duress to do so."

"How many run-ins with these people have you had?"

"To hear them tell it, too many." His eyes darted toward a barracks, where a man came out to pitch the contents of a slop jar into the woods.

"Maybe closing them down on Sundays will show for once who's in charge."

Again Byron looked up after the bird. "It might result in more board feet." He laughed and kept his face toward the sky. "Do you realize that it's finally stopped coming down?" Taking off his hat in a grand gesture, he leaned his head all the way back. "I am washed by the lack of rain," he cried out.

Randolph put a hand on his brother's arm, ignoring the stares of two buckers walking by, their saws springing on their shoulders in time to their steps. "Come on, By, let's get in the shade."

He ate the housekeeper's supper, an amazing dark stew made with rabbit meat and served over rice. After she cleaned the kitchen and left, he rummaged through the house, finding a locker in which his predecessor had left a cracked pair of waders, a fishing rod, a half box of shotgun shells, and a Hohner piano accordion, ninety-six ebony buttons on the left-hand side. He sat it on the bed where its pearl inlay and the wavy imitation ivory of its waterfall keys blazed absurdly against the plank-plain room. The mill manager, who could play several musical instruments badly, stared at the accordion a full minute before going to the back door to make certain the housekeeper had blown out her lamp. Returning, he put his arms through the shoulder straps and ran his left hand down the buttons, stopping at the hollow-tipped one that signaled C. He popped loose the retaining straps and drew out a big chord that sounded sweet, like little birds singing harmony. Patting his foot, he began "Little Brown Jug," playing the first time through in warbling single notes, and then adding fifths and thirds until he gained the feel of the keyboard. He switched to "Over the Waves," the bass reeds ringing into his chest, and he started to waltz a little, fingering grace notes and rolls, his feet moving across the bedroom as he tried not to sing. Closing his eyes, he began to dance with his wife.

Much later that night, the housekeeper came into his room, a gauze nightcap on her head. "Mr. Aldridge," she said, resting a hand on his shoulder. Always slow to wake up, he responded gradually to the heat in her palm, opening his eyes to a lantern globe hanging like a molten noose from her fingers. Randolph saw her flimsy robe and was struck by how slim she was.

"What?" he croaked.

"You better get down to the saloon."

He came up on one elbow, sleep shedding off his eyes like sparks. "I don't . . . why?"

"Mr. Byron's in there, and I hear a lot of yelling coming out."

He got up and dressed, walking blindly out into the street, stumbling around a broad puddle lying like a filthy mirror, the moon imbedded in it like a vandal's rock. He fell out of step to avoid a mule dropping, and the pile moved, uncoiling toward the canal.

The saloon was almost invisible, darkness within darkness, the green planking reflecting no light, the windows kerosene-dim. Rising shouts rang out of the Negro side and mixed with the sounds of bodies drumming the floor. The entry was blocked by white mill hands looking in. Randolph elbowed through the stinking crowd and into the heat and smoke. Razors winked in the lantern light, and four big men were squared off, beaded with sweat, bleeding, stunned with drink, their eyes showing that the mind had been turned off and something else was in charge. The mill manager looked around him and was afraid. Every Negro in the place—at least fifty of them—was arm-flapping, hollering, toe-walking, whooping drunk and ready for blood, anyone's.

He saw Byron standing against a side wall, staring and motionless. "Talk to them," the mill manager shouted.

His brother motioned with a hand to the center of the room, where fighters were circling, waiting for an opening, blinking their eyes free of sweat. "This is the result of my talk," he called back. All four combatants were lumped and scuffed, as if they'd spent the whole night beating on one another.

Byron pulled his pistol and fired a shot through the floor, calling out for them to stop. A tall wave of surprised cursing broke over the room, and one of the fighters swung his razor at the man across from him. The concussion of the pistol's second shot bent every back in the saloon and the worker fell dead, a bullet hole through the bandanna on his forehead. Byron holstered the Colt automatic, walked over to where the mill hand was jerking facedown in the sawdust, and gathered a fistful of his triple-stitched shirt, dragging him to the front door like an overloaded suitcase. He looked back at a man who was folding up his razor and told him, "If it wasn't for me you'd be holding your windpipe together right now." A cloud of quiet settled over the building then. Even the white onlookers said nothing as he dragged the corpse out to the porch and set it on the splintery boards. "Who knows him?" he called out. No one said anything. The men seemed to be concentrating on the bottoms of the dead man's boots.

Then a saw-sharpener, the target of the dead man's razor, wavered through the doorway. "He go by Griggs. His mamma work for the Palmers over in Shirmer."

"You owe me," Byron said, reaching out an upturned palm. "What's your name?"

"They calls me Pink." He gave up an ivory-handled weapon.

Byron looked down at the body and then at his brother, who was standing speechless on the porch. "If you can find a sober carpenter, tell him to make a box to ship him in." He walked off the porch toward his house, slogging through a lake of rainwater spread out like black fog alongside the commissary.

The mill manager turned to Anthony Galleri, a small, dark man with a tarry mustache. "For God's sake, cover him up."

"All I got's a tablecloth," he said, looking down at the body.

"That'll do. Please."

"Okay." Galleri said, raising his shoulders. "But everybody seen him already."

Randolph returned to his house and sat on the bare porch steps, struggling with visions of the killing. He'd been there a full five minutes before sensing a delicate movement of cloth behind him, and he turned and saw the outline of the house-keeper sitting with her back against the wall at the end of the porch. The thought that it was too hot for her to sleep crossed his mind and kept on going.

"Mr. Aldridge, how bad was it?"

"The constable had to kill a man." Saying this made it real, and he closed his eyes.

"Who was it?" she asked quickly.

"A Griggs boy from Shirmer."

"I don't know him." He heard her stand up. "But Mr. Byron, he didn't need that."

He thought about what she meant. When he turned around, she was gone like a fragrant smoke.

He began to wonder if his brother couldn't have stopped the fight in some other fashion. And why, after the death, had he been so calm? He remembered his grandfather, who had helped Sherman to kill many a Confederate. He was a bilious and crowing old man, crying for every crook mentioned in the newspaper to be reformed on a gallows. He could have passed on some flaw in the Aldridge bloodline, the ability to kill a man as if he were a fly biting an ear. Looking out between the dark locomotive shed and the sleeping mill, he saw the kerosene light in his brother's windows, and wondered if Byron could sleep after what he'd done. As though in answer, from that direction came the thin and scratchy vibrato of a violin pleading in the unforgiving woods, and a cloying, nasal voice singing of a postman whistling up the walk:

He little knew the sorrow that he brought me
When he handed me a letter edged in black.

CHAPTER FIVE

The next morning Randolph walked to the mill, determined to see only the ground and not the saloon porch where a body lay covered with a red-checkered oilcloth, its dreadnaught boots jutting out into the sunlight. In his office he cranked the wall phone and raised the agent.

"Southern Pacific Railroad speakin'."

He looked at the floor. "This is Mr. Aldridge. I want you to call Mildred Griggs at the Palmer House in Shirmer and tell her that her son that works at Nimbus has died. Can you do that?"

There was a long pause on the line. "I'm writing all that down," the agent told him.

"Can you load a coffin on the one o'clock?"

Another pause. "Are you paying the freight?"

"Yes, of course."

"I guess you'll send the box up on the log train."

"No, you ninny, I'm going to fly it out in an aeroplane." He hung up hard, and even though the sun was not strong yet, he went to his desk for a drink of brandy. The office door opened and his brother stood in the frame, unshaven, his hat in his hand.

"Rando. You call out yet?" The voice was cheerful, but the face was not.

"Just now. Have a seat." He motioned him into a chair near his desk.

"I saved that other man's life, you know. The one that calls himself Pink."

The mill manager chose his words carefully. "I was sorry you couldn't have stopped it earlier."

Byron shook his head and looked at his hat. "When they're that drunk, almost nothing will stop them."

Randolph tried to see into his eyes. "You couldn't have done something else?"

"The card dealer had said aloud that Griggs was cheating."

"What dealer?"

"Buzetti's man. I think *he* was cheating and just blamed it on Griggs. He slipped out before you got there." Byron was turning the hat in his hands. "It doesn't bother me that I shot him. I had to do that." He looked up. "What if that roomful had turned on us?"

Randolph remembered the press and smell of wild, drunk men. "My Lord."

"I didn't feel anything after I did it, if that's what you're wondering. Right now, I'm ready to go to the dance." He made a horrible smile, showing all of his teeth at once.

His brother didn't know what to say. If lumber was miscounted, or a steam engine broke down, he could tell someone what to do, but Byron's broken self was beyond his ken. Still, he knew he couldn't give up on finding some way to reach him. He looked over at the assistant manager's spittoon and asked, offhandedly, "By, tell me about France."

His brother flipped his hat on askew. "You read about it in the papers, didn't you?"

Below them in the mill, the big saw cut into the day's first log, and the building trembled, the office windowpanes buzzing in the sashwork.

The weather turned markedly hotter, giving the woods the motionless heat of an oven, and extra boys had to be hired to lug fresh water out to the crews. The camp was overrun with water moccasins, and a box of cheap pistols was sent out to the woods foremen.

Randolph, recovering from an ambush of diarrhea, decided to get away from the mill yard, riding the narrow-gauge steam dummy a mile south to watch a team of cutters take down trees near the canal. At the end of the line he watched two Negroes in sopping shirts smear kerosene on their thin felling saw and swing it against the base of a notched cypress five feet in diameter, working the blade into the trunk until the metal jammed as if welded. They drove wedges into the cut with blunt-backed axes until the blade was free again. A boy gave them several dippers of water each, and they finished the cut, their eyes on the tree, listening for the first deep cracking sound. They backed off as the wood groaned and the body fell away, smacking the swamp like a tugboat dropped out of the sky.

The men looked as though they'd been sprayed with fire hoses, and the mill manager saw mosquitoes riding their sweat. One man pulled a rock of salt from his pocket and put it under his tongue like a lozenge. Two shorter men carrying a wide saw, glossy as a gun barrel and stippled with silver-tipped teeth, topped the tree and bucked it into sections, stopping to blow and drink between cuts, their felt hats sagging to their eyes. Randolph watched a filer wade up through calf-deep water to sit on the stump and sharpen the felling saw, polishing each cutting tooth with a small file and swaging the rakers with a little hammer, his care telling that unless the teeth were like razors, leaving woody ribbons on the ground instead of sawdust, the fallers would work themselves dead on but a few trees.

Randolph felt feverish and slumped against a trunk as his mind juggled and flashed. It was a good thing, it occurred to him, that his brother hadn't killed a saw filer. Immediately his face flushed with the mean truth of the thought, and he slogged back to the wheezing locomotive, instructing the engineer to return to the mill. "I need a drink of cold water," he explained as he climbed into the cab.

"Be sure to check it for wigglies," the old man said, pulling

the Johnson bar against his thigh and cracking open the throttle. The locomotive bunched up its train of four loads and
lurched backwards. The engineer left his throttle and bent
down to toss several wood slabs into the firebox. "When you
going to send me another fireman?"

Randolph drew out a yellowed handkerchief and wiped his
face. "What happened to the man you had?"

The engineer didn't turn from his fire. "Your brother kilt
him."

For days after the shooting, the mill manager spent a great
deal of time looking out the high window of his office into the
trees. His dead worker had been shipped off like a faulty
machine returned to the manufacturer, and no one seemed
to question what had happened. He expected that eventually somebody would come to interrogate him—no worker
could be that powerless, that unloved—so he was not entirely
surprised one day when he finally saw, after the lumber train
had whistled its return from Poachum, a short man with wild
white hair shambling through the mill yard toward the Negro
quarters. When the noon whistle shook the windowpanes,
he heard a knock at the door and Merville, the town marshal from Tiger Island, walked in, his elbows turned out a bit
from his sides, imparting a locomotive-like oscillation to his
corky arms. He was hatless, even though the day was white
hot.

"Aldridge, that right?"

The mill manager nodded. "You're the law in Tiger
Island."

"Today, *oui et non*. The parish sheriff called and deputized
me on the phone." He put his hands in the pockets of his baggy
gray pants. "He asked me to come check on that colored boy
what got shot. I been down in your quarters talking to the
people."

Randolph waved him to a chair across from his desk.
"Why didn't you talk to some white workers first?"

The old man's eyes were little gray balls quick with elemental judgment. "It wasn't no white man got killed."

"What did they say?"

"They said the boy got what he had coming. If *they* say that down there," he pointed to the Negro side of the mill, "then, me, I don't have to ask nobody else."

The mill manager reached into his desk and retrieved two glasses and a bottle of brandy. He wanted to cut his mind loose from its moorings. "Here's a drink, if you want it."

The marshal saw the glass and pulled his chair close. "Colonel Palmer, he called the parish people from over in Shirmer. The momma wanted to know for sure what happened. I'll tell her what the men back there said about the damned dago dealer, and she'll have to live with it." He took a sip of the brandy and shook his head. "*Mais*, you got to tell your brother to take it easy. Ten years ago he could of shot up the whole place and the news, it wouldn't travel much." He motioned with his glass to the telephone. "Now, some people can ring up a newspaper, and it's getting harder to hide every little thing."

Randolph poured another shot into Merville's glass. "He's been out here eight months. How much have you heard about him?"

The marshal tilted his head. "We've had dealings. But I don't much talk about people behind they back."

"Neither will anyone here at the mill."

"What'd *he* tell you?"

"Nothing."

The old man sniffed. "I ain't surprised, no. I just finished talking to him and he said he didn't remember killing nobody. Oh, I talked to him maybe five minutes, and then he walked off singing a song like he's *beaucoup fou*, yeah."

The mill manager let out a long breath. "I don't speak French."

"Plenty crazy. No offense."

"I can't find out exactly what he's been doing."

The marshal looked around at the invoice-littered tables, the black typewriter, then back at the mill manager, his face showing that he felt sorry for him. "In Tiger Island we got a little two-room hospital. One night one of your white pull-boat operators come in with a slug through his leg and his thighbone broke. He'd been beatin' on his old lady when Mr. Byron paid him a visit. Then back in cold weather they brought two poor bastards that work for Buzetti into town in the baggage car, one with a broke jaw and the other with a bullet in his gut. Before that it was Buzetti's poker dealer with his foot half shot off. We got other business like that from your brother. Now, me, I don't know who been hauled out on the train in the other direction, or who holes up back in here to get well." When he peered at his empty glass, the mill manager poured him another inch. "Tell your brother, when his head's a little more clearer, he can pound the shit out of whatever bastard needs it. He's a good man." He swallowed a spoonful of brandy. "But whoever gets the smokin' end of his .45 got to deserve it. And no more better come out in a box. The parish sheriff in Franklin is startin' to pay attention to this place."

"Are they paying attention to you?"

He sucked brandy from the bottom of his white mustache and then laughed. "Minos told me you was watching that from the boat. Me and them rousters. Mister, I let a fight like that get the better of me one time. I went down there in the pitch dark and tried to talk to the crazy *fils de putains* and shot one in the leg with a little pissant Smith & Wesson I used to carry because it can't do no damage." Merville sniffed and shook his head. "They threw my ass in the river. Those big rousters started in on each other with the razors, two crews' worth. By the time I swum to a ramp and crawled up on the bank, Malcolm Brown's steamboat was on fire, three men was bone-cut and ruint for life, and another two was dying and calling for their mammas." His gray eyes grew small and bright with the telling. "You know, I got a friend who's a priest. He says it's a sin to kill. I got no problem with that, but what if I don't kill one, and that one kills two or three? Did I kill that two or three? I can't figure that out, me." He stood up and left a hand on the desk, as though struggling with the effect of the brandy. "I learned early on how men have to do. I didn't want to learn that, but I did."

The mill manager held up both palms. "You know your business," he said. "I'm not from here, and I'm not used to what people like you have to do."

Merville seemed to consider this, then swayed a little like a man who'd just stepped into a skiff. "You no different from me. But where you come from's different, yeah."

The door opened and the housekeeper came in with a plate of food under a cloth. Randolph looked at the old man. "You're finished here?"

The marshal put a hand on his chin for a moment. "No. Joe Buzetti stopped me when I was getting on the train. He said he heard your brother told Galleri he couldn't sell liquor on Sunday."

"That's right."

Merville shook his head. "He don't like it."

"I don't care what he likes or doesn't like."

"The saloon is their territory, yeah. Galleri might run it, but it's theirs. They control it from they little waterfront whorehouse in Tiger Island." He pointed through the window into the mill yard. "This is your territory, and you don't want 'em comin' around. They feel the same way about the saloon. Your brother, he already leaned on them hard, and they don't like that."

Now the mill manager laughed. "Do you really think we have to worry about Chicago gangsters out in Nimbus?"

The marshal watched the housekeeper leave. "They all connected, the Sicilians, and if you mess with one down in Tiger Island, his cousin in New York hears. Maybe not right now, but later on. They already got it in for your brother," he said, looking again at the door. "That a white girl?"

"No, it's my housekeeper. She lives out back."

The old man sniffed. "You better keep her inside your fence. These bucks out here mus' get a hard-on just looking at her shadow."

The marshal walked out, and Randolph toasted the closed door with his shot glass. Pulling an ironed napkin off the serving tray, he lifted a cover from a fine chicken stew sprinkled with chopped shallots and edged on one side with a sprig of parsley, suggesting a flower.

CHAPTER SIX

Merville climbed into the lumber train's empty crew car, a windowed box painted the color of dried blood. As soon as it lurched into motion his vision slid sideways, the car turned like a log in an eddy, and he sagged onto a wooden seat, regretting the brandy at once. "If this is it, I'm sorry," he said toward the ceiling. By the time the car rattled out of the trees at Poachum, he was able to totter into the hot station to wait for the westbound local. His revolver pulled at his waist like an anvil, and he slid the belted holster around to the left side, where he seemed not to feel it at all. Suddenly very dizzy, he lay lengthwise on the slatted waiting-room bench and closed his eyes. The agent glanced at him once but went back to his clacking telegraph, and Merville knew that the boy could do nothing for him anyway. The train would come at its own speed to bring him to Tiger Island and the nearest doctor.

His weapon prodded him in the back, and he thought of how there was no law but what his pistol made—and at once the empty, vagrant eyes of Byron Aldridge came to his own closed sight. He'd been deep in the big war, Merville had heard, the war that the men who returned to Tiger Island refused to talk about. He himself had never done any soldiering, but the thought of it broke loose images that eddied fast and dizzying, and he became truly frightened, for what was it people said, that when a man is dying, when his body slows down, the mind speeds up and everything comes back like a flipped-through album of regretted pictures? He remembered living in a war, the one with the blue devils and the butternut devils riding back and forth through his father's sugar cane fields on Bayou Lafourche. He closed his eyes more tightly against a gathering vertigo and saw himself as a boy but could remember almost nothing about that open-mouth simpleton dressed in homespun. Then a taste formed like a ghost on the back of his tongue, and there it was, cream cheese made by his mother, big sausages, smoked pork, and something else—a sound, the waspy drone of fiddles and dancing on Saturdays, dancing in the yard when it was dry enough, all the neighbors come out for a *bal de maison*.

A window opened wide in his memory and Merville was afraid he might indeed be peering through it into death, but still he would not open his eyes. He waited for the evil things to come back to him, but with a pang he realized that until he was ten years old, already trusted with planting seed cane, there were no evil things, and he could remember no blade used against anything but plant or pig, no gunshot but that which brought a rabbit flopping toward a *sauce picante*. His heart skipped once, twice, and a vision formed of a face sunken around a pipe, his grandfather, old Nercisse, who'd told the hearth one night—a north wind leaning on the mud-and-moss house like God's own foot—that he remembered the 1700s when there were still Indians about, and how they did not understand the Acadians' yards, how they must not go into yards, must not take one thing and leave another thing in its place without asking. He'd told in his whispery French how the red men thought the Acadians should be Indians as well, and not take apart trees and put the little pieces in a rectangle and say, "Inside this is not yours. You have to go around." The grandfather told that one night an ambush was prepared and a group of Acadians shot one of the red men, who later died. The whole race of Indians on that upper part of the bayou told each other in one day of that one death, and some struck their heads and some of the bravest cried like whipped children.

Within the month they were *all* gone from the region, *toute ensemble*, down one hundred miles to the marshy lower bayou where there was not a fence to be seen nor a tree out of which one could be made. In those days, in that place, that was the worth of one life.

A shadow passed over the marshal's eyelids, as though someone was walking past him in the dusty waiting room, but he did not open his eyes, because inside his mind men in dirty blue wool who stank worse than any Indian were knocking flat a year's work in the cane fields to build a three-days' camp, kicking down the fence for firewood and taking shrieking piglets on their bayonets. He and his mother and sisters were hiding under the beds with the chamber pots, silently praying *Notre Pere qui es aux cieux*, and watching the filthy boots punish the brick-scrubbed floors as the soldiers cursed the family for having so little. A corporal grabbed the house's shiny new rifle, and Merville watched as it winked out of the doorway and was gone. His father stood in the yard and shook his fist until knocked down and kicked, left talking blood, his body ruined for two planting seasons, at least. The next day at noon, a hundred and fifty horsemen, some in gray uniforms, most in homespun broadcloth and carrying shotguns, rode over the flat fields from the east, breaking down tall cane in a panic, their animals bleeding at the bits. They had ridden by accident into a large Union force at Donaldsonville and thought those federals were chasing them, though they were not.

After the cavalry men came the supply wagons, cannon and limbers, then foot soldiers, their eyes rolling white, panicking through October's dry cane until three hundred yards beyond the house they retreated headlong into the ignorant bluecoat camp. The Yankees saw the foaming horses and thought they were under attack themselves; they tried to retreat, but were overrun by the velocity of the rebels' fear and so began firing everywhere, a smoky and confused melee erupting almost at once. From the house the shooting sounded like an egg broken into hot grease. Merville ran toward the noise and stink of powder, hid in the broad cross-ditch and saw his first death, a man in checkered pants catching a fat rifle slug in the throat, a neck bone coming out with it, his head tumbling sideways like a flower on a broken stem before he hit the ground and died kicking dust. After somebody unlimbered a cannon, a thunderbolt flamed out of the cane, and a horse exploded under a cavalryman whose right leg pin-wheeled across the field like a blue ax, and then Merville had seen enough and began running down the ditch toward the bayou, away from the hollering and the thump of rifle fire. When he got to the bank he ran north back to the house under the lisp of bullets flying overhead and thwacking the willows across the stream, and his water soaked down his legs when he thought of what the men were doing to each other in the cane. There should have been a law to stop what was happening. He remembered thinking this.

That day, his family woke up in one life and went to sleep in another. Over the next few weeks, soldiers from both sides gradually stole everything they had, and for years there was no such thing as lawmen, and after the war there was still no law, just roving gangs of thieves, or Negro-killers, or sick, saddle-wild murderers doing what wrong they could because there was no one to stop them. Merville saw his father's face shift forever when the old man understood he couldn't sell a crop because the sugar mill had been broken into gravel by the blue army. He saw his older brother, who had come back from war with two white scars under his ribs and empty holes for eyes, sitting on the porch smoking and cursing and staring out at the brambles that rose like wiry smoke where fields used to be. At one time this brother had played the fiddle, but the only sound Merville remembered him to make was a brittle refrain of how he wanted to kill this son of a bitch and burn out that son of a bitch. Merville recalled sun on his back each day for eight years as he beat the dead farm like a lazy mule, but the old man had to borrow money from planters who had turned into bankers the way lizards change color. The gentry lost their slaves and got replacements by loaning money at interest against the next crop; and when his father failed to pay it off, they took his land, and loaned him against the next crop, which came short, and they rolled the debt over into the next year until they owned him and his sons like cattle and he realized he could never clear a cent if he lived a hundred years. Before the war, his father had a dream of a big farm for all his children, but Merville witnessed the last day of a nightmare when the old man dropped dead behind a mortgaged plow, falling tangled in the reins, dragged by the spooked mule to the edge of the field, even in death working to the end of the row.

A far-off train whistle shrieked in the woods and he put an arm over his eyes. He saw the rainstormy day he left his brother muttering on the porch and took his mother to Tiger Island, where she hated town life so much that she died within a month. He became a lawman there in 1895, his job to deal with the leftovers of the great killing, gaunt men who bore in them the poisons of Vicksburg and Port Hudson, Gaines' Mill and Chancellorsville, places where the air itself had sung with gunfire like the ripping of cottonade and thousands of men had jerked backwards into either quick death or the slower mortality of hate, which they would pass on to their children and grandchildren like crooked teeth and club feet.

Someone was talking to him through his eyelids, and with his whole heart he did not want to be alive, but his blood still moved through him like a moon-drawn tide, and he had no choice but to sit up on the bench. A boy with baby eyes was looking at him from under an agent's visor. "The westbound's blowing for the trestle," he said.

"*Quoi?*" The storm in his head began to subside, and he touched the boy's shoulder.

"The westbound," the boy said. "*Ecoute ça.*"

Merville stood and blinked himself alive, stretching one arm and then the other. He was still in this world and gave the boy a marshal's glance before walking unevenly out into the sun. He picked up a cypress slab from the platform and flung it across the tracks into a trapper's yard. His right arm still worked, though his left spasmed with electricity. Looking east for engine smoke, he heard the hoarse whistle softened by the thousand-year woods and saw the train's headlight swim around a curve, turning the rails to silver arrows pointing toward his boots. With his sound right arm he drew his pocket watch, and at once an understanding flooded through him of how Byron Aldridge could bear to open his eyes each morning despite his sorrows. It was time that did it, time that allowed a man to put to use what he'd learned from his suffering. Merville's numb left hand struggled to grip the watch, and he wound it tight.

CHAPTER SEVEN

Anthony Buzetti liked the fact that his office had no windows. His older brother had been shot dead through one in Chicago, and his mother had jumped out of another when she heard the news. He pulled the chain on his desk lamp and began dealing solitaire with a new deck, waiting for Crouch to arrive. The first board he turned up showed three fives and two queens, and he cursed the cards, raking them and dealing again. Five minutes into the next game he saw he couldn't make solitaire, so he tore a fistful of cards in half and swept them with the rest into a wastebasket. For good measure, he leaned over and spat on them, his oiled hair sliding over his forehead.

The door rattled, and his cousin, Crouch, pushed it open just wide enough to slide his tall frame sideways into the room. "Hey, Buzetti," he said, and stopped.

His eye patch seemed like a hole in his face.

"Hey, youself." Buzetti got up and embraced him in a clinch, then pushed off.

"Okay, so I'm here."

"That's good. I want you to stick around on salary for a while, know what I'm saying?" He banged his cousin on the shoulder then sat back down at his desk. "I heard about you."

"I bet."

"You some bad stuff. What's it been?"

"Five years." The man slumped down onto an armchair.

"Crouch. Yeah. I never understood how you got a name like that."

"It's my poppa's, in the old country. What can I say, he's a Crouch."

"He's no *paisan*, I tell you that."

"So what you saying, I'm a half-breed or something? A mixed dog, maybe?" Crouch's face was unreadable and still. "I hear you got some hun in you from your momma's side."

Buzetti took a cigar from his coat pocket and lit it. "Crouch," he said, drawing the word out. "Sounds like something you do before you take a shit."

Crouch's eye narrowed. "It's my name."

Buzetti laughed out a spray of smoke and came around the desk to his cousin, grabbing his neck and jerking it back and forth. "It's all right, you know?"

Crouch waited for him to back off, then threw his leg up over the arm of the chair. "You got a job?"

"I always got a job. Right now there's some trouble. I got three nice little cunts working for me. They turn the money, you know, but they think they're high class. Think they can shit flowers. Sometimes they keep back too much fee. I told them, I get half." Buzetti leaned his head to the left. "But I'm not getting half."

"I'll take care of it," Crouch said.

"Don't mess them up. It ain't good for the business."

His cousin nodded. "But you didn't bring me in from New Orleans to fizz up some split-tails."

Buzetti slid down in his chair. "I got a great little business down at this toilet-hole saloon, some place called Nimbus. No competition. One of these country Tonys owns the building, Galleri, but the only thing we let him have is the beer money. This place is so far back in the woods you'd have to ask directions from a fuckin' owl. I got it all to myself."

Crouch shrugged. "What?"

"It could do better. A lot better. But the constable down

there beats up my dealers, puts my girls on the train when they do too good. Now he's trying to shut me down Sundays."

Crouch's face did not move. "A constable. What, a sixty-dollar-a-month man? Just drop some bills on him."

Buzetti pulled on his nose. "Nah, not this constable. He's sharp and crazy both. I think money don't mean nothin' to him."

"So I press his suit, with him in it?"

"Hey, this ain't some joke. He was in the army."

Crouch raised his chin. "You was in the army. I was in the army." He touched his eye patch.

"We kill a lot of people." Buzetti raised an imaginary glass in a toast.

"*Salut.*"

Buzetti frowned and looked down at his desk. "This guy killed more. The bastard was in longer. A lot longer, know what I mean? Before we got there. Years before. He sat in like a folding chair and watched the Frenchies die like ants on a woodstove. Somebody paid him to watch."

Crouch extended the fingers on both hands and touched the tips lightly together. "So, he's one of them with the spiders in his head."

"He'll need some special handling. That's why I brought you in."

"To send a message to the guy who don't listen."

"Something like that."

Crouch's face became even more unreadable, as blank as a shadow.

Buzetti slapped his chest, then got up again, walked back around the desk. "He got to know who to listen to."

"What kind of people runs the mill?" Crouch asked.

"Pittsburgh money, know what I mean? Whitebread from smoketown."

"No mixed breeds."

Buzetti looked away. "You really do to that banker what they said?"

"What. What lies you heard?"

"The snake thing, which I didn't believe. I can't touch no fuckin' snake."

Crouch dropped his gaze and looked at his shoes. "Oh, that."

"You want a drink?" Buzetti finally asked.

Crouch waved the offer away with the back of a hand.

"A cigar?" he asked nervously, then added, when Crouch looked at him, "Ah, of course, you don't want that. The smoke gets in your eye."

The tall man stood up and put a hand on Buzetti's shoulder. "Cousin," he said, in a voice terrible to hear, "don't try to make me laugh."

The saloon had been closed on Sunday for two weeks straight. The next Monday morning, the mill manager saddled the horse and splashed to the office through a foot of tea-colored tidal backwash blown up out of the swamp by a south wind. The horse stepped into a shallow ditch, stopped, rotated its ears toward the planer whining behind the office, got its bearings, and walked according to the sound. Randolph could handle the horse easily during the day, when all the machinery was steaming along and telling it where things were, but at night the animal would balk in the baffling silence. Galleri had said that the horse was blind because it had been poisoned. A mill hand who had been fired by the previous manager had fed it seed treated with mercury. Sometimes the mill manager envied the horse because it was never spooked by sudden motion and couldn't worry about things it could no longer see, its life simplified by tragedy.

Randolph reined up at the office door, noticing a piece of paper on the step held down by a firebrick. The typed note read, "Open up the saloon. If you not going to do this, you pay." At once he suspected the hard-drinking chief engineer, a comical, red-faced German who wore a little plug hat and roamed the plant studying steam lines for leaks, and who kept a typewriter in his closet of an office. The mill manager balled the note up and tossed it toward a wire basket inside the door.

The German would have to think of some other way to get his whiskey.

A week later he was making his daily round through the roaring mill instructing Jules, who listened and nodded while working a half plug of tobacco around his mouth. In the boiler shed they stopped to watch the men throw slabs into the furnaces, and Jules called the German over, slipping a finger under one of the man's suspenders. "Why you got the water level so high in the boilers?"

The engineer pulled off his canvas gauntlets. "*Die Schwartzen* forget sometimes to run the pump. You want I should let the water go under the firetubes so they melt?"

Jules looked again at the water gauge and then jerked at the suspenders, pulling the engineer toward him. "Listen up, Hans, I don't need to be lied to by no rummy. You're carrying water high so you don't have to watch and can sneak off for some schnapps."

"It is no problem with the boilers," the German said. "I watch them *viel genug*." He backed away from Jules's hand. "And I am not drinking on your time."

"It's all my time, Hans. You got to stay sharp."

"I got to be happy. Here is not a happy place. I sweat and my clothes stay wet all day. The waterways stink and look like dark beer." He straightened his suspenders and turned his back on them.

Leaving the boiler room, the mill manager and Jules climbed into the howling saw shed, where the atmosphere was not air but an excited mist of wood particles. The log carriage flew back and forth, running a trunk against a toothy loop of lightning, a band saw powered by a Corliss steam engine straining below the floor. Overhead, line shafts roared in their cast-iron hangers while a shirtless boy crawled on a timber above the noise, continually filling the oilers and placing his fingers next to bearings to feel for overheating. This boy had replaced another twelve-year-old who had gone up among the pulleys wearing a floppy triple-stitched shirt and was grabbed by a foot-wide belt and dashed against the saw shed roof; the mill manager could not bear to look at the freshly white-washed section of cypress above him.

The lumber flew out of the saw blade, all the men talking in hand signals since no voice was equal to the thunder of the room. They drew pictures in the air and mouthed simple words through the sawdust snow. Randolph had heard that when sawyers went to the silent movie in Tiger Island, they could read the actors' lips.

The head sawyer examined an invoice that must have called for a special order, for he held up a forefinger and pinky, a call for 2½-inch cuts. The man riding the carriage adjusted his grab dogs and began slicing a pink slab of cypress three feet wide. The mill manager's skull vibrated like a bell, and he started up the stairs to his office when the band saw suddenly exploded into a clattering mass of shrapnel, its teeth whistling around the shed like scythes. Someone pulled a cable to stop the main engine.

Randolph turned to Jules, who suddenly was not there but lying facedown on the floor in a spray of blood. When he knelt and rolled him over, he saw a red blossom spreading across his white shirt.

Jules spat out a cud of tobacco and gasped, "What? What?"

"Let me look you over." The mill manager brushed sawdust off him and searched for bleeding. "You've got one bad penetration and a few small places. Is anything hurting on your backside?"

"Naw. Just my chest."

Randolph looked around at the crew. "Anybody else hurt?"

The carriage operator, a short man wearing a bandanna, held up a streaming hand. "I lost the top of a knuckle is all. But I sure nuff ought to be dead."

Someone down the carriage track hollered that he'd taken a saw tooth through an ear. "What kin I do about it," he squalled, holding a handkerchief against his cheek.

"Aw, get yourself a earring," the carriage man told him as he slung blood off his fingers.

Workers began to stand up and to crawl from under the

walkways, and the mill manager saw that things could have been much worse. Two dozen shafts of light fell from the tin roof where pieces of band saw had knifed through. When he bent down and ripped open the front of Jules's shirt, he saw several shallow cuts, and nested in the middle of them was a blue hole over an inch long. Spreading the wound with his fingers, he could make out the pebbled butt of a shard of blade steel.

He and two edgers carried him to the commissary and laid him on a counter between the cheese cutter and the accounts ledger. Randolph scissored off the bloody shirt and poured whisky into the hole.

"Son of a bitch," Jules hollered.

"Yell all you want to." Randall called for a light and the commissary clerk brought over a gooseneck desk lamp. "I think it's just in the meat of you. Now, we can do this here, or you can go into Tiger Island in the next baggage car that goes by."

Jules draped a forearm over his eyes. "Aw, God," he said. "There's more goes in to that place than comes back out." He dropped his arm and looked at the manager. "You like this doctor stuff, don't you?"

"Maybe I'm in the wrong business." He wiped the chest down with medicinal alcohol the clerk had found for him. "But my father wanted a lumberman."

"What in hell did the saw hit?"

"We'll find out." Randolph walked over to an oak display case filled with bright tools and chose a pair of needle-nose pliers.

Jules's glossy eyes followed him. "Can I cuss you?"

The mill manager clicked the pliers once in the air and studied the fit of the jaws. "If it helps."

The small pieces came out while Jules bunched and hollered under him. A mill hand came over with a second lamp, holding it high above the wound, as the clerk mopped the counter to keep blood from running under the cheese. When Randolph found a purchase on the large fragment and pulled, Jules called him things that made the toothless clerk laugh. But the hook of Disston saw steel would not come out straight, and the assistant manager began to pant and flail and curse. Randolph motioned for two filers to come over and hold down his arms.

"Maybe I ought to go into Tiger Island after all," Jules gasped.

"Well, we've started in on it now. If it takes several hours to find a doctor over there I'm afraid you'll get an infection. Hang on." The mill manager pushed the blue steel pliers deep into the welling blood, grabbing and then twisting the sap-stained tooth out of the muscles. Jules crossed his eyes, arched his back above the counter, and screamed out like a mill whistle, all of which gave more urgent strength to Randolph's hands. When at last he tugged a bright, corkscrewed shaft out of a rill of blood, two black firemen behind him laughed out loud.

"Turn him on his side and let him bleed a while," the carriage operator suggested, cupping his ruined knuckle, and Randolph watched the wound wash itself out. The clerk fetched gauze, patches, and a little war-surplus suture kit while the mill manager washed his hands in alcohol.

"This sewing is going to sting some," Randolph told him.

Jules was still panting. "How much is some?" he croaked. And when the clerk showed him the soft top of a woman's boot, he gripped it between his teeth. Randolph threaded the hooked needle and decided that seven coarse stitches would hold the big wound shut. As he forced the first suture through, the only sound in the room was Jules's ragged breathing as his teeth ruined the boot. The mill manager took his time, figuring the better job he did, the sooner Jules would be back at work. After bandaging the wound tight, he handed his patient a big soda to drink all the way down, and a half hour later, Jules was sitting up, and the clerk was using handfuls of cotton waste to mop the sides of the counter. Tending the man with the wounded ear, Randolph ran a wad of alcohol-soaked gauze through the hole and told him to go back to the mill and help install a new blade. Meanwhile, Jules's wife, who had just returned from town on the log train, walked her husband to their house with the help of one of the filers. After doing what he could for the sawyer's knuckle, Randolph took a long time cleaning blood from under his own fingernails, looking through the window at the mill, then back at his trembling fingers. He decided to walk to his brother's house.

Byron was at the saw shed, Ella told him through the screen door. He could smell that she'd been drinking.

Putting his face close to the screen, he asked, "He hard to live with?"

She looked past him to the mill. "You ever see a big fine passenger train run downhill without any brakes? It'd be a sad sight if you'd see that, now wouldn't it?"

"I'm sorry."

She looked at his coat, which his housekeeper pressed each day after supper. "You come down to help him?"

"Yes."

"You better get to it. I can't do a thing for him." She raised an arm, and started to say something else, but gave up.

"He's a good man," he said.

She pushed her sandy hair from her eyes with both hands and held it at the sides of her head. "Let's just say he's worth the effort."

He found Byron standing on the log carriage, digging with a long pry bar in a slab of cypress, working a round metal shaft out of the wood. He picked up the steel and banged his left palm with it. "Looks like a case-hardened transmission shaft, ground to a point. Someone drove this into the tree and countersunk it so nobody would notice."

The mill manager remembered the note left under the firebrick, and told him about it. "When I found the message, I thought it was from the German."

"You know who it's from now, don't you?"

Randolph looked over at what was left of the ruined saw

blade. The millwrights were already truing up a new one. "Just because of maybe a hundred-dollar take on a Sunday?"

"It's not just about money with some people," his brother said quietly.

"What, then."

Byron smiled a wide, wide smile that was even more frightening than a shattering saw blade. "It's a little habit a man picks up or is born with. He can't be told no."

"Well, I'm telling him. That damned saloon's staying closed."

"You want to wait around for another accident?"

The mill manager regarded his fingernails, still faintly outlined with dried blood. "Maybe you're right. We can't do to him the things he can do to us."

At this, Byron walked off, stopped in the bright doorway, then turned and pointed the shaft at his brother. "You want me to talk to him, at least?"

"I think you better stay in camp, By, where you're safe."

Byron motioned to the holes in the roof. "Safe?"

Randolph thought about saw blades, nights in the howling saloon, his brother's midnight rounds. "But you can't talk to men like that. Talking won't do a damned bit of good."

"It depends on how you talk."

The mill manager looked up at the whitewashed patch on the ceiling. Jules said the boy had been a careful worker who didn't take chances. "So talk to him, then."

After supper Randolph had the housekeeper heat water for the washtub, where he sat and scrubbed his assistant's blood off of him. It had run up his wrists, ruining his shirt, and his face was speckled with it. He threw the water out the back door himself, put on an undershirt and a pair of khakis, then sat down in a hide-bottom rocker on the porch. The housekeeper came out with a damp hemp sack, lit it with a kitchen match, and threw it on the ground to smoke away the mosquitoes. He looked at her as she came up the steps and passed into the house and saw that her features were white. Her old father, he'd noticed, was not a dark man, his skin a smooth butter-scotch. She was thin and elegant, precise in everything she did. He guessed her bearing came from intelligence and the fact that she knew she was smart. When he was finished with the two-day-old newspaper passed to him every morning by the log train's engineer, she would take it to her cabin porch and read every article, some of them out loud to her father, who suffered from arthritis and rarely did so much as walk a circuit in the yard.

All the squalling machinery was shut down, and he rocked, enjoying the quiet. From out of the twilight came the sound of the Victrola, a male opera singer's voice winding out of place over the stumps and mule droppings. Later, a hillbilly song strummed the air faintly, followed by—given enough time for the box to be wound thoroughly—a military band and Billy Murray's declamatory plea:

> *Keep your head down, Fritzie boy,*
> *Keep your head down, Fritzie boy.*
> *If you want to see your father in the fatherland,*
> *Keep your head down, Fritzie boy.*

And then an anguished roar cut across the mill yard, his brother crying out, "A joke! Nine million skulls spread out like gravel, and it turns into a joke sung through the nose and sold for a dollar." A record sailed out of a window like a bat, and Ella ran from the rear door and stood in the yard, staring at the house as though it might explode.

> *June 12, 1923*
> *Nimbus Mill*
> *Poachum Station, Louisiana*

Father,

Lillian has written to say she is not happy with my being gone so long. I hope you can tell her to be patient, that when there is an

inevitable decline in the market I'll come to see her and make
substantial plans. Of course, I have written as much to her, but it
always helps to hear it from someone else. As of now, however, sales
are very strong, and the stands we are cutting out are some of the
purest grades I've seen, fine grained, easy on the equipment, each
board a coin for us. We are taking everything down that a blade
can cut.

As for the incident with the spiked log, Byron is investigating.
Something has turned him mean, and I wouldn't want to be the
man found out by him. The spike was a warning, and I am
beginning to wonder if I should let the saloon reopen on Sunday.
That would not sit well with Byron, though. He is very unhappy
about the saloon causing workers so much trouble. I had him over to
dinner two days ago (May, the housekeeper here, is a preternatural
cook) and he was sociable enough, but is still not my old brother, the
one who taught me to ice-skate and ride a horse. Gradually I am re-
cementing the family connections, but as of yet he won't begin to
consider a return north.

I have to send into town for a cage of chickens, since a large
alligator has broken down the back fence and killed nearly all I had
here. Tomorrow I meet with a representative of the Yazoo and
Mississippi Valley Railroad, who will pay a premium price for
200,000 crossties. It seems a shame to put such beautiful wood under
a greasy railway, but that money will spend like any other.

Your loving son,
Randolph

The housekeeper was fueling the stove with cypress lath
while the mill manager sat at his kitchen table watching her
hands move above the flames. He looked up when his brother
came in through the screen door wearing a dress shirt and a
.45 automatic in a shoulder holster. "Go back and tend to your
old man for a minute," Byron told the housekeeper, who read
his eyes and left.

Randolph motioned to the stove. "By, had breakfast yet?"

He was trying to pretend everything was normal, that his brother was not shaking and white-fingered.

"I've eaten." He tightened his hands on the back of a chair. "The man who runs the rafting steamer, I want you to order him to do what I tell him to for the next twenty-four hours."

Randolph's eyebrows went up. "What do you need the steamboat for?"

"You really want to know?"

"It's not that important, By. We can let them open on Sundays."

Byron slammed a fist onto the table, the blow turning over an empty coffee cup. "It *is* that important. I know they're going to put another game in and more slot machines. And two Negro whores to add to the two white girls in the cabins. You think you have cut-up and dizzy workers on Mondays now? Wait till they expand."

Randolph held up a hand and said quietly, "By, I just want you to be safe. But I need you to calm down."

Byron threw his arms out from his sides and began speaking in a preacher's voice. "Little brother, I'm calm as can be. The only thing I want is to talk to the Sicilian gentleman in Tiger Island so we can *all* be safe."

"Talk?" Randolph flicked his eyes down to the pistol in Byron's armpit.

"In their language."

"Oh, damn it." Randolph turned away and stared at the stove.

"Do you know that Negro I saved, the one who calls himself Pink? Out along the canal today, before daylight, he saw a man spiking a tree. He came right in and told me on the sly, and I went to the woods and drew it out, just an hour ago. It was the same as the last one."

"Did he recognize the man?"

Byron shook his head. "Not enough light. But it was a white man, he could tell that, and he had some kind of bandage on his face."

Randolph stood up, poured himself a cup of coffee, and walked to the back door, looking out into the yard at his new chickens, Dominicks, their feathers patterned like mattress ticking. "You ought to be glad you weren't in the saw shed when that band saw exploded. We were lucky on that one. Another time we'll have dead men." He watched the chickens peck the ground between each other's yellow legs, then turned around. "What *do* you need the steamer for?"

"Just a boat ride, maybe. Buzetti's boys might be chasing me home." He walked close and stooped as if in submission, a joke from their childhood. "He calls them soldiers."

Randolph smiled, shook his head, and put a hand up on his brother's shoulder, starting to say something, then changing his mind. "The pilot's wooding up at the lower end of the pond. I'll speak to him on the way in."

"Rando," his brother sang out, bolting upright to squeeze his neck so fiercely that his eyes flashed with pain and he spilled his coffee across the linoleum.

Five minutes later, May came in through the back door and saw him on his knees with a dishrag. "Mr. Byron's going to town?"

"That he is," he said, standing up and tossing the rag next to the dish bucket.

"You going to let him?"

He looked at her. She was staring past him out the front window. "He's got business there."

She nodded. "If I had a clock wound tight as he is right now, I couldn't stand to stay in the room with it."

He put a palm on his neck, drew it away, and looked at his hand. "May, would you look and see if I've got a scratch?" He sat at the table.

She came close and pulled down his collar. He felt one cool pass of her fingers, and the motion surprised him, raising the hair on his arms. "Nothing back here but a little pink," she said.

"All right, then." He stood up. "Byron grabbed my neck," he explained.

She looked at him without expression. "Still brothers," she said, turning to the stove.

At sundown Byron got off at the station in Tiger Island, bareheaded, wearing a suit coat. He sat in the waiting room and stared at the night agent, who after a while looked up and spat. "You think I'm pretty, bub?"

Byron didn't smile. "You're a sight, all right."

The man wagged his bald head and went back to writing train orders.

Byron turned to look out the open door, and before long saw two men in striped suits and round felt hats hustling up River Street. Out on the platform, a little boy in knickers, about six years old, was playing on stacked boxes of muskrat traps. Byron called out to him.

"What?"

He held up a coin. "If I give you a nickel, will you sit on my knee and talk to me?"

The boy nodded and came in, pulling on Byron's lapel and climbing onto his thigh. He smelled of mud and his nose was running. "Where'd the nickel go?"

"You have to say the abc's," he told the child, keeping an eye on the door.

"Don't know 'em."

"Can you count?"

"I can count to a nickel," he said, putting a sooty finger in his ear as two olive-skinned faces appeared in the doorway and stared at Byron and the boy like hawks. Both stepped inside, and one checked the men's room, then they looked at each other, shrugged, and slouched back out.

Byron thumbed up a dime and the boy counted to thirteen for him.

"You can get down now," he said.

When he was alone, he looked at his cooling, empty lap. The heft of the child had anchored him, but now he could stand and do what he would do. He walked up to the agent's counter and snapped down a five-dollar gold piece.

The man picked it up and turned it in his inky fingers. "I ain't seen one of these in a long while."

"You know who I am. But if someone asks if you've seen me, you haven't." The agent's face did not change, and he nodded.

"If I find out otherwise, when they pull you out of the river there'll be five dollars worth of telegraph wire wrapped around your neck."

"Message received, damn it." The agent turned away as a telegram rattled the sounder.

Byron walked from the station into a neighborhood of large, somnolent cypress houses, five or six of them boasting columns or gingerbread galleries—the homes of mill owners, he guessed. He saw a soaring brick steeple three blocks away and walked to it, pulling open an arched front door and stepping into a fragrant Catholic dark. He chose a pew in the middle of the empty church and studied saints soldered in the lightless stained glass, and standing flat and dark as negatives.

The last time he'd been in such a church was south of the Meuse when he'd been observing a buildup of French troops for the U.S. government. Desperate for shelter, he'd packed in out of the February wind with over a thousand soldiers. Several priests came in to hear confessions, and lines of penitents flowed around the blocks of pews where others were smoking and talking, boisterous and tipsy with fatigue. He was seated in the middle of a loud group, couched in his Presbyterian reticence, when a sixteen-inch shell landed outside, turning eight hundred years of stained glass into a lavender-tinged hailstorm. The great concussion knocked the film of water off his eyeballs, and when he stood, blinking, the first thing he saw was the glassless tracery of the rose window over the choir loft, a naked suggestion that German artillery was erasing all of history. Then another shell hit, and the air filled with pinwheeling gilded pipes and spruce flutes and tin oboes. Soldiers were screaming, afraid that this was some new type of delayed-fuse ordnance—not a blown-apart pipe organ raining down on the surging raft of men. One of the church's great doors sailed open, and Byron joined a press of bodies in the aisle, helmet rattling against helmet as he and others formed a living cobbled street. It was then that the roof's back was broken by a smaller shell into an unholy avalanche of masonry and roof tiles, killing lines of penitents, burying priests in the confessionals like beetles in sorrowful wood.

That freezing night and many times since, Byron wondered if the unconfessed men had passed unhindered to Paradise.

About nine o'clock a nun gently touched his elbow and he jumped up.

"I'm locking the doors," she said, looking at him curiously. "Did you want something?"

His head moving like a bird's, Byron glanced around at all the intact windows. "Do they hear confessions here?"

"Yes," the nun said. "Do you want me to summon Father?"

With a start he saw the ranks of organ pipes intact above the loft. "Not yet," he whispered.

Sometime after twelve o'clock he walked back to the station, crossed the tracks, and passed south of the railroad bridge, following the star-glossed river and its muddy breath. A weatherboard nightclub rested its chin on the levee, its rear half propped on spindly pilings over a shallow bend of the Chieftan River. Backed by a thumping jazz band, a vocalist was singing "Do What You Did Last Night." Byron listened for a minute, finding the song unlike his records, even frightening— a music that had cast off sentiment like a white dinner jacket and strutted, half-naked and sweating. Crossing the stinking apron of oyster shells, he came out of the dark and into the dark, where six couples clung and drifted over the dim floor. Through a door frame in the back wall he could see two felt-covered card tables ringed by men wearing white shirts and arm garters. He bought a beer and drank it halfway down, remembering that Randolph at one time liked cold beer almost too much; thinking of the ordinary, patient face of the brother who'd come to this netherworld to save him, he was overcome by a melancholy anger. Gulping down the rest of his beer, he slammed the mug to the bar and pulled from his pants the rod he'd extracted from the log.

With wild swings he shattered the glass fronts of two old slot machines by the door and beat down the mechanisms before moving quickly to a Buckley quarter bandit, pounding the pot-metal top and smashing the jackpot window, the quarters flying like ice chips. A woman screamed and the two men he'd seen at the railroad station came rushing from the back room. One of them said, "Hey, you crazy?" and moved toward him.

Byron slammed him on the shoulder with the rod, and the man's false teeth flew across the room as he went down. "Never say that to a crazy man," he said, coming up with a pistol in his left hand in time to make the other one freeze and withdraw his empty hand from under his coat. "Give," Byron said, and the man handed over a large revolver. He took a nickel-plated automatic from the man with the broken shoulder and walked on toward the back room where players at the green tables had begun to stand and mill. He brushed past the band members and the dancers as they moved toward the door and stepped around him in broad arcs as though he were hot enough to set them on fire. In the shallow back room he tossed the guns through an open window into the river and then upended card tables, spilling waterfalls of poker chips and yelling at the men to get out or get shot. With the rod he began to break out windows, swinging it through sash work with great, crashing arcs.

One man stayed in the room, his hands up. He wore a straw fedora and a cream-colored suit over a dark shirt. After Byron finished the last window, he looked in his direction and smiled. "Mr. Buzetti," he said, "would you please step over here a minute." He motioned to the door and the two of them went back out into the bar.

"You fuckin' nuts or somethin'?" Buzetti asked.

Byron holstered his pistol and held up the shaft. "I found something at the mill in Nimbus that might be yours."

Buzetti finally lowered his hands. "I got nothing to do with your piss-hole of a mill."

He raised the steel bar up to the man's face. "A thing like this can cause a lot of damage." He walked behind the counter and beat starbursts into the back-bar mirror, exploded the rod through the leaded glass in the side cabinets, and raked the liquor bottles onto the duck boards. Buzetti made a break for the door, but Byron pulled his pistol and stopped him. "Now that you understand how dangerous this rod is, I want you to tell me we're not going to run across any more of them out at Nimbus. Galleri stays closed Sundays, and we don't have to worry about some Sicilian gentleman spiking our trees, is that right?"

Buzetti took off his hat and looked around the shattered room. "I can swat you like a fly. I was in the big war." He tapped his chest with his knuckles. "Like a fly."

Byron walked up to him and grabbed the left lapel of his bright suit, dragged him into the back room, and raised the Colt against his forehead. "A fly can't shoot back, you pimp asshole."

"You a dead man," Buzetti hissed.

"You're not going to leave us alone?"

"Fuck no."

Byron raised his elbow on his gun arm. He had smelled coppery blood on his face before. "You know, a month ago I wouldn't have thought twice about doing this, but then I bought some Caruso records in the mail and found that Italian is good for more than selling whores." He was thinking, though, not of Caruso's voice, but of his brother's worried expression rising above a celluloid collar. Suddenly, Byron began singing loudly into the gangster's startled face,

La donna e mobile
qual piuma al vento
muta d'accento
e di pensiero.

"You crazy!" Buzetti cried, his confidence melting. He glanced over his shoulder toward the river.

Byron stopped singing and his eyes turned to little rocks. He held the .45 out the window and fired a skull-cracking shot into the air.

"You no can scare me," Buzetti said, his voice reedy. "What you smiling like that for?" And then he heard it, the faint sound of a gong striking and a tingle of engine-room bells. "Hey," he said, his shoes shuffling as he twisted to the window. In the river, a low grate of running lights was backing away from the bank and the water erupted in a silver line as a three-inch hawser sprang taut out of the current. Beneath the floor the nightclub's timbers began to groan and crack like giant knuckles. "Hey," Buzetti screamed. "Hey, hey! Okay, okay, let's talk."

"Scuzi," Byron told him, as he climbed through the window and jumped for the river. The mill's rafting steamer was backing on a wide-open throttle, jets of steam spuming out of its escape pipes as the paddle wheel dug water, the boat's heaviest rope straining in and out of the nightclub's supports. The first piling broke like a cannon shot, and the rest of them leaped out bringing along the main sill, the building breaking in two right in the middle of the dance floor, half of it tumbling into the river with a great clattering of slot machines, liquor bottles, card tables, and the screams of a drunken whore as the restroom wall fell away and revealed her seated on a commode, high and pale in the night air.

CHAPTER EIGHT

Ella heard water splashing in the kitchen before daybreak and went in to find Byron naked and washing himself out of a small tub on the counter. She walked up and pressed against his damp back, running her narrow fingers over his nipples. As she expected, he jumped when she first touched him.

"I've been with you for two years, Kansas Queen, and I still can't tell when you're creeping up."

She smiled against his shoulders. "Why are you washing now?"

"I've been for a swim."

She backed away a step. "I thought you went into town."

"I did. Then I came back and swam in the millpond."

"Ugh. You better put on some turpentine, then."

He turned and embraced her, putting his huge hands on her backside.

"Has your brother told your father we're married?"

He tried to look at her then, and she raised her face to his. "I don't think so. It'll make the old man want to see me and you both. He's like that. He'd pick out a cottage for us somewhere in a crowded neighborhood and get me a job counting trees or selling wood to people, and that I couldn't take."

She felt tremors in his arms, something left over from the

shell shock, though it appeared he didn't realize they ran all through him like messages, every day. "Where did you go tonight?"

"To see Buzetti."

She closed her eyes. "Oh, no."

"I was steady as a post when I handled him. When I'm going up against a real bastard, I just feel the rightness of it. Tonight, well, it was like France was supposed to be." He reached out and she handed him a towel. "No one got hurt very badly."

"Amazing," was all she said. He drank a glass of bourbon and they went to bed. She asked him again to talk to her, knowing he was exhausted and would sleep until noon.

"I might tell Rando what happened tonight," he said. "You know, he makes me feel stronger. I just might tell him." And with that he was asleep, his back to her, a dim surface botched with white scars.

Later, she watched the ceiling boards develop out of the gloom above the bed one by one and prayed he hadn't found another war. The bed jittered, as if from a minor, distant earthquake, and then was still. From down at the boiler house came the sound of the furnace doors banging open and the clank of iron rakes as firemen dragged out the ash.

Merville had gone to bed around eleven, and his arthritic bones floated on the mattress like dying coals on a grate. From a pack of muskrat trappers come to town for women and fistfights he'd taken a three-dollar pistol, a claspknife, three sets of brass knuckles, and a slapjack. As usual, he'd tossed the weapons over the top of the tall armoire standing against a corner of his room.

He woke at five, dressed, dripped coffee, fried eggs, and boiled a pot of grits. At six he walked through the damp air to the office on River Street where the walls, the bars of the cell, and even the stove were sweating. Then the door swung open and the tall priest stood there on the step.

The marshal smiled. "You playing hooky from seven o'clock Mass, you?"

The priest sat down and set up a game of checkers on the desk. He made a move, looked up, and said, "Have a seat, please."

Merville gave the priest a look and did as he was told. He pushed a checker forward and waited.

The priest was frowning at the board as though stumped by a complicated move. "The women who clean the church in the mornings, they're Sicilian, mostly." He glanced up. "Very devout." He nudged a piece over the board.

"Yeah?" Merville moved again.

"Did your phone ring last night? Buzetti, perhaps?"

"No. I pull the wire on the son of a bitchin' thing when I go to sleep." He saw sweat beading on top of the priest's shiny head.

"It didn't ring when you hooked it up at five?"

"*Non.*" He jumped the priest's lead man.

"Then he's decided to settle things himself. So." The priest put his hands in his lap. "I've got something to tell you."

Merville settled back in his chair and looked at the office's rack of obsolete rifles and shotguns. "Them ladies, they talk a lot, yeah. When they think they alone."

The priest nodded glumly, his long German face sunk in folds of skin as he stared down at the board. "Oh, yes," he said, almost in a whisper. "I feel almost like a traitor for what I am about to tell you."

The old man watched the priest move a checker and leave his finger on it.

When the lumber train rattled back from Poachum with its empties, the mill manager heard the whistle and saw through his office window that the marshal was standing in the locomotive cab, a suitcase next to his leg. The fireman helped him down and carried the valise for him toward the office.

"Hot damn, I don't know if I can make it," he said, collapsing on a chair just inside the door, the fireman backing into the hall with a touch to his sooty cap. "Had to drive the town's car to Poachum."

Randolph studied the scarred tin trunk. "What did Byron do in town last night? I tried to see him this morning, and his wife said he wasn't to be wakened."

"He pulled Buzetti's bar into the river with your steamboat."

The mill manager swallowed hard. "Oh my God, he—"

"Buzetti didn't complain to no lawman about it." Merville pulled out a nickel-silver watch the size of a biscuit, yet he still squinted. "In a hour and a half the westbound's coming in to Poachum with four men on it from New Orleans what gonna put your brother in the ground." He held up his watch for emphasis. "They's only one thing that'll run 'em off and keep 'em off." He looked at the ceiling and thought a moment. "Maybe."

Randolph stood up. "What?"

"Get a bunch together, colored and white. With guns. Send them down to stand at the station. The chicken-shit bastards on the train will see it's not just three or four men they up against."

The mill manager pinched his lips and wondered how one might do such a thing. "Will you go to the station with us?"

He shook his white head. "No. Hell, no. I got to live next door to them slimy bastards. You way out here in the woods where they just about got to paddle a boat to get at you." He bent over and opened the suitcase, which held six short-barrel Winchester pump shotguns with full-length magazine tubes.

"Trench brooms," the mill manager exclaimed, for even he recognized what they were, recalling from magazine articles that the only firearm the Germans complained about during the Great War were these same weapons filled with double-ought buckshot.

"That's a fact, yeah. The mayor bought these for the city from his brother-in-law. They loaded up with deer shot. Double-ought to start with and two slugs at the end of the row."

Randolph picked up one of the guns and turned it over. "I can't put sawmillers out there with these. It could turn into a war."

Merville stood up. "Tell 'em just to flash these things. Them dagos'll back off."

He shook his head. "No."

The marshal sniffed his mustache, his gray eyes ranging over the mill manager's rounding shoulders. "Then order your crazy brother's headstone," he said, kicking the suitcase closed.

Randolph studied his eyes for a moment, hoping for a way out. "You couldn't bring deputies to stop them?"

"Who's gonna volunteer to get they house burnt down?"

"The parish sheriff?"

The old man walked to an open window and spat. "Let's just say he likes spaghetti. Now, can you spare a colored man to ride me up the track to Poachum on your handcar? I got to get the Ford back to town."

Walking down the roughcut stairs into the noise and dust of the saw shed, Randolph worried that if he told his brother about the assassins, he'd deal with them himself and get killed. Merville's plan might short-circuit that threat and demonstrate to Byron that he was far from alone, so he pulled the stop whistle, told the head sawyer to kill work on the line, and began gathering the sweating saw crew, the engineer, assistants and oilers, the trimmers and chip-covered planer crew from the floor below. He told the men to go home and get whatever guns they had, then board the train.

The German engineer stepped up onto the log carriage. "What you expecting us to do?"

"Some of the bunch that spiked the log are coming to give Mr. Byron some trouble," he said. "I want to show them that we know who they are, and that they can't get through us." The men moved uneasily, and no one said anything, sawdust settling like dry snowflakes. The mill manager glowered, momentarily at a loss for what to say, what dollop of self-interest to heap on their plates to convince them to go along. "Of course, maybe you all want to be around when that blade hits the next steel rod," he told them, pointing to the band saw that was still idling down, trembling like quicksilver.

The head sawyer, a little man, the front of his hat brim pinned back with a box nail, drawled out, "All right, then." He turned to his crew. "Let's show the tree-spiking bastards some of our own iron." The crews broke up without enthusiasm, but in a half hour the flatcars were loaded with nearly seventy workers: the cutoff men, a woods crew, millwrights, stackers, and pond monkeys.

The mill manager was waiting next to the drizzling locomotive when the engineer, a rawboned man named Rafe, hung out of the cab window and spat next to him on the ground. "You sure you can run this show?" the engineer asked.

"It looks like I'll have to."

Rafe looked doubtful. "No offense, but you ain't no lawman, Mr. Aldridge." He turned to check the water level in the boiler, then leaned back out of the window. "And you ain't been in the war."

Randolph didn't answer for a long time. The locomotive's air pump thumped six strokes, stopped, and a safety valve began sizzling steam. Everything seemed ready for release. "Mr. Merville told me how to set it up," he said, feeling weak for saying so.

"Well, that's something."

He felt the blood rise in his face. "It'll have to do, won't it?"

"If you say so, Mr. Aldridge." Rafe leaned into the engine to adjust the lubricator.

At Poachum station the frowning agent stood at the west end of the platform holding aloft a willow train-order hoop with a message attached. His arm shook as a westbound locomotive barked down on him, hot and mountainous. The fireman hung off the cab steps, squinting through the steam, and put his left arm through the hoop as the engine coasted five car lengths past the station and stopped with a hiss and a squeal. The engineer read the order and hung his questioning face out of the gangway, scowling back at the agent, who nodded his head and scurried inside.

The platform was empty, and when the conductor put down the step stool, four men slouched off with their hands in their pockets, looking as if they'd just bought Poachum for a great deal of money and didn't think much of it. They wore new suits and white shirts, their pants shoved down into sleek black boots. The hats were right out of the box, round, felt, with a deep chop in the middle that seemed to go into their skulls. As they walked toward the waiting room, the mill manager stepped out, Merville's borrowed revolver stuck behind his buckle. "Do you have business around here?" he asked.

The men stopped, rolled back their shoulders. One of them wore a patch over his right eye, and he held out a hand, the fingers bunched and pointed up. "Yeah," he said. "We got the business."

"If you work for Buzetti," the mill manager said, his hands at his side, "you have no business out here. You'd better keep on riding."

Another man unbuttoned his coat. "We tired of riding."

There was a shuffle of boots as five white workers and the largest black faller in the mill filed out of the station holding the Winchester pump guns, the hammers pulled back on each, sunlight sparking on the cyanide-blue frames. The men in suits looked at one another, then back at the lumbermen, licking their lips as they thought out the math. When Randolph saw this counting in their eyes, he knew they hadn't seen enough and probably were very good killers, former Chicago men maybe, and a thrill of fear spread through him. He'd thought running them off would be easy, but now, in a sudden spell of dizziness, he suspected he might be wrong. The train orders that the agent had handed to the engineer, Randolph had written himself. The crew was not to pull out after the passengers disembarked, and they were to do one other thing. He looked west, raised his hand, and the fireman gave a jerk on the bell cord. From the other side of the station's roof came a rumble of hob-nail soles, and forty men appeared on the peak carrying .22 rifles, rabbit-eared double-barrel shotguns, lever-action Marlins, rusty Bisley revolvers, break-action Smiths with half their nickel plating eaten off. From around the east and west sides of the station came big overalled men carrying more long guns, a few holding axes and adzes overhead like Vikings. A man off the train turned his head slowly to the one wearing the patch. "Hey," he said.

"Shut up," the other said calmly.

"Get back on the train," the mill manager told them. "Don't let us see you around here again."

Passengers in the seats next to the station began to slide below the windows. The conductor stepped back down out of the vestibule and replaced the step stool without a sound. He stared west at nothing and said very gently, as if a yell would fracture the sugar-shell calm that encased the station, "All aboard."

The big locomotive hissed like a fuse, and the four men in the new hats slid their eyes along the roofline as though still figuring odds. Randolph worried about all the cocked guns behind him; if just one accidentally went off, what hailstorm of lead would envelop him? After a moment, the man wearing the eye patch extended a forefinger and thumb and made a brief pointing gesture toward the mill manager, then turned to board the coach.

The workers were told to knock off until three o'clock. After eating the tender fried chicken the housekeeper had left on his desk, the mill manager walked over to see his brother, who was sitting in his boxy front room reading the labels on phonograph records.

"You should have seen them, By," he reported. "The worst kind of men, down from Chicago, I'm sure, backing onto the train like they thought we were about to blow the coach to pieces."

His brother took a drink of coffee, spilling a little on his pants leg. "A nice little party. Who told you how to set it up?"

Randolph fell into a chair. "The marshal. Merville."

He nodded and said, "You could've been killed."

Randolph frowned. "I don't think so."

"Then think again."

"Well, what would you have done? Derailed the whole damned train?" He got up again, put his hands in his back pockets, and walked to the window, gazing out.

Byron held up four trembling fingers. "He sent this many men," he said quietly, waiting for his brother to look back at him. "So you showed your strength, and they took off. And you think you've won?"

"That's just it," Randolph said, settling back in a chair. "When they saw we had the guns, the jig was up." As he said this, he felt like a character in a dime novel, and looking at his hands, he saw that they were pale.

"Well, that's something," Byron said in a mocking voice. "It could have been like that in 1914. The Frenchies could have said to the Germans, 'Boys, look at our guns,' and everybody would have been home in time for dinner." He threw his head to the side and closed his eyes.

Ella came to the door and gave Randolph a worried look. "I think I'll make another pot of coffee."

Byron opened his eyes and smiled easily. "I'll have a fresh cup. Bring him one too; he needs to wake up."

"What does that mean?"

His brother pointed at him. "Did one of those fellows wear an eye patch?"

"Why, yes."

Byron dropped his hand. "Tell me, did you have any doubts before the men stood up on the roof? Did you think 'Oh my God, this is going wrong'?"

Randolph looked away. "I wasn't aware of thinking much of anything."

His brother stood and put a finger on the turntable. "Those four men were in the war," he said in a low voice. "They could've killed you and fifteen others in about six seconds." He shook his head. "You didn't know what you were doing. *Everybody* should've been out in the open when that train pulled in."

Randolph looked through a window at a bank of cindery clouds coming up from the south. "I suppose that's what you would have done."

"Maybe, if I'd known a thing about it." He gave his brother a baleful look.

"Well, that's just what I didn't want. Had you shot them up out of your jurisdiction, you could've been jailed."

"Jail," his brother said with a bitter laugh. He reached into the cabinet below the Victrola, drew out a disk of "The Prisoner's Song," and soon a sorrowful, thin voice began to fill the room, the high notes sharp as a razor. "This fellow seems to like it well enough. It fills him with a sadness that he enjoys."

Randolph rubbed his hands together, beginning to understand what he had almost done. "By, do you think they'll come back?"

"Do you still have those wonderful shotguns you told me about?"

"No. The marshall instructed the agent to gather them for return shipment."

Byron shook his head. "Too bad. We could use some good ordnance to—well, let's just say it would be good to have them in the closet."

His brother put his head down and stared at the cypress floorboards. "How in the world did we get into this?"

"Shhh, that's not important. Listen to the song."

"But what if they—"

"Hush, now."

And after that record, he played John McCormack's "I Hear You Calling Me" and another sad ballad by Alma Gluck. Randolph was fidgeting in his hard chair when a whiff of whiskey snapped in his nostrils, and he turned. Ella leaned against the door frame, pouring liquor into her coffee, and he looked at her pleadingly, holding a thumb and forefinger apart the thickness of a two-by-four. She nodded, returning in a few moments with straight whiskey for all of them, placing the bottle on a small oak table next to the talking machine.

After four more records and a generous glass, the mill manager was ready to weep, and he wondered what solace his brother found in such music. He thought of Byron's letters from France. He'd gone over in 1914 as an observer for the Zeus Powder Company, which paid him to study ammunition consumption so they could plan their factory expansion and production lines. After traveling in France for two months and watching Germany grind Belgium into meal, he wrote home that the U.S. government, nervous about the expanding, ceaseless slaughter, had hired him to provide intelligence. At this point he began to see much more of the war than any American soldier ever would, and his letters detailed a conflict pinwheeling out of control. Then, for a few months, he stayed away from the front, and his letters contained long messages about the countryside, the cathedrals, the canal boats and ancient fortresses, but behind these descriptions Randolph could sense that something unspeakable was being left out. The accounts abruptly changed back again to graphic dispatches, one describing a train of boxcars loaded with wounded soldiers, stalled for two whole days in the winter weather, blood pouring through the floors, and that train moving off at last only to be followed by another, loaded down, creeping over the red snow.

In Pittsburgh, Randolph and his father watched the mails, but the slow stream of letters froze and shrank to terse notes, little frigid drops of despair: "Still here among the bodies," one began. When the American army went over in 1917, Byron wanted to come home, but at his father's rigid insistence he signed up in France, and that was the last the Aldridge family heard of him until he got off a troop train in Philadelphia in 1918.

The record stopped with the click of the turntable brake, and Randolph watched his brother down the last half inch of his drink. "By, will you tell me what happened in the war?"

"What—you think I'm like one of these records?" He

wagged his glass before the Victrola. "Life puts the grooves on you and you play them back when you get drunk?"

"I want to know what happened."

Byron poured another drink. "That would take years to tell." His voice was coming slower.

"Don't," Ella said, pulling up a spindle-back chair next to her husband and resting a hand on his shoulder.

Randolph tried not to look at her. "It would help us understand."

"Maybe, if you can keep from interrupting me, if you just let me drone on like a bee in a bottle, I could give you a slice, just a sliver of what you might call my war experiences." He put his head back in the Morris chair and closed his eyes. Ella poured herself another drink and retreated into the bedroom, the floorboards popping once under each of her steps. From across the mill yard came the whine of the planer section coming back on line. "In February 1916 I was ten miles to the rear, as usual, checking ordnance reserves, transportation, and hospitals. Oh, I wanted to get on the front line, even though I saw all the bodies that the fireworks produced, as well as the armless, legless, jawless casualties."

He opened his eyes and sat up suddenly, as though something behind his lids had startled him. "Maybe I wanted to see the men going down. One morning, I struck out on my own. Verdun had been going on like a thunderstorm for two days, and the confusion was nearly total, but in my observer's uniform I could go pretty much wherever I liked. I walked to a section of the battlefield that night with the seventh and twentieth corps of the French army. I don't know how many thousands of men. A whole civilization's worth, if you could call it that. Most of them were pretty young. They were sent out into open country that showed five hundred shell craters to the acre and few trenches or any type of protection, and when the Germans realized what was in front of them, why, they fired their artillery as fast as they could load. At dawn I stuck my head out of a fragment of bunker, and my field glasses showed me what I'd come to see. Naturally, the first French columns were shot down, the bodies like piles of rags, maybe ten thousand piles of rags."

He put a hand out in front of him, palm down. "You know how a pasture looks with a whole herd of cows spread out across it, down on their bellies before a rain? From the distance, that's how it was, those French soldiers in their big coats." Byron drew the hand up to his head. "And the noise. I know you've heard a boiler explode. Well, imagine two thousand explosions like that every five minutes, because the artillery was packed in there, eight hundred pieces on that part of the line, and several hundred machine guns and a hundred thousand Mausers, Lebels, and Enfields." He lowered his hand and rolled his head sideways to look at his brother. "Remember Grandfather telling us that at Cold Harbor the opening volley of the infantry was like—what did he say, tearing silk? At Verdun, the rifle fire was like many pieces of silk ripping and ripping without end, the pistols, machine guns, grenades, and cannons joining in one tearing thunderclap that continued day and night. Shells of phosgene gas formed white clouds on the field, and I saw about a thousand of those French boys gagging out their lungs into little lakes of blood."

Randolph was beginning to sweat, but when his brother turned to look at him, he gulped his drink and said, "Go on."

"It was a long day, Rando. You sure you want to hear this?" He took a swallow from his glass. "Well, silence means assent. When the men out in front of me were mostly shot up or poisoned, the French generals sent in another wave of thousands, and the new men struggled up to the dead and wounded and just milled around. They couldn't move forward and were afraid they'd be fired on by their own side if they retreated." He took a breath and let it out slowly. "So they stayed and were shot to pieces. I saw artillery shells vaporize soldiers into red mist. I saw pieces of men spinning into the sky. And then another wave of maybe five thousand was sent in, and by then there was a pavement of bodies, and in my field glasses I could see mouths working around final words, and I thanked God I was too far away to hear. The third wave came up and began firing from behind the piles of dead, but once the big German howitzers got their range, and listen to me, Rando, because I don't know if I'll ever tell this again, I watched whole groups of men disappear body and soul. The shock waves from the explosions were like mallets in the face, even at my distance. Later in the day, another wave of troops went in on top of all of that. I began to vomit from just a whiff of the gas, so I crept back and stayed low, thinking it would end soon and medics would gather up the wounded. But the shelling continued, and toward nightfall the roar became more intense. For days they kept it up in that part of the field, and for weeks and months afterward the whole place stank of corpses. By the next year, they told me, men fighting on that same ground in new-dug trenches hung their canteens on the hands of skeletons sticking out of the walls."

Randolph turned his head as though he'd been slapped. "By, this won't—"

"I want you to be quiet," his brother told him. "You and Father have always begged me to talk about this. It's why we're here, isn't it?" He put down his empty glass and filled it from the bottle. "I stayed away from the front after that trip, until late 1917 when my services as an observer were no longer necessary and the whole country was filling up with Americans whose eyes worked as well as mine. Then I started to receive long letters from Father, each proclaiming my duty to enlist—to make the family proud. And because of his all-fired pride I did, as a private. I think I felt guilty because all I'd done was watch people die, and somehow, I thought I'd get used to it, you know, to things like the entire British Fifth Army being slaughtered in one offensive. But I got more frightened with each engagement. Watching, I found out, is nothing like being in battle.

"And then there was my big one, the night thousands of us moved along a rutted road, filling it from fence to fence, and I could see our close-packed helmets moving on the hills in front like the scales on a snake. In the dark we filed into mud-swamped traverses, and before dawn everyone was packed into the forward line of trenches. The Argonne forest looked like this place here will look when we're finished with it. I heard there were four thousand pieces of artillery on our side only, and when they opened up, well, I don't have the words for that sound. The concussion from a siege gun behind our trench split the seam of my canteen and the water wasted down my leg. As quickly as the barrage started up, it stopped, giving us an awful few minutes of dark empty silence. In the middle of it I heard hail hitting an iron roof far off to the east, but the sound traveled toward me, growing louder in the blackness. I asked myself, *What is that rattle?* The hair on my neck stood straight up when I realized it was men fixing bayonets. Tens of thousands of bayonets. Whole cities putting knives on their guns. The order was given at the distant end of the line and the noise itself continued the command as men heard it and understood what to do. The fellow next to me clicked his over the muzzle of his Springfield, and I slammed mine on and turned my head to see pale hands rising and falling in the dark, the clatter diminishing all the way down toward the Meuse River. Next to me, my best old buddy, Walter Liddy, a Pennsylvania man, began to pray aloud. The sergeant came down the line lugging a box and stopped next to me. Without a word he began to hang grenades about my coat by their spoons, stuffing them in my pockets, until he'd given me twenty or so. The weight was staggering, but I felt protected by all the bombs I had to throw. Then the cannons kicked the air out of our lungs and the sergeants began screaming and pushing and we went over the top right as the German artillery laid down a wall of shrapnel in front of us. A man behind me took a shell all by himself and flew off like a rag doll in a tornado. I went down then, my back on fire with bits that had blown through my pack and clothes. It was Walter Liddy who'd got it, they'd told me later, old joking, pipe-smoking Walter. After twenty minutes, getting angrier by the second, I gathered my strength and plunged on, as they say, a hundred yards or so, to the first coil of wire where three or four dozen men hung dead and those coming up behind were stepping on their backs to get over. Some bent down to the bigger corpses and started plucking grenades from them. I saw that our loaded-down first wave was *supposed* to get shot and tangled in the wire, our bodies serving as depots for the other waves coming up, you see. That's when I learned the worth of one life to a damned general. I threw all my grenades away unexploded, picked up my Springfield, and went over the wire myself, stepping square on the back of a fellow from Aliquippa, an excellent harmonica player named Angeloz. Bodies were twisted on the ground like trash paper, everywhere you could see. We all should've gone crazy, I guess, but there wasn't time to go crazy, with the air around us flying with Mauser bullets. Crazy came later."

Byron put down his glass and it fell off the table, bouncing away from his shoe, but he seemed not to notice. He turned to his brother, whose hands were covering his face. "I killed a lot of men that day, Rando. I got good at putting a 30.06 round right under the rim of a helmet, and that afternoon it was like shooting pumpkins in a field, but every pumpkin was a Dieter or a Fritz with thoughts in his head just like mine." He stared down at his spilled glass, and his face seemed like something carved by wind out of the side of a mountain.

The mill manager put down his hands and gazed through the front door toward the saw shed where each puff of steam told of a board cut out of the heart of things. "Is that the day you took your worst wounds?"

Only his lips moved. "I passed out at sundown from loss of blood. My pack was soaked and I didn't realize it."

"Shrapnel?" his brother asked.

"In the hospital tent," Byron said, moving his face fully toward him at last, "what they cut out of my back was five of Walter Liddy's teeth."

They heard the back door open as Ella stepped out into the muddy yard. Randolph could imagine her there, hoping for a heron to fly, a whistle to blow, for anything to move through the burdened sky and distract her from the things she knew.

CHAPTER NINE

One Saturday night, the mill manager sat on his porch, playing the accordion in the dark, annoyed that the only songs he could remember were Italian. He found the left-hand buttons for "Come Back to Sorrento," and the deep reeds of the instrument lamented against his chest. May was sitting on the edge of the porch floor, listening silently. Randolph thought of the code down here, that if he spoke first, it would give her permission.

"Do you have a request?" he joked.

She answered as though she'd expected the question. "Do you know 'Sweet Hour of Prayer?' "

He ran his left fingertips over a town of ebony domes. "Is that a favorite?"

"It's what they sang when my husband was buried."

He played the hymn cautiously, thinking about the long anguished letter he needed to write his wife. She had threatened to separate from him because he'd gone where she couldn't follow, and he planned to tell her once again that after this mill cut out its incredibly rich tract, and after he'd somehow drawn his brother back into the family, he would return to her permanently. The mill manager pulled a lonely chord out of the instrument and wondered if he was creating a fairy tale for his wife. Maybe Lillian could not be made happy, nor his brother sane. His wife was a slim woman with silky dark hair and intelligent eyes, a loving person who could

not function living alone. Just the memory of her light perfume made him want to board a northbound train and leave
behind his brother's haunted face, this brother he loved, who'd
pulled him from under the ice of the family pond when his
cyanic heart was one beat away from stopping. He understood
his wife's need, but thought, too, that she must respect how
much money his family was making from this tract. The accordion breathed out its old breath, and he closed all the stops
but the highest reeds, pushing the start of a German waltz.
As he trilled the bee-like notes, Randolph remembered the
touch of his wife, the hand of his brother on his pond-wet
shoulder.

A single gunshot thudded down at the saloon, followed by
a gumbo of fiery voices. Across the mill yard, the door of
Byron's house swung open, and Randolph slid out of the
accordion's straps and jumped off the porch, running to inter-
cept him. "By, hold up," he called. "I want you to give me your
gun."

His brother, who'd just reached the little street heading
out of the white section, stopped and looked back. "It's two
trappers causing trouble. I saw them when they came out of
the woods."

Randolph put out his hands, palm up. "Try and handle it
some other way."

Byron stared into the open palms, his eyes pulsing. "You
know, the angel of death is still an angel."

"Good Lord, don't say things like that." The mill manager
did not know what to think or even how to think about such a
statement.

Byron suddenly handed over his pistol, muzzle down.
"Sometimes there's no other way," he said simply, then moved
on through the dark toward the rising flurry of voices, his
shoulders pushed forward like a man chased by a cold wind.

The next morning the mill manager sat quietly at the table
while May prepared his breakfast. "You heard?" she finally
asked.

"Lord." He put his hands in his lap.

"Before he went in the white side, they say he got him a short-handle shovel. They were fighting like cats in a sack in there, and he made two big round swings and laid them out. The strangers didn't wake up till sunrise." She poured the coffee and glanced at his eyes. "He threw their guns in the millpond, and those men are long gone. You want some bacon with your grits and eggs?"

Because the room was bright with sunlight, he looked at her closely. Her greenish eyes showed flecks of yellow, and her complexion was so close to ivory, and her features so small, that up North she would be a different person. To have a new life, all she needed was a train ticket. "You get your gossip at the fence?"

"I know a little colored water boy. He tells me what's going on."

"Which one is he?"

"Floyd. He's got curly hair and wears what you call a golf cap."

Randolph looked through the window at the mill, which was starting up, long ribbons of white smoke rising from the boiler-house stacks. "That little boy's white."

"News to him," she said, flitting by his elbow on the way to the stove.

In July the heat bore down hard on the woods gangs. The mill manager traveled to New Orleans to hire a doctor, knowing that only a derelict or a graybeard poorly read in recent medicine would consent to work in a place like Nimbus. Sydney Rosen, who'd been an army surgeon in the Spanish-American War but had lost his commission for saving a general's life without benefit of anesthesia, climbed down creakily from the log train one hot afternoon, wearing under his felt campaign hat the sagging, gentrified face of a Confederate commander too long in the field. The carpenters had built a boxlike surgery on the side of the commissary where the man could deal with heatstroke, flu, pneumonia, malaria, broken toes, and severed fingers, and he set up his instruments there and waited inside the open door, out of the sun.

Randolph continued to watch his brother and to visit the saloon like a bored sawyer, though always alert for the flash of a shovel blade. Saturdays spawned fights the way a hot afternoon brewed thunderstorms. The men were young and strong, so built up from the daylong swinging of saws that nothing could stop them once they were drunk and brawling. On the last Saturday in July, the white side of the saloon was noisy with boots and skidding chairs as thirty or so men cursed aloud, played cards, and drank in a burled fog of hand-rolled smoke that stuck in the room like backlit cotton. Everyone was sweating in the soppy air, the floor was slick with sloughed-off mud, and the bar, a long, roughcut cypress plank thirty inches wide and set up on metal barrels, showed a puddled jumble of bottles and wet hats. At a big table in the corner, Vincente, a man with sleek, olive hands, ran the poker game, smiling thinly at the men as he raked in their tokens and drew the cut for the house, smiling even when he lost. He was drinking too much, and so was everyone else. Around eleven o'clock, a furniture-breaking contest erupted, a big ham-fisted faller slapping a stool to fragments. When a sawyer broke a chair back over his knee, a spindle popped out and struck the dealer on the ear. Vincente jumped up and shouted something that nobody understood, pulled a Colt automatic, and fired in exclamation, the slug striking a slot machine across the room.

The mill manager was nursing a hot beer at a corner table by the door when he saw his brother step in from the porch and bring up the little D-handled shovel. He walked to the back of the long room, ignoring two fistfights, and rested the tool's point on the poker table. "Let me hold that gun for a while," he said.

The gambler's eyes were Tabasco red and small. "I no think so."

Byron raised the shovel and buried it three inches into the center of the table, cutting a clay chip in half. "*I* think so." The Italian looked at the blade a moment, then handed over his blue pistol in a fey, mocking manner. Byron walked to a window, ejected the shells into the dark, then tossed the gun back on the table as a bottle neck flew past his head and gouged the wall. Turning to the fighters, he grabbed the nearest one and hurled him halfway through a window, pulling out the prop stick; the heavy sash banged down on his back and pinned him squalling in the frame. The other pair stopped trading punches and stumbled out to the porch and down the steps. A boiler fireman climbed onto the table, rocked out the shovel, and tossed it to Byron, who used it to pry up the window and retrieve the fighter, a big cross-eyed boy who cursed him and took a drunken swing. Byron jerked on the straps of his overalls and threw him down in the spit and ashes, then grabbed a boot and dragged him into the yard, where he dinged him with the flat of his shovel. "Calm down, you son of a bitch, or I'll flatten you like a dollar watch." The boy yowled and held his head.

Randolph returned to his chair inside and sat alone watching the room come to rights, men ordering new rounds and rolling fresh smokes. No one acknowledged that he was present, and he wondered how many of them knew who he was, since Jules did all the hiring and supervising.

Galleri came over with another beer and set it down. "On the house," he said, kneading his thin fingers in his filthy apron.

Randolph bobbed his head.

"I'm glad he didn't hit the dealer." Galleri swiped at the table with his bar rag.

"Why?" The saloon keeper was Italian, but according to Byron, his family had emigrated a hundred years before from northern Italy, and he hated Sicilians.

"For one thing," Galleri said, "his damned shovel didn't need oiling."

The next morning Randolph awakened feeling slow and dizzy, sat up in bed, and rubbed his skull hard with both hands, still tasting Galleri's beer, which must have been brewed in a rusty drum. He looked through a curtain across to his brother's house. In the backyard, a sleeping man was chained sitting against a one-ton flywheel.

A water boy passed by and threw a potato at the prisoner, hitting him on the head, the man waking with a yelp and twisting around like the sick, confused thing he was. Byron came into the yard holding a coffee mug as his brother walked up.

"What you got here, By?" He smiled at his brother, figuring that someone needed to.

Byron looked down at the prisoner and took a sip of coffee. "A slow learner."

The man on the ground, who was very young, Randolph realized, looked at the dirt between his legs. "My head's fixing to blow up."

Byron dumped out his cup. "You're lucky I didn't snap it off and roll it into the privy."

The prisoner held up his shackles. "What'd I do to get locked up?"

"I think you owe Galleri something for broken furniture." He looked over at Randolph. "This is his second fight this month."

"Do you know who I am?" the mill manager asked.

The man raised his head as though it might topple off. "You the boss."

"And you're fired. Draw your pay and get on the train to Poachum."

The chain jingled. "Hey, I won't fight no more. You need good buckers like me, Mr. Aldridch." He squinted up, showing his bruised face, the olive lakes of blood pooling under his leathery tan.

"But I don't need trouble in the saloon."

The man wagged his shaggy head and held up one manacled hand. "I got to keep work to send money home. Hey, give me another shot, mister. I won't go nowheres near that dago's bar."

The mill manager was ready to turn away, but something in his brother's face stopped him. "What do you think?"

Closing one eye, Byron peered into his empty cup. "I think we ought to let the sun burn this fool up in the yard, then cut him loose for the one o'clock shift." He nudged the man's shoe with his boot. "And if he comes in the saloon again, I'll skin him for a fricassee."

"We don't need him in camp."

Byron squatted down and looked the hungover boy in the eye. "You can't ever tell," he said.

"Let me keep my job," he cried, "and I'll wear out my saw."

"What's your name?" the mill manager asked.

"Clovis Hutchins," he said, leaning away to spit. "Can I use that privy?"

"You can piss on yourself," Byron told him quietly.

The man closed his eyes at some interior pain. "I'll piss barb wire in a light socket if you keep me on."

Byron looked at his brother. "Well?"

Randolph sucked a tooth and figured the bucker's worth. "If you think you can finish growing up without getting killed, you can stay."

The two men walked toward the porch, and Byron asked, "You all right?"

"What do you mean?"

"Kind of pale, little brother."

Randolph frowned. "It's the damned water. And that castor oil they serve for beer doesn't help. In fact, I'll have to tend to business right now."

Quickly, he walked back to his house in a straight line, through puddles and all.

Since he'd arrived in camp, the cistern water had been the ruination of his digestion, and he stormed the privy, sitting in there for half an hour. Later, Jules came looking for him, and the mill manager told him to take charge for the day, to phone out the delivery invoices and line up a saw schedule for the orders. Next, he told May to boil jars of water for drinking and to keep them in the cooler on the back porch.

The next day dawned cloudless, and by noon was a continuous white-hot flash. After lunch the mill manager was again camped in the privy, daydreaming of Pennsylvania's dry air and steep green hills. His head was pounding, and thoughts of his slim wife haunted him until he looked down and saw that he was hard as a carrot. At that moment, the privy door snapped open and the housekeeper stepped out of the blinding white light and into the darkness. She was lifting her skirts, but then her eyes adjusted enough to see him, and she simply pushed back out the door.

Flustered, he covered himself after the fact, deep in the grip of a cramp. "She could have excused herself," the mill manager said aloud.

After supper his strength returned, and he wrote his weekly letter to his wife, read a copy of *Southern Lumberman* until he grew drowsy, and turned in at nine. The bedroom's board walls were dark with condensation, and he could feel the air between his fingers. Randolph lay uncovered on his back gasping in the swampy atmosphere, falling asleep at once and floating into a dream of logs drifting slowly in the pond toward the mill, and then of his wife as she slipped under covers with him in a cool Northern room, blessing him with her soft skin. The bed seemed to sway slowly like a hammock in a sailing ship, and the motion was delightful beyond all measure. He was gliding smoothly through a warm sea, his blood itself a tingling tide coursing throughout him. He gave a little groan and opened his eyes, which were clouded, and at first he didn't see May, and thought he was still dreaming as she squatted in her cotton gown over him, her face calm and watchful as she undulated in the dim light. After a few instants, he knew he was awake and stopped his own rocking motions, but his mind refused to work, and she kept on, closing her eyes as though her thoughts were far away from him and the creaking bed.

The next morning, he found her in the kitchen. He thought it impossible to say anything that wouldn't sound crude, though he had to speak to her and sat at the table as she cleaned the ashes out of the stove. Finally, he ventured, "Was that a housekeeping service enjoyed by the last manager?"

When she looked at him he realized that he knew nothing at all about her. "He came knocking," she said, "but I never let him in the door."

He turned up a palm. "Why me, then?"

"You're smart. You're not ugly." She bent close, as though to admire his face. "And you're white." Then she nodded toward the yard. "My daddy, he's about a fourth colored. My mamma was a white woman raised by those Indians over by Charenton." She sat down next to him and laid an arm in the center of the table, letting the window light play over her skin. "Look at this. Just look. If I didn't live with that old man and clean slop jars for a three-piece Yankee, what would you say I was? I'm lighter than that Galleri. Have hair like a Spanish woman."

Randolph thought of his wife and was frightened by the guilt rising in him. He'd been loyal to her during the long separations caused by his work. Passion was not a daily thing for him, but an animal thing, coming on as though caused by changing seasons. "I'm a married man," he blurted out.

The housekeeper laughed lightly. "I'm not after you, Mr. Aldridge."

"And I don't want to buy that kind of thing."

She lowered her face and rolled her eyes up at him. "Do you see me making out a bill?"

He straightened and pulled his hands from the table, now worried. "Do you go with many men?"

She shook her head. "I'm twenty-two and haven't even had it that many times." She stuck out her bottom lip. "I can take it or leave it."

He got up and poured a drink of boiled water from a jug. "Why'd you take it last night?"

"I want an all-white baby."

He dropped the glass and it shattered on the floor.

"Look out." She was up and sweeping before he could take

a step. She pushed him out of the way with a hip and in a moment dumped a dustpan of shards into the tin bucket.

"Why do you want to make a child?" he asked, as she handed him another tumbler. "I mean, like this."

She poured his glass full. "The old man has the breathing disease and rattles all night long. I'm sorry for that, but he's not going to last too long, and then I'll have nothing to do." She folded her arms and leaned against the counter.

"You could get married."

"I could. Around here I'd marry a colored man, and that wouldn't be bad except I'd just have babies and starve." She looked up at him. "You ever listen to me speak?"

He knew what she meant. "You've been to school."

"Eight grades. Two of my teachers were from the North and talked like you. They told me early on about the importance of talking. How it's not just words, but a sign of who you are. Some folks think your words *are* you."

He sat down again, knowing that with a white child she could move anywhere and pass. She could get a white job, a white education of some sort. People would look at her offspring and there would be no doubt. The child would have opportunities and could support her when she grew old. He held his breath, thinking of the possibilities such a life would present. Then he remembered his wife, where he was now, and who he was supposed to be. "I'll not be a part of this," he said. "You can find some other white man."

She tilted her head and started to say something. He imagined she wanted to explain that she didn't want a hayseed's child with red hair and freckles, somebody slow. But what she said was, "Don't worry yourself about my reasons, Mr. Aldridge. I went with you because you love your brother, that's all. And that kind of thing can come to the child." She left quietly and went out to the cabin, and he stood in the open back door looking after her until mosquitoes began to burn on his neck like hot cinders.

CHAPTER TEN

The steaming weeks dragged on, and new workers were hired to replenish the woods gangs that were losing men to fever and snakebites. The mill ran an extra four-hour shift and still couldn't keep up with orders, which Randolph now handled over a new phone line connected to the Tiger Island exchange. At the end of each day he visited his brother, who now owned high stacks of records arranged around his Victrola, new sentimental ballads he would listen to after coming in with fresh blood on his shovel. Amazed by all this maudlin singing, Randolph once asked, "Can people really feel this way?"

The mill manager had tolerated hours of the songs, only once suggesting that his brother send off for polkas or ragtime music without lyrics.

Byron sleeved a Gennett disk. "It's those words I need," he said. "They try to make me happy." His smile, when he said this, showed no irony, and the mill manager rolled his eyes.

"Well, the songs are all right, By."

"Sometimes, they nearly make me feel like when we were going out with the Wescott sisters."

"The silly Wescotts."

He slid the record into the Victrola's rack, his eyes showing a momentary spark of panic. "Did their brother come back from the war?"

"I don't know." Randolph knew that Jamie Wescott was missing in action and at this point he changed the topic, wondering aloud whether Buzetti would send someone to cause them more trouble.

Byron pulled out a glossy record made of orange shellac. "If he does, we'll know about it, won't we?"

"What've you got there?"

" 'Down the Lane and Home Again,' " he said, giving Randolph a penetrating look. "You know, Jamie would've liked this one."

The mill manager began latching his bedroom door at night, and once, before he fell asleep, heard it rattle softly, the hopeful sound filling him with fear and longing.

Weeks passed and the September downpours came hard. For all of one Saturday he stayed indoors, watching the lightning and straight-down rain. The swamp overflowed and streets became shallow runnels flowing toward the mill, which had to be shut down so the saw crews could sandbag the boiler room and the dynamo. While the rain needled the roof, Randolph sat watching May move about in her ironed housedress, passing him here, moving close there, until he could stand her lithe motion no more and reached out and put his hand low on her back.

They were in the little parlor by his desk, and she stopped to assess his face. "What?"

He raised his eyebrows hopefully. "Do you still want to try to get a white baby?"

She batted his hand away. "No need to try anymore."

He stood up and moved his face close to hers. "Why not?" He could smell the starch in her blouse.

"Because that one time did the trick."

"You're pregnant?" he gasped, not believing it. He and his wife had tried for years with nothing to show.

"That's a fact."

He ran both hands through his hair, which stuck to his skull in the dampness. "How do you feel about it?"

"I feel like I want to feel," she said flatly, staring back at him.

He realized he was blushing. "If you need anything, you let me know. I want to help."

She put a fist on a hip and looked at him carefully. "And?"

He swallowed and planned what to say. "If you'll sleep with me again, I'd be grateful."

"No," she said. "I don't need to. If you do, then it's time to get on that train and visit your wife." She picked up the bucket of water she'd been washing the floors with, walked to the door, and tossed it out into the rain. "Now what do you want for supper, pork chops or ham?"

The next day he felt sluggish and moped through the house wearing a pair of khaki work pants and an undershirt, not bothering to shave. It started to rain again in the afternoon and he pushed open the front screen door to watch puddles well up in the shell-covered lane, trying to remember what he'd done on Sundays a thousand years ago in Pennsylvania. He recalled going to church, and on a shelf in his bedroom he picked up a Bible. After reading several chapters, he said a prayer for his brother, then pulled on a slicker from behind the door and strode out into the storm.

Byron watched him slop across the mill yard, and when he mounted the porch, motioned him into a chair. Together they watched the veils of rain. Randolph shrugged out of the sour-smelling slicker and sat back, putting a hand out and tapping his brother's leg. "Have you heard anything?"

Byron's mouth drew in like a purse. He shook his head.

"I called the agent, and he told me he'd ring if he saw the first hint."

"Maybe you ran them off," Byron said, "you and your damned army." He stood and walked inside, and the mill manager could hear him talking to Ella.

The rain lightened up, turned to wind-chipped spray, and Randolph walked home through an ankle-deep lake, feeling like a fish in dirty water. He noticed that the horse had gotten out of the stall and was standing beside the locomotive, listening to the blower as the hostler raised steam for a run. He started to call to the animal, but realized, his mouth open and silent, that it did not have a name.

The next morning, the mill manager was sitting in his unpainted office when his wife walked in. He was so startled that he forgot to stand, and she had to pull him up for an embrace and a substantial kiss that surprised them both.

"Lillian, how in the world did you get down here?" The sight of her made him lightheaded. He studied her tailored traveling suit, the stylish little hat that cupped her head like a hand.

"It's easy. You get on one train and then another and then another, and after three days you're here. I went all the way to Tiger Island and got a room at that little hotel on the park."

"You should've called me into town."

She pulled off her dark kid gloves and waved them at him. "Aren't you glad to see me?"

"Of course." He hugged her again. "But this is a rough place."

She looked over his shoulder out into the mill yard. "I gathered that. I went over to your house to find you, and the housekeeper told me where you were."

He studied her voice for some trace of suspicion. "It's awfully muddy down there," he said, bending to look at her narrow boots.

"And it smells," she said after a pause, mouthing the words slowly. "You probably don't notice, but the place smells of rotten eggs, warm muddy water, oil, that kind of thing." She pinched his nose and kissed him again.

He looked behind her at the door. "Lillian!"

"I got tired of waiting for you. I've decided not to be angry anymore. Mother says I'm growing up at last." She laughed and brushed her fine dark hair from her forehead.

"Will you stay here? It's on the primitive side."

She looked at his eyes. "Oh, don't worry, Rand. I'll set up

somewhere in Tiger Island and you can come see me on week-ends. Maybe I could find a furnished house to rent."

He shook his head. "I doubt you'd find much to do in that place."

She waved this aside with the back of her hand, a motion of dismissal that jolted him. Though he was used to the deference showed by hundreds of workers, he was grateful for this movement. "There's a Presbyterian church in town, and I'm sure they could use a volunteer for this and that. The expense is certainly no worry. Your salary and bonuses have been rolling in at double the rate your father was paying you at the other mills."

She began to talk energetically and in detail about things back home, her father's failing health, news from the other plants. She seemed lighthearted, almost carefree, walked around the office as she spoke, and he wondered what had lifted her out of the subdued state she'd sunk down into over the past few years. He sat down and looked toward the woods. It might be the trip to this place. And with her standing there so crisp and energetic after her journey, he was reminded of how strange and foreign this country truly was.

"Will you be able to manage tonight? If you can't, I can send the lumber train back to Poachum in time for you to catch a local westbound." He raised his eyebrows hopefully, and she bent down and bit him, hard, on the top of his ear.

Randolph noticed that as the housekeeper served supper, she watched Lillian closely. His wife was affectionate, even flirtatious; she challenged him to play cards, and after an hour of gin, she mentioned artfully that she was tired and would go to bed early. In the morning, the smiling mill manager put tonic in his hair and wore a freshly ironed shirt for the first time in days, pulling out the chair grandly for his wife when she came to the plain kitchen table. May, standing by the stove, caught his eye and put a hand over her careful grin, causing him to redden like a schoolboy.

In the middle of breakfast, Randolph heard boots on the porch and looked up as his brother came in. Byron stopped short when he saw Lillian. He glanced quickly at Randolph, then walked over and bent to kiss her on the cheek. She held his face in her hands a moment and looked at him.

"How are you, Byron?"

He straightened up. "Not bad for a sawmill cop."

"I've heard you're married now. When can I meet her?"

"As soon as you like. She's a nice, patient woman." He smiled when he said this.

"She'd have to be to stay with you. Is hunting and riding horses still mostly what you care about?" She pushed away a chair from the table and motioned for him to sit in it.

"I leave the horses to Randolph nowadays."

"Really?" She looked at her husband, who shrugged. "The last time I saw you, you were on Pretzel, that big bay of yours. Didn't you ride a horse out west?"

Byron looked over her head and through the rear door for a moment. "I rode one from Oklahoma to Mexico, and when it died under me I walked to town and bought a used Ford."

Lillian shifted in her chair and frowned. "Were you after a criminal?"

"Sort of. What have you been doing these past few years, duchess? I'm surprised you don't have a brood of kids to boss around."

"Maybe some day," she said quickly. "Right now I've come down South to keep an eye on brother here."

"How long will you be staying?"

"Oh, as long as the trees last, I imagine." She reached across the table for Randolph's hand, who gave it to her, forcing a smile. "And what about yourself?"

"More or less the same."

"And then?"

He stood up and adjusted his gun belt. "That's what we're all wondering, isn't it. Maybe I'll go into vaudeville. I'm learning lots of songs."

"You already know a lot of songs. You don't have a piano out here in the swamps, do you?"

"No, a piano would warp shut in all this dampness. Rando has taken up accordion though." His head jerked toward his brother. "I have to talk to you about something, outside." He tipped his hat at Lillian, and the men walked out.

"Byron Aldridge, I've still got a lot to say to you," she called after them.

He did not smile. "I'm sure I'll hear all of it before long. It's good to see you."

Randolph followed into the front yard, stepping over a brimming rut into the lane. "She's really glad to see you."

"Rando, I know that. God, she doesn't seem a day older than the last time, and still fiesty. She looks like she could brain a mule with her hymnal."

"What did you want to talk to me about?"

Byron motioned to the house with his eyes. "Is she staying out here?"

Randolph laughed. "Would you?"

"Then she's in town? At the Bellanger?"

"Yes, or she will be in a day or so."

"Word will get around who she is, and that's something you don't want. Buzetti will find out."

The mill manager opened his mouth and looked back at the house. "Good Lord. I didn't think."

Byron pulled a cigar from a vest pocket and struck a match, barely able to connect with the flame. His brother reached up and steadied his hand. "If she's determined to stay, set her up in New Orleans. At least she won't be nesting down right in the middle of them."

"How much should I tell her?"

"Enough to make her lock her doors at night." A shout racketed across the open yard, and Byron turned toward the barracks where two men wearing union suits stood next to a stump, pounding each other in the chest as though chipping ice.

September 7, 1923
Nimbus Mill
Poachum, Louisiana

Father,

The new planers have been installed and the siding that comes out of them is like buffed red granite and "most pleasing to the eye," as Mother used to say. After the Gulf cypress is all cut out, no one will ever know such lumber again, unless we send a piece to a museum. The price is up one dollar a thousand just this week.

Byron listens to me. I sense a slow change of heart in him for the better and hope that his war wounds are healing. Though new men come into the camp weekly and fights erupt at the saloon with regularity he hasn't seriously hurt anyone.

I've been forced to hire again from the east Texas mills that have cut out their tracts. These hands are generally single and totally undomesticated, but their arms and backs are like iron. Unfortunately, this quality extends to their heads as well. These are poor people who are as hard as the lives they've lived, but, all in all, worth the expense. I'm continuing the policy of paying them in scrip redeemable in goods at our commissary, to keep them in camp. They live well enough, considering that part of their pay is shelter, fuel, water, and electricity. For anyone who cares for those things, it's better than living in a pasture. I must say that labor is much cheaper and less demanding hereabouts than in our part of the world. The larger, older mills in this region have better men, family men, and they keep them. I could use fewer savages in camp.

I make a point of visiting with Byron every day. We keep waiting for the gangsters to do something, which is like waiting to be struck by lightning. He says he is sorry that you are not feeling well. That is something, at least.

Your loving son,
Randolph

He had rented a suite at the St. Charles in New Orleans until Lillian could find a suitable house to rent. After settling her in, he took a train back to Poachum and arrived at the mill after dark, exhausted, yet still having business to see to in his office. He rode the horse up to the main building and settled in at his desk.

A hard, steady wind kicked up from the south, pushing a tide that crept into the mill yard like pooling blood. He was totaling accounts when from across the compound he heard Galleri's high, excited voice calling out for Byron. He dropped his pencil and clattered down the steps to where the horse stood tethered to a spigot. The gelding began to walk toward a storm of voices coming from the white side of the saloon and when the pop of a small pistol punctuated the general racket, the animal fell into a trot. In the moonless clearing Randolph caught sight of his brother carrying a shotgun, and he reined the horse up hard, forcing it to stumble away from what it heard.

"By," he called.

Byron stopped. Down at the saloon, someone was shriek-ing, *"Gott im Himmel."*

"What?"

"Do you need the gun?"

His brother motioned to the saloon. "Listen to them in there." Another shot popped, followed by a fresh eruption of hollering. The kerosene light spilled through the windows, and the screams were voices in flames.

Randolph dismounted and put his hand on Byron's shoul-der. "Maybe, if you let it run its course, it'll just work out. These events are, well, they're natural, and you're always interfering."

Byron put the shotgun's butt plate on the top of his boot and looked down, leaving Randolph no way of seeing what was in his eyes. "I don't *know* what to do. You're telling me to just stand here?"

"I've never been in a battle. I don't know how it is. I don't understand." He took back his hand. "I'm just worried about you."

"You want me to stand here." Byron looked back at the dark house where they both knew his wife was listening. "Kind of an experiment." Ten or twelve voices rose up in rage and a table flew out of the saloon's dim doorway. "You want me to believe in 'Thou shalt not kill.' Well, I do believe it. But what about those fellows?"

"Let's go back to your porch and sit down." He dropped the reins of the horse, which turned completely around and then stood stock still. The men walked back to Byron's house and sat on the steps. After a minute Galleri appeared in the saloon's doorway and began screaming like a woman. Four rapid reports from a large-caliber pistol followed, and men began flying out of the door and dropping from windows like hornets escaping a burning hive. The mill manager's heart sank, and he suddenly felt both frightened and foolish.

The old doctor came hobbling up, his shoes and pants on, his galluses pulled over gray long johns. Since Sydney Rosen had arrived in Nimbus he'd kept his ears open for shouts and gunfire. "I can't go down there, you know, until someone disarms those sons of bitches."

Byron turned to his brother. "Now?" The word was barely audible.

Randolph looked away, then stood up, and the three of them walked toward the holes of light down at the end of camp, arriving in front of the saloon as two men dragged someone out onto the front porch—the German chief engineer, who'd been shot several times. He was glossy with blood and gasping out in a pleading voice what sounded like prayer.

The doctor knelt beside him and touched each bullet hole, lifted off the engineer's short-brimmed cap, stood, and looked back to his own little house, pulling on his white beard. "Maybe ten minutes."

"There's nothing you can do?" Randolph asked. "Surely there's something. My God, he's our engineer."

The doctor leaned against a post. "He needed a little preventive medicine," he said, staring at Byron.

The big German's eyes grew wide and blind, his lips moving in the old language of death, trying to say the last thing that mattered, and the mill manager got on his knees and put an ear to his lips, surprised to hear, of all things, the thinnest thread of song. A mixed-race gang of tree cutters folded their arms and watched, and a boilerman took off his hat. When the engineer stopped breathing, a tingling panic rose through the mill manager, and placing his hands down on the engineer's chest to shake him alive, he felt only the dead, flowing movement of inert flesh. He then sat up and stared for a long time, saying at last, "Someone wake up the carpenters."

Galleri stepped out onto the porch, his hands wrapped in his dirty apron. He gave Randolph a look of restrained reproach. "You gonna ship this one back to Germany?"

The mill manager's mouth fell open.

Byron stepped over the corpse and entered the saloon, where the Italian who ran the card game was thumbing shells into the magazine of a Colt pistol. "What happened?"

The dealer kept feeding in the fat cartridges. "He was, what you say, nuts. He said I did the cheating on him." Putting down the weapon, he pulled off his fedora, reshaped the crown, and then replaced it, looking at no one.

Inside the door lay a black lumber stacker, moaning, his face pressed sideways against a splash of blood, his left boot nosed into a spittoon. Shivering on the floor next to the bar was a mill hand cradling a broken arm. Byron gestured to him. "What did you see?"

"I didn't see shit," the man slurred, staring at his boots. "Mister Hans lost his pay is all I know."

"Was he drunk?"

The mill hand had the lopsided face of a stroke victim. "It's Saturday, ain't it?" Half of the face was joking, the other as serious as a dead man's.

Byron looked at the dealer. "Who shot first?"

He put out an upturned palm and bunched his fingers.

"Hey, he pulls out a two-dollar pistol, sticks it here, sticks it there. Everybody gets the red ass. At me, at him. Next thing he sets it off. Two time. Maybe three." The Italian lit a cigarette and took a long drag. "He sticks it in my face and that's when I shot." He flicked an ash toward the door. "The nigger was *accidenti*."

"You had to shoot the German four times?"

"Hey, that's defense of the self." He crossed his legs and broke the seal on a new deck. "What you worried about?" He gave Byron a sliding smile. "It's just sauerkraut. I hear you kill more of 'em than me in the war."

Even the mill hand turned his head, sensing the mistake. "I've forgotten your name," Byron said.

"Vincente. What's it to you?"

The mill hand began groaning, trying to rise.

Byron said, "Get out of camp now. Tell Buzetti he can send another dealer."

Vincente smiled out a cloud of smoke. "It's no gonna work. Buzetti's my cousin. This is my, how you say, *territoria*."

Byron walked over to the table. "Listen," he began, smiling too widely, but he checked himself when he glimpsed Randolph's empty face looking in from the porch.

"What?" Vincente asked with his mocking smile.

"Don't come back," he whispered, "until garlic smells like roses."

At dawn, the mill manager, still awake, heard someone walking on his porch, and May rattled his doorknob. "You better get up and see about him," she said.

He found Byron outside, sitting in a rocker, smoking. Without looking up, he said, "I wish you'd been right."

Randolph watched a snake sidewinding along the road. The smell of the mud-choked swamp rose up to him, mixed with woodsmoke and privy. "I don't understand anything, By. I was wrong. From now on, do like you've been doing. Just stop it as quickly as you can." He looked across the mill yard at the breakfast smoke creeping down the roof pitch of every paintless house, and he felt profoundly sad, remembering the drunk German's last minute, the short string of a song, which he now began to whistle, trying to place it.

" 'Lo, How a Rose E're Blooming,' " Byron said.

"A Christmas carol. What was going through his mind?"

Byron rocked back and looked up at him. "I wish I knew, brother."

"Yes."

"If I'd put a bullet in the German in the right place, maybe he wouldn't have died. Maybe the stacker wouldn't have caught the stray shot that ruined him."

"Just do what has to be done. But try not to kill anyone."

His brother rocked forward and closed his eyes. "What if Vincente and the engineer had already faced off, and I had to make a choice? Hans was so drunk he wouldn't have listened to me. What if I had to shoot one or the other?"

"You save the best one, I guess. You've done that before." Randolph studied his brother's tortured profile as he looked off toward the saloon.

And then Byron's voice broke. "You have to decide in half a second."

"I don't know, maybe you should carry a smaller-caliber pistol."

Byron shook his head. "I could empty a .38 into a big tree cutter, and if he's drunk enough it'd be like throwing a handful of gravel at him. That's one thing I learned policing cowboys in their shit-hole bars." He put his head back on the rocker and met his brother's eyes. "What *exactly* do you want me to do?"

"Shoot to wound. If they die anyway, you'll still have tried to do right."

"Leave myself open to the last shot?"

A safety valve opened up above the mill, venting an angry feather of steam, and Randolph squinted toward the raspy sound. "I don't know. I just don't know."

"Just a while ago, I used the new phone line to call the German's folks in Houston. I had to go through about ten operators, a Kirby commissary manager, and a preacher to reach his wife. Lord, that woman cried and cried. I heard the phone's earpiece swing and hit the wall and then more noise after that. When I hung up, I opened the window for air and thought I could hear her screams coming all the way from Texas." Byron put a hand over his eyes.

Randolph bent down and grabbed his arm. "Come inside, By. The housekeeper makes wonderful coffee."

His brother began to cry. "I asked around. That lumber stacker lying in his blood, his name's Georgie. He was a good old boy and could make a two-by-four fly and land like a bird."

"Come on, now," Randolph said, lifting him up as best he could.

In the kitchen, the housekeeper watched the men settle at the table. "Lord," she said, astonished. "A crying man."

That night, when the mill was dead quiet but for the whispery exhale of the boilers, Randolph wandered his house from room to room, brooding about Hans. Back in Pennsylvania, he'd sung the engineer's song as a hymn during Christmas season, sometimes even in German. On the third trip through his bedroom, he saw, behind a chair, a sparkle of pearline finish. He pulled the accordion against him like a lover, his fingers wandering for the melody, and the way a hand finds a doorknob in a midnight hallway, he found the song, playing his way into it, hoping the missing words would come and ride the notes against the silence. He closed his eyes and remembered snow, and then the words came one by one, like birds landing on a wire at sunset.

> *Lo, how a Rose e're blooming*
> *From tender stem hath sprung!*
> *Of Jesse's lineage coming*
> *As those of old have sung.*

Two whole stanzas returned to him, and he recalled a Christmas play in which he'd sung them with his baby voice. He worried that the song was as sentimental as one of Byron's dollar records, another palliative to mask the true hurt of living, but as the instrument's reeds thrummed, he thought of Hans trying to sing it and wondered why, of all the sounds of a lifetime to cling to, he chose this one. Adding another finger to the melody, Randolph sang, with the feeling of a child:

> *Wahr' Mensch und wahrer Gott,*
> *Hilft uns aus allen Leiden,*
> *Rettet von Sund' und Tod.*

He played out all the German in his memory and sang it next in English, opening the accordion's stops and polishing the rhythm until the straps pulled down his shoulders. Then the door to his bedroom swung open, the housekeeper standing there in a flannel nightgown.

"What's wrong with you?" she asked.

Near tears and surprised, he began to stutter. "I—I was singing a tribute to Hans."

May sniffed. "Tribute, is it? Mr. Randolph, you and Mr. Byron have to stop looking at everything on this green earth like it's a moving picture."

"He was a fine engineer," he said defensively.

She put a hand on her hip. "Mr. Hans could make those engines run like a chicken on Sunday morning, all right, but he was a nasty drunk and smelled like a lost dishrag."

Embarrassed, he turned away, the accordion bulging from his stomach. "I guess I was trying to find something redemptive in his death."

She made a face. "You were with him when he died, I heard."

"I was."

"Tell truth. You see anything beautiful about it? Or was it just another sawmill man shot up in a poker game?" She came over and put a hand on his shoulder. "You all have got to deal with what is. Now take this whiny box off and get some rest. I heard this thing from out in the cabin and it scared me half to death."

He unshouldered the instrument and placed it on the floor. As May was going though the doorway, he called after her, "How've you been feeling?"

Over her shoulder she said, "Kind of heavy," and was gone.

Randolph shoved the accordion into a corner with his foot and watched it take a final breath.

CHAPTER ELEVEN

Within a week, Lillian found a large galleried house to lease in the Garden District, and Randolph was glad to have her even further away from the mill because May would soon begin to show. He and the housekeeper had agreed on a story in which she'd been taken advantage of by a white man in Tiger Island. Once such a thing was said in the South, she'd told him, no other questions would be asked.

He began to take the Saturday-evening mail train into New Orleans, and within a few weeks he and Lillian had established a routine. At ten o'clock he would arrive at the house on Prytania Street, where she would have a hot bath ready for him, and afterward, they would have drinks and make love. Each journey was a return to civilization, and he was shocked to get off the train and see people who didn't stink excessively, were not spattered with mud and dung, who didn't walk around with silver-toothed crosscut saws bouncing over their shoulders.

The house Lillian had rented he thought to be wastefully comfortable, so bright it hurt his eyes with its white plaster medallions and ivory walls, brass light fixtures and beveled-glass doors. The deep porcelain tub, however, was a blessing, and he was glad to stand up after a bath and not have his buttocks stippled by galvanizing and impressed with the number 3.

On Sundays they would walk on a real sidewalk to church, but Randolph would still watch his feet, expecting a water moccasin in any sunny spot. The minister was elegant and bright, as straight in his back as he was in his thinking. To the mill manager he looked like some rare intelligence hired for a large fee, and the stained-glass-washed air around him was fragrant with logic.

Lillian began to fit in with the New Orleans culture, learning to cope with the hot afternoons and palate-tingling food. He was afraid that she would be lonely and homesick, but for once she seemed delighted to be out on her own, away from both her dour family and his father, who lately had railed more or less exclusively about responsibility and money. She no longer complained that Randolph was dull and made clear how proud she was of what he was attempting with Byron. Even her complexion, he thought, had improved in the humidity.

Sunday nights he rode the windy coaches of the westbound mail, rocking back into darkness. The train crossed moonstruck alluvial farms by the river, then a grassy, water-haunted prairie, plunging next into the old-growth swamps where everything slowed to the pace of a hunting reptile and the skirted trees threw back at him the crashing of the coaches' wheels. Poachum was only seventy miles from streetcars, jazz bands, sane religion, and theaters pearled with hundreds of lightbulbs, but when he stepped off the train at the station whose only illumination was the backwash from the locomotive's headlight, the settlement seemed to be in the jungles of Brazil.

Sales preparations he previously had completed on Sundays had to be carried over to later in the week. One Monday in early October, an hour earlier than usual, the housekeeper struggled to wake him, her thin fingers set deep in his well-fed biceps.

"What?" He couldn't even see her.

"You have a tying-up to do."

He rubbed his eyes with the backs of his hands for half a minute. "Oh, Lord."

"The men are on the porch."

He sat up, pulled on his clothes and boots, and at the front door she handed him a lantern. Two somber, bearded mill hands and Byron, stiff as cardboard and silent, stepped off with him down to the commissary. Randolph unfolded a big jackknife key and unlocked the store, the bearded men going inside and soon coming back out with a crated cookstove between them that they loaded onto a two-wheeled mule cart. Byron sat on the tailgate, his straw cowboy hat slanting in his eyes. By the time they got to the last cabin in the Negro quarters, a gray light had come up over the treetops. A large black faller wearing new overalls stood between the cabin and the rutted lane, and next to him a woman held herself in a sideways slouch, her head bound in a red turban. The mill hands knocked the crate apart in the yard and assembled the stove, tightening bolts with their fingers. After the lids were on and the lifting keys stuck into them and turned forward, they stepped back and assumed the posture of witnesses.

The mill manager came forward and cleared his throat, trying to remember their names. "Led Williams, do you want this stove to go into this house?"

"Yes sah," the man said, nodding gravely.

"Nellie Jones, do you also want this stove to go into this house?"

The woman put a hand on her hip and looked the mill manager in the eye. "That's a fact," she said, spitting expertly on the stove's long shadow.

Randolph motioned to the men, who picked up the range and walked it through the front door and into the rear of the house, dropping it under a new crock flue pipe set in the wall. When they emerged, the man and woman stepped up out of the yard through the doorway, turned, and stood in the frame, looking outside.

Randolph felt the urge to raise his hands toward the sky, so he did. Then he was at a loss for what to say, feeling pagan, drawing magic from the clouds. Finally, he told them, "You're together now. I guess you know what that means." He brought down his hands. "Congratulations."

"Thank you, sah," the man said. The woman nodded once, spat another brown jet into the yard, and turned toward the rear of the cabin.

Byron replaced his hat and motioned to the doorway. "I won't have any more trouble with him in the saloon. *She'll* keep him straight."

"You think so?"

"Better than I can," he said, climbing back onto the cart.

Randolph returned to his house and ate breakfast, glancing repeatedly at May. "That's the fourth hitching-up I've done. How do I handle a divorce?"

She poured him more coffee with one hand and gave him a dollop of cream with the other. "Get somebody to throw the stove in the yard. Send the man back to the barracks, and give the woman train fare to her mamma. Buy tickets for her little chaps, too."

"That's it?"

She thought a moment, her lovely gold-flecked eyes floating between him and the window. "What else could happen?"

He broke open a feathery biscuit. "How long were you married?"

She pursed her lips and looked at him directly. "Can I sit down?"

He looked behind him through the screen.

"Nobody's studying you," she said ruefully, pulling out a chair and easing into it. "I married a nice, smart boy from Shirmer, a kind, light-skinned boy named James. We came here to work and he spent two dollars to get us married by a preacher. Had to go into town and sign papers because he wanted everything right. About three months later, they had him on the log train and he fell down between two cars and got his foot pinched off above the ankle." She worked her hands in her apron as though trying to scour something off her fingers. "I tried to care for him, but he wouldn't stop bleeding. Mr. Byron, he came over and tried some things they taught him in the war, but it didn't do any good. After two days he got fever, and I wanted somebody to take him to Tiger Island." She glanced out the kitchen window. "I found out the doctor there wouldn't work on colored. Mr. Jules finally got it set up so that the railroad would carry him in the baggage car to New Orleans. But the morning we were going to load him, he passed."

Randolph pushed his coffee cup away and made a face. "I'm sorry."

She looked at him then. "I learned something, though." She reached over, took his empty plate, and placed it in her lap. "I know who I am, and I'm not too proud to be colored. But I know what I look like. I understand that the main reason people know I'm colored is my old daddy out there. But when he's gone, I can take what I've got set aside and head out." She stood and threw the plate into the dishpan. "I'm *not* going to be somebody a doctor won't touch. No, I'm *not*."

He rose and went over to her, studying her face. "You can pass, and when you can get away from here, I'll get you employment elsewhere." She was tearing up, so he took her fingers and pressed a thumb on the back of her hand.

"Mr. Jules gave me the idea last year," she said. "He says up North some of the quality folks are Jews, Spaniards, and all kinds I can be taken for."

"You've been speaking to Jules?"

She nodded, looked at her hand in his, and straightened up. "Some days before you got here, I went with him. But Mr. Jules felt guilty, and he was scared his wife would find out, so we just went the one time."

"You slept with Jules?" He remembered how the big assistant manager would sometimes scream at the saw teams, calling them "rafts of worthless niggers."

She shrugged. "That sap was from good white oak."

At that moment, he sensed how infinitely trapped she must feel, but before he could say anything, he heard the scuff of shoes on the back steps and she pulled her hand away.

A man wearing a pointed hat wrapped with a red silk hatband walked up out of the yard to the screen door and began gesturing with his hands. "Ey. I don't want to in'errupt, but I'm lookin' for the manager." His eyes were dark and hard and bounced back and forth between the two of them in the kitchen. "Can I come in?"

"I'm Aldridge. What do you want?"

"Joe Buzetti." He straightened up and put his fingers through the handle.

The mill manager pushed the door open in his face and walked out onto the porch. "How'd you get here?"

Buzetti looked at him, glanced inside at the housekeeper, then shrugged. "I got a motorboat can come from Tiger Island in about ninety minutes."

Randolph looked over at the canal, where he saw a long skiff and two men in it tending a gleaming three-cylinder inboard engine. "What brings you out here?"

"I got a little business to talk." He looked over his shoulder across the sun-stricken mill yard toward the saloon. "Normally I'd send somebody, you know. But an important man like yourself, I thought I should come myself." He spread his hands out before his waist, as though offering himself as a present.

"What business?"

"My cousin, Vincente, he tells me your constable don't want him dealing in the saloon no more."

The mill manager nodded. "He killed my chief engineer, for God's sake."

Buzetti put up his palms. "Ey. It's a habit. He was in the war, you know? He kill five or six of them Dutchmen before breakfast." He laughed.

"He's killed his last Dutchman around here," Randolph said.

Buzetti raised a thumb and forefinger and brought them together slowly, in front of the mill manager's face. "Vincente. He and me we kind of close, you know?" He lowered his hand and bobbed his head to the right. "If I replace him out here it might be with somebody worse. My cousin, he been out here pretty long, and this the first time you got cause to complain." He made a motion, a little starburst of fingers. "He's sorry about the guy. He told me he had to do it, and tried to hit him where it wouldn't be, you know, fatal."

Randolph put a hand up and leaned against a porch support. "He shot him four times with a .45."

"Hey, you let Vincente come back I'll tell him to carry a Luger. In the war, I seen a kraut dump three or four Luger rounds in a big farmboy and it didn't even slow him down."

Randolph looked at the man's hat as though it offered some clue to the inexplicable reasoning of the brain beneath it. Growing serious, Buzetti turned sideways and looked down. "Ey, your brother pushed Vincente around some already. He coulda done your brother anytime. He held back, you know. He's just interested in the family and the poker game, not no sad sack constable. The next guy I put in could be some young New Jersey guy who don't give a shit. Who knows?"

The mill manager looked at the man's slippery smile and wanted to plant a fist in the middle of it. He glanced over at the thugs, now standing on the canal bank. "You know what I'm thinking, don't you?"

Buzetti shrugged. *"Scuzi?"*

He leaned back against the wall. "I could call up some sawyers to feed your ass to the alligators in the millpond."

Buzetti laughed again, a hacking noise. "Yeah, that's right. You got lotsa people do what you say."

When he heard this laugh, Randolph understood that Buzetti lived in a world where a house could be burned for ten dollars, a tree spiked for twenty, a man sleeping next to his wife shot dead for a wad of five-dollar bills.

Buzetti sniffed, seemingly disappointed. "I thought you had good sense, you know? I thought you was worried about your brother's welfare."

"You could talk to him yourself."

Buzetti blinked. "Last time we talked, my place of business fell in the river."

Randolph looked again at the hat, its foreign angles and too-bright hatband. There were things he did not understand, so he decided to be cautious. "I'll talk to him," he said, turning inside.

"Fine. That's fine," Buzetti called after him.

Randolph watched him swagger over to where his men waited in the shade of a discarded boiler, and they all laughed and started toward the saloon.

Coming up from behind, May cleared her throat and said, "Throw him to the alligators, huh?"

"What?"

"Your talk is changing."

"What do you mean?"

"Look out," she said, hefting a pan full of gray water and heading through the door. When she flung it off the little back porch, her father, sitting in the shade of his cabin, looked up but seemed not to see her. A hot wind began to push down the weeds along the fence. "I mean this place is changing you."

"Nonsense." He followed her out into the chicken-scoured yard, pretending to examine the smoke rising from the mill's stacks. He knew she was waiting for him to look at her, and when he did his eyes fell to her billowing apron, where her hands blended into the cloth.

Randolph convinced his brother that Vincente should continue as the dealer. In return Buzetti told his cousin not to carry his big Colt, that if he felt threatened, he should deal with his back to the corner of the room. But the first night of renewed gambling, Galleri took Byron aside and told him there was a Luger in a cigar box under the dealer's chair.

When he heard this, he laughed and asked Galleri to fix him a tall drink.

The mill manager continued to ride off to New Orleans on weekends feeling as if that were the strange world, the big city, unreal in its pleasures, in the whiteness of his wife's house, in the pale and giving body that enveloped him like a glowing cloud on Saturday nights and sometimes on Sunday mornings when the deep steamship whistles floated up the river and the vegetable man sang out of cabbages and beets, bananas and plums, muskmelons and grapes, the harness of his wagon jingling down the brick streets. But sometimes when he heard the vegetable man's voice rising pure, two blocks away, Randolph thought of the German and his dying song, and again he would try to figure out whose fault it was the engineer was dead: Vincente, or himself, or Buzetti—or a war that had taught so many how to kill.

Randolph began to give the agent at Poachum twenty dollars a month to alert him at once if any suspicious men came into the station, men not dressed for the woods, men with big mustaches, striped suits, flashy hats. When Jules rode into Tiger Island for supplies he brought back the news that Buzetti had repaired his barroom, brought down a new raft of cousins and soldiers. A Chicago madam, yet another cousin, had set up a new whorehouse.

One afternoon the phone rang in the office and it was Merville.

"Mr. Aldridge, you there?"

"I'm here, marshal." Randolph smiled at the old man's voice. "What can I do for you?"

"I got a bill from the city for twenty-three dollars. The burial plot for that engineer what got killed out at your place. Will you pay that?"

Randolph closed his eyes, wondering how long such reminders would show up in his life. "Yes. Send the invoice and I'll take care of it."

"All right." Then Merville's voice brightened. "This new line is something. The mail woulda took ten days. I remember the time I'd have to lug a city bill that needed some face-to-face explaining out to Shirmer on horseback, and it would take me two days on the road. Hell, a car trip would take me a whole day. Now it's over in a minute."

The mill manager thought about this. "That's right."

"While I got you, can you tell me if Galleri got him a big storage shed out there?"

"Why, no. I think he's got a little attic space, that's all."

"I heard Buzetti was bringing in cases of stuff from Cuba. I was kind of wondering where he was storing that. I can't even figure how he's bringing it in."

"Why're you asking? You people don't seem too worried about alcohol."

"I just like to keep my finger on things," Merville told him. "It's the stupid finger what gets burnt."

Even in November the swamps steamed, but overnight the weather came down cold and hard as a hammer on the fingers, a blue wind blowing the long flags of Spanish moss to the south all day as the men worked on in their light clothes. At quitting time, a skim of ice was forming in the shallowest puddles. Two days later, fever swept through the camp, and new men had to be hired. One morning, Jules came into Randolph's office with a large Negro following behind him.

"Mr. Aldridge, this buck wants work in the rack yard." He jerked a thumb sideways. "Says he knows you."

The mill manager looked over at a very dark man in shirtsleeves, barefoot, a hemp cord for a belt. He was about to ask Jules when he'd started recruiting hoboes when the office bulb ignited a black streak of lightning running down the man's face. "So you made it," Randolph said.

"Yas suh. I healed up and stayed on the *Newman*." He turned his head to let the scar catch more light. "You patched me up good." His features didn't move when he spoke. His was a face prepared to show nothing.

"Why'd you quit the river?"

"Boat hit the lock wall at Plaquemine and broke half in

two." He looked at the floor. "You hire me and I be grateful, boss. I got a good back and no rupture no place."

The scar ran thick as yarn. Randolph nodded toward Jules. "Put him on and see how he does."

"All right," Jules said. "What's your name?"

"Clarence Williams. I from 'round Vicksburg."

Randolph thought of something. "Did your engineer live through the sinking?"

"Mr. Minos?"

"Yes."

"He on the bank cussin' right now."

"Jules, go find him and hire him on. He's that old policeman's son."

Jules stood in the door and reached into a coat pocket for his plug. "He any better than the German?"

Randolph looked again at Clarence William's face, at the wholeness of it. "Yes, I'm sure he is."

"I do you proud, suh."

"Go by the commissary and draw a pair of boots against your wages. By the way, what happened to the waiter on that boat?"

"Speck?"

"Yes, that's the man."

Clarence Williams smiled, and the scar belled sideways. "He drownded in the kitchen. I reckon he burnin' in hell right now."

The men left, and the mill manager began thinking about the workers in the mill below, in the woods for miles around, pieces of mechanism that now and again failed, only to be discarded and replaced. He was the chief gear in the machine, where the motion started, and he was not supposed to worry about who was broken or stripped down the line. He reached for his bottle of brandy in the warped desk, found a dusty little tumbler in a file drawer, and wiped it clean with the bottom of his vest.

The horse was tied at the office steps, and at lunch he mounted the shivering animal and rode through the icy slop to Byron's house, leaving the reins on the saddle when he got down. He saw Ella come out the back door and walk toward the two rows of houses in the white section. Inside, his unshaven brother was rubbing his hands next to a woodstove. He watched him for a moment and shook his head.

Byron looked up at him, his eyes worried. "I just noticed your housekeeper. You know, sometimes I'm not very observant." His hands were shaking, though the room felt warm.

"She's getting big, all right."

"Sit down. I've got something to tell you, and I don't know how you'll take it."

Randolph pulled a chair next to the stove and put his hand on his brother's back, admiring the heavy, pent-up feel of the muscles. "Whatever it is, I'll take it well."

"That woman's baby?"

"Yes?"

"It might be mine."

He took back his hand. "Good Lord, By, I—"

"I know, I know." He put up his palms.

"No, I mean, how do you know?" He looked toward the window. "Maybe she's been with others."

"It was back in June, I think. Ella went into New Orleans, and I tied one on. Sat on the porch, got drunk, and sang my records. Ella'd told May to bring over some supper, I guess, and I was capsized in bed when I heard her leave it in the kitchen and come into the bedroom." He looked up sheepishly. "She just got on board."

Randolph looked away again, out at the mill. "Was it just that one time?"

"Yeah. It was kind of a lovely ambush." Suddenly, he straightened in his chair and looked at his brother. "But I was drunk as a noodle, and she knew it."

"Well," Randolph said, getting up, "the odds are it isn't yours. I mean, think of it. Who could be that unlucky?"

"I guess we'll be able to tell soon enough."

Randolph stiffened, his hand on the doorknob. "There's other white men in this camp."

Byron looked up. "Do you, well, do you know if she's seeing anybody? She used to talk to Jules in the commissary, and that toothless clerk."

"She spends the day in Tiger Island once every two weeks, to get medicine for her father. I don't know what else she does there."

"I'm worried sick about it. If Ella left me, I don't know what would happen." He leaned back from the stove and clasped his hands under his armpits.

Randolph started across the compound, so distracted he forgot the horse, the animal following his footsteps like a dog. In his own backyard, the woman was carrying stove wood. He intercepted her between his house and the cabin.

"Mr. Aldridge?"

He barely opened his lips. "How many white oaks have you been climbing around here?"

Her eyes went down. "You starting to talk colored."

"How many?"

She put the firewood on the ground between them. "You found out the third one, I guess." She folded her arms and waited.

He turned and looked at the shingles on his roof as though searching out the source of a leak. "Are you sure that baby's not his?"

"Between him and you the red river flowed."

"What?"

"I had my monthly."

He let out a breath. "I'll have to tell him, I suppose. He's worried about it."

She studied his face, looking in one eye and then the other. "You glad it's not his?"

He jammed his hands deep into his pockets. "I don't know what to be glad of." He wanted to walk away but felt rooted to the spot.

She tilted her head. "You look kind of glad around the eyes."

He glanced over to the cabin door, which her bent father

had opened. "It's chilly," he said. "You better make use of this wood." A white mill hand walking past slowed at the fence to watch them, and Randolph stepped quickly into his own house.

For Christmas, he and Lillian had planned on returning to Pittsburgh, but in mid-December, influenza grabbed her in a hot fist, and they abandoned the trip. At Nimbus it rained every day, and the woods crews suffered like cattle left out in the storm. Randolph played gin each night at Byron's house, talking to excess, forcing out memories of their Pennsylvania hunting adventures, horseback trips, swimming matches, and singing parties with neighborhood girls. Byron would nod, but sometimes his eyes grew hard and dark, as if to ask why he should be interested in someone he used to be.

One February dawn, Randolph sat in his office staring out the window, thinking of how to begin a letter to his father. He watched Byron come out for his first rounds and disappear in the mill steam and drizzle. The standard-gauge shay locomotive headed north for Poachum, and the narrow-gauge dummy bobbled south into the swamp. The rafting steamer—loaded down with men dressed in dark, sagging coats—broke a skim of fog on its way down the canal, the leaking steamboat forming its own cloud that retreated over the black water. Crews fired up donkey boilers and pull boats, and the sooty air was so cold and wet that all the steam exhaust roosted on the mill yard and buildings, brooding and still. The mill manager thought about the twelve boxes the carpenters had to build because of the influenza. Only one other had been built because of the saloon, the weather dampening the drunken meanness in most of the men inclined to kill. He hoped that even in this temporary truce his brother's nerves might relax like the diffusing tuft of steam floating up past his window. As he continued to watch, it occurred to him that Byron's life was a motionless thing. Most people drifted and reshaped like clouds throughout their lives, pushed along by poverty or wealth, disaster or luck. Byron was a self-contained vessel of sorrow that needed to be broken open. Randolph had thought his attention could do it. Byron himself had married Ella with the hope that she could change him out of his haunted self. Neither had done any good.

The mill manager looked down at a new pack of cards Jules had brought from town. He would play gin with his brother that night, even though he knew Byron would not glance at the score.

On a fog-bound morning later that month, he was riding around the back of the millpond when he heard a rifle shot. The horse stopped and rotated its ears. At the second concussion, the animal turned its head and the mill manager spurred it into a meandering amble past tall stacks of two-by-sixes. Riding into the clear, he saw Ella standing on the front porch of their house in an apron, her hands over her ears. A string of shots erupted on the far side, and Randolph rode toward the racket. He found his brother standing in the side yard firing a lever-action Winchester into his Victrola. A window sash was completely broken out where he'd heaved the machine through it. Randolph dismounted near the corner of the porch as Byron began to reload.

A reddened face that had nothing to do with the bitter-cold day flared at him and shouted, "Stay away from me." Again, the rifle bucked and the turntable flew out of the mahogany box and spun along the ground. The next shot ricocheted and gonged against the tender of the locomotive. Not a worker was visible, but the feeling of being watched was palpable in the leaden air. Randolph's horse backed around the porch out of sight as if it had read Byron's mind.

Helplessly, the mill manager looked up at Ella. "What?"

She pulled one hand from an ear and winced as another shot went off. "He was playing a new record when the main-spring broke in the middle of the song." She struggled with the words and began to cry. "He's gone crazy."

Randolph crept around the corner of the porch and could

see that the Victrola was halfway to kindling. The gun banged and another ricochet smacked into the coal house next to the locomotive. He turned back to her. "What was the title?"

"What?"

"The record. What was it?"

" 'Are You Tired of Me, My Darling.' "

It was their father's favorite song, and Randolph remembered the day when he'd played it on the Baldwin upright at home. Byron and his beautiful girlfriend sang, one on each side of the cherry piano, while the old man sat in the parlor across the hall, trying to hide the fact that he was enjoying himself. Now, he looked behind him into the mill yard, where a worker was hiding behind a pile of lath, and then stepped clear of the house. Byron crammed the last shell from a box of Winchester 44-40 ammunition into the rifle's magazine, put a slug through a cabinet leg, and then his fingers froze on the trigger as he heard the improbable sound of his brother's singing.

> *Are you tired of me, my darling?*
> *Did you mean those words you said*
> *That have made me yours forever*
> *Since the day that we were wed.*

Byron closed his eyes for a moment, then lowered the rifle and set the butt plate on his brogan. Randolph walked up and put an arm on his shoulder, took the Winchester, and handed it back to Ella, who'd gamely followed him out.

"Help me, Rando."

"What's the next verse?" he asked, turning his brother toward the porch, where the doctor and Jules had walked up out of the mist.

Byron began to sing weakly, and Randolph sang harmony, their voices rising in strength after the first line.

> *Tell me, could you live life over,*
> *Would you make it otherwise?*

Are you tired of me, my darling?
Answer only with your eyes.

During the next stanza, several emerging workers stood and watched, amazed. When the song was over, Randolph walked his brother to the edge of the porch, where he lay back and put a forearm over his eyes.

The mill manager looked at Jules and shrugged. "The mainspring broke in his talking machine."

The assistant spat a dart of tobacco and nodded. "I'll call the furniture place in Tiger Island and tell that skinflint to load his best Victor on the next train that'll stop for a flag."

The doctor, still standing back watchfully, motioned for Ella to step over. "I'm going to the office to get him something. Give him three drops in a glass of water."

She walked back to the edge of the porch, laid a hand on her husband's head, and looked around at Jules. "He's not some kid you can buy things for and make feel better." She turned her gaze on the doctor, who glanced away. "You can't oil him like some machine that's about to blow up, either."

Randolph levered the Winchester's magazine empty and picked up the blunt cartridges from the ground, wondering if the last one would have gone into his brother's head. "We can't sit around and do nothing." Suddenly, rain began washing down the fog, and Randolph stepped up onto the porch. Everyone except Byron watched as the tree line melted behind the wild, gray spray, and the blind horse stood steaming like a hot rock, all four legs planted like fence posts and its ears pricked forward. With a pang, Randolph saw that it was waiting for the next shot.

In early March, Minos came into the office to give the mill manager an evaluation of the steam plant. He still wore the vest and short-billed cap of a steamboat man, and unlike most of the mill workers he was straight in the back and had all of his fingers. When he stood up to leave, he paused for a moment. "You know, I got to thank you for hiring me."

"Just keep up your good work."

Minos nodded. "They ain't many northerners who treat people like you, no. None that I met, anyhow."

"I appreciate that."

The engineer coughed, and Randolph looked back up at him.

"Your brother's having a rough time of it," he said. "He was in the war, wasn't he?"

"Yes. For a long time, too."

"All that killing—I don't know. Some don't never come out of it."

Randolph knew that the workers had been talking about the Victrola episode and were making of it a camp legend, the kind of thing that foreshadows a terrible event, though none of them could guess what that might be. "You try to help, and wonder if you can ever fix it."

Minos put his hands halfway into his pockets. "My daddy, he lived through a lot of it in the war between the states. That and the wildness that went on after. Mr. Aldridge, I don't mind telling you, getting raised by that old man was holy hell. All when I was a kid he woke the house up screaming in French. He was hard as iron to me and my brothers, and some of 'em still won't waste a penny postcard on him." He pointed at the door. "I seen him be just like your brother, crying and breaking furniture." He looked out the window. "I seen him kill a man, a man that needed killing, but it's hard for a boy to watch his daddy do something like that, yeah. And when he killed him, it was like he was used to it. Like it was a business."

Under the floor, a call whistle shrieked twice. The engineer pulled his pocket watch and began moving toward the door. "I don't want to bother in your business none, but I wanted to say that my mother and me, well, we kind of straightened the old man out. After she passed, I give him one of my children to keep a day at a time. He spent so much time chasin' and fussin' that he wore a lot of the meanness out of himself. I sent the priest around to mess with him, too." A second call whistle rose up, and he pulled the door open. "I just wanted to say, you know, you don't have to write Mr. Byron off."

The mill manager put his hands palms up on his desk. "I don't know what to do that'll help him."

Minos seemed to think about this. "That's the sad part, ain't it?"

On a warm spring afternoon, the housekeeper gathered her strength and heaved a pan of pearl-gray dishwater into the yard, scattering the chickens with the soapy splash. Suddenly, a warm rush of fluid cascaded along the inside of her legs. She saw that Randolph had just come in for his lunch, so she turned round on the porch, opened the screen door, and looked in at him.

"Why," he asked, "are your shoes wet?"

" 'Cause this baby's comin' to town," she gasped, her dark eyes wider than nighttime.

A tidal swell of panic rolled over him, and he led May into the small back bedroom and sat her on the mattress. The next thing he remembered, he was running in his vest and shirt-sleeves across the mill yard to get the doctor, his legs lifting with each bound as though filled with helium. The old man came to his cabin door with a napkin tucked under his furry chin.

"The housekeeper," Randolph gasped. "Her baby's coming."

The doctor swallowed something and plucked off his napkin. "Why you in such a sweat, Mr. Aldridge?" He picked up his bag from inside the door and stepped out into the sunshine. "You can't work that woman's whelp 'til he's twelve, at least."

Randolph wanted to imagine that the doctor was just tired because he'd spent the morning sewing up three men who'd been whipped by a broken cable out in the woods. "Come on." He slipped a hand under the doctor's elbow and guided him off the little porch.

"You know," Sydney Rosen complained, holding back, "any woman down in the quarters can jerk this baby."

"I'm sorry to disturb your meal," Randolph said, hustling him along the lane, "but come on. Now."

When they entered the bedroom, the doctor opened his bag and looked at May, who was sprawled on top of the bedspread. "How you feel, gal?"

"Like I'm about to pass a watermelon." She gave him a look. "You gonna wash your hands?"

The old man stopped short, then turned abruptly for the kitchen.

"Hot water in the kettle," she called after him.

"I don't need to be told about hot water, by damn."

Randolph patted her hand a few quick times. "He'll make it all right."

"I hope so. I'm ready to burst open." She threw her head back, and he could hear her teeth grinding.

The doctor was gentle, at least with his hands, and three hours later came a strong and squalling boy, his eyes already open and wanting to see where he'd got to. Exhausted, his mother held him against her breasts. The doctor and mill manager sat there until supper, and at bedtime Randolph walked May and the boy to her cabin.

The next morning, the doctor came again to tend them. In the new light he took the wriggling, naked baby and held him up to the room's single window. Turning him like a loaf of bread in several directions, he made the child's color come and go, finally provoking him into a wailing fit. Then he handed him back to her and said, surprised, "This one's all cream and no coffee." He gave the housekeeper a questioning look. "Do you know who the daddy is?"

She smiled down and gave the baby a nipple. "He don't have a daddy. I made him myself."

"What you going to name him?"

She gave the doctor a sly look. "I might name him Sydney."

The old man bent down to close his satchel, then sprang upright. "I'll be damned if you will. That's my name. I'd have to move out of the parish."

"Well, then how about Walter?"

"Now that's more like," the doctor said, sliding along toward the door. "With a name like that at least he can sell insurance."

March 23, 1924
Nimbus Mill
Poachum Station, La.

Dear Father,

The weather has faired off this week and the woods crews are free of influenza. Our production will rise a thousand or so board feet per shift. If the men stay healthy and without hangovers, we can maintain the call from Standard Oil for box board and from Williams and Co. for shooks. I am on the phone most of the time with the New Orleans brokers and spend a lot of energy keeping prices down here, though I have had to raise sawyers' wages a nickel an hour to avoid losing them to the Tiger Island mills.

My housekeeper has delivered a boy. I know you don't approve of employees having children out of wedlock, but this camp is such a heap of hell-bent roughnecks that she can hardly cause any lowering of morals. She is intelligent and her son is healthy and fine, and I hope to keep her on as long as the timber around here lasts.

Byron is drifting. I've tried to get him to go on a holiday with Lillian and me, but he says he can't get used to more than one place at a time. He often drinks too much, which leads him to lose control and break up furniture. (Note the enclosed invoice for a new cabinet model Victrola.) I informed him that I told you about his wife, and he wouldn't speak to me for a week. I've given him your letters and he has read them, but will not return to Pittsburgh. He says he must be his own man. I don't know what he means by that. He is so injured in his mind that sometimes I tire of trying to help. At his house the other night, after an hour of listening to his maudlin records, I challenged him to arm-wrestle as we used to do. When he beat me easily, as he had always done, he accused me of giving in and said I was making fun of him, then practically pushed me out the door.

It's been a relatively dry spring and the camp is out of the
water. I haven't stepped on a snake in two days.

> *Your son,*
> *Randolph*

In the evenings, the mill manager held the baby—safely
named Walter, unlike any white man in camp—while May
cleaned the kitchen. He grumbled whenever she offered the
boy but always took him. He often studied the small face when
she was out back in the cabin tending to her father, who was
now bedridden. During the day, the child stayed in the small
rear bedroom that opened into the kitchen, and the baby
became used to the sight of him. Walking into the room to
retrieve a rain slicker or pair of boots, he would pass by the
crib and the boy's arms would fly up. The first time this happened Randolph was startled with longing and regret, and he
backed away, forgetting why he'd walked in to begin with.

Byron would visit whenever he noticed that May was out
hanging laundry, and he'd talk about mill business or problems in the camp, but Randolph knew he wanted to steal looks
at the boy. When Walter was four months old, Byron came in
and saw his brother holding him at the kitchen table, and he
sat down and took the baby himself, laying him atop his thighs
and gazing at his gray eyes and walnut-brown hair. He felt
Walter's ears between his fingers and looked up at his brother.

"No," Randolph said. "Not yours. And there's no telling
whose."

Byron nodded. "Fine looking little tadpole, I'll admit.
Looks like May, pretty much."

"That's true," his brother said, laughing. The baby twisted
his head in Byron's palm to look toward the mill manager,
who at once got up to pour a cup of coffee, keeping his back
to the table. He dared not look at the child when anyone
else was in the room, because he knew what showed on his
face.

. . .

As the heat gathered throughout summer, the saloon fights seemed to generate out of the humid air. Byron had to go into the quarters at night to break up husbands and wives, or husbands and their wives' boyfriends, answering the wink of straight razors in the dark with the ring of his shovel on bone. During June alone, Randolph was required to throw three stoves into yards. Byron had to pack the broken families out of the mill, run off hoboes, shoot snakes and alligators, knock down, handcuff, and ship trespassers and log rustlers off to Tiger Island for jailing and trial. Vincente had to be watched, warned, and sometimes protected from the men who lost their wages and wanted to kill him with their bare hands. No matter how busy they were, the brothers never forgot Buzetti and remained watchful for some toothpick-sucking presence he'd send slouching through the swamps.

CHAPTER TWELVE

After lunch, Randolph and his wife stepped out onto the second-floor porch on a hot August Sunday and watched children playing below on the brick street. Lillian had not said much during the meal, and he imagined a certain grimness around the corners of her mouth.

"Are you feeling all right?"

She nodded. "Of course. It's just that it's time for me to make my monthly announcement that I'm not going to have a baby yet."

He slid his wicker chair next to hers and put a hand on the back of her neck, under her short brown hair. "It'll happen."

"Maybe we're not trying enough. Maybe four times a month isn't enough."

He nodded. "I can take a night train on Wednesdays, then the four o'clock mixed back from Algiers."

"No," she said. "I've been thinking about this. I love New Orleans and my friends in church, but I'm not *doing* anything here." She swung around to him, her dress whistling against the wicker. "I want to come live with you at Nimbus."

He took his arm back. "It's not healthy. It's a slough full of the worst types of men. I only have a privy."

She cocked her head at him. "You know, you squeeze a nickel until the buffalo pees."

He slumped back in his chair. "What's that mean?"

"Build me a bathroom, Rand. Feed it with a cypress cistern. Run the drain to the swamp or the privy hole. And how much would it cost to add a front parlor where I could read and sew and have a little office of my own? The price of nails?"

"You *want* to be down there?" He imagined her in the mornings, the feel of her smooth neck against his lips.

"I can help you. With the mill, even."

He shook his head. "It's just unhealthy."

She raised her chin and glanced at something across the street, then sideways, at him. "Wouldn't it be harder for the Sicilians to bother me in Nimbus than here?"

He stood up and walked to the end of the porch. "Maybe we should move back North."

"So you've stopped worrying about your brother? You'd rather go back to a little hardwood mill where your salary would be considerably less than what it is now? And do you honestly think that pistol you left here for me can protect me more than you and Byron?" She came up beside him, leaned over the rail, and picked a magnolia blossom out of a welter of dark waxy leaves.

"What would you do?"

"I could help your doctor. I could give you advice."

He laughed. "About lumber?"

"About your degenerate mill town. Why don't you hire more men who'd bring their families?"

He looked at her sharply. "It's more expensive. Families need larger cabins."

"More expensive than all the work lost to the savagery?"

"You think the place can be gentled down some, I suppose?"

"It can."

He surveyed the street. "It's no tea party out there," he muttered.

She took his arm and coaxed him around. "Last week there was a man down on the corner standing there looking up at me. He was wearing an eye patch and was smoking one cigarette after another."

He glanced quickly to the sidewalk, then back to his wife. "Why didn't you tell me?"

"I didn't want you to worry."

"Was it the right eye?"

She tapped a finger on her lips, thinking. "Yes."

He slid his arms around her then, drew her close, and put his face into her hair, thinking not of what he was doing but of a man standing on the platform at Poachum and deciding who to kill first. "When do you want to come?"

"How soon can you have carpenters and millwrights do the work? I want a tub in the bathroom." She gave him a peck on the cheek. "How wide is the house in Nimbus?"

"Maybe forty feet." He turned his head to look down at the corner.

"That's enough. I want a front room with windows, and a screened porch about thirty feet long and at least eight feet deep. Put an outside door in the left side of the screened area and leave the one that leads directly into the kitchen from the front. It'll look odd, but we're not going to live there forever."

He looked up and pursed his lips. "Why, I could have the bathroom in by Sunday. I'll have to pull off ten or so workers, but that's all right."

She slipped an arm up high on his back and kissed his chin. "I can take the train back with you next weekend."

He realized that he would have to have a long talk with May and be exquisitely careful around Walter. The thought of Lillian in camp was worrisome but, at the same time, wonderful. He felt foolish for thinking she'd be safe in New Orleans, and now hoped he would be at least a lucky fool.

That same day, Byron was sitting at the desk in his front room, sweating and breaking pencil points as he wrote out an arrest report for the parish sheriff. The sunlight coming through the screen door dimmed, and when Bryon raised his head, he saw Buzetti smiling in at him, the screen imparting a scaly texture to his face.

"What do you want?" Byron said, stepping out onto the porch.

Buzetti's smile widened around the cigarette in the corner of his mouth. "Ey, how's the phonograph? I hear they got you a bulletproof one."

Byron glanced toward the railroad. "How did you get in here?"

"What, you never hear of a motorboat?" He pointed over his shoulder to where a wooden launch idled at the end of the log canal, two men in slouch caps sitting on the bow, watching. "I'm looking for the head man, your brother. Nobody can tell me where he's at."

"He's not to be found."

Buzetti cocked his head. "Aw, yeah. I know about not-to-be-found." He laughed and someone seeing him from a distance would have taken him for a salesman, a politician. "Well, just so's my trip out here ain't wasted, I'll talk to you."

"About what?"

Buzetti looked over his shoulder. "Can we go inside?"

"No."

He shrugged. "You and your brother must think I smell bad. But hey, no matter. Look, I come to ask if you can let Galleri open up on Sunday."

Byron narrowed his eyes. "How fast does that boat of yours run?"

Buzetti's face rippled like a shallow pool in the swamp where a dark millimeter of water rides over a cage of fangs. "I figured we could help each other out. I can use the Sunday business and Mrs. Aldridge, she could use a little protection on the 2900 block of Prytania Street."

"The saloon stays closed," Byron said, but there was a tentative note in his voice that seemed to catch Buzetti's ear.

"Look, I don't want something for nothing. I figure we maybe shoulda took it easier on some of your woodchoppers. So let's say I pay you a fine."

"A fine?"

Buzetti drew a small paper bag out of his coat and spread

open its top. Disbelievingly, Byron looked inside, as if he were being offered a sack of candy. He saw a roll of bills bound with rubber bands, and laughed. "You're trying to buy me?"

"Aw, naw. It's a fine. Do what you want with it, give it to nigger orphans in New Orleans for all I care."

Byron looked through the screen into his empty front room, then turned back to Buzetti and stared over his head at his brother's house across the compound. "No sale."

"C'mon. It's a lot of money." Buzetti held out a palm. "You could buy yourself enough records to tile your fuckin' roof."

Byron grabbed him by the shirt front and shoved him against a porch post. "I don't like the smell of your money, either."

Buzetti's face began to show its blood. "Go ahead, you idiot," he said, "smash my head open in front of witnesses. Then even your brother can't keep you out of the pen."

Byron relaxed his fingers and took a deep, slow breath. "Sunday's out of the question."

"Why?" He held out the bag. "You can sit in there and look all you want. With the five hundred in this bag you can hire another constable to watch Vincente's hands. But he won't see nothing. These chuckleheads you got out here are so dumb he don't need to cheat."

Byron looked at the paper bag. "You think I can do only one thing," he said. "But I can do another." His eyes, lifted up from the money, were two dark disks of tin, but he saw that Buzetti understood his words, and yet was not afraid.

"You can't do shit but what I let you do. I know a million guys like you. You studied the Bible and then went off and killed, what, a hundred, two hundred schnapps-drinking kids, so your brains, they got in a wringer, right? And now your tight Pennsylvania ass is down here trying to save the fuckin' swamp from Joe Buzetti. You want to stop some damage?" Here Buzetti put a forefinger against his own temple. "Well, the damage is already done, you dumb fuck."

"Get off of the property."

Buzetti took a mocking step back. He smiled a genuine

smile, but it was for himself alone. "I apologize to come all the way out here and bother you. You all set up out here with Miss Ella. She don't never come to town. Just now and then, ey? She likes this nice little life you got." He surveyed the mill yard and his face showed what he thought of a nice little life in a place such as this. "And Mrs. Aldridge all by herself down on Prytania, she's okay too?"

Byron stared at Buzetti's bag. "You don't scare me, you pimp."

"Hey, I ain't trying to scare *you*, Jack. Nobody can scare a crazy man what pulls a gentleman's place of business apart with a fucking steamboat." Buzetti scratched his forehead with the little finger of his right hand. "But your brother and the ladies, one of them could maybe wake up with a big reptile in their bed and decide mill life ain't for them, you know? Maybe they'd move out and leave you with the mosquitoes."

"You try that and you won't believe what turns up in your bed."

Buzetti pushed his fedora far back on his head. "Let's get something straight here. This ain't about you. I know I can't do nothing to make you think twice about nothing. You a fucking nutzo or something, I don't know what."

"What's it about, then?"

"Money. Vincente, my cousin, who wants Sunday." He looked past Byron into the house. "With five hundred dollars you could double the size of this shack. Miss Ella, she'd like that."

Byron reached out and took the bag, hefting it.

The sallow face watched him. "What?"

"How many Germans did you kill?"

"Austrians," Buzetti corrected, his voice less harsh. "It was Austrians."

Byron looked down into the bag. "Why did we do it?"

Buzetti cocked his head. "Because somebody gave the permission. That's a great thing, permission. After the war, I learned to give it to myself, you know?"

Byron thought about this and nodded. "Tell Galleri he can open on Sunday. Just leave my brother and the women alone."

Buzetti looked back at his men who were watching but not watching, their eyes aimed to the side of the house. He turned to Byron. "Now you thinking straight."

He stepped inside and latched the screen, leaving Buzetti hovering on the porch like a noisome insect. "No, I'm not," he said, backing away from the door.

Byron got off the train in Shirmer and headed to the rambling store owned by the Spencer Brothers Plantation. The commissary smelled of molasses, coffee, kerosene, and dirt, its rafters hung with harness, cane knives, and axes frosted with dust. Shelves rose to the smoked ceiling packed with everything except what Byron wanted. The clerk, a short, bald man wearing thick glasses, took a long time to walk up from the back and he addressed him in French

"I'm the company law down in Nimbus," Byron said. "What do you have in the way of rifles?"

The clerk put his hands flat on his counter and leaned over them. "Depends on what you need to kill. I got some .22 pumps."

Byron shook his head. "No. I need large caliber."

"Oh, you goin' deer huntin' in the bushes, yeah?"

"Something like that."

"I got some old '73 Winchesters upstairs in 38-40. Nobody buys that no more. I can let you have 'em right."

"That might do."

The clerk looked long into Byron's face. "*Mais*, if you want something that'll put a twelve-point down on his ass, I got the one." He walked to a vertical glass case, opened it with a little key, and pulled out a semiautomatic carbine, a mean-looking rifle with a satin-walnut stock and a short, night-blue barrel.

Byron took the weapon and sighted it. "I've read about these."

The clerk put a finger on the gun's receiver. "Shoots fast as you pull the trigger, yeah. Six times. It fires a soft-point slug that'll knock a black bear's brains out in one shot." He handed Byron a .401 caliber cartridge shaped like a little sausage.

"How many will five hundred dollars buy?"

The clerk glanced at Byron's badge, then flattened out a paper bag on the counter and added up figures, hiding his arithmetic with a broad hand. "I can bring in eight on the train day after tomorrow, with two boxes of shells each."

Byron worked the glassy action on the rifle, studied the fearsome cartridge. He remembered his brother's amateurish standoff at the Poachum station, how Buzetti's men had seen the Winchester trench brooms and had left without drawing a weapon. "Order them," he said.

By Wednesday evening the rifles were locked in his armoire in Nimbus, loaded and rubbed down with Outer's gun oil. His wife watched him wash his hands in the kitchen, then walked into the next room to put a record on the Victrola. As Bessie Smith's "Downhearted Blues" began to fill the house, she came back and poured herself a tall glass of blackberry wine.

"That record you ordered is too sad," he said, squeezing his fingers in the dish towel.

She looked at him, flat and steady. "Somebody's sad is another somebody's happy, I reckon."

He looked through the kitchen window into the dark. "You ought not to drink. It's a habit that gets worse."

She pursed her lips and leaned against a door frame. "Is it the habit that gets worse, or what causes it?"

CHAPTER THIRTEEN

Lillian moved into the logging camp and learned to deal with the captured heat of the place, mosquitoes always floating in her vision, stinkbugs haunting her collar, love bugs flying drunk and sticking to her dress like crawling black snowflakes. She learned the necessity of keeping a shovel on the front porch, which she used to cut the heads off snakes sunning on the steps in the afternoons. The housekeeper she treated as she had always dealt with maids and kitchen women, though she was somewhat at a loss in accounting for Walter. A woman from over in the white quarters had told her the child was probably the son of a millwright who'd quit and moved to Texas back in March. Lillian noted the house-keeper's cleanliness, intelligence, and devotion to her frail father, and made no alteration in her duties aside from teaching her how to bake and boil a few dishes instead of frying or stewing everything. At her urging Randolph hired five married men who brought their families along, displacing rough-neck drunks Byron had escorted to Poachum in handcuffs; she met each new family as they got off the crew car and urged the men, in front of their wives, to keep clear of the saloon.

The mill manager worried that his wife might last only a few days, but Lillian surprised him, and her activity gained momentum through September. On the last day of the month, when he came home riding the old horse, she met him outside with a list of figures. He was still in the saddle when she handed it up with a slender arm.

"What's this?" he said, his eyebrows rising. "What will cost six hundred dollars?"

"A one-room schoolhouse. The parish will let us have a teacher and some old books if we supply the building. And a privy, of course. There's a colored woman down in the quarter who can teach reading and figures to the little black ones at night."

"You've been busy." He looked down at her. "But most of these kids will wind up sawing timber like their fathers. That doesn't require any schooling." He dismounted and began walking the horse around back.

"How much timber will be left when these children are old enough to cut it?" She followed him to the gate of the tiny stall and crossed her arms. "Times are changing up ahead."

He turned to her and sucked a tooth. "You've been reading my *Lumber World*."

"Enough to know that most of the virgin timber will be stumps in fifteen years or so."

He looked at the sun in her hair, the mosquito whelps on her neck. "Where do you want it?"

"Between here and Byron's is a little less swampy."

He looked at the heavy tree line surrounding the site. Nimbus was being cut, unlike most tracts, from the perimeter toward the center, since this would diminish lumbering costs over the life of the operation, requiring less railway maintenance, less cable and fuel for the pull boats and rafting steamer. From where he stood, the timber seemed to go on forever. Turning away from the woods, he imagined a twenty-four-by-forty-foot schoolhouse, open windows, cypress shingles, all number two stuff, of course. In his mind, the benches were lined with shoeless offspring of boiler firemen and loggers, preparing for a life after trees.

He pulled the saddle from the horse, and the animal let out a relieved breath and leaned sideways against the stall boards.

"School," he said. "Next thing, you'll want me to build a church."

"I'm one ahead of you," she told him, putting an arm through his and leading him through a cloud of Dominick chickens toward the back porch. "The Methodist missionary who comes to Poachum can conduct services in the schoolhouse."

May, who was broadcasting chicken feed out of her apron, looked up at her as they passed. "There going to be any religion for the colored?" she asked.

Lillian stopped and looked at her, surprised. "Why, May, I sometimes forget you *are* colored." She reached out and squeezed her forearm. "If you ask around in the quarters and find enough interest, maybe Mr. Aldridge can provide materials for a chapel. Until then, if you can find a preacher, you can use the commissary porch Sunday mornings."

"Shouldn't you ask me first?" When his wife looked at him, Randolph pulled off his hat. "Oh, nobody'll come. You don't know these people. White or colored, they left their religion behind in Texas or Arkansas."

Lillian gave out a scoffing laugh. "Every mill town has a school and church, Rand. It's time you think about providing some civilization."

He looked again toward where she wanted the schoolhouse built and thought of his red-eyed, headache-haunted employees. "I don't know."

"You'll see," his wife said.

By mid-October the school was finished—built of raw, ruddy cypress—and six white children showed up at its door. The teacher the parish sent was an inexperienced stick of a woman, but she knew how to read and write, and after a week, the enrollment had risen to seventeen. Randolph lost a large bet with Jules concerning the attendance at the first church service. He walked out onto his porch at eleven o'clock, sure he would be able to look through the open windows of the little building and see only three or four washed-out hillbilly women. To his amazement, he counted many heads, and as he walked up he saw that the rough benches were filled with women, and their men were standing along the walls. Outside, Negro workers and their women gathered under the windows to hear the spilled-over preaching. The minister was conventional in his sermon, but loud, the homily carrying out the open doors and above the Sunday-quiet mill. A gang of young bucks was sitting in the commissary yard on upright bolts of cypress, watching sullenly. Three white sawyers sat behind them on the commissary porch, quietly chewing and whittling, their ears turned toward the overflowing schoolhouse. The boiler gang lounged about the double doors to the steam plant, far out of earshot, but watching, nevertheless. Above the roofs of both the white and black quarters fewer stovepipes smoked, dinner already cooked and waiting for the service to be over at noon. Maybe less than a quarter of the mill's population was at the service, yet everything turned toward it, Randolph noticed, from the derision of lounging, wild-eyed buckers to the curiosity of single men wandering the barracks yard in their long johns, commenting and scratching. He looked over at the saloon, saw something, and went inside for his field glasses, then brought into focus a man sitting on a nail keg out front—Vincente, flipping cards into his upturned hat. He swung the glasses to the boiler room door, angry that the gang wasn't cleaning the fire and blowing down the mud rings on the boilers, but then remembered that Lillian, now seated on one of the benches, had instructed Minos to postpone that noisy task until the services had let out.

Scanning the yard again he understood that the school and church had become in one day the hub of the rude wheel that was Nimbus. The sermon ended with a ragged "Amen," and a slow gospel song started up like a balky tugboat engine. He focused his field glasses on one side of Byron's porch and there he found his brother, a glass of brown liquid in his hand, working his mouth slowly around the words of the hymn.

.   .   .

Father Schultz liked to play Casino for points, so he and Merville met every Sunday at two o'clock. If someone were locked up in the rusty cell, the priest would offer to visit the prisoner, but on this day they had the mildewed office to themselves.

Father Schultz pulled on his long nose and dealt a hand carefully, squinting at the cards. "You know that you're always welcome to come to Mass."

Merville spread open his hand. "Like you, I work on Sunday."

Casting down a card, the priest shook his head. "You can't arrest me for trying."

"I wouldn't do that, me. You'd sit in the cell and sing to me in that Latin all day long."

"One of these days you'll come back to mother church."

"Maybe so. But it ain't one of these days yet."

The men played four games, splitting the wins. The priest usually talked of his family back in Germany and how everyone was suffering in his country, but today he was quiet, dropping cards without thinking or after thinking too hard.

Merville studied him. "Father, you worried, you?"

"Perhaps." He lay down big casino and when Merville picked it up by slamming down his own ten, the priest's expression didn't change.

"*Quoi?*"

"You know about those women, don't you?"

The marshal shook his head. "Nothing I can do about it."

"I understand."

"The sheriff told me if I brought in a Buzetti prostitute, he'd throw out the charges."

"Of course. I know how things are. But the local girls." The priest threw down his last card and Merville picked it up.

"That's how Buzetti works it. Bring in a professional from up North, and she finds the poor girls, orphans and hop heads." He waved the deck at the priest. "*Mais*, you want to go again?"

"Of course." He pulled his hands off the desk. "Ada Bergeron has become one of them."

Merville shuffled the cards. Out in the river, the ferry whistle shrilled for the landing. "Well, her father's dead," he said sleepily, almost to no one. "He was my cousin, I think." He bit the inside of his cheek and dealt. "We didn't fool with that part of the family much."

"Obviously." Father Schultz leaned back and opened his hand against his stomach. "Still, if there's something you can do for a fallen-away Catholic girl that's got your own blood, it would look good on your record, if you know what I mean."

"I'd be crazy to bother Buzetti about his lady business."

"Could he get you fired or something?"

"Something," Merville said, chuckling. "He would *something* me." He drew out his little Colt lightning revolver and wiggled it in the air above his silver head.

The priest placed his cards on the table and frowned at their red backs. "What could bring Buzetti down?"

"Not arresting him for whores, excuse me." Merville tipped an imaginary hat and then dropped a ten.

The priest flipped over his top card without looking at it. It was big casino. "You see? Everybody's luck changes. One day this Buzetti will be caught with so many cases of liquor, that they can't ignore what he's doing."

Merville shrugged. "Maybe them feds would get interested if the load was big enough. And he brings it in by the ton, yeah." He plucked a card from his hand, then replaced it. "I don't know how."

"It's a funny thing," the priest said, "that if you caught him with a large amount of liquor, everybody—the newspaper, the government—would consider it so important. But if you saved a young woman's soul forever, no one would think much of that."

"Why you so interested in this girl?"

"Ach, I gave her instruction as a child. I gave her her first communion. She's good at heart, but headstrong and desperate."

"Father, a religious man ought not worry so much about cat-house women."

"There's precedent for it," the priest said.

"What's that mean?"

The telephone bells sounded the jailhouse ring, and Merville struggled to his feet. After a moment, he hung up and turned to the priest. "They want you at Murphy Dugas's house. He's sick to death, they say."

Father Schultz stood up and put on his four-pleated hat. "He's dying and mentally ill both. He got hit with both barrels, as you'd say."

Merville sat heavily into a swaying steamer chair by the door. "Crazy's a kind of dead. You can't hardly come back from it, either."

Father Schultz, his hand on the porcelain doorknob, seemed to think of something. "How's your friend out at the sawmill? The constable."

"*Pas très bon*. He's a good man. Just got ruint in France."

"Ach. It really was a world war." He pulled the door open and walked out into a bitter wind flowing up from the ferry landing, where drovers were cursing a large herd of mules onto the wharf. On the other side of the river, a storm cloud rose ragged and swirling like smoke from a wildfire.

CHAPTER FOURTEEN

In late December the mill yard froze into a grotesque, ridged pudding, and the housekeeper's father died while staring out his cabin's frost-foxed window. He was buried in the colored section of the graveyard and the mill manager ordered the mason to build a brick slab over the grave so the coffin wouldn't push out of the ground during high water. He and his wife attended the little ceremony, at which there were more whites than blacks. The old man had no friends in camp, and the people from his real life would never know where he was laid.

Randolph and Lillian returned to Pennsylvania for Christmas, understanding with a mild shock that they were no longer fond of snow and bland food. His father wanted him to consider having Byron committed, and as always, he listened carefully to the old man and then ignored what he said. For a week they endured his complaints and offers of positions in New England mills, then traveled back South to ignorance and good food, poverty and independence, and Nimbus—that place tethered to all of civilization only by a few miles of buckled railroad.

In February, a fistfight started in the saloon after midnight on a Sunday, and Byron was rousted out, tired and half drunk himself, to deal with it. He stood in the sleet before the dark building, holding his short-handled shovel in one hand

and a .38 revolver in the other, not remembering the walk from his house. Yells broke out the saloon door like flying glass, and he digested enough of the agonized shouts to understand that a white sawyer had cut a black whore and she'd shot him in the face with a .22 revolver. A gang of white men came lurching onto the porch, cursing a length of plow line tangled in their boots, bent on hanging the woman from a porch beam while the blacks from the other side of the saloon scrambled out to fight them. The lanterns had been knocked out in the scuffle, and Byron waded into a dark sea of men waving cheap pistols, showing their teeth and screaming, ducking under straight razors that dipped and flashed like bats flying under lightning.

He raised his gun and hollered, but his words were carried away on a boiling flood of voices, so he shot a white man in the side, and then a black man in the thigh, holstering his pistol when they went down and raising the shovel, banging anyone in reach as if batting away hornets. A gun popped and a slug burned into the back of his shoulder. He made a roundhouse swing and felt the shovel toll against a skull, and then two men siezed him, the three of them falling onto the floor of the white section. He smelled the mud and ash, and someone with big stony knuckles began punching him in the face. When he tried to get up, a hobnail boot crashed into his ribs, loosing a shower of sparks in his brain and igniting the thought that this might be the end of it all, and there was a wink of sad comfort in the thought. But then he heard the metallic flutter of a steel wing, and one of the men holding him down let out a yowl. Soon someone else was hollering under the shovel, followed by a general stumbling in the room, and a lantern dangled over Byron, lighting the face of Clovis Hutchins, the man he'd handcuffed to the flywheel in his yard. Behind him, holding the shovel, was a scarface Negro worker.

"Mr. Byron," Clarence Williams said, "come on get up and help this gal out on the porch."

They rocked the constable to his feet, pulling on his hands, and the hole in his shoulder felt as though someone had filled it with a lit cigarette. Out on the porch, the whore was roped but not yet swinging, and several black workers pounded on the two drunken mill hands who were trying in tandem to hoist her up. Someone brought another lantern and Byron drew his pistol into the light to show them all that every trace of fear had been burned out of him. He remembered that he had four loads left in the gun. The men holding the rope, big men, swaying, bovine with rum, glared at him and his weapon. They tightened the rope.

Byron pointed the Colt at them. "I've got some lead tickets. Who wants to go?"

The taller of the two men took an extra turn of the plow line around his wrist and the black woman went up on tiptoe, her hands at her neck. "This nigger bitch shot a white man."

Byron drew back the hammer of the pistol, placed the muzzle in the speaker's ear, and then the men eased the rope and dropped it. The whore threw off the noose, jumped to the mud, and ran for the side of the building, calling over her shoulder, "You all a barrel of motherfuckers." Galleri began shoving men out of the saloon, holding a broomstick sideways to their backs, and when he'd cleared the rooms, he slammed the entrances on the dark energy still simmering in the drunken blood. The men outside heard the heavy bolts knock the night down on all of them, and then a voice rose from across the mill yard, angry as a buzz saw. "Damn it to hell," the doctor called out. "Is it safe to come over and patch the stupid bastards up?"

Within the hour, Byron was lying facedown on a narrow wooden table in Sydney Rosen's office. "Reach under and grab your wrists," the doctor told him. "This is going to sting a mite." He picked up a forceps shaped like a marsh hen's beak and probed a hole high on Byron's back. The room was quiet except for the slow creaking of the narrow table. "All right, all right," the doctor said, turning the forceps. "Don't piss on yourself, here it comes." He drew out a .25 caliber slug, glossy as a berry, and set it on a dinner plate. After bathing and bandaging the wound, he taped up Byron's ribs, and stood back, looking over his glasses at three other patients slumped against the back wall like prisoners waiting to be shot. "Put on your shirt and help me with these other fools." The two of them picked up a groaning black logger and laid him out on the table.

"Oh, hep me Jesus," the man prayed.

The doctor peered close at the wound in the man's left side. "Here, constable, hold this mask over his nose while I pour the ether. Mind, hold your breath." A gasp under the mask seemed to draw the light from the room, and Byron staggered back a step. The doctor gave him an electric light to hold and then cut open the man's belly, running his hands down among his bowels the way a housewife might rummage in dishwater.

Byron sat against a low porcelain table covered with bandages and swabs. "How bad is he?"

The doctor leaned down to the incision and sniffed like a hound. "This is one lucky son of a bitch," he said, straightening up and pivoting a shoe on its heel to avoid a stream of blood coming off the table. "The bullet's in his back muscle and didn't tear a thing open. Hand me those forceps. That's it, use the tongs to grab 'em." He inserted the forceps along a hand he'd left down in the abdomen and twisted out a slug, pulling it into the light. He held it, stringing blood, toward the constable. "You can use this again if you reload your own shells."

Byron turned his head at the doctor's anger. "What else was I supposed to do?"

The slug hit the floor and slid against the wall. "That's always the big mystery, isn't it? Hand me that suture tray." Byron didn't move, and the doctor tried to see his eyes in the dim room. "You know, I've done too much of this in my time," he said, his voice softening. "I guess it's not your fault."

Byron shook his head slowly. "It's either sew up these two or bury that woman."

Sydney Rosen nodded. "Just hold that light for a while and then go find your brother. I've got to sew this one like a saddle so he don't split when he wakes up and starts to vomit."

The next morning, a steady, bitter-cold rain punished the compound. Randolph turned up his collar and walked off the porch before May could set out his breakfast. Sloshing into the doctor's dark office, he folded his arms and leaned against the wall, watching his brother sleep as Sydney detailed the various injuries. The whore had taken fifty-five stitches under the breast and the man who'd cut her had turned up in the middle of the night. The bullet from her two-dollar gun had struck high on his forehead, skidded under his scalp, and come out at the base of his skull. "I ran out of thread on that one," the doctor said. Byron bolted upright on the table like a reflexing cadaver. "Whoa," he said. "What was that medicine?"

The doctor smiled. "Something to round off the edges. Seems like we all could use a sip."

Randolph stepped into his brother's line of sight. "No one got killed."

"A miracle," the doctor announced. "If they'd strung up that gal, you'd have had a race riot. They'd have burned the mill and slaughtered each other. I've never seen such a crazy bunch of juiced-up fools." He dumped a load of bloody instruments into a porcelain bin. "You should've kept them closed down on Sundays."

Jules stuck his head through the door, water running off his hat brim. He nodded at Randolph. "I got the list."

"Get a shotgun and take Minos with you."

"You sure about this? It'll cost us a few thousand feet a day until we can rehire."

Randolph made a face at the floor, thinking about the money. Finally, he said, "I want you to fire every last son of a bitch who was making trouble last night."

Jules shrugged. "Well, if that's what you want."

"If one of them gets on his knees to beg, just walk on to the next man. They're all gone."

"It's pretty cold to put men out."

"I hear it is."

"You the boss," Jules said, backing out into the wind.

The mill manager called after him. "Tell Rafe to get the shay hot and haul them out to Poachum. I don't want them on the property." He looked over to where two wounded men and the woman lay on pallets at the back of the room, floating on a lake of pain. "Even them. As soon as they can walk, I want them gone."

Byron did not make rounds for three days. Each of those afternoons he visited his brother's house where the baby would sit in his idle lap as May cooked and Lillian wrote letters, sewed, or read her husband's business magazines. Randolph saw him there when he came in for coffee at three, and again for suppertime when Ella would finally walk over and nudge him home. One afternoon, the mill manager came home, looked through the screen, and was startled to see his brother lying on the floor, facedown. At first he was paralyzed with fright, but then he heard the baby noises Byron was making. From the next room, just out of sight, Walter threw a cypress block at Byron's head.

Randolph pulled the screen open carefully. "By, you all right?"

"Rando. This little bugger's going to be a baseball player, I believe."

He came into the house and picked up the boy, brushing back his curls. "No, he'll go into business for sure." Randolph looked into the small sharp eyes. Walter grabbed his nose and the mill manager gave the baby's hand a kiss, then bent down with him next to his brother, who sat up. The men each gave the baby a finger and watched him grab on and try to stand.

May breezed in from the yard holding a freshly plucked chicken and set to work at the stove, and the mill manager wondered what she made of grown men playing with her baby on the floor, of what might really be happening there.

Randolph touched his brother's bandage. "You coming along all right?"

"It was just a tiny little bullet."

They both laughed and the baby looked up at the noise, his face questioning one man and then the other.

Randolph stood and brushed at his knees. "I never did figure why you let him open up on Sunday."

Byron pulled himself standing and brought Walter with him. "I'm so optimistic about human nature, I just couldn't help myself."

"Maybe you feel sorry for Buzetti. A little."

"You've been drinking Sydney's medicine." Byron put Walter down, and the boy cupped the constable's thumbs in his palms and stood, trying for balance. "But he was in France a long time. I heard he lost three brothers in one day." He looked away from Walter's bright face. "All bayoneted. They say he watched each one die."

Ella appeared on the porch and pushed open the screen, glancing at Randolph. "Would you tell him he doesn't live in your kitchen?"

"Well, since he's already here, why don't you both stay for dinner?"

"No, I've already fixed something." She touched a finger to the baby's nose. "That child is a weed."

Walter took a handful of Byron's pants and a handful of Randolph's, wobbling, looking up.

By one or two at a time, troublemakers, drunkards, stomp-and-gouge fighters, whore beaters, or dull-eyed gamblers with only lint left in their pockets, were fired and replaced. But still, late at night, down in the kerosene eyes of the saloon, the howls that sprang from insults or sexual deception or sixty hours of work blown away by the turn of a card rose into the mossy limbs ghosting above the iron roof. Every night twenty or so men drank on either side of the wall, but on Saturdays the sprawling building held over a hundred. There were no real women to gentle the place down, no music or dancing, just boozy hollering between addled men who imagined they were telling stories.

Randolph and Lillian were sitting in the new room at the front of the house. He was reading and she was repairing the binding on ragged arithmetic books the state had sent down for the school, and with the windows open, they could hear the saloon's racket. At ten o'clock, he stood up and buttoned his vest.

"Be careful," Lillian said.

"The ten o'clock pass isn't all that bad. I told Byron I'd take it."

She placed a book on top of a stack next to her chair. "The more he stays out of that place, the better."

He walked over and entered the colored side, where a whole woods crew had just come in smelling of mules, hand-rolled cigarettes, woodsmoke, and sap. Vincente's first cousin sat behind a board table that had been hand-sawed round and painted felt green, dealing to a group hunkered under a hanging gasoline lamp. In the corner, a mill hand was playing a cracked F hole guitar, sliding a broken bottle neck over the strings, choking out bluesy rises as the men at the table risked their week's pay. Vincente's cousin was a dark man with a narrow face, carelessly shaven, and he kept a Luger on the table next to him. On the white side of the building, Vincente had also begun openly carrying a Luger to work, but to his was attached a snail-drum clip holding thirty-two rounds.

Sitting to the Italian's right was a faller the woods gangs called Judgment, a man made huge by twelve-hour shifts of swinging a crosscut saw. In the east Texas woods, he'd used only an ax, and his stovepipe arms suggested that he'd cut his way to Nimbus. His skin was the hot, satin black of a locomotive, and his eyes were crimson with both liquor and a steaming suspicion that he was being cheated. Vincente's cousin dealt a hand of seven-card stud, and Judgment bet heavily from the first card, the pot rising with clumps of ones, twos, and fives. Randolph walked up and stood behind Pink, the man Byron had saved from a razor fight months before. Pink was a school-trained millwright, a master at regulating and sharpening the planing machines, and the mill manager was sorry to see him at the table.

It came time to deal the last card, down, and the Italian hesitated. Even the mill manager noticed the break in rhythm. Then he dealt himself a card from the bottom of the deck, a shadowed, subtle movement with the little finger, but not subtle enough. Randolph felt the atmosphere of the saloon turn to molasses, and it occurred to him how a man could walk through a world of logical movement and be distracted by none of it, but when that one motion that did not ring true impressed itself on the eye, it was like a train roaring past. Judgment reached out with an octopus of a hand and grabbed the dealer's neck as the Luger went off with a skull-cracking pop. The little .30 caliber jacketed slug whizzed through the top of the black man's shoulder, but he didn't blink. The dealer's mouth gasped open and his pistol wavered between Pink and a fireman at the table. Shouting "No," Randolph snaked an arm around Pink's chest and pulled him down just as the pistol cracked again and the fireman went over the back of his chair. Judgment tightened his grip, his fingers like black sausages on the dealer's neck, and the Luger bounced to the floor. Randolph ducked under the table past the kicking fireman and seized the gun as the gamblers scrambled away like roaches. He came up on his knees and found the dealer wilting like a crushed flower in the huge black hand.

"Let him go."

Judgment's flaming eyes swung to face him. "He never gonna let me go."

"I'll run him off. Let him go, damnit." Randolph put an elbow on the table, and at that moment Vincente rushed in from the other room, throwing up his Luger. Judgment ducked, and Vincente fired twice and missed, putting two gouges in the green table next to the mill manager's head.

"Drop it," Randolph screamed, pointing the cousin's Luger toward the roof.

When Vincente shot Judgment in the back, he leapt like a

hooked fish and crashed down onto a chair, spindles flying through the room. "You gonna have to hire some more nig- gers when I get finished," Vincente called, spraying the room with dust-raising concussions. Pink yelled and flashed a bloody hand as he rolled toward the door on fire with pain. And then, without thinking whether or not he should pull the trigger, Randolph felt the gun in his own hand jump. Vincente hit the floor all at once like a sack of coal.

The cousin sat up, holding his throat, glancing back and forth between Vincente and the mill manager. "Ah," he cried. "Thisa no good." Then, he looked over at the door.

Randolph turned and saw Byron holding a cocked .45 automatic. Behind him was the silver mane of the doctor. "Who is it this time?" Sydney asked quietly.

Byron's eyes seemed misshapen and sorrow-filled as he looked at the growing pool of blood under Vincente's head, at his brother, still down on one knee next to the table.

Randolph got to his feet and handed him the Luger, dumbly, barrel first. His pulse spasmed like a runaway mill engine, and he felt that everything in his past history was suddenly of no consequence. Judgment sat up, looked at Vin- cente, and despite the blood streaming down his back from two holes, laughed aloud. The fireman was dead and Pink was sitting near the front wall, bent over double. "I'm all right," he said, his voice tight as a fist. "It went through my palm is all."

Randolph turned to his brother, his hands out, pleading. "Let me tell you what happened."

Byron took a quick glance around. "I know what hap- pened." He nudged Vincente's body with his boot. "Just call the carpenters. We'll send this one up to Poachum with the next load of boards."

The mill manager seemed desperate to explain. "He was trying to kill everyone in the room," he said, his voice high and broken.

"I'll see if I can phone the sheriff." Byron motioned to Vin- cente's cousin. "Get out of camp."

The man stood and straightened his collar, which popped off in his hand. "Buzetti no gonna like."

Randolph was feeling washed out, but when he heard this, he grabbed the dealer by the lapels of his coat, whirled him through the door, and threw him off the porch into a water-filled hole. "Tell Buzetti I didn't want to shoot his cousin. It's the last thing I wanted to do. But let him know that if he gives me more trouble I'll make damned sure he never eats another meatball."

The doctor looked up from the dead fireman and called out the door, "Good God, don't tell him things like that."

The dealer stood and slung the mud from his coat sleeves and walked toward the railroad track.

"I've seen this before." Byron's voice was dry and small.

Randolph spun on him. "What does that mean?"

"It's how it all starts," he said. "With posturing. With one shot."

"I didn't want to do it, By."

"You don't have to tell *me* that."

They walked to the edge of the porch, looking after Vincente's cousin.

"Who knows how much trouble this will cause?" the doctor said, as he examined Judgment, who was standing up in the doorway and flexing his back, an annoyed expression on his broad face.

Byron shook his head. "What starts small gets bigger."

Suddenly, they heard a scream rise above the Negro quarters, a high-pitched wail soaring into the night sky as the fireman's woman got the news.

CHAPTER FIFTEEN

Lillian was waiting for him in the kitchen, dressed as though she did not intend to go back to bed. "I know it was bad." She sat down at the empty table and placed a hand over her mouth.

"It was worse than bad."

"Sit here with me," she said.

He watched her in the yellow light of the lamp and held back the news, knowing that after he told her, everything would be different between them. "I think I'll stand a while and look at you."

"Look at me! What's wrong, Rand? You don't seem at all well." Then a shadow passed over her face.

He imagined that there was no good way to say what had to be said. "I killed a man." He did not like the sound of it himself.

Lillian's head snapped back. "I don't believe it."

"One of Buzetti's dealers. The one named Vincente."

She stood up and put a chair between them, her hands clenched on its back. Finally, she said, "You came here to straighten Byron out. Instead you're doing the same—" She bit off what she was about to say. "How could you?"

"It was to save a worker," he said, not sure exactly whose life it was he'd saved, knowing only that Vincente had twenty shells left in his magazine when his head bounced against the floor.

"You killed somebody," she said, crying it aloud.

He held out his arms to her, but she looked to the lamp on the table. Then she turned down the wick, and he felt his real self disappearing, turning to a brown smudge in the background of her life, a monochrome outline of who he used to be.

The mill manager's boots broke ice in the mud holes on his way to the office the next morning. Before he passed in front of the commissary, he heard a noise in the canal, an inboard motor popping along as a bateau arrowed up to the mill's flotilla of skiffs. In it were three men wearing dark fedoras and overcoats. He went out to meet them and helped a stoop-shouldered lawman wearing an enormous mustache get out of the boat. On his left breast under his coat was a small gold star inlaid with what seemed to be diamonds and rubies. The man's face was soft, his features rounded like those of a statue left for centuries out in the rain. Behind him was a cross-eyed deputy, and last, behind the engine, sat Merville, who looked sleepy and sick, one eye stuck shut from the windy ride. When everyone was standing on the bank and stretching out their legs, Sheriff LaBat poked his hat back with a finger and looked at the mill manager. "Did you kill that dago?"

Suddenly out of breath, Randolph looked around at the mill, his kingdom, as though someone had come to take it from him. "Yes," he answered.

The sheriff caught his eye and held it. "Why'd you do it?"

Again there was a flash of panic in his chest, and he began to imagine a trial, a long line of lawyers, the expense and worry. Finally, he said, "He was firing a pistol at a roomful of my workers."

The sheriff spat next to his own foot. "That damned Luger with the snail-drum clip?"

"Yes."

"How many'd he hit before you nailed him?"

"Three."

At that point, the sheriff looked past the mill manager, over to the schoolhouse. He sucked in his lower lip and bit it.

"Would you mind if I put a little five-by-five stand over behind that building? You know, kind of a polling booth for elections? Something to keep the ballot box in?" He put a hand on Randolph's shoulder and clamped it tight. The smell of tobacco and gasoline flooded around them.

The mill manager looked behind him and then at the lawman's expensive badge. "Well, you could do that."

The sheriff nodded. "Your constable, maybe he could register everybody eligible to vote if I sent him the forms? You got maybe a little spare lumber around here to build it? Some number three shingles, maybe?"

"Yes, of course."

"And carpenters?" the sheriff asked, closing his little hand more tightly on Randolph's shoulder and bumping against him with his pot belly.

"I've got carpenters," he said hoarsely.

The sheriff turned him loose and clapped him on the back. "You look like this is the first one you put in the ground." He stepped back into the boat, and the cross-eyed deputy started the engine. "You ought to have my job." The mill manager saw that the deputy wore a shield badge, but it was pinned on upside down. The boat backed out from the knife cut it had made in the mud bank, away into the leaf-stained canal, leaving Merville on the bank making a hand-rolled cigarette and shaking his head.

"Mr. Aldridge," the old man said in his morning-soft voice, "you takin' up your brother's ways?"

Randolph nodded toward the skiff as it swung for the main channel. "He's not too interested in the details, is he?"

The marshal shrugged. "Maybe he figures Buzetti will get at you anyway. A man as smart as you must've figured that out, yeah."

"If Buzetti had been in my shoes last night, even he would have killed his cousin."

Merville squinted at him through the smoke. "But he didn't. You did."

The locomotive wobbled into the back of the yard, and the

men watched it couple to a car of sawn lumber. "I would've given anything not to. You should've seen the way my wife looked at me when I told her what happened. I felt like a stranger in my own kitchen."

"You not the same as you was yesterday, that's for true."

The mill manager put up his hands and let them drop. "What'll I do?"

"You got coffee on?"

They walked to his house, where the housekeeper dripped a fresh pot of dark roast. Walter toddled up to the old policeman and put a soft finger on the handle of his gun.

"Come here, Walt," Randolph said.

Merville watched as the boy climbed with much help onto the mill manager's lap. "Buzetti will go after money or blood."

"What's that mean?"

"You cost him a relative. He'll cost you something. Tell my boy to keep a eye out in the boiler room. Tell Mr. Jules to have a man check the logs coming into the saw shed."

"You think he'll do something to my brother?" He looked over his shoulder and saw that May had left the room. "Or our wives?"

Merville shook his head and took a long swallow of hot coffee. "The sheriff couldn't look the other way if you or your brother got hurt. You got money, and Byron got his little badge."

"What about the women?"

"We got a few White Camelias down west of Tiger Island. They'd come out the swamp and use a rope on Buzetti for that."

"His soldiers couldn't stop it?"

Merville reached over and grabbed the child's hand, studying the palm and then turning it over, looking at the back. "Buzetti ain't God. He's just a mean crook from a family of crooks."

"What are you looking for?"

He dropped the boy's hand. "Nothing," he said, turning to

glance at the housekeeper, who had returned and was stirring a roux in a black iron pot. She stared away, out the door toward the mildewed cabin where her father had died.

The weather turned unseasonably warm and Randolph began to have trouble sleeping. The nights steamed like a cow's breath, and he would wake up with the sheets sticking to his legs like wet paper. Sometimes in his dreams Vincente would slink out of the saloon door, stagger into the mill yard, and throw cards one at a time up in the air, where they turned into birds. Once, Randolph woke up crying, his wife cradling his head against her breasts and telling him it was all right what he had done, that she could forgive him.

"How else could I have handled it?" He twisted his face up to her in the dark.

She petted his slick cheeks and told him, "Let the other men die, I guess," which they both knew was no answer at all.

One morning the agent at Poachum called him on the new line that stretched out to the house. "Mr. Aldridge, your agent in Tiger Island just sent me a telegram."

"What did he say?"

"A man wearing a eye patch just stepped off the westbound there."

Randolph closed his eyes. "How was he dressed?"

"It's him all right."

"Well."

"You didn't hear it from me." There was the sound of a screaming locomotive whistle in the receiver, and then a click as the agent hung up.

He immediately walked over to Byron's, where he found his brother writing a report on the shooting for the parish sheriff, forming block letters like a schoolboy. On the Victrola Lester McFarland was singing "Go and Leave Me If You Want To." Randolph told him what the agent had said, but he didn't stop writing.

"I'm still filling out forms about it. New ones came yesterday." His brother's smile was wide and mean. "You didn't know all that stuff was in a head, did you?"

"What?"

"You maybe thought it was a big noodle in there? But it's not. It's a lot of dark pudding, some of it gray." His hand made a low arc. "A pistol bullet paints the floor with his memories." The record stopped and the Victrola clicked off. Over at the mill, Minos pulled the cable for the noon whistle, and the deep note fell against the window glass, which sang like tissue paper on a comb.

"How can you think up things like that?"

Byron looked down at his paper. "Sorry."

"I wish it hadn't happened."

"It should happen to Buzetti." He picked up his pencil and resumed the childlike lettering. "It would be easy."

"Don't talk like that. You'd go to jail forever."

"Still, it would solve things. Kill the queen and get rid of the hive."

"It's not the way things are done." When Randolph heard the pencil snap in two, he looked down at his brother. "It's wrong, By. It's a sin."

Byron's eyebrows went up. "If someone had shot the Kaiser, would there have been a war? Think about it, Rando. There'd be millions of fat and sane fellows working away in this old world right now." He clapped a broad hand to his forehead. "You know, I recall a story Father once told about Annie Oakley when she was touring Europe, maybe forty years ago. The Wild West Show?"

Randolph looked around and pulled up a chair. "What did he say?"

"She was shooting glass target balls that some chump was throwing up for her." He moved his hands, mimicking the toss. "That's all she did. She'd shoot nine hundred a day sometimes, without a miss. Used a .22 rifle so her shoulder wouldn't wear out." Byron's eyes rounded as he talked. "It was nothing to her, like swatting flies. Well, the way Father tells it, one day she was in Germany, doing some fancy shooting, knocking grapes off a bar at fifty feet while firing backward, sighting through a mirror. Then this odd man steps out of the crowd. Anyone could see that he was odd. Even the cloth on him was arrogant and his mustache was like a piece of tin. He was dressed in one of those grand European uniforms with gold braid and big epaulets. He told her that she had to shoot a cigar out of his mouth at thirty paces. He demanded it. She replied politely that she didn't do such things, and he insulted her. Called her a weak American farmwoman. Somebody in her company leaned in and let her know that the man was very important and it would be a good thing if she would go along." Byron stopped and suddenly looked down at a white scar on his forearm, putting a forefinger to it for a moment.

"I don't remember this story." Randolph turned out a brogan and mashed a roach coming in off the porch, then felt sorry about the mess.

"She told the man to stand off seventy-five feet and then chose a Winchester 73 to do the honors. He put a blunt in his mouth and showed his profile. Annie took aim none too slowly and cut the thing in half with a 44–40 slug, one inch from his lips." Byron thrust his face next to his brother's. "You know who the young man was?"

Randolph shook his head, pulling back.

"That damned crippled woodchopper himself."

"The Kaiser?"

"If she had missed the cigar by two or three inches, my best friend Walter Liddy would be writing me letters about his children, and you and I would be squabbling about hardwood production in the dry woods of western Pennsylvania." Byron stood and raised his arms to the ceiling. "Millions of good and bad fellows would just be going about their own business." He seemed suddenly exhausted and fell back into his desk chair.

"But what would've have happened to Annie Oakley?"

"She would have gone down as a sad joke, brother, one of the world's great idiots." Byron raised a finger into the air.

"But in all truth she would've done more for mankind than Queen Elizabeth, Walter Reed, and Thomas Jefferson rolled into one."

Randolph uncrossed his legs, leaned forward. "A killing started the whole thing, you know. The archduke."

"He was the wrong man to die."

A shadow filled the screen door, cast by a thundercloud of a man, the one called Judgment, who was holding by the jacket collar a small, writhing figure. Minos stepped from behind them and came inside, carrying a cypress slab.

"We got us some trouble, yeah."

"What's this?" The mill manager stood up and walked out onto the porch to look at the olive-skinned fellow writhing in Judgment's hand.

Minos held up the slab. "A fireman saw him walk in from Poachum on the railroad. He pulled this out of a sack and threw it in the pile we use to start up the boilers on Mondays."

The mill manager looked at the wood. "What about it?"

"A scalder," Byron said.

Minos turned one end of the slab toward Randolph to show an augured hole holding a stick of dynamite. "I peeled a gob of mud off the end and saw this."

The little man blurted, "Hey, I didn't know nothin' about that." Judgment twisted his collar, and he stood still.

Byron drew close to the man and looked down on him. "Who paid you."

"Hey. I was walkin' in to ask about a job. The sack was lyin' on the track so I picked it up."

"You know who paid him," Randolph said.

"I want to hear it."

"Nobody paid me nothin'."

Byron shook the dynamite out of the slab into his hand. "A third of a stick." He held the charge up. "With a blasting cap." He pulled out a pocketknife and stepped into his house.

His brother peered through the screen after him. "What?"

After a minute Byron returned, holding two lengths of harness rope and the piece of dynamite, a line of green fuse the length of a rat's tail hanging out of it. "Hold him by the arms, Judgment. Stand behind that porch post while you do it. Mind you don't fall into the yard."

"I gotcha, Mr. Byron."

He knelt and lashed the prisoner's legs tightly above the knees with several turns, and then pushed the stub of dynamite between the man's bound legs so it nested under his testicles, the fuse curling up. Byron pulled out a match and held it against the box. "Now, who sent you?"

The man laughed, once. "You crazy," he said, trying to move his thighs.

"Wrong answer." Byron struck the match and lit the fuse.

Randolph began to flap his arms. "Lord, God," he cried, scurrying to the corner of the house.

Minos took off his cap, bent to look at the sputtering fuse, and stepped slowly off the porch.

The man looked down between his legs. "Come on, pluck that damn fuse."

"Who hired you?"

"Ain't nobody hired me, I told you. Damn."

Randolph called out from around the corner, "By, he's not worth it."

An inch of fuse had burned away, and Byron looked the man in the eye. "Give it up."

"I got nothin' to give up," he said, his voice rising.

Another inch of the fuse had burned away when Ella stepped through the screen door, a glass of milk in her hand. "What the deuce is going on. I—" She saw the fuse, and the glass made a frothy starburst on the porch boards. The men could hear her running back through the house, slamming doors as she went, bedroom, kitchen, back stoop. Only an inch of fuse was left when Judgment cleared his throat and said, "Mr. Byron, I got to wear these clothes the rest of my shift."

At that the man began to urinate and call out *Buzetti-BuzettiBuzetti* as though in a contest to see how fast he could say the name. Byron reached into the man's crotch and plucked away the fuse.

"That wasn't so hard, was it, you lardy bastard? Now, Rando, did you hear him say who hired him to blow our boilers?"

A voice wavered from around the corner. "Yes."

Minos tilted his head into the open. "Did you put him out?"

Byron dusted his fingertips and looked at the dark stain running down the man's pants. "I think he put himself out."

CHAPTER SIXTEEN

The mill manager's wife was fanning herself in her new sitting room, seated on a divan with her husband's head in her lap while horseflies banged the screens, mad to get in at them.

"So, it was an explosion he was after?"

"Yes," Randolph moaned as he soaked up the feel of her palm on his forehead. "Trying to put us out of business—as punishment, I guess."

His wife had grown up among the mechanical chatter of three brothers and had absorbed a feel for the physical nature of things. Something about the sabotage bothered her like a gnat crawling on an earlobe. She bit into her cheek with an eyetooth. "Rand, was that little bit of dynamite enough to burst the boilers?"

He rolled the back of his head against her thighs. "I don't know. Maybe not."

"Why not a half-stick charge?" she asked. "To make sure the damage was severe and wouldn't just blow out the fire."

Her husband turned on his side, and she began to scratch his head. "I'm sure Buzetti knew what he was doing. Those people are crafty."

"Is dynamite terribly expensive?"

"Not at all," he said dreamily. "We've got a shedful of it around here somewhere."

"Well, why not a whole stick, then? Surely he wasn't worried about life and limb if he planned to blow up a boiler."

"Oh, what do you know about machinery?" He reached up and patted her hand.

She stopped scratching him. "I saw what happened when the New Castle boiler ruptured. I was there with Wallace and Todd and they explained to me about reserve heat in the boiler's water which flashes into power when the shell splits open."

"You saw the mess at New Castle?" He bent his head around to look at her. "They say it looked like a battleship had landed a salvo in the mill."

"So why, if Buzetti was trying to blow up one of the boilers, did he use such a small charge?" She folded her arms above his head and waited. Her husband, however, seemed not to want to answer. She grew peeved at him, and looking out her new windows toward the boiler shed, she pondered this little mystery.

The phone rang as Randolph was writing order summaries, and it was Sheriff LaBat calling from his office in Moreau.

"Got some bad news for you."

"What now, Sheriff?"

"That old boy your brother sent down here on the train? Last night somebody knocked the deputy in the head, broke in the jail, and sprung him."

"Are you looking?"

"Hell, yeah, we lookin'. If we find him we'll give you a call."

"He's a dangerous man, not just some drunk we wanted off the property. He was going to dynamite the boilers."

The sheriff sniffed. "Well, we'll look for him, like I said."

"You had him in the parish jail?"

There was a pause on the line. "Yeah."

"That's a big place. How in the world—"

"It was two, three o'clock this morning. We only keep one man on then."

"Was it Buzetti that got him out?"

"What do I look like, a mind reader? All I know is I got a call about sunup, and when I came down here old Boudreaux's sittin' on the floor with a goose egg on the back of his head."

After Randolph hung up, he finished the orders, then slogged over to Byron's house, where he found him sitting in a spindle-back chair on the porch, holding a drink. "Kind of early for that?"

Byron stared blankly at the mill buildings, as though seeing them for the first time. "I like it to wash down those pills the doc gives me," he said, his eyes wide as an owl's.

His brother rested his back against the porch wall. He remembered that Byron had seldom taken a drink when he was living his other life before the war. He was too busy learning the mills, courting women. "Sheriff LaBat called. Somebody broke your dynamiter out of jail, and they can't find him."

Byron spat off the porch. "That so?"

"He also told me he hadn't gotten a statement from him."

Byron took a drink and let it sit in his mouth a moment before he swallowed. "You think the sheriff's fond of tomato sauce?"

Randolph took off his hat and banged it against his leg. "You know, Lillian claims Buzetti wasn't trying to destroy the mill. She says Europeans are more complicated than that. More emotional, maybe."

"What's she think? He wants to make us cry or something?" He took another drink, the glass wobbling on the way to his mouth. "The world is waiting for the sunrise," he said, "just waiting for maybe some two-legged piece of shit to show up carrying a fine German pistol." He made a gun with his right hand, aimed it at Randolph's house, and dropped the thumb like a hammer.

By the first week in March, Randolph was playing solitaire the entire night. He began to watch his fingers and the backs of his hands, noting how different they were from Vincente's, which had been long and flexible and darting. Randolph prayed for the dealer's soul, felt stupid about doing so, then prayed briefly again.

He decided not to return to the saloon, and when the fights, which were becoming less frequent anyway, would break out, he'd let Byron handle the noise and the blood. During the day, at any spare moment, he would check with Minos, to see if he was monitoring the fuel, with old Mackey, the watchman, to make sure he kept an eye on the railroad to Poachum, with the captain of the rafting steamer, who'd put a deckhand in the wheelhouse at night to shine a spotlight down the canal to check for darkling skiffs. Byron came over after supper every day to play a few moments with Walter, as if the child were a poultice he had to apply to an aching wound. The boy was always in the house since Lillian had found it more convenient for her housekeeper to stay in the little back bedroom. Byron was beside himself the first time Walter caught a cypress block he'd tossed toward him.

"Look at that," he'd yelled, so loudly that the baby sat down with a spank.

Randolph received in the mail a manila envelope bearing a newspaper page with an account of Vincente's funeral bordered in pencil. The article gave a tally of flowers, Masses said, hymns sung. He'd been embalmed and sent up to Chicago in an Illinois Central baggage car. Randolph felt a connection with the man as he read the list of relatives and noted the isolated, euphemistic comment that he had worked in the entertainment industry. Again, he felt the pistol leap in his hand, saw the spray of thoughts on the wall. Merville had told him that Vincente was a thug's thug, a man who recruited whores and then beat them up, who won a worker's paycheck in a crooked game and loaned it back to him at daily interest, who sold lead-laced moonshine more likely to blind than intoxicate. Randolph wanted to believe that he'd done the world a favor, but his conscience would have none of it. His only solace was to consider what would have happened had he not pulled the trigger, and to hope that the living men would come to justify his decision. After dark, he thought too much and sometimes drank, and one quiet evening when he heard from across the yard Byron wake howling out of another dreamed bloodletting, he saw that his one killing did not stack up against the ranks of German *Kinder* his brother had packed off to darkness. While this thought didn't comfort him, it gave him perspective on the deep well of foreboding into which his brother sank each time he opened his eyes on a sunrise.

The second week of March came in like a waterfall. Many snakes coiled on the house steps, and Lillian kept a Winchester .22 rifle loaded with shorts behind the kitchen door. Looming over the reptiles, she'd rivet them to the wood with precise head shots. May picked them up with a stick and threw them over the back fence. Before long, the steps both front and back were tattooed with bullet holes. One afternoon Lillian killed a cottonmouth in the middle of the backyard, and May came with a broom handle without asking what had drawn fire. Lillian pumped the empty shell out and set the hammer in the safety notch.

"I don't know why I bother. There's no end to them."

"Women just don't like 'em," May told her, slipping the handle under the coiling, four-foot body. "They give me the chills."

"That one's dangerous."

May smiled and raised the handle. "Aw, Missus, there's snakes that cause more trouble than this one." She gave the reptile a heave and it propellered over the fence.

"What do you mean?" Lillian asked. When she saw the smirk on May's face, she blushed. Later, when the housekeeper came into the kitchen to wipe off the broom, Lillian watched her carefully, the way she moved, the way the light played on her face when she looked out of the window toward where the men worked.

"Something I can do for you, Missus?"

Lillian handed her a pot off the stove. "I heard that you lost your husband."

"Yes, ma'am, that's right."

"Have you ever thought of marrying again? There's no lack of men around."

May lowered the pot into a pan of suds. "I don't think about it, but it might happen. I'd like to move up North and start over with Walter."

Lillian raised her chin. "I see. When the timber's cut out?"

"Yes, ma'am." She reached out for the cornbread skillet and their hands overlapped on the handle. Lillian looked at May's fingers a moment, then pulled her own away.

"I think that might work out for you very well," she said, picking up the kettle.

Each step off the clamshell-covered lanes was a boot-sucking ordeal. One day a steady wind came up out of the south and blew for twelve hours until there was a foot of water everywhere and the camp became a broad, muddy pool where the houses were boxy boats and marooned children stood on the porches watching the tide shift under their filthy toes. That flooded night, when Galleri turned off the lamps in the saloon and shoved the last reeling, tapped-out mill hand off the porch into the end-of-the-world blackness that was the mill yard, it wasn't thirty seconds before he heard the man shrieking like someone in flames. Galleri lit a buggy lantern and jumped off the porch with it, splashing through the sulfurous water. He stopped when he saw the man floating on his back, his arms flailing, the lamplight showing twin ridges breaking the water's surface and the gold dollars of an alligator's eyeballs. The man's screams drowned as the animal towed him under and backed toward the canal. Galleri moved toward his porch but remembered he didn't have a gun in the saloon. Changing direction, he ran toward Byron's place, his feet detonating on the water until he stepped into a rut and fell facedown. His lamp out, he ran on anyway, arriving breathless at the porch, slopping up the steps to bang on the door.

Byron's face appeared behind the screen like an angry smoke. "What?" the face said.

"Sloan got took off by a 'gator," he gasped.

"Where?"

"They're headin' to the canal, *now.*" He screamed a falsetto *now.*

Byron reached behind the door for a rifle and stepped into a loose pair of rubber boots, coming out onto the porch in his long underwear and carrying two nickel-plated flashlights, handing one to Galleri. They moved as fast as they could through the water, past the saloon, stumbling through a patch of floating blocks bobbing on the tide like headless fowl. The beams from their flashlights cut across the glossy flow that slid and stank like crude oil. Byron told Galleri to be still, and they listened, but all they could hear was the wind pushing at the cypress trees behind the saloon, and then the sound of a horse splashing through the water, Randolph coming up behind them on the bare back of the blind horse. "What's going on? I heard someone yelling."

Byron and Galleri waded toward the canal. "A man been pulled down by an alligator," the saloon keeper said, his voice rising. "Just this minute."

"Give me a flashlight," Randolph said. "Maybe I can see him from up here." Galleri tossed him his, and the mill manager urged the horse to step off the hundred yards to the canal, where he called out and swung the light and finally dismounted. The three men wandered for a long time, midcalf in the bitter water, swinging their flashlights until the bulbs shrank to mean, coppery eyes. Galleri ran back to the saloon for another lantern, but when he returned and held it high, the light blinded them and they could see nothing but themselves, dirty and half-dressed, impotent against the great teeming swamp.

At dawn the wind died down and Randolph sent out skiffs to look for the lost man. The mill manager stood on the bank and listened to the oarlocks rattling over in the main pond and around the bend in the black canal, but by afternoon, no one had seen any trace of Sloan, a forty-year-old bucker who had lived in the bunkhouse. The mill manager walked to the man's room to look for the name of a relative or an address, but all he found were four changes of work clothes, a saw file, a pair of dress shoes with one of the heels gone, a bottle of Milk of Magnesia, one work glove, and, under the thin mattress, an autographed four-by-five picture of a naked New Orleans whore.

The camp drained, leaving behind mud-coated snakes and cantaloupe-sized bullfrogs that destroyed everyone's sleep with their bellowing. Gasping choupique lay in shrinking rounds of water, mouthing air for days, trying to swim through the baking sunlight.

On Sunday, the preacher prayed for the lost mill hand inside the packed little church and even preached to the windows, below which a hundred people stood reverently on a fibrous black mudflat as though they thought themselves lucky and blessed to be where they were. The mill manager fidgeted in the second pew, trying to think of his blessings, remembering only that the man who had been eaten was not very important to the mill's operations. Feeling guilty about that thought, he wondered if he should give all the buckers a five-cents-a-day raise. While in church, Randolph understood that he had a small soul, but he also knew that it had been bred and taught into him by his father and by teachers who stressed that every chip of wood was currency and every minute was salary paid out, and that a manager who saved a penny a man per day could live an easy old age, at least as far as money was concerned. When the preacher shouted out that death came like a thief in the night, the mill manager closed his eyes and thought of the cardsharp and the devoured bucker, men who'd met their ends on his watch. He sang the final hymn as best he could, unable to find the tune, but he'd be damned if he wouldn't try.

. . .

Not many days later, Randolph was in bed collapsing into a circle of welcoming, dreamless sleep when suddenly, painfully, as though a rope had been drawn around his neck, he was pulled back toward the troubled sounds of the world. He opened his eyes to the dim bedroom, and Lillian's hands were shaking his arms.

"My God," she said. "You're harder to wake than a statue."

"What?" He blinked at the silhouette of her head.

"Listen," she cried. "What does it mean?"

It was the mill whistle, a big Lunkenheimer triple-chime, droning deep, harmonizing tones. "There's no signal like that," he said. "This is nonsense."

The sound seeped into the wood of the house, into his bones. As he got up and dressed in the dark, he accidentally kicked the bedpost and cursed. The whistle grew louder, rising slightly in pitch as it warmed up, setting the windowpanes buzzing like huge insects. Out on the porch he looked toward the mill, but the moon was down and he couldn't make out a thing. The ground everywhere was slop, so he went out back and bridled the horse, throwing on a saddle without a blanket and climbing up, giving the animal its head.

The whistle cable was above the main catwalk in the boiler room. Randolph rode up to the door of the boiler house and just inside found the watchman unconscious next to his lantern, facedown in the sawdust. When he rolled him over, one of his eyes opened but began roaming as if in search of the thundering whistle. Byron came in, along with Minos and a fireman, all of them shirtless.

"What's wrong with the whistle?" Byron shouted.

Randolph cupped his hands toward Minos. "Do something."

The engineer yelled to the fireman, a young man with blond hair, and he bounded off toward a ladder leading up to the main catwalk. In a few moments, the whistle stopped with a yodel and the fireman came back holding up a twenty-four-inch Stilson wrench for the engineer's inspection. "This here wrench was hung on the cable, Mr. Minos." He held it high for the men to look at like a mystery.

"It's a joke," Minos said. "A son-of-a-bitchin' joke."

Byron bent down and jiggled the watchman's face, trying to bring him around. "A jokester doesn't coldcock a watchman."

"Oh, my God," Randolph said. He and his brother looked at each other and the connecting glance was electric.

Byron drew his pistol and raced toward his place. His brother ran for the horse, which was confused and began to stutter-step until a pistol shot ripped across the dark mill yard, and the animal, now that it had something to aim for, began trotting toward Randolph's house, where a woman's scream rose more frightening than the unbidden whistle. The horse picked up its pace without being spurred, and Randolph was afraid it would run into the side of the house and kill both of them. When he splattered into the yard, he reined up hard and jumped off.

Lillian ran off the porch in her nightgown, screeching, her hands clamped around her temples. Bounding past her into the kitchen, her husband saw the yellow tongue of flame in a lamp on the counter and, below it, the housekeeper sprawled on her back.

He cried out and knelt next to her, his heart falling like a dove shot out of the sky. Her eyes were closed, her lips barely parted, and in the center of her clear forehead was a small bullet hole. He picked up her arm to feel for a pulse, then put his fingers on her neck, but she was inert, empty, no longer there. Looking up, he caught his brother's eye as he came in. "She's dead, By." He could barely say the words.

Byron's unshaven face was the color of lead. "We should've known," he said slowly.

Randolph's head lifted. "Where's Lillian?"

"Ella's got her now."

In the canal a rackety engine fired up, and Byron flew through the back door and across the yard, leaping the fence.

He saw the boat cutting toward the main channel. It was a fast skiff, and Byron realized at once there was nothing at the mill that could catch it. The deckhand on the rafting steamer turned on the big carbon arc light and swung it across the water, missing the skiff but giving Byron enough backlight to see that a single man was running the boat. He flicked off the safety on his .45 and tried a shot, then another, but the boat was a hundred yards away. The first slug banged a barrel on the steamer, the second raised a geyser next to the skiff, and Byron emptied the clip, hoping at least to save some future victim, but the engine didn't waver, and in a few seconds the boat rounded a bend out of sight, its two-cylinder engine rattling into the timber.

Randolph didn't look up when he heard his brother shooting. He knew nothing about the woman on the floor, yet he had taken root in her, and she had made a son for him. He felt this now, fully, a feeling that had come at last simply because she was dead. He'd always thought of the child as hers alone, so responsibility had not blossomed in him. But now, as Walter began to cry out from the back bedroom, he knew he was the one to go to the boy, take his arms, and pull him onto his shoulder. Walter rubbed his face on Randolph's neck, then turned his head away, his arms going slack and trailing down his father's chest.

Byron came into the room and snatched a blanket off the bed to cover May's body, and when he'd finished he stood next to his brother, whose eyes were wet.

"Why her?" Randolph asked. "Why not me or you, or Lillian?"

Byron looked down. "You know why."

He shook his head and put a hand on the child's neck. "I don't."

"She's colored, and they won't chase him hard for that," he said, like a fact. "You or me, or the women, Father would send down money and lawyers to force the sheriff to act." He rested a hand lightly on the child's back. "Put him down, Rando. He's out like a light."

Once the child was in his bed, Randolph began to search for reasons, and when he remembered the day Buzetti had stood on the back porch of the kitchen and looked through the screen at them, a new type of anger swelled under his breastbone like a flaw in his heart. She was dead because Buzetti had seen her hand slide from his grasp, that odd motion that always catches the eye, like Vincente's cousin dealing from the bottom of the deck. He turned to his brother. "He wanted to hurt me deep and close to home."

Byron nodded his head, once. "It's how they work."

They went out and comforted the women, and much later walked toward the mill office to make the call to the sheriff. Halfway there, they realized that the women and child were alone, and Byron turned back, reloading his pistol as he walked.

Merville showed up after daybreak, his white hair tufted up in crazy angles, his mustache drooped over his mouth. As he stepped out of the splintered skiff, its wood not painted but stained dark green with copper sulfate, he squinted up at Randolph. "How'd you know to come out and meet me?"

"A watchman spotted you coming up the canal and phoned the house."

He pulled a white flag of a handkerchief and wiped his eyes. "Phones," he said. "They gonna change every damn thing."

"Where's LaBat?"

"He commissioned me to handle it."

"He doesn't come out for Negro deaths, is what you mean."

Merville drew a pipe out of his vest and lit it as they walked to the house. "I don't have to see nothin'. What you told on the phone last night was plenty."

"You can't find the man with the patch?"

The marshal frowned into the bowl of his pipe. "Did you see him?"

Randolph looked back toward the canal.

"You don't know nothin', do you? Except who did it and who paid him."

Randolph raised his arms and let them slam against his sides. "Is there no law around here at all?"

Merville sniffed. "Yep. We all guilty, and everybody got a death sentence." He went through the porch into the kitchen, bent to the floor, his knees cracking like kindling, and picked up the blanket. "She got any people?"

"She told me no."

"Get a man to make her box, then. Get somebody to clean up the blood off the linoleum and make the women come in and cook a meal." He turned his head and looked into May's face. "If the women don't do it right now, right this minute, they'll never come in here no more. The place will haunt up in their minds." The old man sat down in a kitchen chair and stared at the blanket. "Lord, but she was something pretty."

Randolph glared at him. "I want to get the bastard."

The marshal pinched a hand on his eyes. "You know, some bastards can't be got."

"I'll pay whatever it takes."

Merville took down his hand and put it on a knee. "Money can't do it. Law neither."

"You want me to wait for him to die of old age?" He got up and pinged the back of his middle finger against the marshal's star. "Do *you* want to die, with him still running loose and killing?"

The old man gave Randolph a long, offended look. "You know, they's a lot of dead people what never finished their jobs." He looked to the floor.

"I'm sorry."

Merville stood up carefully. "Let me see what I can find out for us in town," he said. Hobbling over to the corpse he again folded back the edge of the blanket until only the wound showed. "Small bullet," he said. "It's what they use, nowadays, the ones they pay to do things like this." The two men looked down and, had they spoken of it, would have admitted to being haunted by the future, by everything taken out of it because of May's death. She'd believed she could escape. Randolph suspected she was trapped for life, but now there was no hope of seeing what she might have done, and that was the saddest part. He'd wanted, all along, to be wrong.

After a long time, Merville stuck out an elbow, and Randolph helped him up from the floor, easing the breaking stars of pain in the old man's knees.

By noon Lillian was in the kitchen, her jaw set, her hands darting like birds to fire up the cookstove, to pull down pots and skillets, to exorcise the kitchen with activity.

After a few minutes Ella came in warily, wearing her apron like armor over a loose housedress. She found a potato and began to peel it savagely. After a minute, she asked, "Did you ever think why you weren't the one he shot?"

Lillian closed the firebox lid with a stove key. "He knew who he wanted. You heard what Randolph said."

"Still, I believe you'd better carry your little pistol in your apron pocket." She finished the potato and quickly grabbed another, desperate to keep busy.

"I wouldn't even know where to shoot a man to knock him down. And do you actually think a killer who had it planned out, some expert who knows how to do these things, couldn't come in here right now with us both standing with cocked pistols in our hands and not shoot us dead?" She dragged a cast-iron skillet onto a stove lid. "I don't know the first thing about it."

"Still, you might have a chance."

Lillian banged down a lid on the skillet. "There's no chance against people like that. You're fooling yourself if you think otherwise." Her shoulders slumped and she looked at the floor for the first time. "Besides, it's over now. Buzetti's cousin, or whoever that awful man was, is avenged."

Ella began to cut the potatoes into rounds. "So it's over."

As soon as the words were said, Lillian began to picture her husband and his brother, smoking cigars, drinking, talking, pointing to emphasize their facts the way men do, cursing whatever was contrary to them. She thought of the sharp scents on her husband's body, the sweet, burnt smell of sawdust and woodsmoke and tobacco, the earthy emanations of his damp brogans. "If it was left to me, it would be," she finally said. "But men, they act like they smell." She laughed and banged the back of a knife blade on a pot. "Say, could you cut up an onion over those potatoes before you add the cheese?"

Ella wiped her knife and gave her a questioning glance. "An onion?"

"It's what *she* did," Lillian said, her hands trembling over a pot that began to raise a ghost of steam. "And it tasted damned good."

Nimbus Mill
May 15, 1925

Father,

I received your last and was not happy to read your criticism. I was not trying to do Byron's job the night the gambler was killed. I was trying to help him, for God's sake. If you had been in that room with the bullets flying around your head like bees, I doubt that you could have managed as well as I did. There was time only to bend a trigger finger. As for the loss of our housekeeper in retaliation, that has angered me a great deal. There are no witnesses and the local lawmen are unable or unwilling to find any leads whatsoever. Sometimes it seems there is no law down here other than Byron's shovel.

I have replaced the housekeeper with an amiable middle-aged Irishwoman from the white quarters who comes early and leaves late.

The Sicilians have replaced their dealer in the saloon, but he is so poor at cheating I think the loggers will break up his game before too long.

My physical health is holding up in the heat, but I feel downhearted sometimes. Byron of late has taken more intensely to his phonograph. I have asked him what his plans are and he says that for himself, he has only one, to last until bedtime. One bright spot is that he and his wife have decided to try in earnest to have a child, and in that respect Lillian and I are in a similar circumstance. Something has got to come out of us other than boards.

The orders are slowing the past week, except for number one siding. I think by now half the summer cottages of New England must be built of our cypress.

Regards,
Randolph

Moonlight streamed over their bed, and after making love, Randolph and his wife lay toweling off sweat and casting about for cool spots on the mattress. All evening long he had prepared himself to launch the question that now hung in his mouth like a gasp. Finally, he swallowed and asked, "What do you think of adopting Walter as our own?"

In the dark, he imagined her eyes moving toward him, incredulous. "Darling," she whispered, "that baby is colored."

Biting the inside of his cheek, he plunged on. "But when we go back, when the tract is cut out and we go back, nobody up there will know. He's as white as you are."

She rolled over next to him, a cloud of fragrant heat, and laid an arm across his chest. "Byron and his wife know."

"Oh, they wouldn't say anything," he told her, putting his hand on her arm.

"They might, someday. Maybe when he's eighteen and courting a Highsmith or a Vandervoort. It would be a disaster waiting to happen."

He waited a moment, trying to focus on the beaded boards of the ceiling, weighing the risk of what he would say next. "But when I pick him up I feel that he's my own."

She sighed and lay back. "I know. He's smart and well featured for a castoff."

He frowned. "So you think there's not a way?"

"I didn't say that. We could take him in as a ward, that's

all. Put him in schools. When the time comes, we could say we don't know who his parents were. It's been done." She moved again, twisting her head on the pillow. "But why do you want to adopt him, give him your name?"

Suddenly lost in a dark, unfamiliar landscape at the rim of a cliff, he pulled back from the edge and said, "I wasn't thinking," and then, "It just would be nice to raise him. Keep him with us."

After a long silence, she asked, with a tremble in her voice, "Are you afraid we'll never conceive?"

"No, it's not that." He patted her shoulder. "It's just taking us longer than most, is all."

"Bringing Walter into our lives is no small thing, Rand. He might grow up thinking he's white, and that would be fine. But if we told him he was ours and then someday, somehow he found out otherwise, he'd be crushed, turned inside out."

"Yes," he said, "I guess that's true."

"But if he *knew* his parents were a mystery, even if Byron or Ella would let it slip about his race, well, sure, it would be bad, but it wouldn't be as if we'd been living a big lie. Does that make any sense?"

"Yes," he said, smiling, understanding that the boy would be with him, now.

They slept for an hour, and then Walter began crying. "I'll get up," he said, pulling back on his wife's shoulder as she rolled out of bed. He found a clean bottle above the cooler, filled it with milk, and banged around the kitchen until he found the box of nipples. The first he tried to stretch over the bottle slipped out of his fingers and jumped behind the stove. As the cries grew more insistent, he dug out another, this time fitting it on. Walter was old enough to take his milk cool, so he gave him the bottle, changed his dirty diaper, which he washed out in the new toilet, and set it in the covered bucket in the corner. Powdered and with a dry bottom, Walter clamped down on the nipple and stretched his arms out. Randolph gathered him up and settled in May's old rocker. The baby turned loose of the nipple and said, "Wok," and Randolph rocked, inhaling the powder, feeling the flannel gown and the tender skin beneath it, watching the thin, lavender-tinged eyelids grow heavy as the boy floated away. The baby took a breath and sucked in his sleep, dreaming of the business of taking things in.

Randolph knew he should feel like a father, albeit a secret one. He should feel some type of late-night peace brought on by the child asleep against his stomach. Instead, he thought that Walter was his mother's son, with enough of May in his face that Randolph could never forget her and the manner in which she'd been taken out of all their lives. Buzetti had stolen her as casually as he would lift a plum from a fruit peddler's wagon, and Randolph wondered if he would take again, if not from him or his family, from someone else. After the murderer had fled in the skiff, Byron had wanted to catch the train into town that night and kill him, and it had taken Randolph all night to calm him. The mill manager had followed him home and stayed close, asking about his records or how he'd met Ella, pacifying him, keeping him connected to something else, something good. Now, he wondered if he should have left him alone.

He looked through the kitchen door and pictured May standing at the stove. He felt a taste of his brother's anger, but after that moment passed he sensed only frustration at the fact that he was surrounded by hundreds who did his bidding, yet nowhere in that crowd was a man who could touch Buzetti with impunity. The baby sighed, lifted an eyelid, and the mill manager rocked him again, smiling down like someone who'd lost control of his own face. He began to hum a melody from one of his brother's insane records.

CHAPTER SEVENTEEN

At the beginning of June 1925 a telegram arrived, telling that Lillian's father had died. As she and Randolph were packing for the trip home, the housekeeper, Mrs. Scott, a large, hale woman with hamlike arms, fell ill with influenza, so they decided to leave Walter in Byron and Ella's care. When Randolph walked over and handed the child to his brother, he noticed in Byron's eyes a flicker of something he hadn't seen for years, the old prewar lightness of glance. The men stood on the porch without talking, and Ella came out and tried to take the boy.

"Hold on a minute, gal, I just got him," Byron complained. He put his lips against the baby's cheek and made a noise.

Randolph coughed. "I hope we can get back inside of ten days. Whatever you need, go over to the main house and get it."

"We'll make out fine," Byron said. "Stay all year if you want. And tell the old man to go to blazes for me."

"He moves around pretty quick, now. Don't let him tumble off this porch."

Byron sat in a rocker and the boy reached out and grabbed hold of his ear. "Not a chance."

The mill manager and his wife boarded an early train, a ratty mix of passenger coaches and boxcars full of cattle. They crossed the train ferry into New Orleans and took the Southern Railroad to Atlanta, changing trains and lines, and after two days' travel got off in Pittsburgh. Arriving late at her family's house, they rushed to get ready for the funeral. Her father had been dead three days, and the mourners who'd gathered in a stone church thirty miles to the south seemed anxious for the sense of release that burial brings. During the service, Randolph watched his wife carefully, but there was little need for his worry; she was not grief-stricken. Her father had been an official for the Pennsylvania Railroad, a man all numbers and economics who had spent little time with any of his children. Lillian once said that she never cared to understand a thing about what her father did, since whatever it was had cut him off from the family. Randolph had always thought him dull and uncommunicative, and he knew that his Lillian, as she sat next to the aisle in the dark little church, was listening to the minister's comments for some clue as to who her father really was. Toward the end of the service, she reached out a black-gloved hand and almost touched the varnished coffin.

The next day they visited with his father in another town outside of Pittsburgh. His father was not a distant or particularly hard man; he liked a tall glass of rye and water after dinner, but his sole topic of conversation was sawmills. He rode his son down with questions for an hour and a half, until Randolph excused himself when he saw his wife strolling in the yard. He caught up with her and they walked downhill to a rose arbor and sat together on the enameled bench wedged under the latticed arch.

Lillian looked toward a line of dark hills. Even this far from the city, a thin brown haze floated above them. "It feels good to be outside without fear of breaking a sweat." She laughed and leaned against him. "Or stepping on a snake."

"We'll come back before too long," he said absently. "I don't want to build a place on a hilltop anymore, though."

"No," she agreed. "South of a ridge is the place. Out of the wind."

"Maybe we can find a lake. I've grown used to the water, I guess."

"The Lemmon tract."

He made a little sideways motion with his head. "That's a bit large."

"If Byron came back he could have the eastern half. You two used to ride and camp there." She closed her eyes and settled her head against his shoulder.

He was quiet. Looking from hill to hill, then back to the green copper gutters of his father's house, he suddenly felt idle, that everything he belonged to was somewhere else. In Pennsylvania, he had never run a mill completely by himself, had not gone out in the dark to look for a man taken off by a reptile, had not shot a man dead, and no one here had ever carried his child. "Oh, my," he said aloud.

His wife did not open her eyes. "Yes, the air is so dry, isn't it?"

Late that night, Randolph and his father went into the front parlor for a nightcap. The old man was slim, and his dark, vested suit hung wrinkled from the long day's wearing. His white hair was short, brushed off to the side above slate-blue eyes. He was not a bad or shallow man, his son thought, but he enjoyed above all else the complexities of turning trees into figures in a bank ledger. His father believed it was American to make money, a patriotic duty to prosper. In truth, Randolph was most shaped by him, though it was in his older brother that Mr. Aldridge stubbornly continued to invest his hope. This was how things were; Randolph accepted it, and even shared this view. He took what little love his father allotted him and made do with it.

The old man leaned back in an armchair and rephrased the same old question, "How bad is Byron's condition? Is there any change?"

Randolph sat on a piano bench and stared at the keys. "There are days he's worse than others. At times I'll be with him and something simple will happen, I don't know, a whistle will sound or a steam line will pop, and then he's not there."

"Not there?"

"He's standing there, but his mind's thousands of miles away."

"In a trench." The old man scowled. "He should be over all that."

Randolph moved uncomfortably on the piano bench. "There is no way anyone can tell you or me what he suffered."

His father thrust out his glass. "Many others have gone to war and come back fine."

"Maybe they appear so on the surface."

His father took a long pull of his drink. "You want to come home, I know. But if you can do anything at all for him, to get him to return to us, to help his mental state . . ."

His father stopped, and Randolph saw that he was near tears.

"I'm trying and I'll keep trying," he said, nearly angry at the emotion in the room.

"I know, boy," his father said, straightening in the chair. "You're a good son."

"But Byron's the oldest," he snapped. "He's straight-shouldered and handsome, and the one who should take over all the mills someday, is that right?" He was hoping to lead his father toward the realization that Byron had reached a place in his life from which he could never return. He watched him carefully, imagining the words sinking in, waiting for understanding.

The old man let out a long breath and set his drink on the floor. The window was open, and the banshee sound of a Pennsylvania Railroad train whistle drifted in on the cool air. "If only he'd done better in battle," his father said.

Randolph looked through the window into the darkness and could think of absolutely nothing to say in reply.

. . .

They got into Poachum at noon, and the mill locomotive was waiting for them. Rafe Sommers's pumpkin face hung out the cab window, oily and brick-colored with heat. "You didn't bring back no cool breeze in your suitcase, did you?" he called as Lillian walked up to the engine.

She stopped and squinted up at him. "No, Mr. Sommers, but I've got some extra cinders down my neck courtesy of the L&N, if you need them." Once they arrived in camp and their suitcases were carted to the manager's house, Lillian walked down quarters to check on Mrs. Scott, and Randolph went over to get the baby. Ella was in a porch rocker holding Walter on her lap. The child looked at Randolph, smiled, then squirmed down to the decking where he balanced on his rubbery legs, holding on to Ella's fingertips. Randolph reached over and took him by the middle. "Where's By?"

"He's over at the bunkhouse cooling down two millwrights."

"How's he been?"

The woman fluffed her skirt, a full, out-of-date housedress. "Not bad." She looked puzzled, as if she hadn't thought about Byron before now. "Not bad at all, in fact. There was a big row down at the saloon one night, but he went and handled it barehanded. Came back with a drunk and chained him to the flywheel for the evening. But no, no real trouble."

The mill manager hoisted the boy up and watched him put a hand in his mouth. "Did he take to babysitting?"

"He carried Walter around like a watch. Got up with him, even, which plumb amazed me. Not a man type of thing, you know. Matter of fact, he fooled with that young 'un so much he laid off the Victrola a good bit."

Randolph gave her a look. "Is he out of needles for the thing?"

Ella put a hand against a porch post. She was staring hard at the baby. "No. He played with little Walter some. Did paperwork. You know."

The boy squirmed and said something in his language.

"Well, yes, I do know," Randolph said. "The Sicilians cause any trouble?"

"One night a new man was dealing. A sure-enough Chicago man. He told Byron he'd cut his throat if he messed with him."

"What did By do?" He lowered the child onto a dry piece of ground and held on to his hands.

"Came home," Ella said, looking over at the saloon, seeming freshly surprised. "You know, he just came home."

Merville was in his waterfront office putting down pans over the warped floor boards while a thunderstorm spun whorls of water against the sweating windows. His arthritis bound him at the hips and knees, and his chest ached as if a mule had kicked him. Sitting at his desk, he signed the last form he had to fill out for that night. He was trapped by the storm, immobilized into thinking, and he closed his eyes, remembering his wife, who had hated lightning, and his father, who'd been the same way. Now and then, in the long nights Merville's life replayed like a wrongly spliced silent film, an overlong saga that always ended with his sitting in this water-stained office, or sometimes in the empty house two blocks away. He looked up at the flickering bulb on its cloth cord, whose light barely revealed the ceiling's corners where soot-bagged spider webs held leggy husks dead since the war in Cuba.

His arms throbbed and he looked over at the double-barreled shotgun, which had become too heavy for him to carry on rounds. Even his regular revolver made his gut hurt; its shells had turned green in its cylinder, so he had gone through the office's drawers and found a short-barreled Colt lightning revolver in .41 caliber, small, but good enough to knock down a drunk.

Maybe it was the rain causing him to tremble. Merville was aware that most men didn't last as long as he had, and he wondered why whoever was above the clouds was keeping him around. Old age was making him look, at last, for the purpose of things, and he figured there was a job left undone, maybe.

Sometimes he wondered how he would die and when, and

if there would be some realization right before death when he could understand how well or poorly he'd done, because he honestly didn't know for sure. He knew that he loved his sons, though he'd never said that. Minos could make a steam engine run slick as a rabbit's heart, and though the other children didn't talk to him much, he knew they weren't off doing anything bad. Had he seen them all last year—Ralph, Aubrey, Etienne, and Maude? He put a spotted hand on his forehead. His children had passed through him as if he were a doorway, and they did not look back.

The crank phone began to rattle—a long, a short, a long—and he hoped that it would stop and Mrs. Aucoin would pick up. But then another long ring drawled from the wall. He got up and walked around a streaming leak.

"Hallo?"

"Merville, this is Jimmy. Something bad done happened, yeah."

"*Quoi?*"

"*Mais*, Ralph LeBoeuf was walking down to his camp boat and found Ada Bergeron on the levee. You better come."

"What's wrong with her?"

"She been killed."

"Where at?"

"Downriver from Buzetti's new place."

Merville pulled out his watch and checked the time. "That's little Ada what turned whore?"

"Oh, Lord, I guess so."

"I'm coming." He hung up, returned his pistol, pulled a slicker off a nail, and put it on. He hated the floppy rubber hat, but without it the rain would soak down his back. He tried his flashlight and found it dead. The parish wouldn't send him any batteries until next month, so he lit a large barn lantern and adjusted the wick. Across the street, where the river flowed by under a mat of hyacinth, a steam whistle gargled up a slug of condensate and began to blow a series of hoots. He could tell from the sound that the pilot was trying to raise a policeman. Merville sat in a chair and pulled on rubber knee boots. The roof bell began to clang on a rafting steamer. "All right, all right," he shouted, then grabbed a hemp sack that hung from a hook by the door.

He stepped off the sidewalk into a foot of water and slogged over to the wharf, hearing the shouts of a big brawl competing with the rain. When he got close enough to see, he held up the lantern. On a big plank dock between steamboats, two crews grunted and punched and cursed. The old man looked down the river toward Buzetti's and then back to the fight. He drew his Colt and let a round off in the air, causing three or four men to pull up and stagger out of the melee, but the rest were growling like pit bulls, the lamplight showing winks of bared teeth, swinging pipes, eyes torn to red flags. Merville saw that everyone was black except for one overweight white man. He squinted, then shot him in the thigh.

"The hell you say," the man shouted. He started to come at the old man, but the slug had cracked his thighbone and he went down like a tree. The fight came apart at the seams then, and men began to back away, looking at the white deckhand where he lay holding his leg and hollering. A swaying drunk, his shirt torn off of his ebony hide, pulled a jackknife, and Merville fired a shot six inches over his head, the slug taking a baluster off the second deck of the *Cecil N. Bean.*

The lawman threw his hemp sack down on the wharf, and held up the lantern. "I'm gonna say this one time. Put every piece of iron you got in the bag, and the first son of a bitch that holds back a weapon gets shot in the nutsack." He pointed the pistol around at each man in turn, and the bag was soon weighed down by two short lengths of pipe with tape-wrapped handles, a set of brass knuckles, five jackknives, a straight razor, two slapjacks, and a corkscrew. The pilot came down a gangplank holding an umbrella and stopped short.

"Well, shit, Marshal, why'd you shoot my white man?"

Merville spat next to the pilot's boot. "The doctor won't work on niggers. Get your stretcher and bring him over to the clinic." He picked up the sack and dragged it across the street to his office, slinging it muddy and sopping inside the door.

It was a half-mile walk to Buzetti's riverside saloon. He thought about the Model T the parish let him use, but it would never start in the rain. Merville understood that the high sheriff didn't want him to be much of a lawman because somebody with too much ability to inflict justice could cause problems for local government. Crossing the tracks at the railroad station, he continued downriver along the low levee toward the wiggle of a flashlight. The rain slacked off and he came up on the scene and raised his lamp. The man who'd called him motioned to the grass, and Merville bent down.

"You took your own damned time," the man said, taking an extinguished cigar from his mouth.

Merville looked at Ada Bergeron, at the broad cut across her throat, remembering her as a young girl of average looks who had lived with her family in a camp boat north of town. A few years after her father had drowned, she began working as a barmaid on River Street, and after Buzetti set up business she went to work for him. He reached out and rolled her eyelids shut and, before withdrawing his hand, pinched the slick material of her tight dress as if he meant to hurt it. What was under the cloth shifted like meat in a package, and he took back his hand. "Anybody know anything?"

LeBoeuf, the man who'd found her, stepped back out of the circle of light. "Let's put something over her, at least," he said.

"What you know?"

"Nothing. I was walking home, and there she was."

Merville looked around at the other men. "Anybody hear anything about this in Buzetti's?"

No one responded. Out in the river a small rafting steamer screeched for the railroad bridge to open. Merville knew that the man who had found her spoke French and the others did not, so he began questioning him in Cajun. "Come on, you know she was Buzetti's whore. You're in there two or three times a week."

The man's head turned toward the north. "I was in there yesterday and he was telling her to go with his cousin for free. She was a little bit drunk and told him she didn't want to do it. She didn't tell him very nice."

"And?"

The man shrugged. "That's all I heard. He took her by the arm and brought her into his little . . ." He searched for a French word in his head and, finding none, said the English, "office."

"Did you see her later?"

"Oh, yeah. She was working some muskrat trapper from Sugarhouse Bend."

The old man looked closely at the wound. It was a single cut, and the knife had been sharp. Ada Bergeron could have been anything she could have afforded to be, if her father hadn't died and left her and her mother with six younger children. He knew that poverty wasn't the only reason a woman became a whore. If it were, most of the women in town would work on their backs. He took the corpse's hands and turned the palms up to the lamplight. They were soft and the nails were unpainted. The old man recalled that his mother's father was a Bergeron, and squinting an eye shut, he began to sort through cousins until he found Ada's father. Ah, yes, that boy he'd rolled bales with on Giror's steamboat after the war. He looked up and opened both eyes. "This one was Sydney's daughter?" he said in surprise.

LeBoeuf said, "Sydney from Pierre Part."

"Well, I'll be damned. I forgot who that was, me."

"Sydney was your people," the man said. "You spend all your life in that police office, you forget too damned much."

Merville turned his head toward a spurt of garbled laughter rolling down the levee and his eyes brought Buzetti's saloon into focus, a board and batten place painted flat red and built on the repaired foundation of the old business. When he let go of the girl's hands, they stayed up in a gesture of supplication.

"You want me to get the undertaker?"

The marshal stood up slowly, reached down, and rubbed a knee. "Yeah. Get that priest, too."

He then walked over the band of stinking shells at the door of Buzetti's place and went inside. The bouncer put a hand on Merville's open slicker, next to his badge, a pewter-colored star dangling on a few strands of cloth. "You can't come in here."

Merville batted the hand away. "If you make me kill you, I'll be out of shells for the night."

The big man stepped back. "What you want?"

"You know what I want. Where is he?"

The man's bovine jaw clenched. "The door on the right."

The bouncer walked him over and opened a six-panel door, stuck his head in for a moment, said something in Italian, then motioned for the lawman to move into the room.

When Buzetti saw who it was, he seemed annoyed, leaned back in his chair, and spat in the trash can. "I'm busy. What you want?"

Merville drew his pistol, cocked it and pointed it at Buzetti's head, then held out his trembly left hand. "Let me have your knife."

Buzetti became very still. "I got a pistol in my coat."

"I don't give a shit about a pistol."

Slowly, Buzetti drew a long thin jackknife from the region of his right ankle and handed it over. "What?"

"I'll tell you what in a minute." He sprung the blade and held it up under the lamp on the desk. The knife was clean. The old man put it to his nose and sniffed. Grabbing it by the blade, he banged it on the desk and put his finger on a spray of water beading against the wood. "You washed it."

Buzetti spread his arms. "What's all this bullshit about?"

"Ada Bergeron." He watched Buzetti's face.

"What about her?"

"Somebody just cut her throat."

Buzetti cocked his head. "I'm sorry. Hey, it's a bad business, look what she does for a living. When you got a different boyfriend every night, you run the risk, you know?"

"I ought to do it right now." The Colt was shaking, but it was still close to the slick face.

Buzetti's smile slid back over a rack of yellow teeth. "You ain't got no evidence, and you ain't got no balls. And you know that if you shoot me your own sheriff will put you in the can." He stood up, crossed his arms, and bounced, once, on the balls of his feet. "But the real reason is you just a dumb fuck coonass."

Merville winced, uncocked the revolver, and, after two tries, put it in its holster under the slicker. He moved his face close to Buzetti's. "Who shaved you after the zoo let you out the cage?"

"What? Ey, what's that mean?" Buzetti took a step back.

Merville looked at him, his eyes the gray of old bullets. "What's the matter, Ada didn't like your cousin? Maybe she wouldn't mate out of her own kind?" He turned for the door.

Buzetti bowed his back and gestured wildly. "Hey, hey. You live past your time, eh? What, you don't care no more? Listen to me, I can teach you to care about something."

Merville put his hand on the doorknob. "You can't teach a cat to kiss his own ass."

Buzetti brought down his eyebrows. "What can keep you safe?" he asked, in a low, seething voice.

The old man leaned back and mocked him with a wide smile, his upper plate clacking down.

The marshal picked his way across the railroad tracks and through the cloudy puddles of River Street where the wind blew like bad breath over oyster shells piled in the ruts. At his office he retrieved the bag of weapons and began to walk home under crepe myrtles careening in the squalling wind, pattering their stored rain onto the rotten slicker. At his wooden house he walked into the bedroom, upended the bag on the floor, and pitched the weapons one by one behind the high armoire jammed across a corner. He looked briefly at a straight razor before he pitched it, thinking of the inches of man-meat that would go uncut by it, the rolling in the mud and the squalling out in the moonlight for Jesus and Momma that would not issue from the blade. He hefted a set of spiked brass knuckles, then tossed it up and over, listening to it crash down onto years of other weapons. This disposal was what he enjoyed most. It took away from all evil that he had done and felt.

CHAPTER EIGHTEEN

In the late afternoon Randolph was on his front porch watching the child as he pointed at the locomotive, which was coupling up cars of kiln-dried one-by-twelves. Walter's wet mouth formed an O and out of it came the train's whistle.

The mill manager leaned over him from the rocker. "How does the engine go, Walt?"

The boy bobbed his head. "Choo-choo-choo, den na whistle."

"That's right." Together they watched the locomotive slam the cars around, coughing cinders and geysers of steam. Walter sat down and played with his own wooden train, a present Byron had brought from town. Randolph saw his wife come out of the school building across the way, shade her eyes and look over at them, then turn back inside. The knock-off whistle had just sounded and the workers were streaming to their streets, or the barracks, or the gaunt saloon. He watched a black man come out of the road that led from the Negro quarters; the worker took his hat off and stopped a foreman, who listened for a moment, then pointed toward the mill manager's house. He replaced his hat, and when he got close enough, Randolph could see it was Clarence Williams, his scar draining sweat like a switchback road.

"How you?" he asked the child, who looked up at him and was silent.

"Are you doing all right?" the mill manager asked.

He came right up to the porch and stood in a puddle down below the rail. "Mr. Aldridge, they's some talk down in the quarters."

"What kind of talk?"

"That nigger what live by me went with that ho woman back the saloon." Here the man turned away and pretended to study the school building. "He heard she say the debt ain't paid."

"What debt?"

"She say, Mr. Buzetti say one housemaid ain't worth no Sicilian gennelmen. Mr. Aldridge, I wish I knew more what she say."

Randolph put both hands on the rail and looked left toward a stand of cypress, and then above the trees where a mockingbird was chasing a crow. He did not look at Clarence Williams. "Was she drunk?"

"Ho's always drunk," he said. "Ain't nobody drink more and cry more than a ho. Last time I went with one she like to bit my nose in two. I got the blood poison and laid in bed with a fever, breathing through my mouth for two weeks." He looked at the baby, then away. "Most times a ho tell the truth. They just too bad to lie."

"That's all you heard?"

"I wish I ain't heard what I did."

The mill manager looked at the sweat-loaded hat wilting down around Clarence's face and smelled the day's labor on him. "You get any more information, you let me know."

"I hear that," he said, sidestepping back into the lane and starting toward the dark side of the mill.

Before daylight, Lillian heard the chirp of the three-inch Buckeye whistle mounted over the boiler house, the signal for the firemen to roll out of bed and come raise a roaring head of steam before breakfast. She got out of bed and lit a lamp in the kitchen and then fired the stove, heating a kettle for coffee. The yard began to take on the color of a tarnished nickel, and she walked to the screen door to check for a hint of what the weather might be, reaching for the latch, mildly surprised when she found it already undone. She stepped onto the back landing and looked suspiciously at a cottony striation of mist lying like a doily over the wet yard. Turning around, her sharp eye noted that the screen had been carefully cut alongside the latch and then pushed back into shape. Only a bright scratch where the blade had pushed through had caught her attention. She stood in the kitchen and narrowed her eyes, thinking and looking.

Randolph was dreaming that he was playing piano, a ragtime number on the ornate upright at home. He was running arpeggios and trills with no trouble, bouncing the left hand off the right, playing for his own amazement, exhilarated and about to open his mouth to sing when suddenly he felt hands on his shoulders shaking him out of rhythm, the notes falling apart under his fingers, replaced by his wife's muted, splintered voice. He woke and turned his head off the edge of the bed; she was standing back, her hands clapped to her temples, her eyes alight with fear.

"What?" He blinked like a swimmer coming back up into harsh sunlight.

"Walter." The word trembled into the air.

He rolled out and lumbered toward the rear of the house and into the boy's room, looked into the baby bed, and found nothing out of the ordinary, though he was still blurry-eyed and tangled up in his dream. The child was asleep on his back among three wooden blocks, a dark cloth wiener dog Ella had sewn for him, and his green blanket. Randolph started to rub his face, and when he raised his hand something dull moved in the bed, and at that instant he saw the fractured amber of the slotted eye and stepped back. All his senses were shocked awake, and he could hear Lillian breathing in the door frame behind him. "Do you want my pistol?" she whispered.

The spade head was over Walter's foot, its fiery vein of tongue tasting the air. Randolph shook his head slowly. The vast inventory of employees began to reel through his mind and he hoped somewhere would be a name he could summon to reach into the crib and pluck the snake, which was pooling now under his eyes, responding to the boy's motion as he drew the back of a hand across his nose. He recalled grown men puffed out with poison and knocked down for weeks by the venom, the one little bucker who died last year, at least three loggers who had gone out of their heads. Randolph opened his hand and guessed how to grab the snake, and when he extended his arm slowly he heard his wife walk to the front of the house and open the door. Her bare feet slapped the ground as she ran off toward Byron's, he guessed. Walter formed a half syllable, yawned widely; the snake picked up its head and cocked its neck like a question mark. Randolph guessed his thumb and forefinger should noose the head and clasp the jaws shut. It was all a matter of math, of quickness, of figuring what to do, how to master the logic of it, and as his hand pulsed with blood and quickness, he knew he could do it—but in that instant of knowing, the baby kicked, there was a flash of white mouth, and Randolph was electrified by the sight of the reptile pinned to the small foot and by the cry that came at once. His hand shot down on the scaly muscle and it opened to bite him, but he pulled it by the tail high above the bed. Not a large snake, two feet long at most, it was an angry one, and he slung it to the floor where it writhed after his bare feet as he danced backwards into the kitchen. It was then that Byron charged into the room and with the heel of his boot made a red smear of the snake's head.

Randolph seized his arm, stepping over the sidewinding body. "Walt's been bitten." His brother picked up the squalling child and looked at the marks on his heel, putting him down at once and pulling his old pocketknife, opening the little blade, the one he kept like a razor. Randolph remembered the knife, how it had cut twine for their kites when they were children. His brother bolted into the kitchen, cut the cord from the blinds, flipped open a stove lid with the key, and held the blade in a yellow flame. Running to the crib, he tied off Walter's leg below the knee and then bore down with the knife. The child shrieked as Byron incised two X's across each fang hole and then sucked the wound, spitting onto the floor, sucking again as if to drain the leg dry, the child looking up at him, the nightmare, the loving man giving pain, and Byron closed his eyes to shut out that look.

Finally, he asked for whiskey, and to his brother's surprise he didn't pour it on the wound but took a big mouthful and bolted for the back door, where he spat it on the planks like an atomizer.

The doctor, hatless and wearing unlaced brogans splattering water, burst into the room and bent over to peer at Walter's foot, which was already swelling and turning inward. "It been sucked?"

"Yes."

"Your brother did it?" When Randolph nodded, the doctor went through the kitchen to the back porch, where he found Byron gargling and spitting. "You swallow any? You have any sores in your mouth?"

"No more than a match head went down."

"You drain that whole bottle and then stick your finger down your throat," the doctor told him. "You've got to throw breakfast."

The old man came back inside and told Lillian to hold Walter in her lap and keep the foot low. He knelt down, applied salve to the wounds and then squeezed on two red rubber suction cups, wincing at the boy's screams. "We've got to get after that damn poison for thirty minutes, at least. Sometimes that stuff stays up in you like glue." He loosened the tourniquet for a moment, then twisted it tight. Taking the foot and turning it toward the hanging light, he watched a deepening lavender rise from the marks. No one said anything as the rhythm of the baby's crying changed, propelled by shallow breaths. "Ah, Lordy," the doctor said.

"What is it?" Randolph leaned over his shoulder.

"Nothing." He looked down at the snake, its head pasted to a floorboard. "A damned cottonmouth."

From out in the yard came the sound of Byron's retching.

. . .

By noon the baby was pale, one leg twice the size of the other. Byron, weak and nauseated, was sprawled on a sofa in Lillian's sitting room at the front of the house. When Jules came by for instructions, Randolph pushed him out onto the front porch, his hand clamping his arm. "I don't care how the six-by-sixes get shipped today, do you understand me? You can shoot them out of a canon. Just ship them, but first I want you to find out if a stranger's been in camp before daybreak."

Jules looked away. "You think that snake was put where it was?"

"Yes."

"Well, it's a sorry business, but I heard it's been done before." He looked at the mill manager carefully. "You better have Lillian make you some coffee."

That night the child's heartbeat was fast and weak, like a roof leak tapping a pan, the doctor said, and Mrs. Scott, the housekeeper, who normally banged about the kitchen, floated quietly through the house, bringing drink and food to those waiting for Walter to recover. Her quietness frightened Randolph, who was sitting on the porch praying, so scared he couldn't think of revenge, feel anger, or think of anything but how, if the boy died, it would leave a hole in everything forever. He imagined the child as a fine, educated grown man and understood that someone was trying to take all of that from them. At dawn, Byron came through the screen and found his brother asleep on the porch in a rush rocker, the hair on his arms silvered with dew. He sat down next to him and tapped his shoulder. Randolph slowly opened his eyes. "How's Walt?"

"Look what a little nip of venom did to me." He held up a shaking arm. "I'm amazed he's still alive."

"You coming around?"

Byron's face showed several layers of sickness. "If I'd felt good enough last night, I would've gone into town and had some spaghetti."

"You'd have been tried and hung, too."

"I know it."

Randolph sensed that his brother was ready to burn out, like a dying star. A soft rain began to drift over the compound, and the smoke from the boiler-house stacks fell straight down and littered the mill yard. "We just have to figure what to do. I don't want to wake up to any more surprises." Across the yard, the main whistle blew a giant C chord out to the ends of the parish; the sound washed their minds clean, letting them think.

After ten minutes or so, it was Byron who said, "I don't know."

"It's easy to kill someone if you don't have any choice." This sounded like the false cheer of a sickly man.

"It's never easy," Byron said. "But when you're ordered to, taught it's right, at least you don't have to think while you're doing it."

"It's rough to sit on a porch and talk about this." Randolph stood and walked inside.

The old housekeeper looked up at him, her face a moon over the baby where it slept, and she raised her hand from its forehead. "I got some water in the little thing," she said, "and he finally held that down, at least." She looked away just to the right of Randolph's face. "But he won't open his eyes yet. Sure, you think he's got the headache that bad? My old man was laid low by a cottonmouth and he said his head was comin' off his shoulders for three days."

"He feels about as bad," Randolph said, "as you can feel."

She folded her hands in her apron, and he appreciated the motion. "It's a sin and a shame," she told him.

"Yes, that it is."

CHAPTER NINETEEN

Father Schultz was walking in the garden next to the statue of the Sacred Heart of Jesus, reading his breviary. Inside the brick church, the women of the Ladies' Altar Society performed their weekly cleaning of the rooms behind the altar, ordering the vestments, inventorying the Communion wine and hosts, gossiping among the holy objects. The priest's main failing was deliberate eavesdropping; he thought gossip the most interesting noise the soul made, not for any truth it contained, but for what it said about the speaker's character. The day was warm and the stained-glass windows were swung open on their pivot hinges, the bottom canted out, the top in. As Father Schultz made his first pass, the Frenchwomen, Mrs. LeBlanc and Mrs. Dorgenois, were folding altar cloths and talking about Mr. Olson down at the fish dock and how ugly he was acting toward his mother. Fifteen minutes later, two of the Sicilian women came out and sat on the steps with cans of brass polish and four candleholders, beginning an animated discussion of a neighbor's illness. They stopped speaking when the priest walked near, and he nodded and loafed past, his head down to his book, silent in his thin black shoes. Around the corner of the church he went with his rolling gait, disappearing behind a tall ligustrum. The women began speaking again—in English, because one of them was young—and it was this young one whose brother was going to pay her back the twenty-five dollars he'd borrowed.

"And how is he going to raise this money?" the older one asked.

"Ah, Buzetti, he's giving him some work on Sunday morning," she said. "He's gonna be unloading boxes from a boat to a train at the shingle factory."

"These boxes, I wonder what they got inside them," the old woman teased.

"What do you think? It's Buzetti, after all. Do you think it's books?" Here the women laughed, their hands flying along the brightening brass. They said other things, and the priest, who was on the other side of the ligustrum, was ashamed for listening but determined to turn a shameful act to the good. When he came around the hedge, the women fell silent again, and he smiled at them.

Merville labored over his report of Ada Bergeron's death, at the same time worrying about something he couldn't put his finger on. He laid down his pencil and looked up to a furry web fringing the hole where the phone wires entered his office. Deep in the hole, a black spider the size of a silver dollar waited like bad luck. He wondered where the girl was at the moment, if something bad was happening to her because of the things she'd done when she was alive. If she was in a place of torment, Buzetti helped put her there. The lawman was not given to thinking much about an afterlife, but the idea was somewhere in the back of his head, just as he suspected it was in everyone's. There was so much punishment in life, the notion it might continue in the next life had to be taken seriously. Merville again remembered Ada, an honest-looking little girl, hefty and tanned from play, and the memory made him walk to the window to look up at the clouds and wonder if there might be something beyond them, but when he lifted the shade he saw only the big priest slowly walking by, his hand already extended for the door.

"What you know?" Merville said.

Father Schultz sat down next to the marshal's desk and drew two bottles of homemade beer out of a paper sack. "Everything and nothing."

Merville sat down, opened a bottle, and took a swallow. "You not getting better at making this."

"The more I drink it, the better it gets."

"Getting used to bad stuff."

"Something like, *ja*."

The marshal rubbed his fingers to draw blood into them, and then opened a narrow drawer in his desk. When he drew out a deck of cards, the priest shook his head. "What?"

"I have something to tell you." Father Schultz looked at the floor. "And it will probably cause harm."

Merville slid the swollen cards out of their pack and began to deal solitaire. "You think it's gonna cause less than it'll cure?"

"I hope."

When he finished dealing, he looked up. "Say it if you want to."

The priest took another swallow and made a face at the truth. "Buzetti is loading three freight-car loads of whiskey at Cypress Bend switch day after tomorrow, in the morning."

The marshal turned over a ten, played it on a jack. "Loading from what? They ain't nothing there but a open shed. The shingle mill burnt down a long time ago." When the priest shrugged and took another swallow, Merville stood up and put his hand on the phone crank, thought better of it, and walked over to a map of the parish tacked to his wall behind the stove. He leaned close to the yellowed paper and ran a thick fingernail along a black line. "Green Bayou's at the end of that switch," he said to the map. "I forgot they used to take shingles out by barge, too." He looked over and saw that the priest's face was longer than usual, as though weighed down by the news he'd brought. "Three boxcars. Damn." He reached for the beer and drained half of it. "Take your time here, you. I got to go for a little walk."

The priest raised a hand as if in absolution, then let it fall on his bottle. "When are you planning to come to church to be with God?"

Merville checked the shells in his revolver, plucked out three empties, and rummaged in a cigar box on the desk. "How you know God's not in this office?"

"Maybe you had him in jail once?"

The marshal put on his stained hat and went out in the sun, which felt like steam on his shoulders. The motorcar started for once, and he ran it south through the railroad underpass toward something he thought he remembered, a swatch of red wood with railroad symbols painted in blistered paint. On the third street from the main line, backed up to the levee, sat a swayback warehouse covered in green tarpaper, top and sides, a spur track alongside. Set out at the back of the lot were three wooden boxcars, weeds lacing up around their rust-freckled wheels. Merville pursed his lips and rode down Poisson Street until he spotted a tank car next to the seafood-packing plant, then turned around and drove the clattering Ford to the station.

Laney was on shift, and when Merville came through the door the agent shifted his tobacco and spat into a box of sawdust. "Yeah?"

"They's a tank car blocking the road a little bit."

Laney looked out the window. "On Bayer Street, with Santa Fe markings?"

"That's the one. Who's leasing it?"

"It's sitting at the damn fish plant, who you think's leasing it?"

The marshal put his hands on the agent's counter, one atop the other. "If I write them up, I got to make sure. If the car's in somebody else's name, I can't get no order to move it."

Laney closed the ledger on his desk, stood up, and jerked another off the shelf. "Here." He came back to the counter and turned the book around. "Oscar Molaison's got it. I told them to pull the son of a bitch into their lot with their truck. Their siding's so bad the switch engine can't go no closer."

Merville opened the book and peered inside. "Caffery

Mill's leased fifteen flatcars?" And while Laney cursed and explained the rotten situation at Caffery Mill, the marshal turned the page and scanned the names of lessors, spotting three Southern Pacific boxcars on open lease to J. Buzetti. An open lease meant Buzetti could've been using them for months, right under everyone's nose. He turned the ledger around and walked out while the agent continued to complain. Merville crossed the street toward his car and climbed out of the mud, kicking clods off his brogans on the edge of the banquette planks, then stepped under the drugstore awning and looked down the tracks. Day after tomorrow morning would be Sunday. He closed his eyes and inventoried train movement. Three passenger runs in each direction, the first coming in at ten-fifteen from New Orleans. No mixed or local passenger trains on Sunday, but four scheduled through-freights each way, running between noon and midnight. The only local freight was Thirty-Six, a peddler train picking up Saturday production from the mills to be taken along by a New Orleans—bound express Monday morning. Thirty-Six gathered stray cars all the way out to Rick, which was only five miles from Cypress Bend. It would be nothing for the switching crew to make an unscheduled jog out the main line to the Cypress Bend spur with Buzetti's boxcars, where they could be filled with whiskey brought up Green Bayou by luggers or a small barge.

Thirty-Six had the same crew every Sunday, he remembered. George Robinson, a gambling wife-beater he'd arrested more than once, was the engineer. Andy Ledge, the fireman, was as dumb as a box of nails and thought Robinson was the greatest man who'd ever lived. The switchman and conductor, Aldus and Mumphrey LeBlanc, were cousins who dressed like twins, and Merville had known them their entire lives. He couldn't imagine them taking money for unscheduled railroading, but they were meek and could be easily threatened by the red-faced Robinson. He guessed they'd be left in the caboose at Rick, doing their paperwork, while the loading was going on down the line.

The marshal drove back to his office and found that the priest had not waited. In the middle of his scarred desk Father Schultz had left behind a holy card of Saint Stephen, Martyr. He picked it up and studied the tortured expression on the saint's face. "What you whinin' about," he told the card. "What you expect?"

The feelings in the bedroom were as brittle as dry rot. The boy had stopped breathing again, this time for fifteen seconds, and Byron reached into the crib and shook him. Walter made a noise like a bird, took a long draught of air, held it, then let it loose slowly. Randolph's head fell when he heard the breath come out with a soft finality of spirit, but then his brother lowered his face over the crib and said, "He took another one." And the boy had. When he let that one out, he took another, and the brothers watched and counted as though each breath were a lifetime and worth as much as all they had lived. They were as frightened as they'd ever been. The doctor had iced the foot and applied salt meat to the wound to draw the poison. All they could do was wait, he'd told them, and depend on the strength of the child's heart.

Lillian washed Walter's face every half hour and tried to get him to take water. Now and then he would swallow a spoonful, but then gag and throw it up on his pillow, arching his back like a dying animal in a spasm. Once, she'd asked through her tears, "Who could do this to a baby? What kind of soul would you have to have?"

Byron folded his hands where he sat by the bed and put his darkened face on the spire of his fingers. "I know," he said softly. "I've seen them."

She squeezed her hands together hard. "Where have you seen such people? In the war?"

Byron slipped a finger into Walter's hand, and the unconscious child sensed it and closed on it. "I've seen them in the hardware store," he said. "I've seen them standing on the steps of a church."

She bit a thumb and leaned against the bare wall, then put

down her hand. "I wish you'd never shot that man." She was not looking at her husband when she said it, but she didn't have to. He stood up and left the room.

Byron wiggled the boy's fingers. "He didn't start it."

She narrowed her eyes at the door. "He seems sorry to have killed him, but not all that sorry."

"I guess he's just glad to be alive," the constable said dully. "That's a good thing, to be glad to be alive."

The hands on the cheap Waterbury mantel clock, which had been May's, dragged as if moving through glue. But that evening, when the temperature of the room dropped below ninety, the boy's breathing evened out and the doctor shook his head. "Look at him. He's trying to come back." He palpated the swollen leg, which was hot to the touch, then changed the bandage and applied fresh salt meat. Lillian gave the boy a bottle with water in it, and for the first time he sucked.

Randolph and Byron went out on the porch into the dusk, where ash from the furnaces floated like mosquitoes. The mill manager expected to begin to feel relief, but as his fright left him, it was replaced with anger. "By, do you feel thankful?"

"Yes." He looked across the compound toward his house, where a light came on in the front room. "Thankful as a gun barrel."

"If he was going to send someone, why not a cutthroat? Someone who'd just be done with it?" Randolph slapped the porch support. "A snake, for God's sake."

"It's to make us suffer. Nothing pays like suffering."

"I don't understand."

"Neither do I," Byron said, his face half in shadow. "But can't you feel it working?"

The marshal did not leave town through the Tiger Island station but walked over the wharf and caught the paddle-wheel ferry, riding out of sight in the steamy engine room where he visited the engineer, a middle-aged man he'd saved from drowning years before. On the other side of the broad river he

made his way to the tiny station at Beewick and told the operator to flag the westbound local as it trundled across the bridge.
In forty minutes he was at the parish seat in Moreau, again
struggling through the heat, this time to the sheriff's office.

Octave LaBat was wearing a white starched shirt rolled up
above his elbows. He pushed his cast-iron mustache out of his
mouth with two swipes of a forefinger, and didn't offer a chair
to Merville, who was sweating and leaning against the door
frame, holding his stained straw hat in his hand.

"Can I close the door?" Merville looked behind him to
where a surly deputy in a wrinkled uniform was sharpening a
box of pencils, turning the crank of the sharpener slowly.
After every few turns, he pulled out the pencil to inspect his
progress.

"Hell, no," LaBat said. "It's too damned hot."

"It's kind of confidential, you know?"

"I got no secrets."

"Alors, allons parler français."

The sheriff looked offended. "I got no use for that talk anymore. Tell me in English."

Merville put his hat on his head, kicked the door shut, and
sat down. "We got to talk about Buzetti."

LaBat sat up and looked at his door, then back at Merville's expression. "So talk."

The marshal knew that LaBat treated everyone like insects
flying in his vision. "Look, I worked under you, I worked for
the worm that was here before you, and I worked for Dorsieu
in the old days, and I don't enjoy being treated like a dog
turd."

LaBat pointed. "I let you close the damn door."

"I know you don't talk to nobody unless they bring you
something. So I brought something that's gonna make you
look good. Even in New Orleans."

The sheriff swiveled his chair sideways. He lowered his
voice. "You said you wanted to talk about Buzetti."

Merville crossed his corky legs at the ankles and told the
sheriff about the whiskey pickup at Cypress Bend. "It's enough

to get them federal boys involved. You set an ambush and round 'em up, then the big courts take over and you don't even have to jail them here. You'd be famous, yeah."

LaBat looked up at the tall ceiling and shook his head, then leaned forward out of his chair and stood up. He was all gut, a washpot on stilts, and his pleated pants hung like a skirt. He walked close to Merville's chair. "I can't hardly enjoy being famous if I'm worried about some honky-tonk dago burning my house down, or siccing a ghoul on one of my daughters."

"*Mais*, get your deputies out there the night before. By the time them bootleggers show up, they won't know what hit 'em."

The sheriff thought a moment and sniffed at his mustache. "He hires these war veterans. They already killed more people than anybody can count. What you think they'll do to my cane field deputies if the shooting starts?"

"You got to get the jump on him."

LaBat spread his hands apart, as if showing the size of a fish. "Merville, all he does is sell booze and a few pieces of ass."

In the marshal's mind a picture formed of the extra mouth sliced into Ada Bergeron's neck, and he jerked his head to the side. He thought of how easy it would be to go home, lie in the bed, and the next morning get up, go to Breaux's Café for a big breakfast, and sit around afterward, picking his dentures. He could get round and lazy, like his sheriff. He could stop playing cards with a solicitous priest and try to win money at Buzetti's back-room games. Suddenly, he said, "He's giving them Aldridges hell out at Nimbus."

LaBat walked back to his chair. "You want me to get the same kind of hell? For Yankees who gonna take their money and blow out of here in a few years? Let me tell you, that Buzetti is one mean son of a bitch. And the people he knows in Chicago will come down here and play marbles with your eyeballs."

Merville picked up his head and resettled his hat, as though he'd made a decision. "Okay. Then commission me for the parish."

The sheriff laughed. "Old man, you—"

"I want a parish star." He pointed at the desk. "Write me up some authority to make arrests at Cypress Bend. And I want ten other stars so I can deputize people myself."

LaBat looked out his window at the traffic in the dusty street. His voice gentled. "Don't be a fool," he said softly. "They probably know where you are right now."

"No they don't. I made sure of that."

LaBat seemed not to hear. "They probably know what time you walk out of your office down on River Street every day. I'm telling you, you mess with them, they'll break your legs and leave you in a ditch somewhere." He looked at Merville over his shoulder. "If you lucky."

"Then that's my business."

"But I ain't letting you go out and get a bunch of people hurt just because you got the big head in your old age and want to be some kind of son-of-a-bitching hero."

"You don't deputize me, I'll get on the train and go down to New Orleans. I'll tell the people at the *Picayune* how much you like whorehouses and slot machines."

LaBat turned from the window. "They won't listen. You're a little Cajun. What did they used to call your type, *petites habitants*?"

"At least I'm not lint in Buzetti's pocket."

The sheriff's eyes flashed wide, and he stared at Merville hard, as if trying to read his face for the first time in his life.

"Times are changing," the old marshal told him, wagging a crooked finger. "I can pick up a telephone and let people know what you doin'. Things ain't all hid away no more. Maybe Buzetti *is* watching me, but somebody else sure as hell can watch *you*."

"You can climb on a stool and kiss my ass."

"Deputize me and write it up."

LaBat jerked one of the desk drawers open so hard that his lamp nearly tipped over. Merville tensed in the chair, wondering if he was about to pull out an enormous pistol. Instead, he picked up and threw a small canvas bag that rattled against the marshal's chest as he caught it. It was a sack of nickel-plated badges. "Pin those on somebody you can live without."

"I want the authority wrote down."

The sheriff raised an eyebrow. "I'll have Jeansomme type it up for you."

"No, you write it. And don't tell nobody."

LaBat scowled and pulled out a pad. "You don't trust my deputies?"

Merville stood up and began stuffing the cheap stars into his coat pockets. "If you do, that's your business."

The sheriff adjusted a pair of gold-rimmed glasses, bent over, and began writing slowly, a forearm holding the top of the paper. "This is a bad idea."

The marshal reached out for the document. *"C'est pas que mauvais que des autres, non."*

CHAPTER TWENTY

On Saturday morning Randolph watched the boy open his eyes, and in them he saw something wronged. The swelling was down, but the child was crying and pulling at his heel, and always in his gaze was the big question.

Standing in Byron's side yard, he listened to the soaring sound of the Victrola playing a song he had not heard, something slow and raspy.

> *She's taken the steamboat to Memphis,*
> *Leaving me and our two little girls.*
> *She told us that she couldn't take this,*
> *And left us alone in the world.*
> *She pinned on her hat at the door*
> *And told us we'd see her no more*
> *So we've blown out the light, put an end to our night . . .*

The locomotive's whistle roared out a crossing signal, and the rest of the song was lost. Again, Randolph mulled over why his brother listened to such music in the first place. If a man felt strong and comfortable in his life, he might find a little manufactured sadness to be a change of pace. But for someone steeped in profound melancholy to seek out such misery was beyond his understanding.

He went in and found his brother sitting in the Morris chair, one hand gripping the mildewed wood as the Victrola ground out another dollar ballad, the other holding a whiskey glass raised in greeting.

"That breakfast?"

Byron studied his glass the way a chemist might. "Isn't it funny, Rando, that I'm the one hired to arrest the folks who drink too much of this stuff?" He threw back his head and guffawed. "To bring sanity to the great city-state of Nimbus, Louisiana. A pillar of moderation, I am—and a bulwark against vengeance."

Randolph put a hand on his brother's forearm. "I will never understand how Buzetti could hire someone—"

"And I will never understand why I was given carte blanche by the United States government to put thirty-caliber slugs into patriotic German kids, when the law, or guilt, or fate won't let me hunt down and send to hell a one-eyed snake-wielding baby-killer."

Randolph drew back and shuddered, suddenly aware of hell as a real possibility, for he had finally been touched by someone who might be deserving of it. "We have no witnesses and don't know for sure who did it."

Byron raised his glass again. "There you're wrong. The agent just sent down a boy with a note. That Cyclops bastard was spotted in Tiger Island again." He got up and wound the instrument, sleeved a record, and drew another from the cabinet below the turntable. "I just wish he'd come into my little kingdom one more time."

The song began with the tinkle of a mandolin and a man singing through the roof of his mouth about a golden-haired girl riding the train to get a pardon for her father, who'd gone blind in prison. She'd lost her fare, but the conductor started to weep and said she could ride his car anytime for free. In spite of the fact that he'd never known a soft-hearted railroad conductor in his life, Randolph was touched by the song, and then ashamed of himself, for the lyrics made him happy not to be a blind prisoner or penniless child.

"By, if this music makes you sad, why do you listen to it?"

"Maybe I'm waiting for the words to change."

"What?"

"I might be listening one day and the song will change for the better. The little golden-haired girl's father will regain his sight. Maybe he'll never have done something to get put in prison to begin with."

Randolph frowned. "That doesn't make sense."

"That's true," his brother said sadly, "the record can't change. Just like me or you. We're stamped to play out our song, and that's it." Off in the woods, the skidder whistle shrieked like a woman stepping on a rat, and Byron put his head down. "I know the songs are sappy lies, Rando. I guess I listen to them for the same reason a doctor gives you a little poison to make you well. You know—mercury for syphilis, that sort of thing." He lifted his eyes and looked toward the Victrola. "But it's still poison. Like those patriotic songs about war being sweet and glorious. Listening to those got many a volunteer killed, I'll tell you. All that sentimentality, it just leads to oblivion." He placed his empty glass on the floor.

The sound of footsteps on the porch drew their attention to the screen, where a black child stood hooding his face with his hands, looking in. His feet were gray with dust and his short overalls were held up by one strap. "Mr. Julius say you gots a phone call."

Randolph stood. "Someone's waiting on the line?"

"He say to tell you it the direct line. To the outside." The boy waved his arm in an arc, to indicate the outside, the world, and the motion conveyed how trapped they all were, how separated from everything by mud and trees.

In the office he found the receiver lying on his desk. "Hello?" he yelled. Below him the band saw was cutting twelve-by-twelves.

"Mr. Aldridge? This is Merville."

Randolph was annoyed that he'd had to trek across the mill yard, but the old lawman's voice made him forget that he was sweating. "What can I do for you, Marshal?" He listened a long time without speaking, without feeling the floor vibrate, without hearing the safety valve roar its daily test. After a while he said only, "Yes, of course," followed by, "Come on the train. It's safer than the road." He hung up, fought the door, which had swollen into its frame, and bounced down the steps, heading home to look in on the child. When he came into the room, his wife stood up and gave him a kiss in front of the doctor.

"The swelling's way down," she said. "He actually sat up for a moment or two." He looked at her kinked hair, smelled her blouse in which the starch had soured, and thought he had never admired her more. He walked over to the bed, where Byron's wife was changing the pillowcase, said the child's name, and Walter looked up, blinking and exhausted.

"He's worn out, the little bugger." He took off his fedora and ran his finger round the sweatband, looking down at the child.

Ella watched him replace the hat. "Going out again?"

"Back to Byron's. We have some preparations to make."

"I'll walk over with you," she said.

He put his arms around his wife. "I know," Lillian said. "It's a relief."

"Have you moved that accordion?"

She gave him a look. "It's behind our bed. Why?"

He found it and removed it from its case. It banged against his calf as he and Ella walked over, and on Byron's porch he put his arms through the straps and walked in. His brother looked up, expressionless with drink.

"Oh," Ella said, reaching for his shoulder.

Randolph caught her eye. "Can you make us some coffee?" He set the instrument's stops.

"Sure. Say, can you really play that thing?" She smiled at the accordion, and Randolph struck a pose.

"We'll see." He started into "My Bonnie Lies Over the Ocean," missing a few notes. The reeds, like everything in camp, had begun to corrode, and dead bugs were caught under the reed flaps, but the instrument just sounded silly and jolly as it exhaled its mildewed breath into his face. "This is some real music," he called over the notes. Taking a few steps forward, he stood in front of the Victrola, facing his brother, and squeezed harder, until Byron cautiously began patting his foot. He played "Moonlight Bay" all the way through, ending with a wheezy arpeggio that made Byron laugh, and when he began playing "My Indiana Home" both men started to sing; it was a song their mother had bribed them to learn as children. Ella brought in a pot of coffee and ironware mugs, sugar and fresh cream, and they sat and drank in the heat, and Byron—coming around from wherever he'd been—told Ella a story about their Polish music teacher, an earnest gentleman who drove to their father's house in a lopsided buggy and taught them to count time by tapping on the backs of their hands with a pair of chopsticks while they played piano. Randolph stood and tried a polka, playing too slowly, with the left hand a flash behind the right, but it was still good enough, he told them, for a sawmill.

After an hour and two pots of coffee, he pulled out of the accordion's straps and bent over to take his brother's face in his hands for a second, then told him about Merville's phone call.

By two o'clock that afternoon, they had made their plans. The mill manager had drawn a map at his brother's desk, a series of pencil strikes that showed where the Cypress Bend switch left the main line, three miles west of Poachum. Merville would show up with his authority and deputize enough men to carry out the arrests.

Byron examined a railroad timetable and noted that since there were no trains scheduled through Poachum until 9:30, they could take the mill locomotive out on the main line, stop before the curve at Cypress Bend switch, and hike down to get into position before daylight. He stared at the map, trying to focus, rubbing his eyes, then drawing his palms down the stubble on his face. "I don't know. I remember good cover in there, but it's a risk."

Randolph rocked on his heels. "It might work just like the

ambush I set up at Poachum station. You can hand out those cannons you bought in Shirmer to the deputies. Buzetti's men will see the guns and back down. Then we tell them they're under arrest."

Byron stared at the map and pinched his bottom lip with his fingers. "Maybe."

Randolph ran a hand over his hair. "Well, what do you think will happen?" He tried not to imagine the event itself.

"The town boys'll probably run like hell. And Buzetti, once he figures the odds, might decide to let his lawyer do the fighting."

Randolph placed a finger on the map. "And if not?"

"If we do it right," Byron said, "they won't fight a big group. They're not crazy, and they won't be expecting us. They'll be there to load liquor, not to fight deputies."

Randolph began rubbing his hands together. "The little details, you've got to set them up. You and the old marshal." He wanted to think that the arrest was not in revenge for Walter, but it was difficult not to wish that the one-eyed man would be there and would draw a pistol on a sawyer standing over him with a semiautomatic rifle. "I just don't want anybody to get hurt," he said quickly.

Byron looked at his brother. "Did Merville say that one-eyed bastard was along on this one? What's his name, Crouch?"

"The marshal told me everyone was called in. There's something like a thousand cases to be loaded."

Byron walked over to the Victrola and lifted a round tray of discarded needles out of the cabinet. "The kid station agent told me he'd testify that old one-eye walked by the station a few hours before Walter was bitten."

"Did he see him walk the track toward the mill?"

Byron shook his head. "Nope. Saw him carrying a sack, though. Got out of a car with it, walked in front of the head-lights, and the car left."

"A sack? What kind of sack?"

"Burlap," Byron told him, pouring a waterfall of needles

into a wastebasket by the door. "And something in it was moving."

At five o'clock they were waiting at the yellow station in Poachum. The mill manager looked beyond the steep iron roof of a trapper's house into a soaring cypress forest, not his tract, and passed the time by estimating board feet.

Byron followed his gaze. "You want every tree that walks?"

"That's a lot of money standing there."

"A forest is good for more things than shutters and weather-board."

The mill manager regarded him blankly. "Like what?"

"Why, just to look at, maybe."

Randolph turned back to the trees and frowned. "Look at them for what?"

But before Byron could say anything, a locomotive whistle shrieked in the west, and their heads turned down the tracks.

Merville sidestepped down from the wooden coach and shuffled across the platform to meet them, his skin dusty pale. He rolled his shoulders inside his wilted coat and glanced at the waiting room. "Let's step away over there by your engine. I don't want no kind of son of a bitch seein' me here." They walked along the platform and down the steps onto the spur track toward Nimbus. Out of his rumpled jacket he took the high sheriff's document and one of the stars.

Byron nodded. "You've got the authority, sure enough."

They had trouble getting Merville up the steps into the cab of the engine, and Randolph wished he had dragged the crew car along.

Byron looked worried. "You're stiffening up on us."

Merville touched his throat at his open collar. "I feel like chewed tobacco. I'll be glad when we get through with this, yeah."

When the mill manager released the brakes and cracked the throttle, the engine sneezed and drifted backwards toward Nimbus through a tunnel of weeds and willow saplings exploding out of the clear-cut lowland. "I hope your sheriff can hold onto them longer than that other fellow we let him have."

Merville stepped out of the way as Byron threw a slab into the firebox. "You know, since the lines been going all over, I been using that telephone more and more. I got a direct call into New Orleans right to the office of the federal prosecutor, yeah. I didn't know you could do that. Nowadays it's like you think of a man, maybe somebody you ain't seen in ten years, and you just ring him up. The wire finds him." He looked out as the engine backed through a dark grove of cypress. Next to the roadbed, blue herons were stabbing crawfish, ignoring the progress of the locomotive. "Everything's tied to that wire."

Byron threw in more wood and then took off his gloves, tossing them in the boilerhead tray. "And what did this federal man say?"

"He said if we live to do it, we can bring whoever we arrest straight to New Orleans and put 'em in his custody in parish prison. When we round up those boys tomorrow we'll take 'em out on the eastbound. LaBat can kiss *my* ass." He began to cough and settled back in the fireman's seatbox. "That telephone," he said after a while. "I didn't have to get on a train to go see nobody. Just crank the phone and tell the operator to find whatever fool I want."

Randolph looked out the cab window at the single new line running along the tracks on peeled poles. The man who put in the wire had told him that in five years nearly everyone in the country would have a telephone, and he thought about what that might mean. Anyone who witnesses wrongdoing could call for a policeman or a newspaperman. People would know everything, because the phones weren't just ears and voices but eyes as well. He looked again at the copper wire. Like a vein, it would soon run head to foot through the body of the world.

Later in the mill office, Byron decided to use no more than ten men. Jules sat on his desk and listened to the plan, his big cowboy hat cocked to one side on his head. "I don't know," he said. "I done left Texas to get away from the shooting kind of folks. I won't do my wife no good all crippled up with pistol slugs." He kept his eyes low as he spoke, and it was clear to Randolph that he was an employee, not someone bound to this problem by money and blood. An employee didn't take chances for the company after the knock-off whistle blew. The mill manager said nothing and stared at the floor, surprised for a moment, but then realizing that neither the yard foreman nor chief millwright nor saw boss would allow himself to be deputized. Those of higher rank had plenty to lose. They went into Tiger Island, and some had local family. But he had to be sure. He told Merville and Byron to come with him, and together they walked down to the railroad engineer's house in the white section of camp. When they stepped up onto his little porch, he came out, pulling his galluses onto his shoulders. He'd finished his shift but hadn't yet cleaned the locomotive's oil and soot off of him. He looked around, blinking at his company.

The mill manager stepped close, shook his hand, and said, "Rafe, we need to deputize you."

The engineer looked back at his wife, who stood behind the screen door as Randolph explained the deputizing process. "They want me to help get that dago what paid to get the log spiked," Rafe told her.

The woman was rubbing flour off her hands with her apron. "Is there gonna be guns?"

"Yes," the mill manager told her.

"If he gets kilt, you going to feed me and our babies for the rest of our lives? He goes to town and gets stuck, you going to sew up the hole and keep sending his pay till he mends?" Her voice was an experienced weapon, and the engineer turned toward the men on his porch to view its effect.

Randolph stepped back. "I don't want to put any burden on you, Rafe. Just give me an answer and we'll move on."

The engineer motioned with his chin. "Aw, if they was coming in the mill yard up to some mischief, I'd be with you. But this liquor stuff ain't really the mill's business, is it?"

Randolph heard Merville and Byron step off the porch

behind him. He tipped his hat to Rafe's wife and followed them out into the rutted street.

"I'll run y'all down there with the engine," Rafe called. "But I ain't packing no gun."

Byron pulled off his straw hat, looked up at the sun, and replaced it. "It's not exactly like raising an army, is it? The only people who'll go along are the ones who owe us, and the ones with no families."

"And the crazy ones," Merville said. "You got any crazy ones can shoot straight?" He pointed at the Winchester automatic rifle Byron was holding. "Show them that bear-killer and they'll think it's a party they going to."

A crop-eared yellow dog came up close, and Byron held out his boot for it to sniff. "You can't just ask, for God's sake. We've got to go in and tell them what they've got to do for us."

"You handle the next one, then. Where's Clovis Hutchins, the drunk that promised he'd turn preacher if I kept him on?" He pulled his watch. "He's on the first boiler gang, so he's off now."

They walked over to the barracks where the single men lived, a long, two-story box punctuated at intervals with single-pane windows propped open with ax handles. Turning into the bottom hall they walked through the smells of tobacco, liniment, sweat, and unemptied chamber pots until they found Hutchins washing up in a corner of his little room.

Byron pitched a star to him and Hutchins caught it in his towel. "What you giving me a medal for?"

"It's a badge," he told him. "Be down at the locomotive at four in the morning. Wear that and I'll tell you what to do."

Hutchins looked at the shiny weapon dangling from Byron's right hand. "That's a .401, ain't it?" He dried his hands and took it reverently, working the action, finding the safety and flicking it on and off. "Where you want me to pin this here badge on, Mr. Byron?"

"You can wear it on your drawers for all I care. Just be on time. We're going to arrest some fellows, and that's all you need to know. Don't tell anyone about this."

Hutchins handed back the weapon. "I'll be there, boss. Do like you tell me." He drew a hand across his bald chest, holding the badge by one of its points, positioning it over his right nipple.

Outside, Randolph trod on a mule dropping and stopped to wipe his foot. "So you're right. Now there's four of us."

"Five," Merville said. "Minos will do what I tell him."

"Are you sure of that?"

The marshal gave him a look and the mill manager nodded. "Okay, then. Five," he agreed.

In the saloon, Norbert, the young fireman for the narrow-gauge dummy engine, was getting a drink. A new man in camp, too smart for his job, Byron figured he was safe enough to ask. They pulled him out into the yard and talked to him a long time before he agreed to be deputized, and it cost the mill manager a five-dollar raise. Byron watched the big man pocket his star and walk off toward his shack, then said, "Six."

Merville pulled a handkerchief and wiped his neck. "I got to go sit on your porch awhile. I'm done."

"Go on into the house," Byron told him. "Make yourself at home. Ella can fix you a drink."

Randolph bent and looked. Merville's eyes were staring, red-rimmed. "Rest up, Marshal, and we'll finish this."

Byron touched the old man's shoulder. "Make her play a record for you."

"My dancing days is over," he said, giving them a handful of badges and angling away, carefully sidestepping a rut.

Byron looked after him. "Well, we'll have to drop in on the Negroes." They struck out across the dummy line track and walked through the mill to avoid the log ramp and its avalanche of bark and mud. The gangs of men catching lumber and sorting it glanced at them but didn't stop working, because boards were flying through air filled with blinding, cinnamon-colored cypress dust. Threading through the rack yard, they entered the lower camp where brown ducks and fish snakes navigated standing green pools, and everything smelled of wet, burned wood, chicken dung, and Ivory soap. In the Negro barracks they found Clarence Williams's room bare as a pauper's coffin. The man across the hall raised up from his cot and told them he was on shift. They walked back to the rack yard and found him finger-tossing two-by-fours to a man high up on an air-dry stack, who waited for each board to stall in the air next to him and then closed his hand on it.

Byron raised a finger and both men looked at him. "Take a break," he said to the man on the stack.

Williams was running with sweat and stepped back into the shade cast by the pile of lumber. "Mr. Byron."

"Clarence, we need you to be a deputy for tomorrow, to help us round up some of those Tiger Island bootleggers." Byron held up a badge and put it in Williams's long fingers.

The stacker rolled his eyes up. "You ain't gonna let them use me for no target practice, is you, Mr. Byron?"

"Keep your head down and listen to what I say tomorrow, you won't get hurt. I want you on the train at four o'clock."

Williams looked at the needle on the back of the metal. "I ain't never been on this side of no badge before."

Byron tossed him the Winchester. "I'll give you one like this, loaded up. All you do is flick off the safety and pull the trigger."

"Sure enough? You don't got to work nothing? It just reload itself?"

Byron looked around for the other man. "Your partner, will he shoot or run?"

Williams laughed, showing a mouth full of crooked teeth. "He so cross-eyed, he shoot and the bullet be goin' around the rabbit and back again."

Randolph held up a hand and gave him a serious look. "Can you find us three like yourself we can deputize?"

A bead of sweat ran down Williams's scar as he turned his head toward the barracks. "I can show you three Negro gennelmens won't never have to back up to the pay window."

The last one they visited was Minos. At six o'clock they found him in the boiler house disconnecting an injector from a steam line, his shirt off, thick leather gloves dribbling sweat when he reached up to turn a valve. He waved the men off, unable to talk above the roar of the fireboxes and a steam leak from a faulty valve stem. They backed out of the gangway into the slanting sunshine and waited. A few minutes later, he came out buttoning a wet denim shirt, and Byron told him what his father had planned.

Minos pulled a handkerchief and wiped his face hard. "I talked to Daddy two days ago and he was mad."

"He says you'll go with us."

"Then I guess that's what I'll do."

Randolph clapped him on the shoulder. "You're the last man. We're all set."

"Who's the others?"

The mill manager gave the list. A pipe banged in the boiler room, and Minos looked suspiciously toward the noise. "I don't know if the old man can take it."

"He's got to go. All our authority comes from him."

Minos shook his head and looked at his asbestos-covered boots. "Shit, he's almost seventy-five years old."

CHAPTER TWENTY-ONE

Merville sat in a rocker on Byron's porch and watched the mill yard suddenly fold in half like a newspaper and fall inward on itself, the smokestacks tumbling horizontal, workers and mules walking in and out of a seam in the earth. His ears whistled, his eyes went dead and then came back to life. He saw the mill come to rights, but twisted, as if everything had begun to melt. He felt noise and a little breath at his ear, and his head drifted around to a woman who was saying something kind. Was it his own wife? He opened his mouth, feeling he could never again make words, and was amazed to hear himself ask for aspirin and water.

"Surely," Ella said. Her skirt stirred the air, and at once she was next to him again. After he washed down the pills, he saw her looking at him closely and then felt her hands on him. "You come in where it's a little cooler." The next thing he knew she'd sat him in Byron's chair and turned an electric fan toward him. He shuddered as his eyesight squeezed down again, turning the room warped and jaundiced, as if he were viewing it through a film of varnish. Before him was a mahogany thing he did not recognize, bent and angled like a wooden tabernacle, and the woman said she would play some music for him. Merville blacked out and began to dream about the men on horseback who fired his father's barn because he wouldn't tell them where he'd buried his coins. He watched the deserters hang his brother by one foot from a live oak, claiming they would cut him down when the father relented. Little Etienne was not even crying; he was so thin the rope barely cut his ankles, and he swung patiently like a chicken who didn't understand what was coming. His father told them there were no coins and a deserter drew from his muddy blouse an old single-shot pistol. His father went down on his knees and said if they wanted to hurt him, they should shoot his mule instead. So the deserters, having murdered so many men that they considered the death of a good mule a greater tragedy, did as he asked. Merville decided then that if he lived to be two hundred years old he would never be like these stinking outlaws, would never allow a kinked desire for blood to rise in him the way it did in these robbers' eyes before their weapons bucked and his father's fly-bled mule went down in its patched traces.

Merville's ears vibrated with a sound like the moans of a dying man haunted by nightmare. He opened his right eye to the abrasion of a fiddle and words about lovelight and twilight and silver-haired lovebirds riding the train to dreamland and the kiss of gentle years. At this groaning music, his mind snapped open like a windowshade unblinding a sunrise, and he saw his friend the priest, waiting in the dark confessional for truth from the sweet-faced man who told of his stealing, from the woman who wanted her doctor's hands on her, from the wife who dreamed her husband dead, and then he saw himself kneeling before Father Schultz and felt at once gilded like a morning-bright pane because he could not think of one thing to confess. The image faded as the music rose around him like the whir of a saw, the nasal moaning so cloying and false that the marshal struggled to his feet and stretched out his hands toward the dark wood to put an end to the sung lies of the glossy machine.

Ella found him facedown next to the Victrola holding half of the record in each liver-spotted hand and ran out yelling for Byron and the doctor. A group of men came clomping into the house, one of them Minos, his face sweating and unreadable.

He went to his father and lay a hand on his white hair, then rolled him on his back and shook him as if he were an engine that could be coaxed back to motion. He sat down on the floor and closed Merville's eyes, then changed his mind, pushing them open and looking hard and close. "Well," Minos said, lowering the lids again, "he had a good long run."

The doctor came in and knelt to put two fingers on the marshal's neck. He looked up at Minos.

Ella put a hand over her mouth and started crying. "He was here one minute and gone the next."

"That's how it happens," the doctor said, getting up awkwardly and going back outside.

She leaned against Byron's chest and began to sob. "I was playing a love song for him on the phonograph."

Minos leaned over and read the title off the smashed record. "That would do it," he said.

Randolph and Minos straightened Merville's body and crossed his hands over his chest. The light was failing, and the men gradually spilled out onto the porch, Minos staying inside with the body. No one said anything for several minutes, until Randolph announced bitterly, "It's all off."

Minos came through the screen door, slumped into a rocker, and looked up at him. "What you mean?"

Randolph nodded respectfully toward the front room. "Without your father, we've got no written authority to go after Buzetti."

Byron folded his arms and spat into the yard. "Tomorrow, when they back that switch engine down that track, I'll show them some authority."

His brother shook his head. "It's an arrest we were planning, not a damned ambush."

"I'll arrest him, then."

"You mean you'll arrest his motion with a .401 slug. By, I'm not about to let you throw yourself away over this."

"I'm doing," he shouted, "what we said we'd do."

Randolph pointed through the screen into the house. "You have no jurisdiction anymore."

Byron looked across the yard for a long moment. "If the

old man is our power," he said softly, "we can bring him with us."

"What?" Randolph looked down at Minos, who pulled off his nautical cap and hung it on a knee, squinting at it.

Byron spread his arms. "Just put him on the train and bring him along. Nobody can say exactly when he passed away. We can tell LaBat he died after the arrests were made."

"By, that's crazy."

His brother's eyes turned hard. "Someone shoots May in the brain, then puts a snake in her baby's bed, and *you* call *me* crazy?"

Byron took a step forward, but Minos got up and stood between them. He jerked his head toward the front room. "You know what? He'd like the idea, yeah. Going for the last ride. Sort of like working overtime. He was made for that." He pulled his watch. "We gonna leave in less than ten hours." And with that announcement, all that could have been said about the heat and decay was done away with.

"You want to bring him along?" Randolph was incredulous.

Byron turned around and smacked one fist into another. "We'll lay him on a stretcher in the back of the crew car, with his face uncovered. I'll tell the men he's sick and not to bother him."

Minos nodded. "You'd better. If some of them think he's passed, they won't get on that car."

Randolph peered inside through the screen. "I'm sorry about this."

Minos put his face alongside the mill manager's, looking into the room as well. "All my life I was the horse and he was the spur, and I don't know if that's how it's supposed to be, but it's sure how it was."

Randolph could smell the sweet pipe-joint compound on him, tobacco, sweat, and woodsmoke. He smelled of work. "After it's over," he said, "we can tell people he died on the job."

Minos nodded. "Won't nobody not believe that."

Rafe, the locomotive engineer, got up at two o'clock to raise steam, and by ten to four Randolph could hear the machine's safety valves sizzling. The engine was turned on the wye so it could run backwards, pushing the crew coach out to the main line at Poachum. The stars slid behind a mudflat of clouds, and the mill yard was empty of light. One by one the men assembled, and as the mill manager walked up, he wondered if any of them had been able to sleep at all. After he'd gone home and watched Walt sit up drunkenly and point to his still-swollen foot, he'd tried to keep Buzetti out of his thoughts. The child's pinched face brought out May's features, and again he could see her, the soul of his house. In bed he rolled around like a log, and then, along toward the end of the time he'd allotted for sleep, he'd dropped off briefly, the way an automobile wheel rolls off the edge of a paved road, and he saw the hard, just face of Merville fixed on him, his eyes asking for law.

Clovis Hutchins and Minos loaded the marshal into the crew car on a stretcher. Byron handed out the eight semiautomatic rifles and kept his own Winchester lever action for himself. He gathered the deputies by the engine's headlight and explained precisely what they were going to do, how it would play out so that no one would have to fire a shot. He spoke about the weapons, and the men turned them in their hands, fingering the buttons and triggers. While his brother lectured, Randolph looked across the flat-black yard and thought he saw a blurred, nightgowned figure on his porch, holding on to a post, watching. He wanted nothing more than to go to her, take off his clothes, and try once more right then to make a child. But then the engineer released the air brakes, the coach lurched backwards in a heavy, cloudlike motion, and they all began to pile aboard. Randolph pulled on the grab irons and hoisted himself into the cab as the engine began rocking over the sagging rails.

When the train arrived at Poachum, the fireman jumped down with a spike puller and broke off the lock on the switch stand. He opened the switch, and the train backed out of the spur track and onto the Southern Pacific's high rails. As soon as the fireman swung the switch closed again, the engine began to dodder west as fast as it could go, eighteen miles per hour, its gear shafts and connecting rods winking grease in the afterglow of the headlight. Randolph hung out of the gangway remembering the invisible landscape, the moss-haunted trunks rising from a floating carpet of duckweed, the reptile-laced bog that still raised the hair on his neck if he thought about it too much. He wondered if the many-fanged geography rubbed off on people, made them primal, predatory. Had it changed him? Why else would he be out on this errand, risking gunfire? What had affected him if not the land itself that sickened and drowned his workers, land that would eat him alive, too, if given half a chance?

When the slowing train approached the big curve before Cypress Bend, the engineer killed the headlight, and let the locomotive creep along in a white noise of whispery exhausts. At a point where an engineer approaching Cypress Bend switch from the other direction would have no chance of see- ing the Shay, he set the brakes, and with the jolt Randolph's heart bumped up in rhythm. He began to worry about all the men and weapons on both sides and concluded he'd rather be playing accordion on his porch. Getting down on the fire- man's side of the engine and stepping off the roadbed, Ran- dolph could no longer see the black locomotive and he was immediately lost. Away from Nimbus the world was a darker and wilder place, and when Clarence Williams touched his arm from behind, he turned around and saw nothing but a smudge on the night.

"What wrong with Mr. Merville back there on the floor?"

Randolph reached out to find the man, so he would know where to send his words. "He's very sick. Unconscious, in fact."

"Why ain't he at the doc?"

"We can't do this job without him."

Byron came up and turned on his flashlight, playing it along the coach to where Minos and Big Norbert were taking the old man down the steps on the stretcher, Norbert on the ground, holding the handles high.

The mill manager watched the light ghost over his brother's face. He hadn't said a word. "Are you all right, By?"

"I've done this with a hundred thousand men," he whispered, reaching into a shirt pocket and removing a police whistle. "One blast and we all stand up."

"Yes."

"Yes, *sir*." Byron struck off west down the main line, followed by his brother, Clarence and three other Negro mill hands, then Clovis, with Minos and Norbert at the rear.

Rafe, the engineer, who'd just struck a match for his pipe, looked down at the stretcher as it passed under the cab window. "Y'all must be hard up for lawmen."

Minos spat on a driving wheel. "Some people don't never take a day off," he said, then disappeared past the steaming front of the locomotive.

It was a quarter mile around the curve to Cypress Bend spur. Rafe had predicted that George Robinson would run the Tiger Island switch engine around the wye at Rick and back down the line into the spur so the boxcars would be close to the wharf. They all came to the switch stand and walked the spur away from the main line into the uncut woods, staying in the center of the track. From the left came the rum-rum of a bar pit full of bullfrogs. Grass spiders and crickets textured the dark with their noise, but after a half mile of walking, the men heard the wall of sound fall away. Byron snapped on the flashlight and lit up an open area, a broad apron of clamshells on the left, and down near the end of track, the jutting roof of a storage dock where the wisteria and poison oak squeezed the rotting roof braces in weedy fists. Fifty feet behind the clamshells and parallel with the track was a low, overgrown levee, and Byron signaled with his light for the men to spread out as he'd instructed, twenty feet apart in the tallow trees and privet, keeping behind the mound. Minos and Big Norbert lay Merville far back in the roundgrass, taking their rifles out of the stretcher. Randolph crouched in the dark and heard the men settle in, shucking shells into the chambers and clicking the safeties on and off, on and off, another insect noise.

He didn't know the time, but when he noticed the outline of a thistle appear next to him, guessed it was five o'clock. Light glazed the treetops in the east and after a moment he could see flat, lead-colored reeds leaning against his gun barrel, and then a live oak formed out of the night sky across the tracks. He worried about standing when his brother blew the police whistle, about trying to arrest everyone in a show of force, and whether the surprise would indeed paralyze Buzetti's men into preserving themselves.

Hearing the thump of an engine, he rose up to look toward the slate-colored bayou where after a minute the ghost of a small tugboat appeared, pushing a deck barge toward the landing. The boat drifted in at an angle like a careful drunk and landed sideways against the plank dock. Two men stepped off carrying rifles in a careless fashion, holding them parallel to the ground, one-handed. Randolph backed down into the brush as the men walked slowly up the track, looking to the north. He could hear them speaking, trying to guess the time as they sauntered up the line and then returned to the boat where two other men had thrown off a gangplank and were off-loading wooden crates.

A wren scolded, and then a crow flew low overhead. The mill manager froze as he saw movement in the dense grass to his right where the hatless head of his brother broke through the greenery. "Remember," Byron said, panting, wide-eyed, "this is an arrest. No shooting unless one of them fires first."

Randolph drew back, alarmed. "You don't have to tell me that."

"The mosquitoes are making everybody jumpy. The sooner the train gets here, the better."

"Yes."

"Rando."

"What?"

"Are you all right?"

Randolph looked toward the dock. "How'd you feel before you went over the top in France?"

"There was always a moment when I wondered if I was making a mistake."

"I was trying to make a joke."

Byron licked his lips and peered through the weeds. "A joke. Well, we'll see who laughs, won't we." Then he backed down through the path he'd made in the wet grass, and when he was ten feet away, the mill manager could see nothing of his movement.

The mosquitoes burned like droplets of acid on his arms and neck, but he didn't slap at them. His ears were on fire with the stings when he heard a train whistle calling a long way off at the road crossing in Rick. Ten minutes later came the heavy clack of boxcars slowing out on the main line, and the woofing exhaust of the locomotive died as the fireman dropped off to throw the switch. Through the cypress stand came the sing of wheels as the train backed down the curve toward Green Bayou. The exhaust of the switch engine drummed four times, and then there was the slowly growing rattle and creak of the approach. The mill manager took off his hat and laid it on the ground. Looking above the levee he saw the first boxcar wobble into the clearing a hundred yards away, and he clicked off his Winchester's safety and gathered his legs beneath him. Mosquitoes were lined up and drilling on his ears, but he didn't feel them. The engineer backed the cars all the way to the end of the rails, the fireman dangling from grab irons on the last car and giving lazy hand signals. With a hiss of compressed air the train stopped, and a boxcar door slid open in a complaint of rusty rollers as Buzetti jumped out along with four others, all of them wearing pistols in holsters. Randolph looked under the cars and could see no one on the other side of the train, so he listened for his brother to blow the whistle for the deputies to stand up. He was sure Byron would call out in his big musical voice for everyone to stand under arrest, and it would all be over. Randolph could taste the relief on his tongue. His ears yearned for the signal.

Perhaps the whistle was in his brother's mouth, but Byron must have seen what Randolph suddenly noticed on the far side of the train: a dark hat passing in the rectangle of new light between two boxcars. No whistle sounded, and there was only the rattle of another boxcar door and the grunt of a man hefting a wooden crate of whiskey from the dock and struggling with it toward the tracks. Despite the mosquitoes propellering in his ears, all the mill manager could think of was catching Buzetti's men on this side of the train, the surprise both complete and safe. He held his breath and watched the legs moving along the far side of the last boxcar, then stopping; the man might be urinating, or maybe just dodging the work. It was a shame, Randolph thought, that several lives could depend on the fullness of one man's bladder.

The first crate of whiskey arrived, and someone in the boxcar pulled it inside. Seven men formed a walking line between the barge and the train. Twenty-five, fifty, then a hundred wooden twelve-quart boxes arrived, and the mill manager began to rock back and forth, his legs cramping and burning. He ignored everything except the movement on the other side of a willow sapling in front of him, thinking of how he would describe this motion years from now—and at once a shiver vibrated along his shoulders at the idea that there might not be any years ahead, and he looked up to see vividly for the first time the grasses around him and the smudge of train beyond.

Someone stepped from around the back of the last boxcar, a man with a small, dark mustache and a darker eye patch, a piece of material so black it seemed to be a hole showing the lightless insides of his head, and immediately the police whistle warbled out from the brush—the same whistle, Byron had told him, that had belonged to his sergeant on the line at Chateau Thierry—and the nine of them stood and stepped over the embankment together, Byron in the lead and shouting, "You're all under arrest, put your hands up." For one moment, an angry churning seized Buzetti's face, his hand moving to his side, but the sun was full up, and even the man wearing the patch could see the huge muzzle holes and box magazines of the sleek Winchesters and how they were designed to kill at once. Buzetti's hands drifted up, shaking in the yellow light, and then the men who were loading put down their boxes and hesitantly raised their arms, as if they were only following their boss's lead. The boatmen reached their hands the highest, and Randolph looked over this dream of the whole batch of them being rounded up without a shot fired, even the dark one with the eye patch stepping out into the light, his coat falling open to reveal an automatic pistol in his belt, but his hands on the back of his head like a military prisoner. The mill workers were rigidly aiming, every one of them scared of death and standing firm only out of loyalty to the sawmill boss or a paycheck or some connection to the pile of smokestacks and boilers and saws gnawing daylight out of the swamps. Randolph fixed his sights on Buzetti's forehead and tested the curve of the trigger with his forefinger, but there was no resistance in the criminal's eyes. He was giving up, as they all were, Buzetti perhaps already thinking of his lawyers, of how paying a few thousand dollars to a jury foreman was better than swapping lead with a sawmill gang so ignorant in the ways of killing people that they might be lucky enough to manage it. The event looked to be over. Byron was the first to step ahead of the line, hollering for the bootleggers to bunch up, making sure the morning's work was finished.

But then, the wife-beating engineer, the foul, balding man with blotched, peeling skin who craved the admiration of gangsters, lifted above the ledge of the locomotive's window a large break-action revolver, drew back the hammer, and fired, knocking Byron to the ground. The concussion ran through everyone like lightning; the men by the train dropped their hands to their guns, and all the deputies panicked, jerking their triggers as one shot, and pulling them again and again, not really comprehending automatic rifles that kept reloading themselves. The mill men seemed to lose track of how many rounds they were firing and as long as guns went off kept banging away.

The engineer's skull cracked open like a watermelon and the heavy slugs broke planks out of the boxcars, rang the iron wheels like church bells, thundered against the locomotive's tender as Buzetti and his men fell down firing their pistols wildly, at anything or nothing, as if it would be unthinkable to die with unspent shells. While the deputies filled the air with spinning brass, the mill manager fired at Buzetti and the recoil kicked the next shot into the top of a car, and when he felt a bullet thwack through the cartilage of his left ear, he brought the muzzle down and pulled the trigger until his last casing winked through the air and the firing pin snicked down on an empty chamber. He spun dumbly to the right, heard the roaring fade through the trees, and smelled the mockingly pleasant odor of smokeless powder filling the windless clearing. A few shocked moments passed before he saw that no more shooting was called for. Everything had changed forever, and the gunfire had lasted six seconds.

He ran over to his brother, who was sitting up in the clamshells looking at his shattered left elbow, crying out "Aw, no" while trying to move his left hand. Randolph saw the lower arm dangle and pour, that the elbow was simply missing. Byron's rifle was at his feet, unfired.

"Hold on, By. Just be still," he said, going to his knees beside him. Clovis Hutchins came over and held the arm together, but just then Byron slumped over, unconscious. Randolph looked up and saw the fireman's boots in the gangway of the locomotive, and at that moment the entire clearing began spinning around him. At the end of the train a man lay facedown with his neck across a rail. None of the whiskey loaders was moving, and Buzetti was doubled up like an infant, his arms folded around himself, his lips moving. Randolph got to his feet and walked over to where Buzetti lay staring sightlessly and muttering in Italian, blood seeping from a ragged hole in his coat. The mill manager got down on one knee, in an attitude of apology or prayer. "If you live long enough," he said at last, "I'll get you a priest."

Buzetti stopped speaking, and his head turned, trembling, toward the voice. "You," he said, and the live gloss of his eyes clouded like cooling lead.

Clarence Williams walked up, shaking, holding his empty rifle by the barrel. "Mr. Aldridge, this went bad. I didn't know it was gone be like this. Somebody shure to come after me for killin' a white man."

Randolph looked over to where Big Norbert was sitting on the ground, a red hole in his overalls strap. "No one's coming after anybody."

"You sure?"

"Look around," he said, motioning right and left to the twisted bodies. "Who's left?"

Clarence shook his head and began to reload. "The one-eye gone."

The mill manager stood quickly, all guilt and sorrow panicked out of him. Quickly he got over to Norbert and saw that the bullet had gone cleanly through him under the shoulder bone. "Where's Minos?"

"He's all right." Norbert glanced up. "You better see to yourself."

Randolph examined his own blood-sopped shoulder and felt his sodden ear, then walked over to where Minos, unhurt, was sitting in the weeds next to his father's body, staring at the hissing train. "We killed the engine crew," he said.

Randolph's ear began to throb, and he pulled his handkerchief and pinched it against the wound. "Did you see the one-eyed man?"

Minos shook his head. "Been busy on my end."

The mill manager stood drunkenly in the high grass, tying the handkerchief around his ear. Clarence Williams came up and they walked down past the end of the train, searching the tugboat and barge and scouring the trashwoods around the ruins of the shingle mill for signs, but Crouch was gone, whether along the alluvial shelf of the bayou, through the swamp, or flown off on leather wings, the mill manager couldn't tell.

He sent Clarence hiking out to the main line to tell Rafe to shove the crew car down into the woods, then he moved over to his brother, who'd come to and was sprawled on his back over the sharp-edged shells.

"I'm going to lose this arm," he cried.

"Easy," Randolph told him, feeling for the first time how big a part dumb luck plays in a man's life. He looked around and felt good in spite of everything.

"I was shot at by a half-million soldiers," Byron was saying, "with the most accurate rifles in the world, and not one of them could do what a puke-brain engine-jockey did with a fifteen-dollar pistol." He closed his eyes and tears rolled down into his ears. "I was hoping I was through with the war," he sobbed, "but this whole damned world's turned into one."

The mill manager shifted his gaze toward the woods and flicked off the rifle's safety. Only when he heard the crash of drawbars as the mill locomotive backed down into the clearing did he turn around. Fifty yards away, Minos and Clovis Hutchins carried the old marshal out of the brush and one of the black workers who knew Merville walked over to them, staring down at the still figure on the stretcher, then waving his arms above his head and crying out, his voice keening with surprise and fright.

The living loaded onto the train, which pulled out for Poachum. When they arrived, the operator came out onto the platform yelling about the jimmied switch lock, but Rafe ignored him and watched for the rails to be aligned so he could take his train into the weeds toward Nimbus.

When they rattled out of the woods into the mill yard, Randolph stepped off the train and had to sit down on a spike keg to wait for his head to clear. Along with Byron and Big

Norbert, he was brought to Dr. Rosen, who tended Byron first, giving him an injection to make him sleep. After studying the wound for a long time, he finally bound it to stop the hemorrhage and sat against the wall on his examining stool, his forearms on his thighs, wagging his white head at the floor.

CHAPTER TWENTY-TWO

Jules was at his desk sharpening the third pencil of the morning when Minos opened the door, came in, and sat down at the mill manager's desk.

"Don't tell me," Jules said, laying his pencil on an open ledger. "I don't even want to know."

"We wound up killing every damn one of them." The assistant manager held his hands up like a man with a gun at his back and walked out of the room. Minos listened to his boots clopping down the stairs to the saw parlor, then picked up the earpiece from the phone. He looked out the window and politely asked for the connections to the sheriff's office. After two transfers, he reached the big deputy stationed outside the sheriff's door.

"This is Minos, Merville's boy. I want to talk to LaBat."

"You can talk to me."

"I don't want to talk to you."

"Then you ain't talkin' to nobody."

Minos took a breath. "When LaBat finds out you didn't put me through, he'll shove that pointy badge of his sixteen feet up your ass, jewels and all."

There was a pause and the sound of a receiver being thrown down, and the next voice was LaBat's. "What?" Over the phone came the sound of paper being grabbed and manhandled into a stack. Minos winced at the thought of a man having to work for a living by moving little squares of paper.

"Merville and some old boys he deputized went down to Cypress Bend to arrest Buzetti and his bunch. Buzetti's man shot first and blew Mr. Byron's arm off, so the deputies opened up and killed everybody what was shootin' back." He stopped, figuring he'd said enough.

"Son of a bitch," LaBat screamed. "What you mean, everybody?"

Minos ran down the list.

"You killed the fucking locomotive crew?"

"Robinson shot the mill constable down with a pistol. Him and that fireman was in on the deal."

LaBat yelled something incoherent and vile, then the line went quiet. "What about that man with the patch, Crouch?" the sheriff finally asked.

"That one got loose."

"Got loose? What you mean, got loose? He was the only one worth killing."

"He probably swimmin' to Cuba after he saw what the others got."

"Bullshit. That one-eyed bastard is Buzetti's first cousin. I'm telling you right now, you better start wearing eyeglasses on your asshole."

"They can't watch for him no harder than what they been doing."

There was another pause on the line, and the sound of papers being batted around, as if the sheriff was scattering them with a stick. "Can we get into Cypress Bend with a car?"

"Hell, no. Call the railroad and tell them what happened. Maybe they can hold the westbound and get your deputies in there on the Beewick switch engine."

"You left them all in there?"

"Except for my daddy. He dropped dead when all the shootin' started." The mill engineer imagined the sheriff forming a question on his face.

"Why'd you take just him?"

Minos looked out the window at the sooty crew car that still held his father. "He was the only one I cared to pick up, yeah."

A mist of new-hatched mosquitoes rolled out of the swamps and stippled Randolph's neck as he helped lift his brother's stretcher to the baggage car of the eastbound, which would take him to New Orleans. The camp doctor climbed in beside him wearing his tan suit. Ella boarded the day coach ahead, fanning at the mosquitoes with a soggy handkerchief. After the train pulled out, its whistle howling at an ox standing down the main line, Randolph sat on the station bench and waited patiently for the sheriff.

LaBat and his driver came along in a mud-spattered patrol car at five o'clock and parked next to the station. He got out slowly, then brushed at dried mud on his pants legs and knocked clods off his boots on the edge of the platform. He sat next to the mill manager, and they waved away mosquitoes as they talked, Randolph listening with his unbandaged ear.

"I'll have to talk to your men."

"Come and speak to them."

The sheriff looked at him sharply. "You got together with everybody already, I bet."

The mill manager looked over at the driver, who was scraping his boot on the bumper of the patrol car. "How much of a stink will this raise?"

The sheriff hunched his shoulders. "People gonna ask why *I* wasn't down here after Buzetti." He shook his head. "I never seen so much liquor in my life. Bonded stuff. Canadian, some of it."

"Oh, but you *were* down there."

"No I wasn't. What you mean?"

"Your authorized agent, Merville Thibodeaux, and his deputies, *your* deputies, pulled the raid. You stopped the biggest shipment ever seen in these bayous."

The sheriff froze for a moment, narrowed his eyes. "No. I don't want to be hooked up with this deal. Not with the worst of the lot still loose."

"He's just one man."

"So's the devil. That half-blind bastard ain't crazy. He's ruined, is what he is."

"Ruined." Randolph said the word slowly.

"Buzetti himself told me the guy was captured by the Austrians, and some fancy officer put a gun to his head and made him shoot Italian wounded. I heard he fell down and started pukin' after he'd killed twenty, maybe twenty-five." The sheriff turned a palm up, and shook his head once, uncomprehending. "Now, don't look at me like that. I know this is bad stuff. An officer gave him a pistol, told him he could get out of shooting the rest if he would kill himself. And you know, he put that gun in his mouth and when it went off, it fried the inside of his throat. The Austrians all started laughing because it was just a blank cartridge."

Randolph put up a hand and closed his eyes. "I've heard enough."

LaBat glared at him. "You got to know who you dealing with. Them Austrians give him a little lecture about bein' Italian, then they got some bread, soaked it in the blood of one of the men he just killed, put it on the bayonet of a Carcano rifle, and made him put it in the mouths of the wounded. They'd bring him one man at a time, you see, and while each one of them was eating they made him—"

The mill manager jumped up. "How was his eye put out?" he asked, his voice breaking.

LaBat ran his smart, mean eyes over the mill manager. "I kind of like you, Mr. Aldridge, so I don't think I'll tell about that. It's worse than the other."

"Why do you like me? What do you mean?" Another question, he figured, would stop the storytelling altogether.

LaBat raised a hand and gestured toward the woods. "You come out here and buy this shit swamp for fifty cents an acre and you make money off of it. Hire a few folks so they don't starve for a while. Without people like you all this would just be woods." He looked around. "Woods ain't good for nothing unless you a woodpecker."

Randolph swallowed and looked down the tracks to the east. "What will you tell the New Orleans papers?"

"If they hear about it, I'll just say everything was done legal."

"How can they not hear about it?"

The sheriff shook his head. "Look where it happened. Nobody saw. No phone line for a man to call out and tell about something right when it happens." He stood up. "I'll send Buzetti and his three to New Orleans for a quick autopsy and then storage in potter's field, the wet part where the maggots are busy. Those three other slugs from Tiger Island, their families won't want it to get out, maybe, what those guys been doing. I can make the local paper say they drowned."

As he listened, Randolph felt that he was indeed living at the end of a thousand-mile road in the jungle where everyone is anonymous and unrecorded. "What about those men on the tugboat?"

LaBat shrugged. "Out of towners. Florida men. We'll get 'em embalmed and mailed home and let their local papers say what they want. Now, the railroad men, I don't know. Maybe the Southern Pacific won't raise hell, considering what that crew was doing on company time."

"Impossible. There are too many ways for information to get out."

The sheriff looked up at the single wire running down the poles toward Nimbus. "Not that many, not yet." Then he looked at his driver, who was leaning against the radiator. "Hey, Percy. Bring us a drink of that new whiskey."

Randolph's head jerked toward the automobile, a cold nausea rising in his neck.

"Oh, hell," LaBat said, "I'm just kidding."

. . .

The next day the mill manager turned a saw team into watch-men for his house and the plant, issuing them pistols and new flashlights. He set about working the backlog of sales orders, and every time he hung up the phone he expected it to ring, but it didn't—until two o'clock. It was a judge in New Orleans, inquiring about the authority of the marshal who led the raid, and Randolph spoke carefully, every fact in his voice a decision. At four, a reporter called from Baton Rouge, and the mill manager said he could not release any information about the incident. That he should call Sheriff LaBat. The reporter said that he had been trying all day. The next morn-ing, the station agent at Poachum rang up and told him that two newspapermen were on the platform and wanted to know when the log train was coming in. The mill manager told him no train would come that day, nor maybe the next, and he sent Jules to tell Rafe not to run, to let the lumber stack up on the flatcars. For the rest of the week, each day was punctuated by phone calls and careful answers. One man, wearing a tan suit and cursing the cloud of mosquitoes circling his head, came out on foot down the spur from Poachum to where Judgment was stationed at trackside a mile from the mill. He was sitting on a stump under a chinaball tree when the reporter tried to walk by. "Can't nobody get past me," Judgment told him, stay-ing seated.

The reporter was both cocky and heat-addled. "Says who?"

Judgment held up a new Blue Grass ax handle, said noth-ing, and the reporter turned around.

The Poachum agent sent down a copy of the *Picayune* that ran an account on page three of a squabble between deputies and bootleggers, noting two fatalities, one of them Merville, and an unspecified number of wounded. Randolph thrust the paper into the cold woodstove and lit it. The next day he, Lillian, and Jules traveled to Tiger Island for the marshal's funeral. Though he was not a regular parishoner, Merville received a funeral Mass, old Father Schultz singing the Latin in a strong but sorrowing voice that should have broken but did not. They rode out to the graveyard for the burial, and afterward, as Randolph and his wife were getting into the hack for the ride back to the station, Minos walked up. He didn't look like himself in his pressed suit and bare combed head.

"Seems like they's somethin' we all ought to say that ain't been said yet." He looked over at a pile of dirt and the men leaning on shovels behind it. "I can't make the words, you know? But can you follow me and Father Schultz to the old man's house? We want to show you something that says it all."

They rode back into town and parked in front of a galleried frame house shedding paint, its green shutters latched shut. Randolph got out and told Lillian she could wait in the cab if she preferred. Father Schultz and Minos went in first and held the door. The hall floor popped and squawked as they walked down to the marshal's room, and Randolph noted that the place already smelled empty, carrying an odor that was the history of every cooked meal mixed with tobacco, sweat, and the dusty emanations of the housewood itself.

"You see that?" Minos pointed toward a broad walnut armoire, ten feet tall, shoved against the corner of the room. "Help me move it." The priest put his shoulder against a side panel while Randolph and Minos pulled a corner. The armoire was stuck in the varnish of the floor, sunk into the original coat and glued to the spot with subsequent layers. Eventually they rocked it loose and swung it shuddering away from the wall.

"Good Lord," the mill manager said, stepping away from an avalanche of weaponry so dense and dust-bound that he hardly knew what it was—a coral of straight razors, skinning knives, spiked knuckles, break-action Smith & Wesson, Iver Johnson, Hopkins and Allen pistols, pocket shotguns, machetes, ice picks, hat knives, cabbage knives, corkscrews, lever-action rifles, slapjacks, scalpels, pump guns, giant scissors, single-shot shotguns bound together with string and tape by men poor in everything but revenge, pieces of metal shaped to stab or slice, innocent pipe and tie-rod sharpened to death.

Minos looked down at the heap. "Every week he'd throw these things behind there. When we was kids, if we tried to get at it, he'd wear us out with a belt, let me tell you."

Father Schultz bent over and examined a bayonet. "What will happen to these things?"

Minos kicked a cotton hook back into the pile. "A long time ago, he told me what to do. I'll get a couple men to help me put it in skiffs and we'll throw it in the middle of the river."

The mill manager sat on the edge of Merville's bed. An arsenal, he was thinking—enough to equip a crazed, primal army. He watched the priest place a finger on the razory edge of a hatchet, and with a shudder Randolph began to imagine all the things that had never happened.

After ten days, the mill phone jingled only with orders for siding and not with the concerns of judges or reporters. Randolph understood the cliché that news, like fish, becomes less valuable with age.

LaBat still called every day to report on his efforts to find Crouch, the one-eyed snake carrier and killer of housekeepers. And he informed the mill manager that the railroad's investigation into the raid was stopped dead in its tracks when a Southern Pacific accountant discovered a combined total of $52,000 in the train crew's bank accounts. The one morning LaBat did not call, Randolph was relieved, as though beginning to believe the subject no longer worth a daily consultation. But after lunch, he stood in his kitchen and stared long at the swirling linoleum before the stove, deciding to use the new phone on Lillian's desk to call the sheriff himself. A deputy told him the sad news, how LaBat had somehow cartwheeled down his stairs at home and broken his neck.

"It was an accident?" the mill manager asked, his voice sailing up.

"You know, it's a funny thing," the deputy said. "A man goes up and down the same stairs for twenty, thirty years. One day he misses that top step, maybe. How do you suppose that happens?"

Randolph found Byron on his porch, his legs crossed, his bandaged stump propped over a knee. He received the news with no expression. Turning in his rocker, he yelled through the screen, and the nasal hillbilly voice that began to unwind on the Victrola sang of a railroad engineer's head burning up in the firebox of his engine. Randolph thought of the image. A head in a firebox, flames for eyes.

Ella came to the screen. "This is the sixth time," she announced, shifting her gaze to Randolph as he eased into a chair. "He cried through the first three. He's getting used to it, I reckon."

"I went over to see little Walter," Byron said. "He's recovered almost all the way. Amazing how they are at that age." He looked at his brother for the first time. "I got him up in my good arm."

"By, what do you think?"

"About what?"

"That last man." Just saying the words made him tired, because he wanted to be through with it all and think only about his wife, Walter, sawing timber, and moving home. It scared him the way his brother looked when he talked about the boy.

"He's got to do whatever's in him."

"What will that be?"

Byron frowned. "You're asking me to predict him like a line in a song I've never heard before." He closed his eyes and listened again to the keening record. From the woods came the call of a pull boat's whistle, far off, pained, like a white egret caught in the jaws of an alligator.

Ten days later, August came in damp and airless, capturing the camp in heat. Machinery sweated at sunrise, beads of condensation rolling like bugs off every iron thing, and the mill-wrights stepped up lubrication as the air itself washed oil from the mill's many bearings. The locomotives required more sand on the water-slick rails, the women spent more time at their wash pots as towels and bedsheets soured overnight and never seemed to dry on the beaded clotheslines. On some days, clothespinned and spiritless overalls gathered more water from the atmosphere than they gave up. Jules and the mill manager worked orders and figures in their shirtsleeves, a series of lacquered engine nuts holding down their paperwork against a battery of oscillating fans. Randolph was happily distracted, calculating profits on an unexpected order for water-tank lumber. He was engaged like a machine in his mill, a moving part of the process leading from stump to farmstead in Minnesota. His work shut out worry, became again life's real adventure. He remained on his guard, but nothing could happen in the mill yard, which, after all, was being watched like a fortress.

One day in mid-month he walked home for lunch, ravenous, empty of care, looking forward to a conversation with his wife, and came through the rear door into the kitchen, whistling, just in time for Crouch to step from behind that same door and call out "For Buzetti," as he fired a shot into the mill manager's back with a .30 caliber Luger. Randolph felt a narrow spear of fire in his heart and then the floor struck him like an onrushing train, the busy and blurring design of the linoleum forming the connected shards of his great final catastrophe. He arched his back and turned his head in time to see another slug shock through his left forearm and to hear his assailant calling out a rhythmic and spiraling string of Italian punctuated by another ear-splitting pop that gouged splinters out of the baseboard, a deliberate miss, he knew, to make him suffer through a last few moments of hope. Randolph saw a soft flow of white cotton at the door leading into Walter's room and then a red blossom as his wife's little .32 loaded with black-powder shells banged a slug into the one-eyed man. She fired the pistol four more times, once missing her target and spearing Randolph in the back of his left hand, this bullet causing the most painful wound of all. Feeling for a moment the warmth of safety, he then heard Crouch raring in pain and scuffling with someone, cursing, flinging words like *bitch* and *stupid fucking whore* and worse, his wife screaming under blows. He tried to turn over, and after two attempts, air rushing out of his mouth with a cupful of blood, he did, only to see the one-eyed man looming above, grinning like a death's head, the dark Luger pointed straight down at him. "Have a look where you going," Crouch said, bending closer and with his bloody fingers raising the black leaf, revealing a tortured, waxy ball, a fat yellow worm on its surface, some infected scar caused by a flame, perhaps gunpowder poured in and lit by a man wearing absurd epaulets and a gilded sword. Randolph stared at the eye, this jaundiced pain that Crouch carried with him like a fiery coal to burn whomever it could—and he was not afraid, but simply sorry. His hand ached so much that he was distracted from his approaching death, and he opened his mouth to speak—of what, he had no idea—when a church bell tolled and the yellow eyeball revolved completely back into its skull, Buzetti's cousin falling onto him and rolling off, as slack as jelly.

Above Randolph hovered the rocky face of the Irish housekeeper, the big woman holding an eleven-inch Griswold skillet with her two chapped hands. "Sure I've sent the poor fellow to blazes," she cried, turning to Lillian, who Randolph could see was also down on her back.

The doctor, drawn yet again by gunfire, cautiously stepped in through the screen door, looked around, and touched his chin. "Well," he said, kneeling down next to Randolph and opening his shirt, glancing the while over to the still figure next to him. "That one's head is completely flat. What'd she do, drop a stove on him?"

The mill manager opened his mouth and tried to answer, but the air for his voice was coming out somewhere else. The doctor became more focused, thumbed his patient's eyelids, counted his pulse, watched the blood spread out from his shoulder across the olive and red curls of the linoleum. Randolph could hear his wife's healthy crying, then doors rattling open and the sound of boots and a despairing, angry flux of voices above him in the failing light. It occurred to him that he was listening but not seeing, that the great pain welling up inside him had nothing to do with a bullet.

CHAPTER TWENTY-THREE

Many of the sawmill's workers seemed bogged in a relentless hangover for days, as if caught up in the misery of the people who controlled their lives. Minos moped along to the commissary for cheese and bread, then came out to sit on the steps next to the doctor, who was eating sardines and crackers off a blinding square of waxed paper, neither man speaking as they washed down the food with swigs out of sweating soft-drink bottles. From down at the saloon came the sirenlike howl of a drunk. The doctor rolled his sallow eyes. "Damnation." He bit a cracker as if he meant to hurt it. "It's a trapper in there with Big Norbert's cousin. I saw them go in earlier."

Minos threw his cheese under the steps and stood up. "I'm surprised the place hasn't been fought to pieces the past week, what with no law." They walked to the corner of the commissary and looked over at the saloon, each understanding that the low, odorous building had lost its invisible power the minute Buzetti died. Only the momentum of the camp's hard drinkers kept the place open at all.

The doctor put his hands in his pockets. "You know, that place's a menace to health."

The engineer spat into a wheel rut. "Galleri done run out of bonded and beer both. He's down to a couple oil drums of moonshine." He looked back to his house, down the row from Byron's. "Wait here a minute while I check on something." In ten minutes he was back, carrying a twenty-four-inch Coe's wrench. Another round of hollering came up from the saloon.

"You can't do better with a shovel?"

"It's all I could find in the house. If it don't work I got the old man's pistol in my britches."

At the saloon door, they were met by a millwright, coming out, who looked at the wooden-handled wrench. "Better not, Mr. Minos."

"Let's just see," he said, sliding past, followed by the doctor. The trapper was a dark Indian who was straddling Big Norbert's cousin, sitting on his back and drawing hatch marks on his neck with a skinning knife. Several men were trying to stop the fight, but whenever one pulled on the Indian's arm he was met with a whistle from the blade.

"All right," the doctor hollered, his face filling with blood. "I'm tired of fixing you dumb asses." He grabbed the wrench from Minos and raised it high, addressing the Indian. "Drop that knife or I'll wind up digging this out of your skull."

The Indian turned his red eyeballs toward the doctor and stood. As the wrench came down, he grabbed the handle with his left hand and threw it spinning across the room, as though it were a playing card. "You couldn't whup me with no two wrenches," he said, pushing the doctor backwards through the door and off the porch, where he fell to the ground onto his back. He tried to get up but felt a brogan on his shoulder, not heavy, and looked up into a face frowning under a steamboat man's cap.

"Stay down," Minos told him. He wheeled and hollered at the trapper, who was turning on the porch to go back after Big Norbert's beaten-down cousin. "Ay, muskrat."

The trapper faced around and stared, his eyes crossed as though one of them had been beaten out of line by a sledge.

"What you gonna do with that knife?" Minos asked.

"Skin me a hide."

"No you ain't."

"How you gonna stop me?"

Minos pulled his father's Colt lightning and fired a round

into the trapper's shin, right over his mud-caked boots. The man yelped and threw his arms aloft as if he were slipping down on ice, the skinning knife flying up and sticking in the underside of the porch roof.

The doctor got up and walked through the puff of gunsmoke into the black side of the saloon, where he put a hand under a saw filer's overalls strap and dragged him out into the sun, instructing him to fetch two five-gallon cans of kerosene from the commissary.

Galleri stepped out on the porch, his hands making questions in the air. "What's going on?"

"Clear every worthless jarhead out of that bugger hole," the doctor told him.

"What? What you going to do?" His lardy face bounced back and forth between the two men.

"Your floors are unsanitary," the doctor announced. "We're going to clean them so people can say you run a healthy place."

Minos searched the writhing trapper's pockets and stepped down off the porch. "Coal oil. Ten gallons ought to clean things up some."

Galleri looked into the men's faces. "This a joke, right?" Then, after a moment he hurried inside. From the back of the saloon came the sound of breaking glass, and the doctor and Minos dragged the bleeding Indian off the porch and dumped him out in the lane next to a pile of mule droppings.

When the kerosene arrived they went inside the white section and found that Galleri had broken out the jackpot windows in the slot machines and was scooping quarters and nickels into a sombrero. The saw filer set down a can in the middle of the floor, and Minos shot a hole into it near the bottom; next, they walked over to the black side and did the same, the slug bounding through the other side of the can and shattering a mirror behind the bar.

A tipsy, barefoot whore wandered out from the back, holding a pint can of pomade, come to see what the racket was about. When she smelled the kerosene, her feet froze to the floor, and she looked at the spreading silvery pool. "What you crazy white folks doin'?"

The doctor smiled at her. "Do you have a ready-made, my darlin?"

The woman drew a soggy cigarette from her bodice and held it out as though expecting someone to light it. "You wants to fire me up?" she asked, wavering.

Minos stepped around the running fuel and dug a kitchen match from a box on the bar. "Come here, girl." He led her around to the front door and struck the match, the doctor following and putting his hand on the knob.

The woman leaned over and inhaled noisily, then let the smoke slide from her mouth and drift up her nostrils. "You gennelmens want something?"

When Minos took a step backwards and dropped the match to the floor, a yellow lip of flame grew patiently across the boards as though following a giant wick. The woman stepped onto the porch without making a sound, an expert at leaving trouble, and the men stayed in and closed the door behind her, then walked quickly along the wall to the spring-loaded back door. They strolled out casually, moving toward the canal, where they sat down on a bulkhead. For a long while, nothing seemed to be happening inside the building, but then the fire began to drum and snap, gray smoke snaking out around the closed windows. Something detonated with a thud, and after this noise every crack and seam in the saloon began to spray smoke. The mill's fire whistle started to whoop, sliding up and down the scale, and the two of them walked around to stand with the gathering crowd, feigning surprise. A stretcher crew showed up for the wounded trapper, while the whore, trying to be inconspicuous, sauntered around to her cabin in back.

Minos pointed at her. "Looks like she's going to pack, yeah."

"She'll be all right," the doctor said. "Nobody'll bill her for a burnt-up saloon."

A team of workers rolled down a hose cart from the boiler

room and began to hook up to the one hydrant in the mill yard. Minos walked over and grabbed a man by the arm. "Take your time," he said.

The man looked over at the building, which was now a huge blossom of seething, slate-colored smoke. "You gone Baptist on us, Mr. Minos?"

"Go on back to the mill for that big wrench hanging by my chair. You got to get that hose on tight." He looked at the other men. "All of you go get yourselves a wrench." They did as he asked, moving toward the mill in no particular hurry. Meanwhile, the saloon hissed and boiled, sap running like water out of the knotholes, the tin roof crinkling and banging as if someone were inside throwing billiard balls against it. All at once the fire burned through a side wall, the air got in, and every board bled red and yellow flame. The onlookers scrambled back to escape the flash of heat and the ragtime notes of bottles breaking, the building lighting up like a paper bag and disappearing in a roaring bloom. The hose crew reappeared with their wrenches and proceeded to wet down the roof of the commissary, the two whore cabins out back, and three smoking-hot privies. The porch posts burned away upright, the window sashes fell out and flamed in the yard, and the saloon pulsed hotter, a giant tulip of crackling orange light, until its roof collapsed in a tornado of sparks. Everyone not on shift was in the yard, watching respectfully as if the blaze were a play they'd paid good money to see.

Full dark showed only a bank of red coals, and the next morning revealed a rectangle of ash littered with giant rusty flakes of tin and the partially melted hulks of eight slot machines canted in the cinders like one-armed torsos. A bucker glancing at the debris on the way to his shift remarked that it looked like the day after Hell burned out.

That afternoon several thirsty men stood around the ashes like dogs whose bowls had been taken away, and Galleri, smudged and sick, appeared at the mill office, straw hat in hand. Jules asked what he could do for him.

"I didn't have no insurance," he said, turning his hat in front of him.

Jules threw down his pencil. "Hell, you the only man around here with a bank account."

"Okay, I was ready to move on, but you got to admit, the building was worth somethin'. You got to admit that."

"Aw, go on and move to Shirmer, or Tiger Island. Build yourself a barber shop or a little grocery store."

"Hey, you know what happened."

"I don't know what you're talking about."

"I can't get no free lumber?"

The assistant manager looked up at him for a long moment. "All right. I can let you have some number two stuff, siding and some joists."

Galleri rocked from one foot to the other. "What about tin?"

Jules squinted meanly. "Hell, no. Your place was a boil on this mill's ass, and you're lucky to get a four-penny nail out of me."

Galleri put on his hat. With his hand on the doorknob, he said, "One time, Buzetti offered me a thousand dollars to kill Mr. Byron."

The assistant manager's face snapped up. "Why didn't you take it?"

"You know, livin' out here with the owls, I thought about it a while. Not real serious, you know? But still, a thought like that wouldn't never popped into my head if I lived in a town." He rattled the knob. "A thousand dollars is a lot of money." Galleri laughed. "That's how you get to thinkin' when you work in the woods sellin' booze to the animals."

Jules began filling the little voids of an invoice. "I guess."

"Is it workin' out in the woods makes you crazy?" Galleri asked. "What you think?"

Jules did not look up. "I think you're glad you didn't take that money."

.   .   .

The mill manager rose to wakefulness the way a Louisiana coffin pushes up out of the mud after a week-long rain. Lillian was there holding his hand, one of her eyes blacked shut, a narrow bruise across the bridge of her nose and fourteen bristling stitches marking her cheek. He tried to speak, but his mouth felt plugged with wax. "No," she said. "Don't try anymore." She told him this as if he'd tried for many days already and had failed, and this frightened him. He saw behind her a figure the size of Byron, and beyond, against the wall, a man holding a book who was perhaps a minister. The room came apart and drifted away, and Randolph prayed for forgiveness for whatever he'd done wrong in his life, and then suddenly, when he felt his brother's touch and voice, the walls came back together, light again registering in his brain and his eyes seeing as if through broken water. He thought of things he had yet to do, hundreds and hundreds of things, but realized, in his trough of weakness, that he had better think of the two or three most important. He willed his lips into a shape and aimed his one working eye at his wife, who lowered her face to his.

"Love you," he whispered. She kissed his cheek and put a finger on his bloodless lips, but he spoke around it. "By," he said, like a call.

His wife backed away and Byron stepped closer, his eyes wide on some grief-killing drug the doctor had given him. "Rando," he whispered. "The man who did it, Mrs. Scott hung up his guns for him. I'm thinking of giving her my badge."

The mill manager struggled for a breath. "No."

"What is it?"

"Walter," he said slowly.

"He's safe, brother. And he'll be safe."

It cost him a great effort to form the words, "I lied."

Byron's brows went up, and his eyes were dark moons. "What? What lie?"

"May told me." He felt the room warping apart, so he gathered his breath and said, "He's yours."

Byron turned and looked behind him, and Lillian put the heel of her hand on her forehead. She took the minister's arm and led him through the door into the hall, then came back alone. She looked at her husband, who had closed his eyes and gone under, then at Byron. "I consider myself a loyal wife, but I'm not stupid. It occurred to me that it could have been one of you." She looked to the window, where a rainy sky darkened toward sunset. "I just tried not to think about it."

Byron put his hand on Randolph's shoulder.

"Let him sleep." She pulled him away from the bed.

He sat down next to the cold radiator. "I've got to think straight." He pointed at the bed with his stump. "Why would he lie to me?"

"Maybe he figured you had enough troubles." She looked down at her stomach. "Or he wanted the baby for himself," she said bitterly.

"This is some news."

Lillian looked at him a long time. "What kind of news, Byron?"

He raised his face to her, smiling a regular smile. "Tall headlines," he told her quietly. "Like they used at the end of the war."

The mill manager groaned and stirred under the sheets. The rubber tube snaking down into a bloody bottle on the floor quivered with his pounding pulse, and the two of them continued to wait for him to die.

A week after his brother entered the hospital, Byron returned to Nimbus and found his wife waiting for him on the porch with Walter in her lap. He walked up carrying his grip and stood still in the yard.

Ella looked down at him and hugged the boy. "It's a fine thing to hear about over the telephone."

He stepped up onto the porch. "I told you what happened, how and why. I can't do any better, but if you want me to say or do something else to make it right, I'll do it."

Walter squirmed out of Ella's lap and grabbed Byron's hand. "Come see," the boy said, tugging him to the far edge of the porch. "Take me to the train."

Byron looked over to where Rafe was setting the packing nuts on the locomotive's cylinders. "Sure. We'll go in just a minute."

"This might take more than just a minute to fix," Ella said. She was biting a thumb, looking away.

"I'm sorry. It was that one time, and I told you how she came on to me."

Out of the side of her mouth, she said, "Kind of like an ambush, was it?"

He took this hurt and squeezed Walter's hand. "I guess so." He moved closer to her and looked at her freckled skin, her sandy hair curled above her shoulders. "Can you forgive me?"

He could tell that she was trying not to cry, and she didn't answer him. He was afraid of what she might say, the longer she would not say it. She was studying the child.

"Ella?"

"It sure would be hard to let you off the hook if we were in one of our hometowns." She looked around the mill yard, then raised an arm. "But here, well, where the hell are we, anyway?" She stood up, putting a hand on Walter's head. "I guess someday we might have that's mine too. They say one like this can cause another to come on."

Byron looked over to the flat blanket of ash that was the saloon. "I wonder why he never told me the truth."

"You don't have to ask that, do you?"

He stepped off the porch and let Walter pull him toward the tracks. "I guess not."

Randolph Aldridge did not die. For two months a fluid pressed around his heart like a spongy fist. The bullet had passed through the center of his chest, and all the tissue around its path had been shocked black. No one expected him to recover, and after thirty days a young Spanish doctor began to experiment, holding back his injections of fluids, and slowly, like a boat bailed by a thimble, Randolph began to come up.

His father, delayed by his own ill health, arrived by train and went straight to the hospital, doddering down the hall peering at numbers. He came up behind Byron, who was outside the room leaning against the wall, and grabbed him by the arm, turning him gently around. "Son, it's good to see you."

What surprised Byron most was how unsurprised he was, as though he'd always expected to be touched and turned in this manner, to be found. When his father embraced him, he let his arm dangle toward the floor as he smelled the train ride on the old man's clothes, all the soot and lounge-car smoke between Pittsburgh and New Orleans giving him an idea of how hard the journey had been. His father looked weaker, older. For this he gave the old man one pat on the back, then pulled away. "It's been a while," he said.

His father opened his mouth, then closed it. Finally he said, "I don't know what to say. I don't want it to be anything that will run you away."

"Don't worry. I'm already away."

The old man nodded. Straightening his back, he looked toward the door. "How is Randolph?"

"Out of danger, but he's seen a lot of damage." Byron put his hand on the knob and they went in.

After giving a pale Randolph brief greetings and reassurances, the old man spotted Walter, who was on his knees in a shaft of window light and drawing in a buff-colored tablet. "Byron," he cried out, walking around the bed, "why didn't you or your wife write me about him?" He looked at the child closely and smiled a claim on him, placing a hand on his head. "Why, he looks exactly like you. I'd have known him anywhere on earth."

The mill manager witnessed this exchange from his bed and felt that he'd been shot once more. Over the past weeks he'd slowly come to realize that he was going to live, and had begun wondering if it were possible to tell Byron the truth and retrieve his son. But now, with his father's recognizing cry, he felt that Walter's identity, his place in the family, was sealed. His father would never visit Nimbus and find out otherwise, and once the trees were cut out and the mill broken down, the place itself—Walter's source—would no longer exist.

His father picked up the boy and brought him close to the bed. "You rascal," he said to Randolph. "You should have written something to me in your letters."

Walter swung a hand out, and Randolph seized it. "Yes," he said, closing his eyes. "I should have told."

"I've got a grandson," the old man blurted, bouncing the boy who studied him blandly, trying to place him, looking around to Byron for some clue as to how to take this new face.

Randolph watched the trio gathered against the window, the boy's thumb up the grandfather's nose, his brother's old grin come back.

CHAPTER TWENTY-FOUR

In early October 1925, when the black swamp water was bleeding south and the cypress tops were burning into their coppery change, the mill manager returned to Nimbus. In a rocker on his front porch he listened to his wife tell him what she had been doing with the church and the school and how she'd been helping Byron hire good people. Since the saloon had burned, there had been nothing much for a constable to do, though Big Norbert, his shoulder wound healed, had taken a badge and was making rounds at night. Byron had been called in by Jules to help with the office tasks, duties he'd dreaded all his life. After a week on the job he'd made a mistake and shipped three carloads of lath to a customer in Missouri who'd wanted shutter material. When he got the phone call telling of his mistake, he picked up a Remington typewriter with his one hand and hurled it through the window sash. He turned over his desk, and pencils, order books, and ledgers exploded across the floor. Jules opened the office door for him like a porter as he rushed down into the mill yard and stood for a moment, staring at the mill manager's house and the potted flowers Lillian had placed out front. He looked over to his own place, at two pair of little trousers flying in the breeze out back, and seeing that, he turned back, taking the stairs two at a time to the office where he and Jules uprighted the big desk. He shuffled around on his knees gathering pages and books, paper clips and rubber stamps while Jules went down into the yard and retrieved the typewriter; together they dug mud from between its keys with their pocket knives.

"Type a nasty letter to someone owes the mill money," Jules said, "and that'll shake the rest of the dirt out of it."

Byron stayed in the office nine hours a day, and when he got home he sat on the floor with Walter or took him on his lap in the Morris chair to read to him. Most of the time he was too tired to listen to the Victrola. Work exorcised the sad music and much of the maudlin streak from his life, and when he did play the machine, he found its voice hoarse and wavering, for the humidity of the camp had corroded the nickeled mechanism and turned its internal grease to varnish. He cut back on his drinking because he didn't want to perform the morning's desk work with a head swaying on his shoulders like an anvil, but mostly because with the saloon gone, liquor of any sort was a commodity hard to find. In truth, he was too busy to drink.

Five weeks into the job, he rode to Tiger Island on the local and was fitted for two suits. He traveled into Mississippi and gave a presentation to officials of the Vicksburg, Shreveport and Pacific Railroad. During that trip he became reacquainted with the world outside of Nimbus. The day he rode through New Orleans, he felt like a monkey set free from its cage. On the train, the dining-car steward seated him among strangers, and when the man across from him asked what line of business he was in, for a long moment he didn't know how to answer. He was Randolph Aldridge's brother, doing his brother's job until he got well or died, he started to say, but then thought better of it, and shook the man's hand too hard over the sugar bowl, saying, "I'm in cypress, the wood eternal." In Vicksburg he could tell that the railroad men thought him odd with his pinned-up coat sleeve. He knew he was abrupt with them but couldn't imagine what to say other than what he was there for. What finally mattered was that his calculations squeezed the price of a crosstie down to a cent better than his competitors. On the train back, with the signed contract for 200,000 ties in his jacket, an army officer in full dress sat in the aisle seat next to him and tried to make conversation, but Byron wanted none of it and looked away from the man's uniform only to see it reflected in the darkening coach window. He closed his eyes and saw two men killed next to him, a single Mauser bullet passing through one heart into the next, and suddenly he was fighting the urge to force up the sash and plunge into the speeding, cinder-strewn darkness when the officer said, "Excuse me, but were you wounded in the war?"

Byron turned on the man rudely. "Yes."

"Chateau Thierry, I bet."

Byron looked into the young man's eyes and saw he'd never been in combat. "Nimbus Wood," he told him.

"Ah, yes." The officer's smile was jolly, thoroughly absurd.

Byron looked back out the window, where stumps littered a dark pool of cut-over swamp.

At the middle of October the mill manager was still frail, able to get up the office steps only twice a week, and then only with Lillian pushing him. Jules and Byron ran the mill together, and Randolph found himself with time on his hands, dropping in at Byron's house once each day to see Walter. He would teach him a new word or read to him with whatever expressiveness he could muster. The boy would sit still for one story but otherwise wanted to move down into the weedy yard to play. Randolph wasn't up to chasing him, so Ella would have to keep an eye on them both, which made him feel like a child himself.

A cool spell breezed through the swamp late that month, and after lunch he and Lillian sat on the front porch, looking around at the dry air as if they could see it. Months earlier, she had detailed men to haul off some of the brush and dress down the stumps in the mill yard. A tough, long-legged grass came up in the sections of the compound not crushed to mud by wheels or hooves, and the clearing began to look civilized and green. The playground behind the church and school had been covered with masonry sand she'd ordered from Tiger Island, brought in by rail.

She laid a hand on his arm. "I saw you over there with Walter."

"He's spinning out whole sentences. Pretty good ones, too."

She drew back her hand to wave away a mosquito, and he could tell she was trying to figure how to ask something. After a long while, she said, "When you were in the hospital, why did you tell Byron about the boy? Did you think I wouldn't have taken care of him?"

He turned in his chair toward her, alarmed. "No, not that. I'm not sure exactly what I was thinking, but not that."

"I'd have taken him as a ward. As I told you I would."

"Of course." Wincing, he reached out to her the stiff hand she'd shot a bullet through. "You'd have done a fine job."

"At the time I thought it wasn't a good thing, telling him like you did. I mean, he's not well enough to raise a child. But when I see Ella walking with him down to the commissary, and certainly when I see Byron come home and ride him on his shoulders around the house, well—"

"Look." Randolph pointed across the way as Walter ran naked out onto the porch, Ella right behind him with a billowing bath towel. They watched the chase, heard Ella's entreaties and the boy's squealing laughter.

Lillian put a hand over her mouth. "Just look at that little fool," she said. "I almost wish he *was* yours."

Randolph bit the inside of his cheek until he could taste blood under an eyetooth. He kept watching until Walter was pinned against a post and Ella swept him up in the huge towel and carried him inside with her face down in the squirming bundle. He watched the door they entered for a long time, even after Lillian got up, regarded him closely, and then dragged a finger over the back of his scarred hand.

CHAPTER TWENTY-FIVE

By January of 1926 the mill manager was riding the blind horse on daily inspections, handling a few sales calls on the phone and helping Lillian with what she called personnel. It was the low-water time, and on a Saturday morning he rode the animal through the clacking palmettos to Cypress Bend, walking it up and down the area of the shootout, trying to remember who had killed whom, staring at the rails rusting off into the dead weeds. The horse was tired and got its hoof caught between two angled crossties, and Randolph knelt there for half an hour, talking to it, finally working the animal free with a pocketknife. At noon, the mill's whistle sounded over the brush like a chord played on a giant faraway organ, and he sat down under the overhang of the vine-wracked shingle mill, pressing with his fingers the place under his sternum that still ached when he took a deep breath or started to laugh. For a long time he stared at the spot where he'd killed Buzetti and wondered if he would be punished by God for the deaths he caused or if the killing itself was the punishment.

The thought occurred to him that it was no longer necessary to stay in Nimbus, that he wasn't doing much and could move back to Pennsylvania, but he'd be just as idle there, and Lillian had not suggested that they move. He felt there was still unfinished business with his brother. The horse nudged

his back, as if he'd read his thoughts and judged them unwor-
thy, so Randolph mounted up, reigning through the trash-
wood saplings rising from the wrecked land.

In 1927 the rains came and never left. The mill was awash for
months, and when the main levees broke on the Mississippi,
Nimbus was submerged for sixty days. Randolph watched
the water rise, boiling in from the north through the railway's
culverts. The Negro section went under first, the water coming up slow, an inch or two a day. At the flood's crest only
the mill manager's place was dry, though he could hear the
water popping against the bottom of the house. At night he
and Lillian listened to the backs of turtles bumping against
the floorboards or the blind thud of garfish caught between
the joists.

The water was two feet deep in Byron's house, and the
Victrola's veneers delaminated and peeled like dark sheets of
skin, leaving the machine workable but twisted and decom-
posed. When the floodwaters doused the fires under the boilers, everything was shut down. Workers moved to tents along
the tracks in Poachum, to the second floors of the dormitories,
in attics and crew cars. The tracks were still open, so some
families gave up and headed to New Orleans. To Randolph's
surprise, Byron's was one of these. Five cases of typhoid had
sprung up in camp, so he took Walter and Ella to a hotel on
Canal Street, where they ate in restaurants each night, walked
along the swollen river, and felt as though they were in Paris.
The mill manager admired the logic of their escape, even as he
and Jules stayed in the mud-haunted, swirling nightmare to
direct the movement of livestock and the roundup of lumber
floating out of the rack yard. He was thankful for the extra
work, because it kept him tired and sent him spiraling to sleep
at night like a thrown shingle, too exhausted even to dream
back the faces of the men he'd killed. At times, when he was
taking a rest, leaning against a wall or climbing up on the
horse just to be someplace dry, he would watch the egg-
smelling water leaching around him and think of Buzetti's

cousin, knocked dead at once in the saloon, or of Buzetti himself folding up into a resentful oblivion.

As soon as the water receded enough for Minos to raise steam, they began to cut trees and fill orders, running longer shifts, even nighttime shifts, with stackers working in the boot-sucking yard wearing headlamps, some carrying pistols and scanning the borders of light for the luminescent eyeballs of alligators.

They continued cutting the tract from the outer edges in toward the factory, and early in 1928 the mill manager studied the maps, saw what was happening, and fired the first two woods gangs. In May he sold the big rafting steamer to a sugar mill, because all the timber that could be rafted had been cut. The steam winches on the pull boats spat and chuffed along, dragging the trees away from the cutting crews and into the canals where they were handled by a new little gasoline tugboat and shoved to the mill. The compound began to fill with herons, egrets, owls, bullbats, marsh hens—any feathered thing that had lost its cypress home. Grackles lined roof ridges and stared off at the remaining trees crowded with crows and chicken hawks. Three Indians were hired to shoot and haul off alligators, just to keep them from under people's houses where they hid from the noon sun, waiting for house dogs and chickens. Nothing edible could be left out for fear of the starving raccoons, possums, rabbits, and squirrels that were eating the hides off porch chairs, boots left on the steps, magazines in the privies, and the bright contents of flowerpots.

In July more woods crews were laid off as the circle of timber around the mill shrank to a mile wide. The narrow-gauge rails were unspiked and the little locomotive shipped away to another mill on a flatcar, the timber cars stacked and burned, their wheel sets sold for scrap iron. The single men were let go first, Lillian saw to that, and the dormitories, white and black, were sold, winched onto barges by the pull boats and hauled off by an oil-company steamer down the long canal to the main channel. Randolph and Byron stood on the company bulkhead and watched them drift away, their gables dragging moss off the cypresses still standing on the bank. A limb raked a line of slate-gray birds off a roof ridge; they circled the unpromising swamp, and returned to their moving roost. The mill manager turned around and looked over his dwindling compound. "Well," he began, "Oregon will be quite a change for you."

"It's a good mill," Byron told him. "I read the whole bill of sale last night. One of the better tracts Father's bought." He moved two steps over into the shade of a ragged willow. "I can cut and sell more fir than we sold cypress here."

"You're moving up in production, all right."

Byron smiled, knowing the veiled reference to Ella's pregnancy. "You think I can get out before she delivers?"

Randolph spat into the black canal. "You don't want it connected with this lovely place?"

"What do you think?"

There was a detonation at the mill, yells, and then half a length of band saw shot through the roof like a steel snake. The men froze, hearing the piercing stop-engine whistle and, a minute later, two short moans from the big whistle, a signal that the line was shut down but no one was hurt. The mill manager shook his head. "We're wearing out. The main engine needs new bearings and belting."

"Minos was telling me he's got so many leaky boiler flues plugged with wooden stobs he's having trouble keeping up steam."

"I'm not paying for a flue job this late in the game." He motioned to the rust-streaked roof of the saw shed. "You better go see what the damage is." Byron nodded and walked off.

Five minutes later Randolph was in Ella's kitchen, teaching Walter to drive a nail into a piece of kindling, using the child's hammer that Byron had bought.

The boy turned up his hands. "Uncle Rando, the nail keeps jumping away." He picked up a number four finishing nail, tapped it with the red hammer, and it glanced sideways out of his fingers.

Randolph took the tool and studied its head. "Why, your hammer face isn't broken in yet, Walt. It's too slick." He reached over and made a show of scraping the face on the rusted leg of the woodstove. "And you should practice with a nail that has a bigger head on it." He chose a box nail from the boy's kit and started it for him in a piece of one-by-four, show-ing him how to place his fingers. He froze then, in a brief seizure, remembering the touch of Byron's fingers on his own, the first time he'd ever hammered a nail.

Ella began pulling plates down from a cabinet. "I hope he grows up to be more than a sawmill carpenter," she said.

Randolph sat down and stared over the boy's head and into the years he would not see him. "You and Byron have to make sure of that," he said. "There should be good schools in Oregon in that city. What is it?"

"Portland."

"School's the key. And bring him to church."

"He's goin' to Sunday school." She looked down at him. "Randolph Aldridge, you're just a boy yourself. You're grind-ing ashes into your suit pants."

The mill manager got up and dusted his seat. Walter bammed the nail halfway through the board and was trying to pull it out with his fingers. "Here," Randolph told him, "let me show you what the other side of that hammer head's for."

He came out of his front door late one morning and started to walk the edge of the muddy lane toward the mill when some-thing unusual in the air arrested his motion, a new quality he couldn't quite put his finger on. He looked around at the houses in the white section, at the mill itself, and decided it was the light. The woods around the compound were no more than a windbreak, a scrim of trees a hundred yards thick. When he'd first come to Nimbus he could not imagine what was beyond the great cypress swamp, and now he could see through the trees to the plateau of stumps on the other side. Giant bars of light stood on the eastern camp, and he under-stood that soon the factory would steam away in an enormous clearing, that Poachum would be visible in the devastated distance. The mill manager now felt under constant scrutiny, and he wondered if all the savagery would still have happened if he'd cut outward from the mill, if the light and a wider view would have stymied the bloodshed.

He walked over to the commissary and went inside to stand by the long counter. Byron was there, and the manager, who was wearing a white shirt and arm garters as he silently counted bars of soap.

"Well," he sighed.

The commissary manager looked up. "I know why you're here. I've been through cut-out before."

"I've still got to say it. Don't order anything else. Let everything you have go out at cost. I'm sorry."

The man nodded and continued to count soap.

Randolph turned to his brother. "You in on the betting?"

"I don't care when they cut Last Tree."

He looked down at the stained counter. "It might be next week."

"Does Father know?"

"Of course. He wants me to come up afterward, to help him retire."

"Well, God knows you both deserve some rest."

The only remaining saw gang gathered in the mist at daylight at the foot of the Last Tree, a gray giant six feet through the middle at a man's waist. It was between the mill and the railroad to Poachum, right in the compound, and was the final cypress standing anywhere in sight, a beautiful tree with the red blush showing under the splintery bark and a pool of apple-green foliage at the crown, which was so high up that the egret perched in the topmost branches looked no bigger than a jaybird. The mill manager mounted a stump and made a speech, saying among other things that the mill had fed and clothed everybody for a number of years and that they had to be grateful for what they'd taken out of the swamp. Not many seemed convinced by his words, and he knew that no common mill worker had a bank account, that nearly all of them had only the same belongings they'd owned when they'd signed on. He looked at the barefoot children and the faded overalls of the men as he talked, and he became longwinded, saying things about how industry helped build the country, as if ideas would make them all feel better. He couldn't imagine what would.

Two black axmen swung in perfect rhythm, notching the tree to make it fall where they wanted it to go, which was directly onto an empty wooden barrel a hundred feet away, part of a bet the saw gang had with the boilermen. For twenty minutes chips spun off the trunk and then the fallers stepped away and rested their double-bit axes on the toes of their soppy boots. Two men poured turpentine on a Disston Cougar felling saw and went against the tree, sawdust boiling out of the cut in long pale ribbons. When the back of the blade was deep inside, a man stepped up and placed four wedges, painted silver for the occasion, into the cut and swung his sledge, opening the incision so the saw could work through the back half of the tree without binding. At a certain point a mystical and inevitable feeling touched the crowd, and everyone gravitated to the safe side of the tree and began looking up its straight trunk. The mill manager did the same, wondering if the clouds were drifting or the tree's top was beginning to move. Along his shoulders he felt the pressure of Byron's arm, smelled the soap in his fresh shirt, and the mill manager put out his own arm behind his brother's back, as if to pose for a photograph, both of them looking skyward. The long saw soughed through the heartwood, the fallers so used to the motion they hardly broke a sweat as they tossed the blade back and forth, letting their ropey arms do the work.

"How are you, By?" Randolph asked, his face still raised to the treetop.

"No better," he said, "but gladder to be here." He, too, kept his head up. "You?"

"Selling lumber, is all."

At the first subtle crack from the trunk, Byron took back his arm. "That's better than nothing."

"I've heard that."

A wheezing creak came from the wood and the fallers stopped for a moment to listen, then swung in several quick strokes on one corner of the cut and stepped back, leaving their saw in the tree. Byron and Randolph imagined a drift to the crown, which slowly became real movement, ponderous, giving true meaning to a man's puny weight, the feathery top beginning to flutter as if the tree were beating its wings to stay aloft. The cracking intensified to the sounds of bridge timbers tearing apart and the tree came down in the muck like a lightning bolt, exploding the barrel to toothpicks. Lillian applauded weakly, glanced around at the somber workers, and crossed her hands behind her back. The mill manager felt as though a giant electric switch had been thrown off, stopping everything in his life. The buckers climbed up on the trunk like ants, bringing their heavier crosscut saws, the toppers went after the limbs, and in a half hour one of the last mules limped up, towing the steel cable from a pull boat's winch. The cut-up tree was dragged into the pond, where it waited its turn with a hundred others to be made into boards, dried, shipped out to be nailed into churches and whorehouses, hospitals and jails.

Two days later, the Last Tree was sent through the band saw, and after the final skull-ringing gnaw of the blade, the master sawyer pulled the stop whistle, the big steam engine down under the floor slowed, the belts whined lower in pitch, the overhead pulleys and line shafts and idlers rotated slower and slower into a paused quiet that ached in the men's heads as if a powerful vacuum had been applied to their ears. The saw-shed crews began to wander, stunned by the stillness, then one by one they pulled off their gloves and walked out into the sunlight like mourners leaving a funeral. They went home, where most of them had already taken apart stoves and crated chickens. They washed the mill off of them and got ready for the morning's train out. A few would hang on to help with the end tasks.

Minos kept pressure up for a week until all the lumber was kiln dried, then he turned the two-foot valve wheel to shut off the main steam lines, pulled a long soulful note out of the mill whistle, threw his gloves into the firebox, and walked with the boiler crew upstairs to the pay window. The mill manager was spelling the accounts keeper when Minos walked up.

"If you need a reference," Randolph told him, "tell them to call me." He reached under the grill to shake his engineer's hand.

"I got on at the Tiger Island power plant. I been studying them diesel books and tested for my license."

"You give up on steam?"

Minos drew his pay and counted it. "Times is changing, yeah."

"I doubt they'll change that fast."

Minos pulled his watch and glanced at it, then laughed. "Look around. This damn mill turned a whole forest into window frames and water tanks in six years."

Randolph looked down to the ledger and drew a line through *Minos Thibodeaux.* "You were the best steam engineer I ever hired, I know that much. I'm just sorry you lost your father here the way you did."

Minos wound his watch tight. "The old priest come to see me and said for me not to worry about his soul. I told him, hell, if he missed out on heaven nobody else in this parish got a chance." The engineer turned toward the door.

"Take it easy," the mill manager hollered after him.

"Ain't no such thing," he called back.

Two days later, the machinery buyers and scrappers came down in the crew car and walked the mill, drawing yellow chalk lines on every piece of mechanism left in the compound, one man writing his company's name on a flatcar even as a crew stacked lumber on it. A week later, the mill was coming apart like a wedding cake eaten by ants. A few of the better shotgun houses were winched up onto flatcars and sent to Shirmer; the rest were knocked down, the lumber sold to trappers who took it out in small rafts on towlines behind their skiffs. The steam pipes to the kiln were pulled up, the brick structure itself left behind, where the mill manager imagined it would be found by hunters in a hundred years and puzzled over as if it were a pyramid.

Byron and Randolph did not have to stay around for the end, but they did. Jules was sent to a new Arkansas mill, even though they could've kept him on to close Nimbus out. The brothers felt they could not leave until this place where they had fought and killed and created was completely gone. Their wives and Walter had moved to a hotel in New Orleans the week before crews began cutting the better homes into quarters and loading the pieces on flatcars. On the sunny day when the locomotive pulled the dismantled houses out of camp, Randolph looked into his kitchen as it drifted by, open to view, the stove still in place, nailed into the blazing linoleum where May died and where he lay pouring blood.

Day after day the brothers watched something else leave. The boilers were pulled to the canal and skidded up onto a steel barge. The mules were taken by a sooty steamboat with cattle rails nailed around her unpainted deck. The privies were chopped up to fuel the locomotive on its run west to Shirmer and its buyer, the track to be pulled up by the Southern Pacific in a month.

Byron and Randolph slept in the agent's extra room in Poachum, and on the last day they borrowed a hand-pumped track car and labored down the rails to Nimbus, which by then was just a flat tract of engine foundations and house piers, broken boards, stacks of cast-off furniture, timbers, cable, dragged-over mud, and the hollow vault of the drying kiln looming above a vast plain of stumps. They were to receive a buyer's check for the sale of the pull boats, which were the very last things to go. As they rolled to the end of track, the mill manager noted that the blind horse's stall had been knocked apart for its boards, and he was surprised to see the animal standing in a gray square of earth where the building had been. When the horse heard the ringing wheels of the track car, it spun like a compass needle and faced the men.

Byron gestured with his nub. "I thought it was sold with the mules."

The mill manager looked at the horse and felt accused. "The dealer didn't want it once he saw its eyes. One of the stackers said he might take it, but I guess he changed his mind." The animal had listened to everything coming apart and knew what was happening, that the human world was a temporary thing, a piece of junk that used up the earth and then was consumed itself by the world it tried to destroy. When Randolph understood what the animal knew, a bottom-less sadness crawled over him like a winter fog come out of the swamp at night. He thought of the cottages and shutters made out of this woods and of the money in his Pennsylvania bank account, but looking at the horse he could see no worth in any of it.

"If we had a gun," Byron said, "we could put it out of its misery."

"I'm not sure it's miserable," Randolph said sharply. "It's just blind." He whistled but the horse ignored him, as if obedience was now beside the point.

"There's no way we could walk him out over those little trestles," Byron said. "He'd fall through and break his legs." He looked to the canal bank, where deckhands had lashed together two barges and three steam pull boats, ready to be towed away by the gasoline tug. "Maybe they'd put him on a barge?"

"They're not going to any place different from this one, By." The purchaser—a bearded man from the Texas border-lands, where they were taking down longleaf virgin pine—walked over and paid them for the pull boats and the tug, then motioned for his deckhands to cast off. The tug revved its engine, pulled the slack out of the towline, and the greasy flotilla straightened out and headed up the canal, disappearing around a westerly bend.

Byron looked around at all the silence. "Looks like France when I left it."

"My God, is that a joke?"

"Sometimes a fact *is* a joke."

Randolph scanned the site. "It'll grow back," he said.

"Sure. In fifteen hundred years it'll be just as we found it."

Randolph put the check in his wallet and then took off his coat because he was sweating. He started back to the handcar, stepping around a coiled water moccasin sunning itself on a broken flywheel. He and his brother mounted the car and faced each other on the pumping handles. They both looked at the horse as it turned its head and listened for them. They became quiet and watched the animal pivot.

"He can go into the kiln to get out of the weather," Byron whispered. "There's no lack of green things to eat."

"Don't go softhearted on us."

Byron looked up the track where it pared through the stumps. "Come on, that old thing's trying to look at us." He pressed down on his handle, putting all his weight on his one arm, and the car began to jingle down the track. The horse heard and came toward them at a trot. They stopped, and the horse did the same, listening, and the men wondered what to do to keep him from following and getting killed. Finally, Byron stepped off, motioning for his brother to follow, and walked two hundred yards to a stack of twisted tin that had been thrown over a heap of crippled tables, water-ruined pie safes, and a huddle of porch stools.

"What are you looking for?" Randolph asked, wiping his face and neck with a handkerchief.

"Here. Help me pull off some of this tin." Underneath, tangled up with kitchen chairs and a rabbit cage, was the hulk of the Victrola. They stood it upright, its four legs sinking into the mud, and heard a few records rattling in its case. The doors had swelled shut, and Byron pried them open with his pocketknife and cocked up the top. "Let's see, we'll need a good while to get on up the track." In the cabinet he found "Love's Perfume," a twelve-inch Columbia record, and read the tune's length off the mildewed label. "This one will give us four minutes." The machine balked at first, but once it was wound as tight as it would go, a death rattle of a waltz began to escape its grille, a rising dirge of clarinets and trumpets, tubas and French horns. The horse, which had followed the men within fifty feet, picked up its head, its ears rotating toward the music. The brothers walked away in an arc as quietly as they could, got on the handcar, and began pumping the handles hard. Randolph's last glimpse of Nimbus was over his brother's bobbing head, and he saw the horse staring at the leaning machine, deceived and abandoned, but with a bright sun gleaming in its coat and a reedy grass springing up around its legs out of the demolished world.

The mill manager threw all his strength down against his handle, pressed until his feet left the deck, as if to outdo his brother. Byron saw the game and bore down on his side of the handle, then pulling up as best he could with his one arm. After a hundred yards the men rose and fell like pistons, building velocity and putting their backs into the rhythm for more, the wheels singing and jittering along the track, the brush and trashwoods a green blur, the wheels banging the rail joints like gunshots, and they kept at it, equal in strength, grimacing or grinning, who could tell, trying their hearts, gaining speed on a straightaway for a whole mile until they gave up the handles together, sweating like rain, flushed, panting, and heartsore as the handcar coasted out of the swamp. Byron threw back his head and hollered like a train whistle down the track to Poachum, where the main line's rails ran east and west to the rest of the nation, all the way to their hates and loves, toward what they would have and what would have them.